A BUMP IN THE ROAD

To Rachel,
Thanks for
reading!
xoxo,
Maureen Lipinski

A BUMP IN THE ROAD

From Happy Hour to Baby Shower

MAUREEN LIPINSKI

Thomas Dunne Books
St. Martin's Griffin 🐾 New York

This is a work of fiction. All of the characters, organizations, and events portrayed in this novel are either products of the author's imagination or are used fictitiously.

THOMAS DUNNE BOOKS.
An imprint of St. Martin's Press.

A BUMP IN THE ROAD. Copyright © 2009 by Maureen Lipinski. All rights reserved. Printed in the United States of America. For information, address St. Martin's Press, 175 Fifth Avenue, New York, N.Y. 10010.

www.thomasdunnebooks.com
www.stmartins.com

Book design by Rich Arnold

Library of Congress Cataloging-in-Publication Data

Lipinski, Maureen.
    A bump in the road : from happy hour to baby shower / Maureen Lipinski.—1st ed.
        p. cm.
    ISBN-13: 978-0-312-53391-5
    ISBN-10: 0-312-53391-8
    1. Pregnancy—Fiction.   2. Chicago (Ill.)—Fiction.   I. Title.
    PS3612.I635B86 2009
    813'.6—dc22

                                                            2008044634

First Edition: June 2009

10 9 8 7 6 5 4 3 2 1

For Kevin and Ryan

Acknowledgments

. . . .

My mother always told me to say "thank you" as a child, but I was never very good at it. Yet there is so much gratitude to go around when it comes to this book, so here goes.

To all my friends, especially my old college roommates Pam, Sheryl, Barrie, and Carrie: You all provided me with endless hours of laughter and hilarious moments, a fair amount of which made it into this book. Drinks on me!

To my editor, Katie Gilligan: You are one of those people who "gets it." You have effortlessly guided me through the sometimes dizzying world of publishing and continually put me at ease.

To my super-agent, Holly Root: This book certainly wouldn't have happened if it weren't for your amazing persistence, humor, and dedication. You are the ultimate cheerleader and one of the coolest people ever!

To all of my teachers: Thank you for giving me the confidence and support to believe my writing dreams could be a reality. You have helped me in more ways than you know.

To my family, especially the Kilmer-Lipinski clan of Mom, Dad, Patrick, Mary Claire, and Christopher: Your love and support gave me the strength and comfort to pursue my vision of writing a book. I love you all very much. Without you all, my writing would be just thoughts in my head instead of a reality. This book is just as much yours as it is mine.

To the entire extended Leurck family: I'm so thankful for all of your warmth, compassion, and love. You all inspire me in different ways and continually remind me to strive to become a better person. I'm so blessed to have in-laws that are nothing like Clare's!

To Kevin: Your endless love and support astound me each day. Thank you for always insisting I pursue my dreams, picking me back up when I fall, and helping me to laugh at all of life's little bumps in the road.

And to Ryan: Your sense of irony and timing is just brilliant. I love you more than the stars in the sky, even when you had colic for three months straight. I'm constantly amazed by your independence, intelligence, and charm. With that said, please don't repeat any of the bad words in this book.

A BUMP IN THE ROAD

Sunday, April 22

· · · · · · · · · · · · · · · · · · ·

Earlier on the plane:

"This is why we're never having children," Jake said as he lurched forward in his airplane seat again.

"Relax. Didn't you hear? Li'l Mikey is experiencing a personal tragedy. He wants to watch *Cars* but the DVD player is broken." I stifled a laugh.

"You're hilarious. I'm going to put a muzzle on that kid if he doesn't shut up," Jake said.

Li'l Mikey stopped screaming for a moment and everyone collectively exhaled.

"NO! NO! NO! NO! MINE! MINE!"

Jake rocked forward again thanks to Li'l Mikey's short and fat toddler legs. He turned around and tried to glare at the parents through the half-inch gap between our seats.

"Mikey, you're making these nice people upset. If you don't stop, you're going to get a time-out. You don't want that, Pooh Bear, do you?" his mother cooed to him.

"NO TIME OUT!"

"Do you want some candy?"

"CANDY!"

We heard rustling and Li'l Mikey silently chewed for a moment, until we heard what sounded like marbles dropping on the ground as all of his M&Ms dropped to the floor.

"WAAAAAAAAAAAAAAAAAAAA!"

"Can I start screaming, too?" Jake asked me pathetically.

I opened my carry-on, pulled out four Tylenols and a Gatorade, and handed them to Jake, who wordlessly gulped it all down. After forty-eight hours of debauchery in Vegas, I had prepared to battle the Mother of All Hangovers but not Damien, Evil Spawn of Satan.

"This is God punishing us for spending a drunken weekend in Sin City," I moaned as I jerked my thumb back toward Li'l Mikey.

Jake closed his eyes and leaned back in his seat. "Wrong," he said, his eyes still shut. "This is God punishing us for sneering at the parents whose kid was screaming in the restaurant last night. It's like Dante's Inferno, except with annoying children and mothers instead of hornets and wasps."

"Oh, please. They absolutely deserved to get kicked out of the restaurant. I mean, it's somewhat difficult to enjoy a fifty-dollar steak when Junior next to me is screaming 'Fie truck! Fie truck!'"

"I agree. But like I said, Dante's Inferno: the poetic justice of two hungover assholes suffering through three hours with Li'l Mikey."

"Speaking of which . . . ," I said, reaching forward again into my carry-on to pull out my birth control pill.

"Yes. Please. The only thing more frightening than other people's obnoxious children is the prospect of dealing with one of our—" Jake stopped when Li'l Mikey reached forward and gave him a good solid bop on the head with a stuffed Buzz Lightyear doll. Jake didn't seem to appreciate it.

He also did not appreciate when I laughed so hard I choked on my birth control pill.

"You think this is hilarious, but I'm the one who has to give a presentation on Logitech's new software application to about fifty executives tomorrow," he whispered as he fiddled with his wedding band.

I smiled at him. "Maybe you should bring Mikey as your secret weapon."

"What, like, 'If you don't buy our product, I'll give the kid a Jolt cola and turn him loose in your employee break room'?"

"Exactly. See? Children can be useful," I said as I opened *Newsweek*.

Once the plane landed, the airplane doors opened like the gates of heaven. As Jake and I stepped off the Jetway into the terminal, I felt a tap on my right shoulder.

"Are you Clare Finnegan?" a short, chubby woman with round chipmunk cheeks asked me.

"Yes," I said, moving aside to let people behind me keep walking.

"From *Am I Making Myself Clare?*"

"That's me," I smiled at her.

"I'm Melanie. I just love, love, love your blog. I read it every day at work. I think you're hilarious."

"Thanks, that's great to hear."

"I started reading it after the article in *The Daily Tribune.* I've been hooked ever since. Do people recognize you a lot?"

"Every now and then, more since the article came out last month." I straightened my wrinkled pants, hoping she wouldn't notice the mustard stain on my hip.

"Hi, I'm Jake," my husband said, and extended his hand.

"I recognize you, too. It's nice to meet you." She giggled. "How's your car?"

"It's fine. All taken care of," he said, turning a little red.

"Well, I just wanted to say hi. I don't want to keep you. I can't wait to read the next entry," she said, then gave a small wave and disappeared into the mass of people in the terminal.

"She was sweet," I said to Jake.

"Yep. Thanks again for writing about my accident."

"No problem."

"Which way's baggage claim?"

"I think to the left." I pointed. "I guess I should start looking somewhat presentable when I go out. I hate meeting people when I look like a homeless person. Do I look OK?"

"You look great."

"Really?"

"Well, except you split your pants when you bent down to pick up your carry-on." Jake saw my look of horror and started laughing. "I'm just teasing. You look fine."

"Don't harass me when I'm hungover, Jake. I will not hesitate to sic my legions of fans upon you."

"I'm terrified. Let's go before someone else recognizes you, Internet Rockstar. Besides, I fear the consequences of keeping your sister waiting outside."

"I do, too. I've read a teenager's patience window is around ten minutes. Sam won't hesitate to use her Tiffany heart bracelet as a weapon if pissed off."

In the car after we collected our bags, Sam began to rant. "Holy shit! You are majorly, effing kidding me right now, aren't you? What a loser! He is such a complete freak show! He's so totally emo it's not even funny." She flicked her long blond hair, perfectly straightened due to a several-hundred-dollar Japanese straightening treatment, rolled her eyes, and snapped her Swarovski-encrusted Sidekick closed. She threw it into the backseat, narrowly missing Jake's right temple. "So what the eff took you so long? I had to go around the airport forever and this ginormously obese policeman kept blowing his whistle thingy at me."

"Sorry. We were at baggage claim for a while. The airline lost one of our bags."

Oh, but Rosemary and her baby sure got their bags promptly.

Jake leaned forward from the backseat and whispered, "What does 'emo' mean?"

"How should I know? I don't speak teenager," I hissed at him.

Sam's blue eyes narrowed as she sized me up. "Did you guys get fatter over the weekend or something? You look all puffy."

"Probably just the hangover. It's great to see you, too. Where's Mom and Dad? I thought they were coming."

"Hel-*lo*, do you think their lives, like, *revolve* around picking you up from the airport? They're being so annoying today. I have, like, a jillion things to do tonight and they made me come and get you. How am I supposed to get Chris to ask me to KOH when I look like a corpse?"

"What's KOH?"

"*Duh!* King of Hearts? You know, the dance? God, how freaking old are you, anyway?"

"I'm twenty-seven, Sam."

"I effing know how old you are, OK? It's called sarcasm, ever heard of it?"

Assuming her question was rhetorical, I glanced back at Jake with a slightly amused smile. He didn't miss a beat.

"So, Sam, did you go out and get *wasted* this weekend?" He held up his right hand, his fingers making the Rock On! symbol.

"You guys are so weird." She rolled her eyes and grabbed her M.A.C. Lipglass out of her Coach purse and applied some using the rearview mirror.

"Um. Sam. Car. Look."

"What? Oh, whoops," she said as she swerved away from a parked car.

"Pay attention, OK? I don't want to die in a massive pileup. Besides, I think this hangover is enough to kill me."

She opened her mouth to retort, but the Blackeyed Peas' "Don't Phunk With My Heart" started blaring in the backseat and she reached behind her to grab her phone while cruising through a red light and nearly ramming into an open car door.

Jake handed her the phone and the last thing I heard before I drifted off was "Yeah, yeah, yeah. Totally. So fugly."

I jolted awake when we reached my parents' house and Sam flattened the newspaper in the driveway.

"OK, bitches. Get out," she said, and jerked her head, her palette earrings swishing back and forth.

My parents were inside, putting away groceries. Sam immediately went upstairs to her room to lie down from the extreme effort it took to drive us home.

"Welcome home!" my mom shouted, her head halfway in the fridge.

"Hey! There they are! The two Vegas whales!" my dad said, slapping Jake on the back.

"Oh, right. We're up two hundred bucks. I'd hardly call us whales," I said.

"You two want a beer?" my dad asked.

"No way. I've had enough beer for a while," Jake said, pointedly grabbing a bottle of water from the fridge as my mom closed it.

"We're so hungover," I moaned, and laid my head down on the kitchen island.

"Three Tylenols, flat soda with lots of ice, frozen peas on the head, and a little hair of the dog. You know this stuff. Didn't I teach you anything?" My mom thrust a two-liter bottle of Coke in front of me.

"Mom, this hangover is impervious to the effects of caffeine or sugar. It's like I'm dying."

"What the hell did you expect to feel like after coming home from Vegas?"

"Like shit. She's just whining," Jake said.

"Has your sinus infection gotten any better?" my mom asked.

"The horse-pill antibiotics cleared it right up. Now, instead of my head exploding from sinus pressure, it's throbbing due to the virtual bottle of vodka I drank last night."

"That one, my dear, is your own fault. No sympathy here. And stop complaining, you're not the one who has to get up at the crack of dawn tomorrow to make a six A.M. flight," my mom said while trying to shove a container of ice cream into the already bulging fridge.

"Flying out?"

"Yep."

"Where to this time?"

"Hospital in Austin, Texas. We're implementing a new HR database."

"Sounds thrilling."

"Always. I'll be gone all week so your father has to wrangle Sam himself. I know he has a couple of late meetings so keep your phone on in case she needs to get ahold of you."

"When are you going to realize she's seventeen and not six?"

"When I stop watching my oldest daughter's cat while she's getting drunk in Vegas over the weekend."

"Funny. Hey, guess what? A fan recognized me at the airport," I said.

"That's so great, honey! Your last blog entry was hysterical. Very funny. How's the car, Jake?"

"Fixed, thankfully. But I have a feeling the accident is going to live on via Internet lore." He turned to my dad and said, "Is the game on?"

"Let's go," my dad said, and they walked into the other room to commandeer the big-screen television and watch whatever game was referenced.

"Staying for dinner?"

"Of course. Free meals taste the best. What are we having?"

"Pepperoni, sausage, and cheese."

"Is Mark coming?"

"No. He's staying in the city. It's one of his roommates' birthdays." She paused. "At least, I think that's what he said. I think it's just an excuse to go out on a Sunday night."

"Mom, when you're twenty-two you don't need an excuse. The fact you're legally allowed to drink in bars still has some luster."

"Just as long as he doesn't end up in the gutter somewhere."

"Clearly you haven't heard some of his college stories."

As we sat down to eat pizza an hour later, I watched as Sam picked at the cheese on her plate, not daring to touch the crust for fear of osmotically ingesting a carb. She felt me watching her and snapped her head in my direction and narrowed her eyes. "Do you know your cat is gay?"

"What?" I said. Jake choked a little on his pizza.

"Your. Cat. Gay. Did you know?"

"What is she talking about?" I turned to my parents.

My father had an amused smile on his face.

"What?" I asked him.

"Oh. Nothing. I have no idea what she's talking about," he said.

"Mom?"

"Well, let's just say Butterscotch is *very* interested in women's fashion."

"Huh?"

"We came home from dinner the other night and—"

"*No!* Let me tell the story. Mom and Dad came home the other night and your totally weird cat was all bored while you were in Vegas and we were stuck watching him. Did you know he is so fat and afraid of everything?" Sam said.

"Point?"

"Jeez, relax, psycho. I wasn't done yet. Way to interrupt me. Anyway, he went into everyone's rooms while we were gone and brought stuff downstairs and left it on the kitchen floor. Like presents or something. He brought down your old ugly frilly prom dress, mom's gross black underwear, and my thongs. Mom and Dad came home with the Andersons and tried to explain why there was lingerie and weird crap all over the kitchen." She took a swig of her water and sat back in her chair, arms crossed.

"Seriously?" I said, and looked back and forth.

"Unfortunately," my dad said. "It was pretty difficult trying to blame all of that on the cat."

"Yeah, I don't think we'll be seeing the Andersons any time soon. They left pretty quickly," my mom said.

"I'm so sorry, he's never done—," I started to say.

"Don't worry about it. Like I said, maybe he's just interested in fashion," my mom said.

"Why couldn't you have a cat that was interested in normal fashion, like Citizen Jeans or something, rather than ugly nineties prom dresses and lingerie? Your cat is a freak show."

As if on cue, we heard the unmistakable sound of Butterscotch howling. We all froze and looked at each other, cautious smiles on our faces. We waited, silent and still, as the howling got louder. I took a sharp breath in and my mom elbowed me to be quiet. Butterscotch rounded the corner into the kitchen, dragging Sam's hot pink, sparkly feather boa from Halloween behind him.

We jumped up and cheered and Sam let out a snort. "What is wrong with you people? Hel-*lo*, that cat has serious problems. He is so freaking annoying. Aren't you like totally embarrassed to be associated with him?" she said, turning to me.

"Not really. I've been associated with you for seventeen years. I'll get used to it."

"You're such a loser. Just like your cat," she said, and stomped off, wrenching the boa from Butterscotch, who looked confused that his latest present wasn't gratefully accepted.

I turned to Jake, who looked positively thrilled.

"This. Is. So. Awesome. That cat can stay," he said.

1:00 A.M.

Finally, back at our apartment, gay cat and all, I opened my computer and checked my blog's comments. I yelled to Jake in the bedroom, "Wifey1025 offered to drive you to work tomorrow if your car isn't fixed yet."

"Thanks. Tell her I prefer to get hacked into little pieces next week instead of this week."

"Will do," I told him as I walked into the bedroom. I jumped into our fluffy marshmallow bed and snuggled underneath the comforter. "How great does it feel to get in bed?" I asked him, my face buried in a pillow.

"Pretty damn good," he said, and stretched his arms over his head.

"I know, but Jake?" I poked him in his ribs.

"Yeah?"

"I'm kinda hungry again," I said, and smiled at him.

"Jesus, we just ate a few hours ago." He flipped on the television.

"I know, but it's the hangover. I've gone from extreme nausea to ravenous hunger pains. My body is finally ready to accept food. There's all that leftover pizza my mom gave us."

"OK, fine," he said as he casually turned off the television. He slowly sat up in bed. "The deep-dish slices are mine!" he yelled as he scrambled out of bed and nearly trucked over Butterscotch lying in the doorjamb.

"NOT COOL!" I yelled as I chased after him.

He got to the kitchen first and yanked out the pizza box so forcefully the leftover slices slid out onto the floor.

"Nice going," I laughed.

He looked at me and shrugged. "Ten-second rule?"

We both paused and smirked at each other before diving onto the floor and trying to salvage the slices not covered in cat hair. We leaned against the kitchen cabinets and silently munched on the cold pizza.

"Leftover pizza is nothing short of amazing," I mumbled as I wiped pizza sauce off my mouth.

"I'll show you amazing." Jake smiled wickedly at me as he took the pizza crust from my hand.

"Kitchen floor? I don't think so. When's the last time we actually cleaned this thing? Actually, have we ever cleaned this floor?" I said as I tried to grab the crust back.

"Probably not. Who cares? Let's have fun."

"Well . . . what the hell," I said, and allowed him to pull me closer.

We didn't get back to bed until almost two in the morning. I'm sure I'll be exhausted tomorrow and find cat hair and dust in some very interesting places, but as Jake said, "Who cares?" We haven't even been married a year—we're still newlyweds. We can have sex on the kitchen floor until the crack of dawn while eating leftovers, right? By my calculations we only have a few more years to do things like that, so we might as well take advantage.

Monday, April 23
· · · · · · · · · · · · · · · · · · · ·

As I feared, getting out of bed this morning was quite difficult. Newlyweds or not, four hours of sleep after a weekend in Vegas isn't a good idea. I slunk into Signature Events forty-five minutes late due to a steaming-cup-of-coffee/new-white-blouse debacle. Apparently, even though I have the high and mighty title of Event Director and regularly plan black-tie events with healthy six-figure budgets, I still have difficulty getting out the door without spilling something on myself.

I kept my head down as I tiptoed into my office, careful not to make my keys jangle as I set them in my purse. I threw off my coat and shoved it under my desk; no time to walk over to the coat rack and hang it up.

I sat down at my desk and Mule Face immediately walked in. I looked up with my best *I have been here for an hour already, can I help you?* smile.

"Don't worry. Christina's not here yet," Mule Face said, licking strawberry Pop-Tart frosting off her chubby index finger.

"Oh, um, er, OK." I stared at her, waiting for whatever bomb she obviously had in her arsenal.

She took another bite of her Pop-Tart and the whole thing crumbled and fell to the floor. "Damn it!" She looked down and shrugged her shoulders at the pastry and jam mess sprinkling the carpet of my office. "Anyway, I wanted to tell you Carolyn Wittenberg came in on Friday when you were off." She smiled, revealing the frighteningly large cosmetic veneers that inspired her moniker.

So screwed. I knew it immediately. So, so screwed.

"Carolyn? Really? I wonder what she wanted."

"She was wearing these fabulous shoes, but she came in with the bitchiest attitude, like usual. Anyhoo, she and Christina were talking so loud, I couldn't help but hear them."

Right. I'm sure her coffee cup pressed against the door helped.

"And?"

"Carolyn said something about needing some extra help this year with their Women's Board Gala since they have two new cochairs. I think she wants to hire us." I saw a few strawberry seeds stuck between her front teeth.

"What a shame. Don't you usually assist with their events?"

"Yeah, but I've got Isabel Castle's sweet sixteen party in two months. I'm swamped." She continued to smile at me. "I wonder who Christina will assign?" She tapped her finger against her cheek.

"I don't know, Annie. I'm sure we'll find out soon." I turned away from her and started to type an e-mail, hoping she would leave and make someone else miserable.

"Don't worry. I doubt she'll give it to you. It's a huge project and she'll want someone with well-developed attention to detail."

"What does—"

"Just kidding!" She turned on her heel but stopped quickly. "I almost forgot. Here." She shoved a Mary Kay catalog at me. "Our new spring line is fabulous."

"I'm sure it is, but I told you I'm pretty happy with the makeup I use."

"We all could use a little fine-tuning!"

Yeah, especially her, the overweight hag whose ex-boyfriend was in jail for credit-card fraud.

"You might be interested in our complexion-smoothing mask. It's made out of pure cucumber extract with pomegranate seeds— wonderful for exfoliation. Just take a gander at it and let me know if there's anything you'd like to order. Feel free to link to it on your blog."

"I'll let you know," I said, and threw the catalog on a corner of my desk. I swear, she should give up pushing makeup and sell drugs instead. She'd probably make more money, which would allow her to buy more sweaters with cats knitted on them.

"You know, I didn't enjoy your last blog entry. I think _Reba_ is a really good show."

"Oh, well. It's just my opinion. I'm sure a lot of people enjoy _Reba_."

"When are you going to write about work?"

"I've already told you—never."

"Why not?"

Hmmm . . . I wasn't sure how to answer her question. I couldn't really say, "Because there's no way I could write about work without ranting about your Prince Valiant haircut."

So I said, "I try to keep my personal and professional lives separate," in the same manner as Lindsay Lohan or Britney Spears whining about intrusive paparazzi.

"Well, I think you should do a whole entry about how bitchy Isabel Castle's mom is."

"Yeah, right. I'd like to keep my job, thanks."

"Well, maybe you should try coming in on time once in a while, then." She smiled sweetly and lumbered off to raid the vending machine for Snickers.

I hacked through my e-mails by lunchtime—most of them were pointless ones people cc'd me on. One of the e-mails was from Reese, who sent me more pictures of Grace. I looked at them for the required ten seconds, sent back an e-mail proclaiming how cute they were, how we should get together for lunch soon, and then deleted the e-mail. I love Reese to death but I don't need to see a virtual slideshow of pictures of her kid every other week. I mean, Grace is a cute kid and all, but I don't need to see Grace at one month! Grace at two months! Grace at three months! Grace at Halloween! Grace with a flower next to her face!

Jake and I wouldn't have room for furniture if I framed all of the pictures Reese gives me.

Christina finally came in around lunchtime. She breezed past my office, juggling her cell phone and a new Prada bag I drooled over in *InStyle* last week. I swear she has to be prostituting herself on the side to afford all of her clothes. The first time I met her, I felt like she was the prom queen and I was the nerd trying to befriend her. Like I should send her a note: *Will you be my friend? Circle yes or no.*

"Clare, are you free to meet in an hour?" Christina called through my office wall.

"Sure."

I spent the next hour coming up with lame excuses why I couldn't work on the Gala. I already have a trip planned for that weekend! I'm taking a sabbatical to India! I don't like being humiliated!

I walked into Christina's office and sat down for our meeting. She started, "Before I forget, I have a meeting tomorrow around three and I may or may not come back to the office afterward."

Knowing this was code for her leaving early, I smiled and nodded, looking forward to spending my afternoon at Banana Republic.

"I'm glad you're smiling. You might not be in a few minutes. On Friday I met with Carolyn Wittenberg, the president of the Women's Board of Chicago Samaritan Hospital. They would like to hire us to do their annual fundraiser black-tie Gala. I told them we'd be thrilled to work on their event and you'd be a wonderful contributor. What do you think?" She looked at me critically.

"Doesn't Annie usually assist with their events?" Last-ditch lifeline.

"Yes, but she's swamped with Isabel Castle's sweet sixteen party. I know, I know. They are bitches from the deepest level of hell. But we have to do it. I know you'll be a consummate professional."

"Of course." I smiled, but I felt my face turning crimson.

"Thanks, Clare. Round of drinks on me next happy hour."

"Sure," I said, and recalled the Women's Board's spring luncheon when Mule Face washed eighty centerpieces in her dishwasher. At the time, I was overjoyed.

Karma, she is a bitch.

As an event planner, I'm somewhat used to odd requests and wealthy, picky clients. But the Women's Board is a particularly demanding group. Planning this event means fitful, sleepless nights spent dreaming about incorrect invitation assembly, and smiling while being called incompetent because the luncheon napkins aren't the correct shade of hunter green.

I paused a moment before getting up to leave, desperately hoping Christina was going to say, "Gotcha! You should've seen the pathetic look on your face! April Fool's!" She just smiled apologetically, completely aware of the firing squad she placed me in front of, the same smile a sales clerk gives right before she cuts up a credit card.

"Oh, and Clare," Christina called out as I walked to my office, "they're coming in two weeks from now to meet, so that'll be when you can get the ball rolling."

"Sure thing," I called back.

"And, like I always say: 'Please don't publicly bitch about this on the Internet.'"

"Like I always respond: 'As long as you keep the fridge stocked with Diet Coke and don't tell anyone how I used to lust after that dorky graphic designer, we're cool.'"

"Well, he *was* really strange. He used to wear argyle sweater vests, for chrissakes."

"I'm logging on to the Internet now."

"OK, fine. I'll shut up."

The only bright spot of the day was Julie's e-mail, wanting to set up a shopping trip for next Saturday. I love Julie. Most days, I would still sell my left boob to go back to college, when I lived with her and Reese. To go back to the days when waking up earlier than noon felt like medieval torture. The days when a hundred bucks in my bank account made me feel like a millionaire. The days when we were all still friends. I'm sure someday they'll get over all of that shit that went down at my bachelorette party and be friends again.

Scratch that: Do not mention Reese during shopping trip.

Thursday, April 26

Reese responded to my e-mail complimenting Grace's pictures and invited me over for lunch this afternoon. Around noon, I ducked out of the office and drove to the most expensive part of town. As I pulled up to Reese's gorgeous, enormous house, I once again felt like her friend from the wrong side of the tracks. I parked my Ford next to her Mercedes in the driveway and reminded myself of the emotional price Reese pays for every inch of her square footage and felt better about my 1,200-square-foot apartment. It seems like for every extra dollar Matt brings in, he and Reese grow another inch away from each other.

I walked up to the doorstep and rang the doorbell. After waiting for several minutes, I checked my watch to make sure I had the right time.

Suddenly, the door was flung open and Reese put a finger to her lips and whispered, "Didn't you see the sign?"

I looked up and saw the PLEASE KNOCK! SLEEPING BABY! sign for the first time.

"No, sorry, I—"

"*Shhhh!*" she interrupted, motioning for me to come inside.

"Sorry. I hope I didn't wake her." I felt like I was back in high school, in my friend's basement, getting wasted at a slumber party and being yelled at for being the loud drunk.

"It's OK. Come into the kitchen where we can talk normally." We walked inside, through her enormous house, past the Oriental rugs, past her cherished signed and framed photo of George W. Bush I will never stop laughing at, and into her beautiful kitchen, complete with sub-zero fridge and granite countertops.

She whirled around when we reached the kitchen island and gave me a bear hug. "Tell me everything about your trip! The food, the drinks, the gambling, the sex!" She arched one eyebrow into a tiny V.

"Oh my God! It was amazing. All of it, the—" I stopped when I heard what sounded like a goat being murdered coming from the baby monitor and looked in Reese's direction with alarm, but she was already halfway up the stairs to retrieve Grace.

I heard her on the monitor as she went into Grace's room. "How's Mommy's big girl? Did you just want to come and see Auntie Clare? You just wanted a girls' day, didn't you? Uh-oh! I think somebody has a poopy diaper! What a good poo-poo for such a big girl!"

I struggled between laughter and wanting to stab my ears with something sharp.

Reese came down the stairs holding Grace. "Say hello to Auntie Clare!"

Grace took one look at me and started wailing.

My entire life, I've had this effect on babies. For whatever reason, they scream when they see me. Which is just fine, because I want to scream when I see them, too. Sam once told me, "Babies cry around you because they have a sixth sense and know you are a total loser."

Reese quickly whipped out her boob and shoved it in Grace's mouth and the screaming stopped. This is another thing that confuses me about having children. Why is it OK for a woman, just because she has a child, to suddenly feel it is appropriate to start pulling out her boob publicly? (Although, I think it's somewhat hypocritical to be grossed out by Reese breast-feeding since she caught more than a few glimpses of my girls during college spring breaks.)

"So anyway, it was the best trip ever," I finished, keeping my gaze well above nipple level.

"That's awesome, Clare. So what else has been going on?"

"Well, same old stuff. Working and doing the Gala like I told you, ordering takeout, suffering through hangovers. Nothing special."

"Well, you look amazing. Where did you get those pants?"

"Banana Republic. Fifty percent off," I said proudly.

"You always look so well put together. These days, I'm lucky if my pants are zipped."

"Not true. You always look hot."

"Well, still. I wish I could look as great as you do all the time." Right. Reese's wardrobe puts Posh Spice's to shame. "Oh! I almost forgot! I have something for you. It's on the countertop."

"What? Reese, you didn't have to get me anything."

"Don't be silly, I saw it and thought of you. Go get it."

I walked over and grabbed a lavender-wrapped box. Inside lay a beautiful pair of gold-wire earrings adorned with green beads. "Reese, these are beautiful. You really didn't have to get me anything."

"I know. I just wanted to get you something because you've been such a good friend and I know I've been preoccupied with Grace. It's my way of saying thank you."

"You're welcome." I hugged her tightly—well, as tightly as I could with her boob exposed.

"So, any particularly good hangovers lately besides Vegas?" she said.

"Well, I went out with Julie two weekends ago, so that one was a doozy."

"I read about it. Sounds like you guys had fun." Long pause. "Looked like fun from the pictures. God, I haven't been out in ages. We should plan to go out sometime soon," Reese said.

I nodded and smiled, knowing it would probably never happen.

"How's Julie?" she asked, and adjusted Grace.

"Great. Same Julie. Having fun, living life. You know."

She smiled, then her face hardened. "When is she going to grow up? I'm serious. I'm concerned about her. Life isn't one big frat party. We're not in college anymore." She looked at me.

"It's who she is. You guys are different people." I shrugged.

"Well, I still can't get over how rude she acted at your bachelorette party. It was your party and she was off making out with a disgusting man. It was so disrespectful."

I shrugged again. I had zero desire to defend Julie's decisions to Reese or explain Reese's life choices to Julie for the umpteenth time. The bachelorette party was the official Declaration of War between Reese and Julie, and I was remaining Switzerland.

"So, how's Matt?" I asked her casually.

"Fine." She shrugged as the light left her face.

"Everything OK with you two?" I said.

"Fine. Great. Good. All of the above," she said, and looked down at Grace.

"Are you sure? You sound—"

"So, married gal, when are you going to have some little ones running around?" she interrupted.

It is so typical of Reese to ask a loaded question to divert attention away from whatever she doesn't want to talk about. I played along and answered her with my prepared response: "In our thirties, but every time you ask, it's another year."

"Seriously? No way, you should have some sooner. You guys would be great parents."

I just smiled back at her and shook my head.

"Although, it is a huge lifestyle change. Do you know that you can't have sex for six weeks after giving birth? And you remember how horrible it was when I had that infected milk duct a few months back—talk about pain!"

Why, why do new parents always try to convince me to have children and then proceed to tell me every disgusting, painful, grotesque story about actually having children? It's like saying, "You guys should really take a vacation to Thailand! Just be careful of the biting flies, unclean tap water, and child prostitution. Oh, and try not to get sold into white slavery while you're there."

"Although that sounds like a winning endorsement, I'll pass. At least for a while."

"Why not sooner?" She continued to push.

This is when I should've said, "We're just not ready." Instead, I said, "We figure we should wait to have kids until they don't completely annoy us." Which is a valid statement, but probably not a good one to make to someone holding their own child.

I immediately clapped my hand over my mouth and apologized profusely and tried to explain that yes, kids annoy us (Li'l Mikey comes to mind) but that Jake and I love Grace and think she's the best baby ever, etc. She laughed it off, but didn't seem too happy with me after my brilliant comment. She quickly served lunch, I think in an effort to boot me out the door.

Even though I apologized and even though Reese knows I often say things without consulting my brain first, I still feel horrible. Not only because I hurt her feelings, but because today is just another example of the wide chasm between our lives these days.

I think I just need to kidnap her and get her completely drunk. Yes. A bar-hopping night where we can all forget about babies, pregnancy, and diapers.

Friday, April 27

. . . .

I still feel guilty about the way things went with Reese yesterday, and Jake offered no help. His advice was, "Everything will be OK." I stared at him, waiting for more words of wisdom, and after five minutes he turned back to me and said, "Was I supposed to say something else?"

Men are so worthless when it comes to giving advice. They don't realize women just don't brush off conflicts with a six-pack. I think I'm going to send Reese some flowers thanking her for lunch. It will hopefully smooth things over.

Thursday, May 3

. . . .

5:00 P.M.
The flowers had the desired effect with Reese. She laughed off my comment again and thanked me. When I tried to ask her about Matt, she said she heard Grace crying and hung up the phone. I give up.

Rather than get depressed about Reese, I'm going to focus on this weekend. My shopping trip with Julie is finally here and I plan on staying in tonight so as not to be tired for the very important money-spending extravaganza. I plan on waking up feeling refreshed and looking fabulous (i.e., skin all glowy and not at all pasty and white, hair smelling like apples rather than an ashtray). Maybe I will even wake up early and work out and get Starbucks or something.

This is going to be just what I need.

6:00 P.M.
I am so proud of myself. I just got an e-mail from Jake's cousin Carrie, his only normal relative, inviting Jake and me to a martini party

in the city with her and Patrick. It would be fun but I don't even want to go. Who cares if they have five-dollar cranapple martinis and free appetizers? I have some great pasta from Trader Joe's I can make and a new *Dateline* to watch tonight.

6:30 P.M.
I heard that bar is lame anyway.

6:35 P.M.
I don't even like cranapple martinis.

6:38 P.M.
I don't have anything to wear.

6:49 P.M.
I'm having a bad hair day.

7:02 P.M.
OK, we'll go, but just one drink. We can still come home and get to bed at a reasonable hour. One drink each, which is only ten dollars, plus free appetizers. That's like *making* money. I forgot Jake ate all of my pasta last week so we would have to go out and pick something up anyway, which would be more than eight dollars. So, we'll get to socialize with Carrie and Patrick, who we haven't seen in forever, eat dinner, and each drink a cocktail. We can still totally be in bed by eleven and wake up feeling refreshed.

8:30 P.M.
One and a half drinks won't kill me. Jake's already had three. We've only spent about thirty bucks. If we went out to dinner, it would've been at least thirty-five dollars. We're right on track. Next I want to try some of those free appetizers.

Oh, they have four-dollar flirtinis?

10:04 P.M.
Little drunk. Who cares? Early. Much fun. Still can be in bed soon and get good sleep. Drunk=OK, but wasted=no. Grabbed Carrie's left boob. Am lesbian when drunk.

12:17 A.M.
Wasted. Jake hammered. Weird man keeps hitting on me but shoe broke. Think ankle is dead. Love cat. Love life. Love cranapples thing.

Friday, May 4
. . . .

Quoth the hangover: I'm back, bitch.

This hangover has to be the worst of my life. Much, much worse than my epic Vegas hangover. Yet it's not the hangover that has me shaking at my desk.

Last night: awesome.

Today: not so much.

This morning, I said a silent prayer before I attempted to open my eyes, thirst pains having finally gotten the best of me, but mascara had crusted to form a sort of paste that kept my eyes from opening fully. I weakly reached for the bottle of water next to me and immediately chugged it, afraid it would run out and I'd still be thirsty. As soon as my stomach felt the water, it cramped, afraid I was abusing it with more alcohol. I silently thanked God it was Saturday and I could remain in a corpselike state for the entire day, moving only to turn on a classic made-for-TV movie starring Tori Spelling. And . . .

Fuck me.

It's Friday.

I tossed my crusty strands, matted into a new-wave hairdo and reeking of a bar, into a ponytail and threw myself at my desk as quickly as I could.

All of which wasn't a big deal. I mean, I'm hungover, but fine. Until five minutes ago.

When I opened my calendar to check on the date for the meeting with the Women's Board ladies, and my stomach immediately dropped and my hands started shaking for a reason other than the eight million drinks I had last night. I grabbed my purse and started clawing through it before locating what I was looking for and feeling a cold sweat form.

How did this happen? Am I hallucinating or something? How could I have missed it? Not a hair appointment or a painful family dinner, but IT. The Big One. The thing I don't want each month but I don't not want.

WHY DIDN'T I GET MY PERIOD?

I should've gotten it on Monday and tomorrow I'm supposed to start my next pill pack, which means it never came.

I must do Internet research. I'm sure there is a logical explanation. One that doesn't involve anything "developing."

11:15 A.M.

Stress! I *have* been really stressed out lately with cleaning out my closet. And Butterscotch did barf on the couch the other day. Yes. I am stressed.

11:16 A.M.

Exercise! I totally exercised last week on the elliptical machine. Like two miles. Two miles *has* to be pretty hard on the body. I'm so glad I figured it out.

1:00 P.M.

What am I going to do? No, no I can't think like that. I *know* it is a fluke. Life will go on and I'll laugh about this with Julie next month as we sit around with bellinis telling our "I *so* thought I was pregnant when . . ." stories. Yes, this will all be a funny story soon. I know the way my life is supposed to go and missing a period for any reason other than stress or exercise is *not* what is supposed to happen.

2:00 P.M.

God wouldn't do this to me. I've been a good person. I've donated to charity and given good advice to my friends and even pointed out when a sales clerk gave me the wrong change.

8:00 P.M.

I'm at the movies, watching an action movie Jake has been dying to see. I haven't been able to follow it at all, considering I have bigger things to worry about than if the ugly guy is going to successfully kill the other guy. I'm not going to tell Jake. There's nothing to tell. Due to stress or exercise, my period never came this month, so why worry him? I don't want to freak him out over nothing. So, I'll tell him next month when my bastard period finally shows up and I can sigh in relief. Besides, if anything was a possibility, wouldn't I feel different? And I don't feel anything at all, minus the rotting white fear gnawing at the pit of my stomach. And besides, birth control pills are like 100 percent effective. OK, so not 100 percent effective, but really, really fucking close. I'm always reading they're the most effective method of birth control. If they stopped working at random times, people wouldn't use them, would they? I take mine at the same time every day, so I'm sure it's fine.

Except I want to beat the shit out of the voice in my head singing, "You were on antibiotics while you were in Vegas, weren't you? You had lots of very dirty sex while in Vegas, didn't you? Did you really take your pill at the same exact time every day when you were in Vegas? I didn't think so. You are an irresponsible drunk who is most likely pregnant." I mean, what's the chance my antibiotics affected anything? I'd say probably slimmer than the guy with the gun to his head's chances of surviving another hour. I mean, I've never seen articles in *Cosmo* about "My birth control stopped working after a sinus infection and it could happen to you!" I bet the myth of antibiotics lessening the effectiveness of birth control pills is really just an urban legend. I will look on one of those urban myth Web sites when I get home.

8:36 P.M.
OK, some kid was just kidnapped and is being held for ransom. Another reason not to have children: they can be used for ransom when the entire future of our country is at stake. I mean, we could all die because of this dude's weakness for his daughter. That is why it is not a good idea to have children.

9:30 P.M.
Oh gee, darn it. I think I just got my period. Man, I hate when that happens. Wouldn't you know it, I don't even have a tampon in my purse. I hope they have a vending machine in the bathroom.

9:36 P.M.
Fuck.

1:35 A.M.
I bet the antibiotics are the reason I missed it. They killed a bunch of bacteria in my body and I bet they killed some period stuff, too.

Sunday, May 6
. . . .
I went shopping with Julie yesterday. I should've been warming up my credit cards for their ass-kicking but instead spent the morning lying in bed, trying to ignore the acid churning in my stomach.

I kept telling myself to forget it and tell fabulous stories and have a fantastic time with Julie because when I finally *do* get my period, not only will I breathe a sigh of relief, I will have a wardrobe full of new clothes.

Or something like that.

2:00 P.M.

I arrived at Julie's apartment and knocked on the door. She let me in, flame red hair piled on top of her head, wearing bubble gum pink Juicy Couture sweatpants and a black bra.

"Hey, baby! Sorry, I'm running late as usual! I got hung up at work." She threw her arms around me and gestured for me to come inside. "You look fucking amazing! Love the top!"

"Thanks," was all I could squeak out, seeing as how thoughts of diapers and baby bottles still danced through my cerebral cortex.

"Just give me a sec and I'll be ready." She bounded down the hall-way to get changed, her enormous boobs bouncing everywhere.

"Your hair looks great. Did you just get it colored?" I yelled after her.

"Yep. Every six weeks at two hundred bucks a pop is a fucking nightmare but the color fades so fast. I would be a millionaire if I just gave up and went blond like every other bitch in this city."

I sank down on her IKEA couch and slowly took in the comfort of Julie's place. Her apartment still looks like a college student's—full bar, martini glasses, IKEA coffee table covered in *US Weekly* and *InStyle*, heels scattered on the floor, and media cabinet full of Julia Roberts movies. It's perfect.

"So what was going on at work?"

"Car accident plus multiple injuries equals a packed ER," she yelled from her bedroom.

"Sounds awful."

"It was. Good news: Hot Dr. Ben was on call so I got to stare at his ass while he stitched up a patient's laceration."

"At least it worked out."

"For me. Not so much for the patient. He's in pretty bad shape, poor guy." Julie appeared in front of me, arms outstretched, sporting enormous cleavage. "Too much boobage?"

"Possibly, considering it's not even happy hour."

"Sweetie, happy hour isn't a time, it's a state of mind."

I managed a weak laugh, fully expecting her to bust me and ask what was wrong, but her phone beeped and she opened it up and smiled.

"Who's it from?"

"Mark. Saying thanks for the hot sex last night."

"What?"

"Relax. I'm kidding."

"You'd better be. We've discussed that many, many times."

"C'mon, Clare, just once?"

"Sorry, no. You can't sleep with my brother."

"I swear I have nothing but honorable intentions."

"Julie, he's looking for a nice girl, not one who will sneak out in the morning before the sun comes up."

"Clearly you haven't heard his college stories."

I knew I couldn't hide my gloominess forever, so on the walk over to Michigan Avenue I initiated Julie's favorite game: Remember the Time When . . .

Me: "Remember the time, sophomore year, when you did the Walk of Shame at eight in the morning after that Bikers and Babes party and you walked through a group of pre-frosh with their parents touring campus?"

Julie: "Remember the time, freshman year, at the Sigma house, when some guy hit on you while you were peeing in a bush outside? What did he say? Oh, I know, 'I've never kissed a girl while she was peeing,' and then he leaned down and stuck his gross tongue in your mouth?"

Me: "Or the time Reese's mom found a list we made of our hookups, written in code so it said things like 'Sigma Pee Boy.' She thought we not only slept with all those guys, but couldn't remember their names so we had to make up nicknames for them?"

Silence.

Julie: "Reese. God."

Me: "Oh, look! We're here."

3:00 P.M.

". . . so fucking hot and his lips are amazing. He's so hot I'd sit on his face on a Sunday." Julie rambled on about her ongoing lust for Hot Dr. Ben. By this point, she'd already bought two pairs of boots, a pair of gold chandelier earrings, and four cute camisoles, and all I'd bought was a latte.

"Oh, and did I tell you I have another strange coworker?"

Happy for the distraction, I said, "Really? Do tell. I love your coworker stories."

"He's another nurse but can't seem to stop touching his crotch. Like, I'll ask him what he did last night and he'll shift his dong with every other word. He even pulses it a little, like he's humping the air, when he talks to people."

"That's disgusting. Shouldn't you say something to your hiring manager or something?"

"What the hell for? It's entertaining. He loves— Hey!" She stopped and looked at me. "Why haven't you bought anything yet?" She stared suspiciously at my empty hands.

I'd lost the will to spend all of my rent money when I saw a display of maternity clothes in the first store we visited. I knew I needed to buy something immediately. I desperately reached out and grabbed whatever my hand connected with first and blurted out, "I'm so buying this."

Julie looked at me strangely. "That?"

I looked down and realized I had grabbed a *very* unflattering pink hair bow.

"Um, yeah. Hair bows are back in," I mumbled.

After I purchased my stylish accessory, Julie decided she needed some new bras so we headed over to Victoria's Secret. I moped around the store, wishing I was home and curled up in bed.

"Clare. Clare—come here," Julie called from one of the dressing rooms.

"What?" I asked, hoping she wasn't going to show me a thong or something.

"Can you get me the cute flower bra in a bigger size? My nipples are showing in this one."

"I guess so," I said with as much enthusiasm as I could scrape together.

She poked her head but thankfully not her nipples out from behind the door. "What's wrong? Are you OK?" she asked.

"Yeah."

"Why haven't you bought anything? Didn't you say you wanted something for your anniversary?" She stared at me with narrowed eyes.

"Sex is bad. Highly overrated. With dire consequences."

"What?"

"It's bad, Jules," I said, shaking my head and staring at the floor. I couldn't even make eye contact with her; I was afraid I'd dissolve into the pink-carpeted floor.

"What? You're getting divorced, aren't you?" She opened the door and stepped out of the dressing room—thong, too-small bra, nipples showing, and all. A guy noticed, choked on his gum, and dropped a bottle of perfume.

"Maybe we should go in here." I pushed her back into the dressing room and closed the door behind us.

"What the fuck is going on?" she asked, biting her lip.

"Well, I'm sure it's nothing but I'm really worried and I don't want you to freak out or anything."

"*What?*"

"My freaking period is late, OK?" I threw my hands up.

"Oh, God! That's it? I thought you were having an affair or something." She threw her arms around me. "I mean, that totally sucks but it's no biggie, right? Just a fluke."

"Um, yeah. I'm just freaking out."

"You're still on the pill, right?"

"Yeah, but I was on antibiotics."

She waved her hands around. "That is such crap. You're totally fine. I mean, it's like that time that—"

"I know, I know. Hey, Jules?"

"Yeah?"

"I'm gonna go out there because the fact I'm having this conversation while I can see your nipples is disturbing me."

"Oh. Sorry."

I stepped out of the dressing room and took the black rain cloud with me. A few minutes later, Julie walked out.

"Shopping trip is over," she said.

"What? Why?"

"We have other things to do."

"Is this because of what I said? Just forget it. I'm sure it's nothing. I swear, I'll buy something."

"I *know* it's nothing. That's why we're going to get you one of those tests so you can relax."

"No way. I'm not ready for that."

"Are you ready to drink wine and smoke cigarettes?"

"Always, what's your point?"

"Well, my dear, that's exactly what we're going to do once you take that test and life can go on."

"I just don't think I can," I said.

"I'll even take one with you."

"That's crazy. You didn't even miss your period."

"No crazier than you freaking out, since you're totally fine."

"Well, I—"

"Shut up. We're doing it," she said.

4:00 P.M.

"Look at how expensive they are. No way. I'm not doing this. I can't afford it." I tried to walk away from the Scary Aisle in Walgreens and over to the fun section to buy some nail polish, but Julie grabbed my elbow and yanked me back in front of the pregnancy tests.

"I saw you buy a pair of boots last month that cost the equivalent of forty of these tests. Now's not the time to be the girl who cried poor, OK?"

I thought, *Why? Why did I have to tell her? Why couldn't I be trying on lingerie or jeans right now instead of profusely sweating in a drug store?*

"Fine. You pick one," I finally said as I wiped my hands on my jeans. She squinted at all eight million options and picked one out.

"Here! This one says 'early result.' This way there will be no doubt in your mind."

Great, just what I'm looking for—concrete answers.

"Whatever," I mumbled as I grabbed it from her and headed toward the cashier. I picked up a few fashion magazines and some gum to hopefully distract the cashier from thinking I'm a Big Pregnant Ho. I also made sure to use my left hand to scratch my nose a few times so he would see my wedding ring. I thought the first time I bought a pregnancy test would be a time when it was something I'd be hoping for, not praying against like a knocked-up high school student.

Maybe Julie is right. Maybe I'll be drinking martinis and laughing about this in an hour.

An hour later, we were back at my place.

"Did you do it right?" Julie asked casually, sipping a vodka martini.

"How should I know? I've never done this before." I tried to grab the other martini next to her on the table but she slid it away.

"Oh, no. Not yet. This is for after you get your negative and the world can go back to revolving." She took another big swig of her drink. "God, can you imagine if you are?"

"Julie! What the hell does that mean?"

"Oh, whatever. I can say it since you aren't, but what if you are? What would you do?"

"There wouldn't be anything to *do*. Except completely flip out."

"Yeah. Your life would pretty much be over. You'd have to wear high-waisted mom jeans and spend your paycheck on diapers."

"*Julie!*"

"Just kidding. Can you imagine?"

"I thought you said I'm not so I shouldn't even worry about it!" I cried out.

"I know! You're not—don't worry. Has it been two minutes yet?"

I glanced at the clock, wondering if 5:24 would become a signifi-
cant moment.

"Yeah."

"Well, go look," she said.

"I can't. I think I'm frozen. You do it."

"Fine, drama queen." She rolled her eyes and hopped off the stool
and disappeared into the bathroom.

I tried to take a deep breath and calm down but grabbed the martini glass instead and took a big swig. I figured one more swallow
wouldn't hurt.

There was dead silence as Julie came out of the bathroom.

She held the test and stared at it.

"Where's the box?" she said in this weird, almost nonhuman
voice.

"Why? What is it?" I said, my voice shaking.

"The box! The box it came in. Where is it?" That voice again.

"I don't know, it's in the garbage or something. WHY? WHAT
IS GOING ON?" I reached for the test and she jerked her arm away.
"Give it to me."

She just stared at me.

"Give me the fucking test."

She slowly extended her arm and handed me the test. I looked
down and saw two pink lines.

Oh, God.

I started gagging.

"Clare! Get to the sink!" Julie rushed me over to the kitchen.

A million thoughts ran in my head in between heaves.

How could this have happened?

Bleech.

What did I do wrong?

Bleech.

Does this mean I have to stop drinking?

Bleech.

"It's OK, hon. It will be fun! Designer diaper bags and all. And Seven! Seven jeans! Maternity jeans! Just came out! Coincidence? I think not! You'll be super skinny still! You'll probably be smaller than me when you deliver! I should lend you some of my clothes to wear as maternity clothes!" Julie blabbered on, rat-a-tat-tatting like a jackhammer.

I sank down and sat on the kitchen floor, still unable to grasp what was happening. I thought I was hallucinating. I couldn't comprehend the fact I was sitting on my kitchen floor, listening to Julie, while *pregnant*.

A thought raced through my head: *Does this mean there's something growing inside of me?*

Julie didn't stop talking for two hours. I think she was afraid if she stopped talking, I'd flip out and start screaming and running around.

The horrible panic and vomiting had subsided, replaced by a comatose feeling of calm. I started thinking. *I can totally do this. I'll wear designer clothes for a few months, have the kid, be skinny again and buy some baby stuff. I'm not going to be one of those frumpy moms who wears Christmas sweaters and breast-feeds their kid until age four.*

Julie continued on about celebrities with kids. "Reese Witherspoon! Her baby wasn't planned and she's this huge movie star with a gorgeous husband and a size-two body. Having a kid helped her career! Well, she and her husband did get divorced but you and Jake totally won't get divorced so you'll be like Reese Witherspoon but *better!*"

She shook my shoulder a little. "Clare? Clare? Are you OK?"

"Mmmm," I responded.

"And don't worry! Sex is going to be awesome for you! Did you know that being knocked up increases the blood flow to a woman's hoo-ha? So, orgasms will be even better!" Julie flung her hands out.

I slowly turned my head and stared at her, silent. She sounded like her head was going to explode. Amazingly, I remained calm in my Zenlike hypnotic state.

"No, it's true! One time I had to put a catheter in a pregnant woman and she got off from it. Shit! We all should be so lucky, right?"

I narrowed my eyes at her and she shut up. We sat silent on the kitchen floor, staring at the clumps of cat hair skittering by our feet like tumbleweeds across a Western plain. I realized the irony of my situation now, compared to the last time I sat on the kitchen floor. I couldn't wrap my mind around what was happening. It wasn't supposed to be like this. Finding out I'm pregnant is supposed to be an exhilarating, thrilling, and *wanted* moment. But all I could feel was fear. Fear about how Jake would react. Fear about how I was supposed to react.

After several minutes, I cleared my throat. "Well, I guess—," I started to say when I heard the front door open.

"Hey, Clare! Guess what? The liquor store was having a sale on that Riesling you like so I bought a case of it." Jake was home.

I looked at Julie, my face going pale and forehead beginning to throb. The acid in my stomach churned again and I swallowed quickly to keep from getting sick again.

We both quickly peeled ourselves off of the kitchen floor and stood up just as Jake walked in.

"HI!" Julie yelled, making Jake jump a bit.

Jake's eyes shifted from Julie to me. "Hey. What's going on?" he asked.

I'm not sure what tipped him off, Julie's fake high-pitched voice or my inability to lift my pale and sweaty face and meet his eyes.

Or maybe it was because both of us were covered in an inch of dust and cat hair from the kitchen floor.

"What's going on?" he asked again.

I wasn't going to say anything. I figured Julie could tell him.

But that damn bitch smiled and said, "Well! Gotta run! Call me later!" and kissed me on the cheek and clocked Olympic-sprinter speed running to the front door.

It's already happening. People have already started to ditch me since I'm pregnant.

Jake took a step toward me and tried to grab my hand but I pulled it away. I knew if he touched me I'd fall apart.

"Please tell me what's going on."

I waited a few seconds until I knew I could speak without sounding squeaky. "Let's go over here," I said, and pointed to the couch. We sat down and I saw his hands shaking.

"I have some news and I don't want you to freak out. It will be OK."

He nodded slowly, and I could see his right eye twitching slightly.

"It's no big deal but I took a test today and, um, it wasn't negative."

I studied his face for a reaction and all I saw was confusion.

"For what?"

"What?"

"Not negative for what?"

"Jake, it wasn't negative for, um, pregnancy."

He leaned back and his look of shock almost broke my heart.

"What?" he finally whispered.

"Yeah, apparently we are going to have a baby." I could barely say the word "baby."

Long pause.

"I guess I should return that case of wine I just bought."

It was a start.

"Yeah, I guess so."

We sat there in silence for several more minutes. I twisted my hands in my lap, the fear tightening its grip on my shoulders. I was afraid I ruined the moment. I was afraid I was expected to lead the way and act happy and excited. I was afraid he'd ask me if we should keep the baby.

"Are you OK?" I asked.

"I'm fine."

It must've been the Zenlike comatose state.

Around midnight, after five hundred and eighty-seven more "fine"s, Jake broke down. He started sweating and asking questions about Scary Things like day care, breast-feeding, money, and who is going to baby-sit during the annual St. Patrick's Day Pub Crawl. I certainly didn't have any of the answers. After exhausting every angle, our heads were about to explode, so we watched the Weather Channel for an hour and went to bed.

God, we're already acting like parents.

3:00 A.M.

Neither of us slept much. I desperately wanted to, in dramatic fashion, fling myself down on the bed and curl into a ball, but I knew if I let my emotions out of the corner of my brain where they were so tightly bound, I'd never be able to rein them back in. I'd walk around for the rest of my life as an emotional wreck, unable to process my sudden loss of freedom. I'd be an elderly old lady, yelling at the kids who stepped on my lawn, "Get off my property, you punks. Did you know I got pregnant when I was on BIRTH CONTROL? DO YOU KNOW THAT CAN HAPPEN?" and they'd say of course they did and spit on my daffodils.

So, I've chosen to remain not completely in denial, but really fucking close.

I woke up in the middle of the night thinking, *It was a horrible nightmare. Yes, dreamt all of it, like the time I dreamt that the Backstreet Boys called me up to ask if Jake could be a member but I said no because he had to make pancakes for the cat. Maybe it is a secret lesson designed to make me appreciate my youth? I dreamt all of it.*

Except I knew it wasn't a dream. I could feel Jake throwing himself around in bed, making it obvious he was awake, meaning he wanted me to talk to him. But I couldn't. I was too scared and freaked out.

Sometime in the morning, Jake poked me and whispered, "You awake?"

"Yeah."

"Do you want to talk?"

"Not really," I mumbled.

"Oh. Okay."

I rolled over and snuggled against Jake's back and wrapped my arm around him. I buried my head in his T-shirt and breathed in the smell of Tide Ultra. He put his hand over mine and brought it to his mouth and kissed it.

I want to freeze everything right now, when things are quiet.

I know things are going to be different. I know we're about to go down the rabbit hole and the whole universe is going to kick us in the ass.

I took a deep breath and gave him a little squeeze. "I love you," I said.

"I love you, too," he whispered back. "You know I want to keep the baby, right?"

"You do?" I lifted my head off the pillow a little.

"I do."

"I'm scared, but me too," I said, my voice wavering.

"It's going to be great," he said.

We finally fell asleep.

Monday, May 7
. . . .

I can't help but feel like I'm on a roller coaster that just pulled out of the station. The car hasn't even gone over the first hill, but I'm already ready for it to be over.

I don't have any philosophical reasoning why all of this is happening, but I know we're stuck for the ride.

Julie left a million messages on my cell phone but I'm not ready to talk to her yet. She'll just ask me a bunch of questions I don't have the answers to and name more knocked-up celebrities. And forget about telling my parents or, God help me, Jake's parents. No, I'm not ready to share this info yet. I'll tell them eventually, like right after I deliver.

"I'm just fine, Marianne. Oh, I almost forgot to tell you, I birthed a child earlier. Congratulations! You're a grandma! Yes, I'm going back to work and no, I'm still not changing my last name."

I can't even think about this right now. Work, I must focus on work right now.

11:30 A.M.

Mule Face totally knows. I can feel it. When I saw her in the conference room, she glanced at my stomach. Why would she do that? I bet
she knows. It would be so typical of her. She probably went through
my trash last night and found the seven pregnancy tests I took, praying that one, just one would come up negative, meaning I could dis-
regard all of the other positive ones and have a cocktail. But those
little buggers came up positive each time.

2:00 P.M.

Google. Google is my friend. (I had to break up with my old best
friend, Belvedere vodka. I told him I'd write and in nine months, we
could totally hang.) I'm going to Google "pregnant tips" and the
learning will begin.

2:06 P.M.

I'm super pissed off. It's amazing how hard it is to even get pregnant.
The average woman (who is *not* on the pill) has a less than 25 percent
chance each month of conceiving even if everything is timed perfectly. Which makes me the most fertile asshole on the planet. I
should become an infertility counselor. I'd tell people all they have to
do is take birth control pills while on antibiotics. Hmmm . . . I
might be on to something. Maybe I can invent a new fertility treatment. The money would certainly help with the upcoming diaper
expenses. It might also help fund a personal trainer, tummy tuck, and
breast lift. I checked those prices, too.

4:00 P.M.

I must update my blog, although I have no idea what to write about.
Maybe I can do a random mundane entry about my extreme distaste
for bulk-shopping grocery stores. It has to be somewhat coherent,
since my last entry was written at two in the morning on Friday and
titled "Crann3p#ples Rules!"

Tuesday, May 8

· · · · · · · · · · · · · · · · ·

Still in shock, Jake and I went to an Italian restaurant for dinner last night. I hoped the public setting would eliminate the possibility of sudden crying jags or flipping out. We tried to talk about things other than the pregnancy, but the conversation sounded something like this:

"So, Jake. How's work?"

"Fine, Clare. Thanks for asking. How's your work?"

"Splendid." I swear, I almost said it with an English accent. "Your sweater is very lovely, Jake."

"Thanks, Clare. You look very nice yourself."

Five minutes of polite conversation, and I cracked. I put my hands up to my face and said, "What are we going to do?"

"Nothing," Jake said simply.

"What?" I peeked in between my spread fingers.

"There's nothing to do. We just need to accept it and plan accordingly."

"How can you be so calm about this?"

Jake shrugged. It was so like him to be the rational one.

"But what about money and day care and the fact that we have no idea how to be parents?" I moaned.

"Like we said the other night: we'll figure it out."

"Haumph. You're way too OK with all of this." I crossed my arms over my chest.

"Don't get me wrong, I'm freaked out, too. I'm just keeping it to myself. One of us needs to keep you away from the ledge."

I glared at him. I started to retort, but I was distracted by a waiter walking by with a glass of red wine. I immediately became depressed and desperately wanted to jerk my hand out, grab the glass, and down it. I settled for shoveling a huge bowl of pasta into my mouth. I rationalized it was for the baby—the one huge benefit of pregnancy.

My depression over the prospect of nine long red wine–less months continued today, when Carrie e-mailed me some pictures from the infamous Cranapple Night, a.k.a. Clare's Last Night of Drinking Ever. Extreme sadness pricked behind my eyes as I looked over the pictures of all of us holding our pretty red drinks and smiling drunkenly for the camera.

I became so entranced by the pretty colored drinks, I nearly forgot about my first meeting with the Women's Board ladies at nine until I heard Mule Face lead them into the conference room. I quickly grabbed the event file and rushed down the hallway, just in time to hear Mule Face gush over Carolyn Wittenberg's Gucci loafers. Carolyn, President/Head Bitch, greeted me coolly with a limp handshake. I saw her eyes quickly dart to my shoes as she sat down. Thankfully, I anticipated this and wore my Lanvin flats.

Betsy Fallon and Jessica Greene, the Gala cochairs, were close behind and rushed in and sat down, each looking as though the Neiman Marcus catalog barfed all over them.

"Clare, I'd like to begin by giving you a brief overview of this year's event and then we can get into the specifics regarding your responsibilities." Carolyn placed her alligator-rimmed glasses on the tip of her nose and peered down at me as Betsy and Jessica poured themselves cups of coffee.

"Sounds great." I smiled a little too widely as I placed my hands under the table to hide my chipped manicure.

"The Women's Board Gala is the premier event in the Chicago area. It is the gold standard to which all other black-tie events are compared. We not only represent ourselves and our community at this event, but also the fine tradition and long history of the Women's Board." Carolyn stopped and stared at the tiny pen mark on my sleeve.

I nodded my head. "Absolutely."

"That said, I cannot tolerate any mistakes or errors or omissions for this event. It must be completely flawless." All three of them stared at me silently and I realized I was supposed to say something.

"Absolutely," I said again.

"Clare," Jessica began, "this year's theme will be 'An Evening in Asia' and we are planning on incorporating an Asian theme into everything from the decorations, to the food, to the silent auction. It promises to be a fabulous event."

"The theme is fun. We really like it," Betsy said. I once heard Christina refer to Betsy Fallon as having the personality of a houseplant. A very accurate assessment.

"Clare, here is a list of responsibilities we've been told that your company will handle for us." Carolyn slid a packet of paper three inches thick toward me. Except it only made it halfway so I awkwardly half stood and groped around the table until I reached it.

Carolyn continued, "We've usually handled most of these tasks, so there are very specific ways that we want these things accomplished. This year we've had an unprecedented number of members who had personal crises, so we have less manpower than before." I nodded my head, thinking, *Personal crises? What, like, someone's gardener quit and their favorite rose plant died? Or, someone had to fly coach when first class was sold out and they became disgusted by the mealy communal pillows and blankets?*

"It's going to be such a wonderful event and we're looking forward to working with you," Jessica said, and nodded her head enthusiastically. I shot her a grateful look.

I opened the thick packet, which detailed the next few months of hell and included everything from stuffing their invitations to assembling favors.

"That said, Clare, this is a lot of work and we've been assured your full attention until the event. Betsy and Jessica," Carolyn turned toward them, "think of Clare as your sort of personal assistant to help you through the event. Anything you need, you call her. She is here to be your support system."

Four years of college, seven of working in event planning, and I'm called a personal assistant? Awesome.

Jessica and Betsy smiled at Carolyn and beamed at me.

"Now, ladies, you must excuse me, I have an appointment at George's that I cannot miss." Within seconds, Carolyn left the room and all that remained was the smell of her perfume and my churning stomach.

"So, what's the first order of business?" I asked carefully.

"Well, we'd like to get the letters out asking people for silent auction donations as soon as possible, so that would be great," Jessica said.

The silent auction each year is the crown jewel of the entire event. The auction is where most of the proceeds from the event originate. The women use their connections to secure extravagant prizes, with everyone trying to outdo each other. Last year alone the prizes included a trip to the Seychelles, a private catered party for one hundred and fifty, and a week-long stay in the Presidential Suite of the Four Seasons. Since the guests are some of the richest people in the city, and are usually pretty intoxicated, the prizes usually go for well over market value, which is rare in a silent auction.

"Certainly, we'll have those completed by the end of the week." Suddenly I had a horrible vision of the next few months, a vision of me saying, "Absolutely," "Yes," "Certainly," and "Of course," like some robotic prostitute.

Three hours later, Betsy and Jessica left. My hair was thrown back into a haphazard ponytail, my makeup was running, and my head was pounding from nodding and smiling.

Man, I wish I could go home and have a glass (or two or three or, OK, a bottle) of wine tonight. After I'm done being pregnant, I'm going to focus on inventing a safe-for-pregnant-women wine. I'll be a millionaire.

Wednesday, May 9
· · · · · · · · · · · · · · · · · ·

My cravings for wine are still going strong and continued as I drove home from work today. Unable to satisfy my longing, I settled on indulging another addiction: books. I peeled into the parking lot of the first bookstore I saw, tore inside, and headed straight for the pregnancy section. I blindly grabbed every single book I saw. I ripped through them when I got home and quickly came to this conclusion: pregnancy books are the equivalent of the Homeland Security Alerts on the news.

I mean, after reading all of the inflammatory warnings, I felt like I should be stocking up on canned goods and building a bomb shelter in my parents' basement.

Many of the warnings are common sense (*Really?* You mean it isn't good for the baby to down this bottle of scotch and smoke a joint? Seriously? Well, what about half of the bottle and a few puffs? What if I don't inhale? You're joking!), but others are downright ridiculous. Apparently, lunch meat and goat cheese are the equivalent of smoking crack, according to some books. Do people actually buy that crap? I'm sorry, but no alcohol or cigarettes means I can have a turkey sandwich if I want. No one is going to convince me I need to exist on organic granola and fruit for the next nine months. And I pity anyone who tries to pry my diet pop out of my soon-to-be-fat pregnant fingers.

Besides all of the food warnings, these books go into graphic detail *with pictures* about labor and delivery. I actually threw one book across the bedroom in shock when I read that something like 80 percent of women poop on the table when they're pushing during labor. Horrified, I showed Jake, who laughed and thought it was hilarious. Why does it seem pregnancy is one small indignity after another ending with one giant loss of pride? Isn't nine months of discomfort, nausea, hemorrhoids, varicose veins, stretch marks, profuse sweating, and heartburn enough? Why must God give us one final kick in the teeth involving bodily functions in front of everyone right before the baby comes out? Is it because having your girly parts on display just isn't humiliating enough?

I'm wondering how difficult it would be to sew my knees together.

Why are there no helpful books on pregnancy? Why are there no books called *What to Do When Your Husband Impregnates You But You Can't Have a Baby Because All of Your Furniture Is a Collapsible Death-trap from IKEA and Plus You Don't Even Like Kids That Much?* Now *that* is a book I'd find helpful.

It reminds me of right after I graduated high school and everybody gave me these books about college and the "Real World" (grown-up world, not the TV show). These books were all totally worthless because they had advice like "Make yourself stand out in class. Introduce yourself to your professor on the first day." Now, anyone who has actually attended college knows standing out is the last thing to do in class because then the professor will notice absences. I could've used a book outlining things like what to do when your roommate is having loud sex when you're in the room or what to do when you oversleep and miss a final. That is shit I actually *needed* the answers to.

So, I ask: Why can't there be a pregnancy book that tells me what to do when everyone else is partying on the Fourth of July? What to do to ensure I'm back to my prepregnancy body no more than one month after giving birth? How to convince everyone I'm still cool to hang out with even though I'm the fat, knocked-up one? Who the fuck thought giving us a child would be a good experiment?

Because these are things I need to know. Immediately.

Thursday, May 10
. . . .

I gave the pregnancy books another shot today. Once I got past all of the disgusting details about labor and delivery and the inflammatory warnings, I started to actually learn a few things. For example, my child currently has a tail. I'm pregnant with a little tiny dragon. Which is kind of awesome.

I wanted to do nothing more than spend the day on the Web learning about the very strange process of growing a baby, but Mule Face provided a very compelling distraction. Apparently, she has a new boyfriend she met on the Internet. His name is Dwight but she calls him "Big D." It's his screen name, and I will assume the "D" stands for his name and not anything else. He's from Wisconsin and only drinks champagne cocktails when he goes out. He also, based on the photo she e-mailed to everyone, has a severely receding hairline and slightly resembles a frog. Nothing gives me more pleasure than watching her show Big D's picture to someone, seeing their initial re-action of shock/horror, and then watching them quickly try to cover it up by complimenting his orange striped shirt or something.

She put a picture of him on her desk and periodically says things like "Look at how cute he is!" and "I could just lick him!" throughout the day. I also listened to her talk to him on the phone in a high-pitched baby voice in between slurps of microwave oatmeal. Occasion-ally, her voice drops down to a whisper and I hear things like "hot" and "can't wait." Like they're having phone sex. Sick. It makes me want to cut off my arm and throw it at her.

It was kind of all worth it though when I heard Isabel Castle's mother ask her if she is color-blind because the wrong tablecloths were ordered for Isabel's birthday.

It's times like these that I wish I could talk about work on my blog. I'd love to post a picture of Mule Face's feathered bangs and watch the comments fly. But I'd like to keep my job, especially in light of the Dragon. I can't talk about that, either, so I'm going to write an entry recapping one of my old drunken college stories. Besides, right now? An entry on the pregnancy would look something like this: HELP ME INTERNET PEOPLE! I'M PREGNANT. SEND HELP. AND DIA-PERS.

I have to write something, because I've gotten twenty e-mails ask-ing if everything is OK since I haven't updated as frequently. Wifey1025 offered to drop off some of her famous chocolate chip cook-ies if I would please just give her my address and phone number.

Friday, May 11
. . . .

I was so busy Googling Mule Face's new boyfriend yesterday I com-pletely forgot about this weekend's trip: the Famous In-Law Week-end Camping Extravaganza with the Grandalskis. Unfortunately, my recently discovered "delicate condition" does not, in any way, preclude me from participating. I've asked Jake many times.

I am so *not* looking forward to the campfire sing-alongs and the eating of nonperishable food. We aren't sleeping in tents or anything but we're staying in a gross cabin with bare-bones indoor plumbing while being expected to do "outdoorsy" things like sit around a campfire while battling giant woods-dwelling insects and wildlife. I am also not looking forward to sharing a tiny cabin with my husband and my in-laws. Oh, and Natalie, Jake's sister-in-law, who I only recently stopped wishing would fall into a deep, dark hole. My mother-in-law, Marianne, invited her to stay with us since her husband, Doug, is out of town this weekend.

Recap: Five adults crammed into a tiny cabin in the middle of the woods.

It sounds like the opening scenes of a slasher movie.

I hope I get killed first. (Although I realize I probably won't since I will be sober all weekend. The sluts and the drunks always get killed first. Lucky bastards.)

My readers thoughtfully suggested some tips to make the weekend easier, all of which include massive quantities of alcohol and/or illegal drugs. They would normally be very good suggestions. Wifey1025 asked if she could come. I had to tell her no, I don't think the Grandalskis would be open to inviting strangers from the Internet. Also, please stop asking me if I want to take knitting classes together.

11:00 P.M.

I haven't fallen asleep yet thanks to Jake's dad. Moaning. In his sleep. All night long. Seriously. As though he's having some erotic dream. One I'm sure doesn't involve his wife.

It's been a horrible start to a sure-to-be-torturous weekend. Even the drive out here was painful. It went something like this:

"Look! See! I told you!" I shoved my cell phone an inch from Jake's face and hysterically pointed at my continually weakening signal as we tried to find the campground.

He pushed my hand out of his face. "Jesus, I can barely see the road." He squinted and leaned forward.

Ignoring him, I continued my cell phone tirade. "Jake, what did I tell you about my phone signal? That anywhere you can't get a signal is probably not a good place to be! What happens if I accidentally chop my finger off and need to be rushed to the ER? What will happen then? Do they even have 911 out here? What if there's an emergency at home, like our apartment burning down? How will anyone get ahold of us?" I sadly watched the last bar of my signal disappear, and peered out the window into the darkness. "This probably means I won't get a wireless signal either, huh?"

"Did you honestly expect to be able to use the Internet while camping?"

"Yes, I did. The entire civilized world has wireless. Except for this hillbilly pocket in the middle of nowhere." I paused. "I don't think we're going to find it. I mean, it's already late and we should probably stay in that nice Holiday Inn Express we passed a while back."

"Lake Park Campground!" Jake turned into a fenced-in area and an ancient old man waved us through the gate. Apparently they have security guards at campgrounds. Do people actually try to sneak in? Or is it to keep people from escaping once they see the bathroom facilities?

We drove through the campground and *Christ*.

I swear I heard banjos playing as we passed a giant RV with neon beer signs (which made me quite sad since it served as a reminder that Bud Light is, indeed, cold and refreshing), some plastic lawn animals, and a NASCAR sign.

"Hey look! There's Julie's relatives!" Jake said.

"Leave Julie alone. She may have grown up in a trailer but at least she has the smarts to stay the fuck away."

"I swear, I didn't know it was going to be this bad," he said.

I looked over at him. His eyes met mine and he spit out an explosion of laughter as tears poured from his eyes.

"YOU KNEW IT WAS LIKE THIS, DIDN'T YOU? RIGHT? RIGHT?"

He didn't answer me; he was too busy gasping for breath and hyperventilating.

I poked him in the ribs and stuck my finger in his face. "You owe me BIG TIME for this. And I mean Big. Time. Big time like chick flicks for a year, new designer bag big time."

He nodded, still coughing from lack of oxygen.

"Do you think Carrie is here yet?" I asked. "Thank God she's coming."

"Ummm, mmmm," Jake responded.

Which was Not. Good.

"She's still coming, right?"

"Yep. She and Patrick are still coming," pause, "tomorrow."

"WHA?"

"Oh, look, we're here." I continued to stare at him as we pulled up to a giant buslike RV thing surrounded by a few tiny cabins and a bunch of those pop-out trailer/camper things.

I peered through the windshield out into the darkness and made out a shitload of Jake's elderly relatives. They sat all circled around the fire, probably telling stories about how kids today don't appreciate nature the way they did and how our society's tolerance of gays will bring us eternal suffering in the afterlife.

I also saw enough kids to fill a day care center, running around and beating each other with sticks.

I'm so lucky. I get to spend the weekend with old farts and a bunch of kids.

And Marianne.

I got out of the car cautiously, like an animal testing its surroundings. One of the stick children spotted us and ran over to the old people.

"SOME WEIRD PEOPLE ARE HERE!"

Marianne saw us and ran over.

"Welcome, Mr. and Mrs. Grandalski!"

"Marianne, it's still Finnegan."

She tittered. "Oh, you modern girls! I just don't know what to do with you! You know, in my day, there wasn't such a thing as a stay-at-home mom or a stay-at-home wife. You were just a wife and a mother. Your family was your priority, you know. Not your career, you know."

Another "In My Day" story. She forgets she's the same age as my mother, the bra-burning, protest-attending, card-carrying member of NOW.

"Er, uh, yeah! Hello to you, too. Where's Natalie?"

"Oh, she's lying down in the cabin. She has terrible morning sickness. You know, her pregnancy is considered high-risk."

Yeah, probably because she could stand to lose a couple hundred pounds.

"That's too bad."

"Yes, dear. I've really had to be there for her lately. You know, since her own relationship with her mother is not so strong. She's really become the daughter I've never had."

"Where's Doug again?" Jake asked.

"On a business trip," she said.

Right. He probably just wanted a weekend away from his wife. I'm sticking to my theory that when Doug proposed he was either (a) severely wasted, or (b) a contestant on an unaired reality show.

We made our way past the children accosting each other with lumber, who are apparently all Jake's third cousins or something, and over to the old people. After a quick hello, I settled down into a folding soccer chair and within sixty seconds a gross beetle thing landed on my boob. I screamed and jumped up, frantically trying to bat it off my chest. Jake came over and knocked it off. All the little kids, watching me very intently, exploded in laughter because I yelled, "Get it off! Get it off! It's on my BOOB!" while flailing around as though on fire.

I decided five minutes of nature was enough and Marianne showed me the way to our cabin.

I pushed the door open and immediately saw Natalie inside, sprawled out on the couch, moaning.

"Well, hi! How are you? How are you feeling?"

"Oh, hello, Clare." She didn't look thrilled to see me.

"How's my sweet girl doing?" Marianne asked.

"Horrible. I have excruciating gas pains."

Jake walked in behind us. "So, is this our place? Hey, Natalie," he said.

She responded by farting.

"Yes, it is," I said, a little too quickly.

There was a long awkward pause as we all stood there, shoulder-to-shoulder in the tiny space, silent except for Natalie's ass.

"Well, we should go," Jake said, and practically shoved me out the door.

Marianne followed us out and a thought suddenly occurred to me.

"Marianne, where are we supposed to sleep? I saw the futon and the loft with the air mattress but what about us?"

Her mouth twitched. "Well, the table and benches fold into a bed."

Yes, the table and benches MacGyver their way into a bed. A bed I am expected to sleep in with a six-three man for two nights. It is such bullshit. The futon was supposed to be ours and that bitch Natalie is sprawled out on it like a princess while Jake and I sleep on a table. She wasn't even supposed to come this weekend but Jake's brother had to torture all of us by going out of town knowing his fat pregnant wife can't possibly be alone for more than an hour.

"Maybe Natalie could sleep on it since there's two of us?" I suggested.

Marianne looked surprised. "Clare, she's preparing for childbirth. She needs some space."

I should've slept in the car like a homeless person.

Jake did the polite thing and joined the old people around the campfire while I leaned against the RV and tried to block out what I was hearing—something about how Pat Robertson and the *700 Club* are so inspiring. I looked around at the other campsites, located surprisingly close to ours. I thought this was supposed to be a quiet, relaxing time in the woods, not hanging out with our family *and* the weirdos next to us.

After an hour, I decided it was time to go pass out. Natalie was already asleep, snoring lightly. I fiddled with the bed/table/bench until I got it somewhat flat.

And so here I am, lying on an incline, listening to Frank's erotic dreams and Natalie's occasional farts.

Saturday, May 12

. . . .

Oh, thank sweet Jesus. Carrie is coming today. At least I'll have someone here who won't try to convince me hiking is really peaceful or sleeping in the open air is refreshing.

9:30 A.M.

Me: "Where is she? You said they'd be here in the morning."

Jake: "Relax. Patrick and I have a noon tee time. They'll be here."

9:45 A.M.

Me: "Maybe they're lost. I could call them if this horrible phone would get a signal."

10:05 A.M.

Me: "Let me try your phone. Ah! Praise the Lord! I think you have some juice. NO! Fuck. I just lost it."

11:01 A.M.

Me: "Where. The. Hell. Are. They. Your mother is trying to convince me to go to some Amish cheese shop with her. I need someone NORMAL to hang out with."

11:20 A.M.

They're here!

2:00 P.M.

I love Carrie.

When she and Patrick arrived, I raced over to their car before it even came to a standstill. I saw their looks of slight alarm behind their sunglasses. I'm sure I'd be afraid, too, if some crazed woman wearing lotion-smudged sweatpants threw herself in front of my car.

"Hi! Hi! Hi!" I spurted, waving vigorously.

Patrick rolled down his window and poked his head out. "What the hell happened to you?"

"Screw you," I said.

Carrie got out of the passenger side and pushed her sunglasses back onto her head, fanning out her perfectly highlighted hair.

"Hey, Clare. Looks like you've been having fun."

"You have no idea. I'm *dying* here! Thank the dear Lord that you guys are here. You won't *believe* the things I've seen!"

"Hey, everybody! It's some of them city folk we've been hearing about!" Jake yelled across the campsite in a fake twang. He walked over and bear-hugged Carrie. "How's my favorite girl?"

"Fab. I think you should be asking your wife that question."

"Whatever, you have no— Whoa!" I shrieked.

All three of their heads snapped in unison to look at me.

"What is THAT?" I grabbed Carrie's left hand and nearly went blind from the sunbeams coming off of the giant diamond.

A smile appeared on her face. "Just last night."

"Congratulations!" Jake slapped Patrick on the back. "Welcome to the family. Let's get you guys settled in so we can hear the details." He grabbed their bags and headed over toward the throng of campers.

After Patrick and Carrie got settled in, the guys left to make their tee time and Carrie and I found some lawn chairs and started leafing through all of the trashy tabloid magazines I brought.

"So, where's Natalie?" Carrie asked me while picking up a copy of *InTouch*.

"Locked away in the cabin farting."

"Ew. Natalie." She wrinkled her nose.

Seriously. I love her.

"Hey, girls! Do you two want to come antiquing with us in town?" Marianne asked.

"No thanks," we both answered quickly.

"So what's new, Aunt Marianne?" Carrie asked.

"Oh, you know. Spending time with Natalie and looking forward to our first grandchild. I've also joined a book club."

"You know, if you ever want something new to read, Clare's a great writer."

"Oh, really?"

"Her Web site is hilarious. You should really check it out. It's really popular, too. How many hits do you get every day?"

"I don't know. It's never the same."

"How many on average?"

"Something like twenty thousand."

"See, Aunt Marianne? Twenty thousand people read it every day."

"You know me, I don't have time to check my e-mail. I'm just so busy, busy. You know who is also very popular?"

"Who?" Carrie asked, rolling her eyes slightly at me.

"My friend Sally's daughter Amanda. She writes columns for our church bulletin. She is such a good writer. You should call her sometime and get some writing tips."

"Yeah, maybe," I said, not looking up from my magazine.

"Are you girls sure you don't want to go antiquing with us?"

"Positive," Carrie said.

As soon as Marianne was gone I said, "Thanks for trying."

"No problem. Don't let her get under your skin. It's not worth it. She'll be in the nuthouse in a few years anyway."

"I'm so glad you're here. Jake doesn't understand why his mother makes me want to drink myself to death sometimes." As soon as I said it, I got very sad again when I realized I'm going to spend the next nine months dealing with my mother-in-law without the aid of any intoxicants.

"No problem. I feel your pain. Marianne asked me last week after my photography exhibition why I take pictures of boring things like the sky and clouds instead of babies dressed as flowers like that Anne Geddes."

"Nice. So what are we doing tonight? We should probably make plans so we don't get roped into corn husking or something of the sort."

"I already know what we're doing tonight and it doesn't involve any cranapple martinis this time," Carrie said, and smiled at me. She flung her magazine on the ground and laid her head back.

"Oh, uh. Good. I mean, what?" I said, suddenly uncomfortable.

"We're going to this bar about five minutes up the road. Patrick and I passed it on the way here. It's practically in the middle of a cornfield. It's one of those places without a name or address, just neon beer signs in the window."

"Huh? You want to go to some weird bar?"

"Of course! It will be a blast. We can get drunk off of two-dollar beers with all of the alky locals."

"Oh, um, yeah." I shifted in my chair and thought, *How the hell am I going to get out of this one?*

She opened her eyes, assuming my hesitation meant ambivalence. "Fine, stay here and sing campfire songs with the mosquitoes while the three of us hang out in the air-conditioning."

"I'll probably have to be designated driver since it's my turn." Yes! I found a loophole!

"Whatever. That's fine. Too bad for you, though."

"Yeah, gee, too bad," I said. Looking back, I'm surprised she didn't bust me right there with how horribly I delivered the line. I should've just snapped my fingers and added an "Aw shucks."

But Carrie just looked down at her hand and said, "My ring is amazing."

Sunday, May 13

. . . .

We left to go out around nine last night. Despite my fears the entire place would stare and the music would stop with a loud *riiipppp* when we walked in the door, no one even looked up when we entered. In fact, there were only two other people there, and they looked too hammered to even lift their heads up.

"What do you want?" Jake asked.

"Diet Coke."

He signaled to the bartender.

"A Diet Coke and a Bud Light bottle."

The bartender shook his head and wiped the sweat dripping off his forehead. "No glass in here. Cans only."

Jake looked at me and shrugged.

"A can is fine," he said to the bartender.

"What are you guys getting?" I asked Carrie and Patrick.

"Three vodka shots please," Carrie said to the bartender.

An hour later, they were all pretty buzzed. By ten thirty, the bar became as packed as a gun show in Alabama. Someone unplugged the jukebox and a DJ started playing.

The DJ got on the microphone. "All right fel-las! It's Saturday night and you know why you're here, dontcha?"

A loud cheer erupted from all of the men. I swear I heard a "Yee-haw."

"It's time for our world-famous THONG CONTEST!"

I prayed, *Oh, God, please, please tell me I heard that wrong.*

No, I didn't.

In fact, the DJ passed around a hat for donations to give to the lucky winner, and asked for volunteers.

I practically had to sit on Carrie so she didn't run up to be a contestant, although she would've won hands-down. The four girls who volunteered looked like they were straight out of a *Jerry Springer* panel. And not one of them came in under three hundred pounds.

The DJ started the music and Sisqó's "Thong Song" came on.

"Contestants, show your stuff!!" he shouted, pumping his fist in the air.

"Those chicks could be wearing shorts and they'd qualify as thongs in those asses!" Carrie hissed at me.

All four girls started simultaneously wiggling around on the dance floor, unbuttoning their Jordache jeans and lifting up their T-shirts. One girl decided she *had* to be crowned "thong bitch" (as she told her friend), and went for the gold and took all of her clothes off. I realized I'd hit a new low as I sat there, drinking my Diet Coke, watching a naked fat chick hump a peanut-shell-covered floor.

Carrie, of course, egged the girl on. "Go for it, girl! *Aw-huh*, that's right! Work that shit!"

Naked Fat Girl won the contest and she was presented with the money in the hat, which totaled fourteen dollars.

"Can you believe that girl did a porn show for fourteen bucks?" I asked Jake.

"Clare, that girl would've done that for a quarter," he answered.

"I wonder what she would've done if you gave her a Snickers?" Carrie asked.

Twenty minutes after the porn show, the DJ put on the song "Black Betty."

"You know what to do!" he shouted.

I thought: *No, what? No, seriously, what?* Please *don't take your clothes off, portly biker man. Everybody, keep your clothes on. I am sober, people. Please don't do this to me.*

Everyone except us jumped on the bar and started line-dancing, or at least, I think it was supposed to be a line-dance but it really just looked like a bunch of drunks hopping around on one foot. We all sat at our table and obligingly clapped along and cheered when it was finished, thinking the show was over. Oh, no, the DJ played that song every half hour, which made it somewhat difficult to get a drink since we were afraid to put our fingers on the bar, lest they get separated from our hands by the heel of a cowboy boot.

Eight thousand cans of Bud Light and a few more shots later, it was time to leave. We did realize at some point that the "no glass ever" rule was one we'd recommend they keep since we witnessed three fights by the end of the night. One I think was over cigarettes or something. All I know is the skinny guy beat the shit out of the fat guy and made his girlfriend cry.

Oh, and the thong contest winner had sex with some guy in the bathroom while I was peeing but I was too exhausted to care.

We made our way back to the campground. Carrie and Patrick immediately went to their cabin to pass out while Jake and I decided to stay up for one more beer. Fueled by the massive quantity of alcohol Jake consumed and the fact we couldn't fool around in the cabin, we started making out. The klassy surroundings inspired us and we wound up doing it in our car. Yep, I have become a broad who goes camping, watches naked chicks compete in thong contests, and gets it on in the backseat of a used Ford Taurus.

I am officially pregnant white trash.

Tuesday, May 15

· · · · · · · · · · · · · · · · · · · ·

The camping weekend thankfully behind me, I posted pictures from the hillbilly bar on my blog. The overwhelming favorite is the one of the thong contest winner licking Jake's face. Wifey1025 said she's jealous.

I'm moving from one extreme demographic to the other today and attending the first Gala meeting with the entire committee at one of their estates. I've tried to dress up, wearing my best suit and shoes, and twisted my hair into a knot. I pray they stare at my chipped manicure instead of my eyebrows, which I forgot to pluck last night.

2:30 P.M.

The meeting did not go well at all. After I arrived twenty minutes late due to extremely poor Internet map directions, I tried to quickly smooth my frizzed updo into submission but it was to no avail; strange wiry hairs kept poking out of the sides, giving me a Medusa-like appearance.

I booked it to the front door of the gaudiest house I'd ever seen. Easily ten thousand square feet of real estate, giant round pillars evoking a Taj Mahal feeling, accessorized with two seven-foot-tall Adonis statues. I tried not to stare at Adonis's giant marble penis as I rang the doorbell.

A woman in a maid's uniform answered the door and silently led me through the gold-embossed foyer to an opulent living room, where ten Women's Board ladies sat.

". . . and then we will have Asian lanterns—" Carolyn looked at me with disgust and abruptly stopped while all of the other nine perfectly coiffed heads turned to stare at me. "Clare. So good of you to make it. Thanks for coming." She shot me a look of death.

My eyes spastically darted around the room as I desperately searched for a place to sit until Jessica smiled and waved me over to share the ottoman she perched on. "Thanks," I whispered to her, and she gave me an amused smile.

Carolyn's ice-blue eyes narrowed as she waved me away with a dismissive motion of her pale white hand. "This, ladies, is Clare Finnegan. She's from Signature Events and will be helping us to make this event a great success." She smiled tightly at me. "Assuming, of course, she arrives on time."

The other ladies tittered as I turned three shades of crimson.

Carolyn continued about the importance of the Gala and I began to steal glances around the ornate room at the other women. Each was attractive, some with obvious nip-and-tuck work and some naturally pretty in a pinched, constipated, WASPy sort of way. Nearly every woman was dressed in a Chanel or St. John tweed jacket in a shade of pink.

As I pretended to take notes on what Carolyn blabbered about, I passed the time by mentally assessing what each woman's outfit cost. I wondered if anyone would chase after me if I ripped Betsy Fallon's shoes off her feet and made a run for it, since I'm pretty sure alligator Manolo Blahniks are worth more than what I made last month.

I snapped back to reality when Jessica stood up and passed out packets containing the invitation list.

"Everybody, if you could look through the packet and let us know if there is anyone you'd like to add to the invite list." She flicked her long dark hair over her shoulder.

"Clare, you'll be assisting us by personally delivering the VIP invitations." Betsy Fallon's nasal voice stabbed through the room.

I gritted my teeth and gave my usual reply of smiling a bit too brightly and chirping, "Great!" while mentally envisioning running out of the house with the Tiffany lamp in my arms.

Afterward, we all retired to the dining room for a lunch of "Salade Niçoise," which pretty much just looked like canned tuna atop a bunch of lettuce. Some of the women took pity on me and tried to be friendly by asking me where I got my suit, but quickly lost interest when I told them I got it on the sale rack at J.Crew.

Halfway through the cold pear soup, I became temporarily blinded in my right eye from Stephanie Cohen waving her left hand with what had to be a twelve-carat diamond on her finger. The freaking thing looked like an ice cube. I glanced down at my own ring, which suddenly looked very, very tiny.

I drifted off again during their conversation about the best boarding schools ("definitely in the northeast") and began to wonder what it would be like to have as much money as these women. God, what would it be like to have summers in St. Tropez, winters in Telluride, country club memberships, BMWs, and a beach house on Hilton Head Island? Seeing as how I'm "in the family way" now, I have no idea how Jake and I are going to afford day care *and* running water, let alone private schools, college tuition, an emergency fund for when our dear child rams our new car into a telephone pole, a new iPod when he/she gets his/hers stolen at school, sports gear, field trip money . . . We seriously need to win the lottery. (Although I don't think obsessively playing the state lottery will do anything for my new "pregnant white trash" status.)

The meeting finally wrapped up and I was released early due to good behavior. Driving away in my Toyota Camry, I kind of felt like the poor girl from the wrong side of the tracks on *Beverly Hills, 90210* who Kelly, Donna, and Brenda pity.

Saturday, May 19
· · · · · · · · · · · · · · · · · · · ·

Well, another work week is behind me, which means I'm facing another weekend of No Drinking Ever. It's so strange. Normally, I'd be stocking up on bottled water, Coke, crackers, and aspirin to fight the inevitable hangover. Instead, I'm stuck with an armful of books detailing every delicious bodily function I'll get to experience over the next several months. I'm not even sure what I'm supposed to be doing right now. I know what I can't do, but I feel like I should be doing something other than sitting around my apartment in my sweatpants and eating ice cream straight out of the carton. Jake keeps staring at my stomach as if he's waiting for it to spontaneously grow outward. I've resorted to giving him the finger every time I see him looking at it. It seems to work.

I haven't told anyone yet. I figure it is better to wait until I can give a reaction other than "Guess what we did! Man, are we freaked out! Can you lend us some money?"

Julie took pity on me and came over today, although I'm pretty sure she's never coming back. She came prepared, showing up at the front door with every celebrity magazine she could find and a pint of Chunky Monkey.

"How are you?" she asked, furrowing her brow and giving me a look she'd give to someone who just found out their cancer is terminal.

"How do you think?" I said, barely letting her get inside before I grabbed the ice cream and threw myself on the couch. I was having a particularly hormonal day and declared: "Never again. Never again will I reclaim my youth. My life as I know it has been ripped from my hands. Never again will I be able to buy designer purses. I'll have to buy diapers and bras resembling straightjackets. I'll have to attend Tupperware parties and host book club meetings. And forget about having long hair anymore. I'll have to cut it off because it'll be encrusted with baby food and poop."

A touch dramatic, yes.

I'm such a mess.

"Would it make you feel better if I showed you my boobs?" she laughed.

"NO! Because it will only remind me of how enormous mine are going to get when they fill with the milk I'm supposed to feed to this child. Is it bad that breast-feeding kind of creeps me out?"

"You're asking the wrong girl. The only human I ever want to touch my boobs is one with a fully grown penis. Preferably attached to Hot Dr. Ben. Or your brother, Mark."

"You're disgusting."

"Anytime."

"What movies did you bring?"

"All eighties movies. Nothing like a good teen comedy from the 1980s to take your mind off of anything baby-related."

We started to watch *Sixteen Candles*, surrounded by a million pillows on the couch, pints of ice cream, and a bowl of popcorn. For the first hour, I was fine. Then, the part in the movie happened when the popular girl is all wasted and gives the nerdy guy a birth control pill and I became really sad. Why did Anthony Michael Hall get to have birth control pills when mine punked out? Then I was fine again until the end of the movie, when the waterworks came on. It was like I was floating above my body, unable to control my emotions. Just remembering it makes me want to kick my own ass.

"Such a sad movie!" I blurted out in between sobs.

"*Sixteen Candles*? It's not supposed to be a tearjerker."

"But IT IS! The sister's wedding is RUINED because she's so loaded. And the popular girl's hair is SO MESSED UP that she'll have to practically shave her head to look normal again. And Jake Ryan probably dumps Molly Ringwald the next day. And it's not like they'll stay together anyways because he's a SENIOR and going away to COLLEGE soon ANYWAY."

She stared at me, looking like I'd just told her Butterscotch recently started his own Internet business and would she like to become a primary investor? She tried to rationalize that Jake probably did stay with Molly Ringwald's character, but I just got more upset and she finally gave up.

Jake came home soon after my meltdown and Julie left. The whole afternoon resembled what I would imagine it would be like to be possessed, minus all of the head spinning and crotch stabbing.

I'll be lucky if Julie doesn't start calling me Sybil.

I tried to explain to Jake how messed up *Sixteen Candles* is but he only gave me a nervous half smile accompanied by some awkward back patting. Is this how things are going to be? Me sobbing hysterically during teen comedies where nothing remotely sad happens, my friends thinking I've lost it, eating entire pints of ice cream, and Jake petting me like I'm a pit bull trained to cage fight?

None of this is happening the way it was supposed to. I thought when I got pregnant, it would be something so joyous, so exciting, so *wanted*, the happiness would cut out my heart with one clean slice. I thought I'd get to come up with some cute way to tell Jake, maybe wrapping up a rattle or something, and when I told him, he'd cry and hug me tight and give me the smile that makes my stomach jerk. I thought I'd feel different and a test would only confirm what I "knew." Instead, I don't feel any different—no spiritual sense of the life growing inside me, nada. Just an ice-cold panic and tears that won't stop coming. And a husband who hasn't slept in days. But we should probably get used to it, since every book has told me a baby = never sleeping again.

I need more ice cream.

Wednesday, May 23

As I struggled with more silent auction item descriptions today, Julie called. Happy for the distraction, I listened to her rant about another weirdo coworker. I swear, her HR manager must patrol comic book conventions, Star Trek fan Web sites, NAMBLA meetings, and KFC parking lots for new-hire candidates.

"Clare, she's dead. I'm going to murder her or at least cut off her fucking hand! You think I'm kidding? I could swear that a fucking gray hair just popped up on my head. I'm going to hear that voice in my head while I'm trying to sleep tonight!"

"Jules, can't you just ignore—" Christina walked past my door so I quickly spread the Gala linen invoices out on my desk to make it look as though I was actually doing something.

"Already tried that. The walls here are paper fucking thin!"

"I don't—"

"Holy shit! She just hit it *again*! I've gotta go. I have some ass to kick."

As I hung up the phone, I let out a laugh I'd been holding in for the entire conversation. Unfortunately, it was right when Christina walked past again, so it appeared I was sitting in my office laughing to myself. She shot me a quizzical look and kept walking.

Julie was freaking out because a vendor dropped off some marketing materials that included a button that, when pushed, said, "Metrotab is the easiest choice you'll ever make! See? Wasn't that easy?" in a male voice apparently sounding like Michael Jackson on anabolic steroids. Only higher. And gayer. One of the other nurses thought it was hysterically funny and had hit the button every five minutes for the past four hours.

I feel bad for that woman. Julie can be frightening when pissed off. In college, she peed on the toothbrush of a girl in our dorm because she tried to convert her to Scientology.

I took a deep breath and wearily turned back to the silent auction item descriptions when I heard Mule Face's unmistakable voice wafting down the hallway outside my door.

". . . Medieval Castle for dinner and then went dancing at Shooters until two in the morning. So tired today but it was worth it. That boy can *move*."

For the second time today, I laughed alone in my office. (Of course, Christina happened to walk by again and I'm sure she now thinks I have some kind of hallucinogenic drug/uppers addiction.) The image of Mule Face bumping and grinding with Big D was hilarious enough, but the fact she went to Shooters made me want to lie on the floor. The killer is they went to dinner at Medieval Castle, one of those places where actors joust on horseback while patrons eat their dinner with their hands.

". . . meeting him for lunch. I'll introduce him to everyone."

Yes! I cannot wait to meet the man who is clearly seriously medicated.

12:00 P.M.

Mule Face just brought Big D into my office, introducing me as "*This* is Clare, you know, *Clare*, right?"

I quickly stood up, hoping my shirt covered my unbuttoned pants. (Again, my bloat is from the *baby*. Not all the burritos I've been eating.)

He warmly stuck out his right hand, met my eyes, and smiled. "Nice to meet you, Clare."

I smiled back at him as Mule Face did a terrible job of hiding her clear disappointment we were being so civil to each other. I'm sure she was hoping that her contempt for me could be shared with another human being. (Note to Mule Face: It is. Just call my mother-in-law.)

I surveyed Big D up and down. Dressed very plainly in rumpled khaki pants, a white button-down, and blue striped tie, he certainly wasn't a movie star. But he seemed to have a calming and patient aura about him.

Obviously, our encounter disturbed Mule Face. Normally, she would've brought up topics like the time I infected the entire office with a computer virus because I downloaded an attachment called "Prostitute Arrested for Assault on Dildo" or the time when I spilled an entire grande gingerbread latte on myself seconds after buying it and minutes before giving a presentation. I know this from experience. Her last boyfriend knew about every boneheaded thing I'd ever done publicly and would inevitably end up drinking too much at corporate events and loudly regaling everyone with reenactments involving wild hand motions with high-pitched shrieks while Mule Face laughed and looked at me with fake sympathy. For whatever reason, I can't picture Big D doing the same thing. But there has to be something massively wrong with him for choosing to date her. Maybe he's a secret cross-dresser or had scientific experiments involving plutonium done on him as a child?

1:00 P.M.
He's not listed as a registered sex offender in the state.

1:45 P.M.
LexisNexis search brings up no criminal history.

2:16 P.M.
He didn't appear to be hypnotized and/or under the influence of psychedelic drugs.

3:27 P.M.
Undiagnosed brain tumor?

4:47 P.M.
Severe untreated mental illness or schizophrenia?

5:15 P.M.
Possible immigrant in need of a green card?

6:00 P.M.

I'm completely baffled how Mule Face found a guy willing to date her who doesn't belong on *Dateline*'s *To Catch a Predator*. I've decided to table the issue until further research can be done. Besides, Jake and I are going to dinner tonight and I need to concentrate on what I'm going to wear. I'm thinking my stretchy new jeans, unbuttoned of course, and a black-and-white top, with my favorite black jacket. I'm figuring I might as well wear my cute things until I'm forced to wear maternity muumuus.

7:00 P.M.

My apartment is officially a black hole. My things keep disappearing. I can't find my black strapless bra anywhere. I thought I put it in my laundry basket last week but I ripped apart everything and can't find it. So, I guess no black-and-white top tonight. Gah.

11:52 P.M.

Jake and I left to have dinner at the wine bar around eight. I know a wine bar seems like an odd choice, but besides serving excellent parmesan-crusted scallops, the place is dimly lit and perfect for snuggling into a booth and talking. I'd taken two bites of our appetizer when I felt a strange cramping. I ignored it, thinking it was merely growing pains, and continued to shovel the artichoke dip into my mouth. Before I could eat another piece, the pain came again, only this time much, much stronger. I set the chip down on my appetizer plate.

"What?" Jake asked as he saw me pause.

"Nothing. I mean, I'm not sure," I said.

We sat silently for a few moments.

"I guess it was nothing," I said, and picked up my water glass. "Who knows what my body is doing these days."

"Are you sure?" he said.

"Yep," I said cheerfully. As we finished our appetizer, I stood up and went into the bathroom. I came out about fifteen seconds later, white-faced. "Jake, we need to leave. I think something's wrong."

"What?" His hand froze as it reached for his wine glass.

"I'm bleeding pretty heavily. I'm not sure what's going on." My hands began to shake, matching my voice.

As we walked to the car, Jake started freaking out. "What should we do? Should we call the doctor? Do you want to call your mom?"

"I don't know. My mom doesn't even know I'm pregnant, remember? And I haven't even seen Dr. Clarke yet—I just made my first appointment yesterday—but I guess I'll try to give her a call. I'm sure it's nothing." My voice belied my confident words.

I called information and was connected to Dr. Clarke's office. An answering service picked up and said they would page the physician on call, who would call me back. Jake and I sat in the car in the parking lot, unsure of what to do.

"Should we go home?" he asked.

"I don't know. They might want to see me. Let's just stay here for a minute."

"But aren't you, um, bleeding?"

"Yeah, but I'll be fine for a few moments."

We sat silently in the car, watching the minutes tick on by. I wondered if this was it. If the pregnancy was over. I wondered if Jake would be relieved. I wondered if I would be relieved. But mostly, I wondered why I felt so terrified if this pregnancy wasn't something we planned.

My phone beeped and we both jumped. I answered it and Dr. Gwam, Dr. Clarke's partner, told me to go to the ER to get checked out. He said most likely I was fine, but I should still get checked out just in case since it is still so early.

On the way to the hospital, I twisted my hands in my lap and watched my knuckles turn white. In the ER, a very sweet-faced nurse led us into a room and let me know a doctor would be with us shortly.

"Are you OK?" Jake asked as he gripped my hand while I sat on the exam table.

"I don't know," I said quietly. I tried to focus on the lettering on a blood-pressure monitor.

Dr. Hoffsteder, the attending ER physician, came in and asked for my history. His face told me he thought I was miscarrying. He started most of his sentences the same way: "I'm sorry, how many weeks are you?" and "I'm sorry, who is your regular OB/GYN?" Jake flinched each time he spoke a pseudoapology.

Since the baby is still so tiny, Dr. Hoffsteder explained the only way to see what was going on was through an internal ultrasound. It didn't sound pleasant and certainly didn't appear pleasant when they whipped out what looked like a dildo attached to an imaging machine. I laughed in spite of the situation as they applied what looked like a condom to the dildo-camera.

Immediately, an image appeared on the screen. A grainy, black-and-white, snuff-film image of this little circle with a flickering inside.

"Is that it?" I said, and tried to sit up. Dr. Hoffsteder motioned for me to lie back. I looked over at Jake and whispered, "Do you see it?"

"I do," he said, his mouth open.

"It is OK?" I asked Dr. Hoffsteder. Suddenly, I felt as though my insides liquefied and in the two seconds it took for him to answer, I realized I'd never wanted anyone to say yes more than in that moment.

"Looks pretty good. Yes. It was probably just some ancillary bleeding. Baby looks healthy." Dr. Hoffsteder said, smiling at us.

"Is that its heart?" I pointed to the flickering on the screen.

"Yes, it is. And this mass next to it is the egg sac."

"I can't believe I made a heart and an egg sac!" I shouted.

Dr. Hoffsteder and Jake laughed. Jake audibly sighed.

"So, we're good, right?" Jake said.

"Looks that way." He switched off the machine and turned to us. "The risk of miscarriage is highest in the first trimester, so keep an eye on things and don't hesitate to call your doctor if this happens again."

We nodded at him and he gave me some prenatal vitamins and discharged us.

As we walked back to the car, Jake grabbed my hand.

"Relieved?" I said to him.

"Very," he said.

"Are you surprised?" I said softly.

"That I'm so relieved?" We stopped next to our car and faced each other.

"Yes."

"Is it OK if I say yes?" He studied my face.

"Yeah. It doesn't make you a bad person," I said to him.

"Are you?"

"I'm relieved, but mostly totally surprised because for a moment, I really thought it was all over. A very small part of me said well, OK, that's fine, but most of me couldn't imagine losing the baby. Weird, huh?"

He leaned forward and hugged me. "This whole situation is weird to us. We'll just take it one step at a time and try to figure it out."

"Jake," I said into his rugby shirt, "I'm really glad everything's OK."

"Me too," he whispered. "Me, too."

Thursday, May 24
. . . .

Last night and this morning, I've felt something new since I found out I'm pregnant: gratitude. I'm grateful for Jake, for being such a great husband. I'm grateful for the doctors, who took care of me last night. I'm grateful that everything's OK with the Dragon. I'm still somewhat surprised at that last one. Not that I wanted something to happen, but I just didn't realize I'd already become attached to the baby. Or at least, the idea of having a baby. I don't know. I don't have anyone to bounce these strange ideas off other than Jake or Julie. And I won't for a while because we've decided to wait until after the first trimester to tell our families. Last night was just too scary to start announcing the news right now.

I desperately wanted to remain in bed this morning in a vegetative state and let my body rest, but dragged myself to the office since the Trio of Torture came in today to discuss the RSVPs for the Gala.

I was already in the conference room when they all arrived. I could hear their six-hundred-dollar heels click-clack against the floor; each knock filled me with more anxiety. I straightened my cardigan and smoothed my wool pants quickly. Finally, they arrived at the door.

"Clare, hello. So nice to see you." Carolyn's tone betrayed her smile. She was dressed perfectly in a black Chanel knit suit. Betsy and Jessica were behind her, scurrying around in her wake. They both waved casually and smiled, turning to Carolyn to take the lead like two puppies following the alpha dog.

"Clare, as you know, we are here to discuss our invitation list." She stopped and stared at me for a minute until I realized that I was supposed to say something.

"Absolutely." My old standby.

"Now, what we need you to do is to keep meticulous records in a certain format," she looked in Jessica's direction, silently giving her a signal, and Jessica slid an Excel spreadsheet across the table, "and coordinate the requests for table seating. They should be tracked in this specific way . . ." She looked over to Betsy, who slid another Excel spreadsheet across the table. I couldn't believe how well trained they were. "Is this something that you can handle?"

"Of course." I was back into robotic prostitute mode.

"Well, good. I need to run now. Felicity is home from Europe and there are things that need attending to."

Having no clue who the hell Felicity was or why she was in Europe, I simply said, "Good luck."

With that, Carolyn left the room and I could swear the temperature increased at least six degrees. I looked at Jessica and Betsy and asked, "Is there anything else you'd like to go over at this time?"

They looked at each other and raised their eyebrows. After a long pause, Jessica leaned forward and asked, "Is she driving you nuts?"

"I'm happy to help you guys out however you need it." I smiled angelically at them.

"Well, she's driving us crazy!" Jessica said.

Wanting to hear more but not wanting them to stop for fear they'd gone too far, I tried to be casual. "What do you mean?"

"I mean, she's insane! She won't let us make any decisions without her. We're the cochairs but we have to run everything by her first. We are not allowed to meet with you without her present. She insists on leading every committee meeting and shoots down all of our ideas. We originally planned on a Brazilian Carnival theme for this event and she turned it down and said we were using this ridiculous Asian theme!" Jessica's usually porcelain face began to turn pink.

I shook my head, shocked, still trying to look even-keeled so she'd continue.

"She treats Betsy and me like we're her slaves, not to mention how she treats you!" Betsy nodded. "I'm sorry, but we've just about had it with her."

There were a few moments of silence.

Still trying to be professional, I said, "Well, she certainly is a woman with strong opinions. I know this event is very important to your organization and I'm sure she's just trying to ensure its success."

I really wanted to say, "She's a big fat bitch and I hate her, too! Let's draw mean pictures of her and prank call her cell phone! I bet she sleeps in a coffin at night!"

"I know you have to say that since you're the professional, but you know she's completely impossible!" Jessica said.

"She is!" Betsy chimed in.

"I'm sorry, I'm sure that this is the last thing that you want to hear. You have enough on your plate right now," Jessica said.

"Don't worry about it, being in charge of something as enormous as this event has got to be incredibly stressful," I said, even though I was thinking: *Stressful—what do they know about stressful? I spent last night in the ER and didn't even take the day off. They can leave here and get manicures and massages all day long if they want while this pregnant working schlub is going to be chained to her desk for the next six hours.*

"This event is going to be a huge success and you guys are both doing such an awesome job," I said.

"Thanks so much for saying that, Clare. We appreciate everything you're doing, really. We honestly couldn't do it without you." Jessica smiled warmly.

"We really couldn't!" Betsy said.

"Well, thank you, and don't worry, I'll be sure to get this invitation piece out the door ASAP."

Jessica and Betsy stood up and turned to each other.

"Lunch?" Jessica said.

Betsy nodded.

Jessica turned to me. "Clare, would you like to join us for lunch? Our treat!"

It sounded wonderful, but I didn't think I could sneak out for three hours, so I turned them down.

As I walked them to the door, Mule Face called out, her voice garbled by the omelet sandwich she shoved into her mouth, "Good-bye, ladies! It was lovely to see both of you!"

Jessica looked at me for a split second and rolled her eyes slightly before leaving.

I think I'm starting to like Jessica Greene. Even though I sort of hate her for owning fifty pairs of Manolo Blahniks.

Saturday, May 26

10:00 A.M.

Today's my first anniversary. Harumph. Most couples I know spent their first anniversary in Hawaii or somewhere exotic. Jake and I are spending ours at home with Blockbuster's latest. My life is so exciting I can barely stand it.

1:00 P.M.

So, OK, our anniversary might not be so terrible. Jake just surprised me with a reservation at the Four Seasons tonight as a present. He said we both need to get away, which I find funny since the last time we got away was the Conception Vegas Trip. I laughed when I said this. Jake did not.

Anyway, I cannot wait to lie around on million-thread-count sheets and order room service. If I can't have a glass of champagne, I'm going to stuff as much food as possible into my body.

My life has become so romantic. On our honeymoon, Jake and I barely wore clothes at all, alternating between lying in bed, rubbing aloe vera on our sunburned shoulders while surrounded by international newspapers, and making out and having delicious middle-of-the-afternoon sex and then falling asleep until dinner. A year later, I am looking forward to lounging on two-thousand-dollar sheets, wrapped up in the comforter like a burrito, and gorging on room-service cheeseburgers. In one short year, I've gone from tanned sex goddess to Jabba the Pregnant Hut.

7:00 P.M.

Ooooohhh. I think my stomach is going to explode. I hate the Four Seasons. Why do the sundaes have to be so tasty? And the nachos? Oohhhhhh.

Besides destroying my gastrointestinal functions, I think I've officially made the transition to Scary Pregnant Wife in Jake's eyes—as if the whole *Sixteen Candles* episode wasn't enough. I think it was the sight of his formerly sexy, hot wife lying in bed pigging out, not even caring when nacho cheese dripped on her chin. I'm pretty sure I looked like one of those fatsos on talk shows, who've lain in bed for the past three years because they're too fat to fit through their bedroom door anymore. So Maury or Jenny or Sally Jessy has to hire a crane to rip off a side of their house and airlift the blob to the nearest hospital because Oh. My. God.

It's true, I saw it once.

12:00 A.M.

Despite everything, Jake still managed to have sex with me. Men. They're so predictable, but I guess it's how ugly girls get laid.

We hadn't done it since the whole "oh, by the way, I'm pregnant" discussion. (No, the In-Law Camping Trip didn't count, because he was so wasted he would've humped a tree log.) It was good, but Jake continually stopped and asked if I was OK, really meaning if the baby was OK. Afterward, I explained to him the baby is still about the size of a grain of rice or something and *please*. Your penis is lovely but it isn't gonna puncture whatever organs are holding the rice in place and injure it.

Well, at least I hope not. It would be terrible if the child is born with a dented head and we have to come up with some half-assed story about it being hit with a baseball as a newborn.

Sunday, May 27
· · · · · · · · · · · · · · · · · · · ·
Sadly, we checked out of the Four Seasons this morning, but I was cheered, and mildly surprised, when Reese called me and invited me to lunch.

I arrived at the restaurant fifteen minutes late but it wasn't my fault. It was Banana Republic's fault for having such an amazing sale. I tore through the restaurant and found her already sipping a glass of Merlot.

"Sorry! Sorry! Have you been here long?" I set my shopping bags down on the bar stool next to her.

"Half an hour, no big deal."

"Shit! I'm sorry. I didn't think you'd be early."

"It's OK, I wanted to get out of the house before Grace woke up from her nap. I haven't had an afternoon to myself in what feels like years." She smiled and took another swig of her wine.

We got settled at a table and ordered some food.

"So how's everything at home?" she asked me.

"Nothing exciting. Just the usual—work, in-laws, family, going out."

"Well, enjoy your free time now because once you guys have kids, things get crazy," she said quietly.

I bit my lip and the back of my neck got prickly. I desperately wanted to tell her, but I knew I couldn't say anything yet. I wished I could say, "Reese, I'm pregnant. You have to help me. I don't know what to do or how to be a mother or anything. As a mom, please, please, please tell me it's going to be OK."

"Happy to be out of the house?" I said instead.

"Yep! So, how's Jake?" Quick change of subject. I ignored her question.

"Is everything OK, Reese?"

"Couldn't be better! Let's order!" She gave me a bright smile and I didn't press any further. I knew from experience it would take an oyster shucker to get information out of Reese before she was ready so I sighed and opened my menu.

By the time we finished lunch, Reese had downed her second glass of wine and was hovering on the line between drunk and tipsy. After telling me all about Grace's latest cute faces and sharing a thousand new pictures of her, she finally started to open up a little.

"What are you doing after lunch?"

"Probably shopping, I don't know. Jake and I are going out to dinner tonight."

"Matt and I used to have so much time for each other. Now all we

do is talk about things like babysitters and diapers. I can't even remember the last time we went on a date."

"Things will be easier. You guys are still just figuring everything
out." I didn't know what the hell I was talking about, but it seemed
to help a little.

"Of course we are. I don't know what I'm talking about. I'm just
being silly. My whole life I've wanted to be a mother and a wife. I
have a gorgeous husband and daughter and my life is just perfect."

It was a typical Reese rationalization. I squeezed her hand. "It's
just a rough patch. Besides, you are totally a MILF."

"Oh, right!" She laughed and her gloominess seemed to break.
She downed the last of her wine and I could tell she was officially
drunk.

I suggested we do something totally frivolous like shop for bras
or something but she said she had to go home to take care of Grace
since Matt wanted to go golfing with some friends. So, we waited
until she sobered up and then parted ways, me to go find some new
bras and her to go find a hangover cure.

It was great to see her but I can't stop thinking about what really
must be going on between her and Matt. She deserves every ounce of
happiness; I'll kill him if he's being an asshole.

Tuesday, May 29
. . . .

This morning, as I walked into the office, I got a frantic phone call
from Betsy Fallon's assistant, Lois.

"Clare! You *have* to help me! Ohpleasehelpme!" She ran every
word together as her voice rose five octaves.

"What's going on?" I unbuttoned my jacket and examined a
hangnail, not alarmed in the slightest, since Lois recently went off
her meds or something and lately I'd been operating as her stand-in
psychiatrist for problems like the one she had yesterday—a fax machine running out of paper.

"This time, it's really, really bad. You have to help me."

"Yes?"

"You're going to kill me."

"Most likely. Do tell."

"Well, you know the cocktail party Betsy is throwing at her house in two weeks for the committee?"

"Yeah?"

"Well, you know the invitations for the party? The ones that Carolyn picked out herself and gave to Betsy? And you know how all I was supposed to do was print the envelopes, stuff, and mail them?"

"Yeah?"

"I printed the envelopes upside down by accident and now we can't mail them."

"What?"

"We can't use them. We need to get more of these exact envelopes or Carolyn will know. I'd go and pick them up at the stationery store but I have to pick up Betsy's dog at the groomer's in an hour. Please help me." She sounded like a bleating lamb.

"Fine. Give me the directions."

An hour and a half later, I was on the expressway, cursing the construction workers who had the nerve to close down two of the three lanes. They seemed really busy, too, with all of them gathering around to smoke cigarettes and stare at the one guy operating the crane.

My cell phone rang and I snapped it open with one hand while simultaneously turning down the radio. "Hello?"

"Oh, good, Clare, I got you." It was Lois again. When the hell did I give this woman my cell phone number? "I wanted to make sure you knew to buy the envelopes with the Chinese symbols in the upper right-hand corner. Not the one with the Chinese dragon across it. They're both from the same manufacturer."

"Yeah, I got it. Number four-seven-eight. Gold leaf and navy blue."

Unfortunately, my role in assisting on this event has turned me into a virtual safety net for everyone involved. "Clare, can you get me reservations at NoMi?" "Clare, can you secure Trotters to Go for our committee planning meeting?" and "Clare, do you know where I could find a twelve-year-old prostitute who makes house calls?"

After I found the envelopes it was nearly five, so I had the extreme pleasure of sitting in rush-hour traffic on the way over to Betsy's house. I wordlessly shoved the envelopes into Lois's fat fingers and downed several Tylenol on my way home. My cell phone rang again and I hurled it into the backseat, fatally cracking the battery. Which sucks since now I have to shell out several hundred dollars for a new one. The upside? New pretty pink phone.

Despite ruining my cell phone and cursing everyone from construction workers to the politicians who authorize road work, today wasn't anything I haven't dealt with before. Being in the event-planning industry means handling odd requests, last-minute changes, and, inevitably, incompetent people with sky-high expectations. And I do all of that. Usually really well.

Sometimes it feels like I'm really good at my job but really bad at my life. I can pull off a black-tie event regardless of the curveballs thrown my way, but when life throws me one of my own, I'm all, "Oh, shit! What are we going to do? How are we going to handle this? We're so screwed!" I think it relates to being really good behind the scenes, horribly bad at being the star of the show. Although some refer to me as an Internet Rockstar, the blog is so indirect and passive, I usually don't feel too exposed and in the forefront so that doesn't count. But being pregnant? Kinda hard to be behind the scenes. And labor and delivery? Well, that's just a Julia-Roberts-winning-the-Oscar kind of moment. Everyone's staring at you, waiting for something to happen. And only you can give them what they want.

Oh, man.

Wednesday, May 30

I've made it through this morning without any more phone calls from Lois, so I consider today a success so far. Which is a good thing, after my realization yesterday about labor and delivery being kind of a one-woman show that I will soon be starring in. I stared at the carpet in my office and wondered if I could get an epidural preventatively, as in, before labor starts. Like, if they could just insert it into my back when I hit nine months. But then I realized you can't move your legs with an epidural, so I'd have to wheel my ass around in a wheelchair for a month until I had the baby.

Thus, I was grateful for the distraction when I heard this conversation wafting down the hallway outside my office:

"Do you or do you not understand the importance of this event?"

"Um, yeah, sure."

"Well, then do you or do you not understand why it is so important that my daughter's entrance is upon a pure white horse?"

"Yes, I do."

"Good. We are in agreement. I will trust that this detail will be closely attended to and taken care of."

I was so engrossed in listening to Isabel Castle's mother berate Mule Face that it took me several seconds to find my phone, which was buried under a mock-up of the Gala invitation design.

"Clare Finnegan."

"Clare! I'm so glad I caught you. I thought for sure you'd be at lunch!"

It was Marianne.

"Well, I haven't really had time to take lunch these days. So busy."

"Oh, you working girls! Always on the go!"

I wish she would try to remember that next time she makes a joke about how much I sleep in.

"So, what's going on?"

"Nothing really."

"OK, did you need something?"

"Oh, yes! Actually, I wanted to start talking about the big party coming up that we have to start planning."

I thought: *Party? What party? Plan something?*

"What do you mean?"

"Natalie's baby shower, of course."

Shoot me. Kill me. I can't do this. I absolutely despise baby showers. Actually, showers in general. I had to be practically drugged and tied up to go to my own wedding showers. All that oohhhing and ahhhing, sandwiches with the crusts cut off, pink décor and degrading games. No thanks. I'd just as soon go over to someone's house with a case of beer and some pizza. At least at a wedding shower there's usually something decent to drink but at a baby shower it's all sherbet punch and sparkling water because apparently everyone has to treat the expectant mother as an alcoholic who can't be near anything intoxicating. Plus the whole passing around of gifts bordering on embarrassing, like nipple cream and breast pads.

"I was thinking we could have it at Kingsley's Bistro. What do you think?"

"Marianne, I don't think the grandmother is supposed to plan the shower. It's usually not supposed to be an immediate relative, according to Emily Post." I thought I'd found a loophole.

"Of course not! That's why only your name will be on the invitation. But don't worry, I'll help you plan everything."

I blinked silently for a minute, trying to comprehend what was happening but it. Did. Not. Compute.

"So," she continued, "Natalie said she wants an all-pink theme since she's just positive she's having a little girl. Isn't that sweet? She's such a stitch! For the food, we should definitely have mini sandwiches, probably chicken salad, cucumber, and turkey. We'll also do a green salad and Caesar salad, with cookies and brownies for dessert. What do you think?"

Thankfully, she had already planned everything. She just wanted me to throw my name on the invitation and cough up some cash.

"What about drinks?"

"I'll have Aunt Sally make her famous punch and we can do the usual soft drinks, sparkling water and such."

"What about cocktails?"

"It's a baby shower, people won't want to drink! If the guest of honor isn't drinking, nobody else should be, either."

"Well, if I'm throwing the party, I'm going to have alcohol there." If I have to fund and help throw a party for Natalie, there sure as hell is going to be alcohol present. Even if I can't drink it.

"Well, I certainly can't stop you if that is what you want to do. I hope people would refrain from drinking out of respect for Natalie, but it's up to you." I could practically *hear* her pursing her lips together.

"Great! I also think we should make the shower co-ed." I didn't really want to have a co-ed shower, so it wasn't a big deal. I mean, why torture the men also? I just brought it up to drive her nuts.

"Oh, no, dear. A baby shower is supposed to be all women. It is supposed to be a time for ladies to get together to shower the mother with gifts and bestow advice. Men would just feel uncomfortable and intrude on our Hen Fest."

"OK, so no men. Anything else?"

"Well, we'll need to compile a list of games we want everyone to play."

"Honestly, Marianne, I'm not really a fan of the shower games. I don't think they're as popular as they used to be. They're kind of considered somewhat corny these days."

"Natalie already said she wants to play games."

It figures.

"OK, well then, I'll leave that up to you, if you don't mind."

"I'll come up with some good ones," she promised.

"How many people are you thinking?" I started to mentally add up the dollar figures.

"You know how large our extended family is, so we'll send out around a hundred invites and I'd expect seventy-five or so to show up."

"Seventy-five people! That could get a little pricey. Is there any way we could cut down the guest list?"

"Oh, no. We can't pick and choose who we're going to invite. That would be tacky."

Of course, now we're concerned about tacky. I hope she's OK with visiting her grandchild in a trailer, since we won't be able to afford our rent after this shindig.

"We don't want to offend anyone. Listen, Marianne, can we talk about this later? I'm really swamped at work right now."

"Of course, dear, call me later tonight. We need to get moving on this!"

I hung up the phone and massaged my neck a little. I completely forgot I'd be expected to throw Natalie a baby shower. We are practically going to go broke funding this party. After the baby comes, we're going to be stuck inside with a screaming newborn, eating baked beans out of dented cans, and screening our phone calls from creditors.

That bitch better get me a nice gift when I have my own shower. No, wait—screw that, there's no way I'm letting Natalie and Marianne throw a shower for me. They'd probably make me wear some weird hat made out of bows and humiliate me by making everyone guess my weight. Screw. That. If they try to throw me a shower, I'll convert to Judaism and get off on the technicality that Jews don't have baby showers.

Thursday, May 31
. . . .

Although I got very little sleep last night, thanks to peeing every half hour, I'm supposed to go into the city today to meet with the band leader and approve the choreography for the Gala. In between courses, semiprofessional dancers will perform lame routines pertaining to the theme of the event. When the theme was Broadway musicals, singers came out and sang show tunes. It is usually at this point in the evening I have to throw my fork off the table to prevent me from sticking it in my eye, but the other guests usually enjoy it. Of course, they've all had a gallon of vodka each.

4:30 P.M.

I arrived at Tony G. Productions this afternoon and Tony G. informed me that Jessica and Betsy were running late due to a backlog at the salon. Tony G. seemed like a normal enough guy, except for an ego the size of an elephant's ass. He calls himself a "Creative Musical Consultant," which basically means he knows a bunch of musicians and performers he hires for events. And that would be fine, if that's all he did. However, his aforementioned ego convinces him he should also take on the role of "party planner" by making suggestions on everything from the flowers to the invitations. He's a total douchebag.

I sat around for twenty minutes listening to Tony G. ramble on about his latest event, a "spectacular black-tie at the Ritz," before Jessica and Betsy walked in.

"We are so sorry. Our mani-pedis ran late." Jessica and Betsy leaned forward and air-kissed Tony G.

"Ladies, are you ready to see the magic?" Tony G. asked, while I rolled my eyes. Apparently it was noticeable and he stared at me. I smiled innocently back at him.

"What do you have for us?" Jessica asked.

"Well! First we are going to watch a presentation of a Chinese dragon, followed by a traditional dance done by geishas and a performance by Chinese drummers." He smiled widely, revealing a gold tooth, and smoothed back his ponytailed gray hair.

"Sounds fantastic!" Jessica exclaimed.

"Yes!" Betsy said.

"Ladies, prepare to be blown away!" He clapped his hands and we settled back to watch the performances, which were so craptastic I started playing Pac-Man on my cell phone. Halfway through the "Geisha Dance" one of the dancers dropped her paper fan and never quite recovered. She forgot half of the steps and almost took out an-other geisha when she turned the wrong way and smacked into her. At that point, I feigned a coughing fit to cover up my laughter. Tony G. didn't verbally react, but his face was bright red and I knew geisha number four would get the axe later.

After the performances, Jessica and Betsy exploded with ap-plause.

"Fabulous!" Jessica said.

Tony G. stood up and bowed. "Oh, thank you, ladies. I live to please you. Anything for the Women's Board! I mean, you ladies *are* the social scene in this town. Without you, parties would be like tax seminars!"

I suddenly wanted to vomit all over Tony G.'s fringed white leather jacket.

"Oh, no, Tony. Any party without *you* just wouldn't be a party at all," Jessica said.

"Tony, do you have a final quote we could look at?" I asked him.

"She's not very much fun, is she?" he whispered to Betsy. "Here it is." He slid it across the table. Thankfully, he came in at budget.

"This all looks good," I said briskly, eager to leave, as my nausea was entering dangerous territory, but no one was listening. Tony G. was too busy regaling Betsy and Jessica with tales of his travels to the Far East.

". . . and that's where I found these girls! In Hong Kong, can you believe it?"

He actually tried to pass the dancers off as being from Hong Kong even though I very clearly heard geisha number four mutter a swear word in a Southern accent.

"Clare, have you found a dress yet?" Jessica asked me as we were leaving.

"A dress? For what?" Oh, right. "No, not yet. Have you?"

"I'm having one made."

I thought: *Right. I'll have one made, too. To cover my ever-expanding ass.*

"Clare, you've done so much for us, we insist you come to lunch with us today," Jessica said, and Betsy nodded.

I was going to beg off, citing my usual workload, but I was too tired to protest. I learned a variety of new things at lunch today, including: the popovers at the Zodiac Room at Neiman Marcus are heaven, a tuxedo is called a "dinner jacket" when you're rich, and I am now cursed with Superwoman-like overactive taste buds, making it possible to identify every ingredient in anything. I'm thinking of parlaying this into some kind of game show on the Food Network.

Friday, June 1

. . . .

When I told Tony G. that he came in at budget, he apparently took that to mean he should call every half hour and try to add "additional services" into his contract and, thus, thousands more dollars in fees. In the past twenty-four hours, he's suggested adding custom-designed spotlights for his band, fifteen additional musicians, four more choreographed dances, and—I'm not kidding—a tai chi demonstration.

As I slammed the phone down after our third conversation today, I heard my cell phone beep with a message. It was Sam, begging me to buy her beer on my lunch hour: "I totally need it like *right* after school because we all want to go to the game tonight completely wasteoid."

I called her back. "Sam, I'm at work. I can't just leave to go to the liquor store so I can buy you and your friends beer." I swear I heard her roll her eyes.

"I knew you wouldn't understand. You and I are too far apart in age."

"No, we're not. Listen, I just can't right now."

"That's fine. I didn't think you'd help me anyway. It sucks that my friends are all close to their sisters," she mused.

"I wish we could be closer. Don't you?"

"Whatever. Forget it. You're so old," she said, and hung up.

I'm concerned my mother abused narcotics while pregnant with Sam but it would explain her serious personality disorder.

Mark called five minutes later.

"Did Sam just call you?"

"Yeah, she wanted me to leave work to buy her beer, why?"

"She called and asked me why you act like you're a senior citizen. And then she asked me to buy her beer."

"Isn't she lovely?"

"The best. One of the many reasons I never moved back home after college."

"Do you think she'll be normal someday?"

"Doubtful. You weren't normal until about two years ago."

"Thanks. I've now been told I'm annoying by my sister and abnormal by my brother in the same day."

"Whatever. I said you *used* to be abnormal."

"As much as I love these sibling chats, I must go. I'm very busy."

"Tell Mule Face I think she's sexy," he called out before I hung up.

Yes. My mother definitely abused drugs while pregnant with both Sam and Mark. Amazing I came out so wonderful.

Saturday, June 2

. . . .

"I don't care if you think your brother's weird. He's still hot," Julie said as she eased back into the massage chair at the Blue Water Salon.

I took a sip of my cucumber water and eased my feet into the bubbling tub below me. As soon as my feet hit the water, I felt my body instantly melt a little. "The answer is still no. Man, I haven't gotten a pedicure in years." I closed my eyes.

"I know. I can tell," Julie said, looking disdainfully at my chipped toenail polish. "So, how are Natalie's shower plans coming?"

"Haven't done anything yet. I'm not really supposed to. I'm just supposed to let Marianne plan the entire thing, then pay for it and show up."

"That blows. How's everything else been going?" The manicurists pulled our feet out of the water and started vigorously exfoliating.

"Fine. Work's a little hectic with the Gala coming up, but fine." I looked at her and shrugged.

"Those rich bitches still giving you a hard time?"

"Shhhh," I said to her and frantically looked around. Thankfully, I didn't spot anyone I recognized. "Yes, but shut up," I hissed to Julie.

"Calm down, drama queen. No one can hear me." The manicurist looked up and gave me a small smile, letting me know that she and everyone else in the room did indeed hear every word Julie said. "And Jake? What's with him?"

"OK, I guess. Still kind of freaked out. But you know what's even weirder than . . . everything? The fact that it's getting to be not totally weird. Know what I mean?"

"Yeah. You're not bugging out as much, which is bugging you out."

I nodded. "I think so." Out of the corner of my eye, I saw a familiar person being led into the pedicure room. Brown hair, well dressed, pretty.

Jessica Greene. I tried to silently communicate this to Julie, but she caught her reflection in the mirror and started adjusting her boobs as she rambled.

"Don't worry about anything. Even though you're knocked up, you'll still be a hot preggo lady. And you and Jake will be great parents. God, isn't it weird that in a few months, you'll be a mom?" Except she said what sounded like: "MOM" as in, "Hey world, did you hear? Clare Finnegan is pregnant! Hey, Jessica Greene! Did you catch that? Please spread the word around."

"Hey, Clare." Jessica caught my eye from three chairs down and waved.

"Hey, Jessica," I said. I smiled back at her and then turned to Julie and narrowed my eyes.

"Holy shit," Julie whispered. She didn't say much until we walked outside of the salon, feet looking beautiful. "Clare, I'm so sorry. There's no way in fuck she heard, right? Don't worry, she didn't hear. There's no way she could have."

"Julie, she definitely might have. Remember, not even my parents know about this yet. You, Jake, and some ER doctors are the only people in the know. I would've liked to keep it that way."

"I'm so sorry," she repeated.

I'd just about forgiven her when Jessica walked out of the salon and appeared next to us.

"Clare, did I hear that right? Are you pregnant?" Jessica beamed at me while Julie looked around for a rock to crawl underneath.

"Um . . . no." I felt my face start to get hot. "Her." I pointed to Julie, who looked surprised. "She's pregnant!" I said gleefully. "Yes. She's pregnant. She's due at the end of the year."

"How wonderful! Congratulations!" Jessica said to Julie.

Julie met my eyes for a second and paused before she turned to Jessica. "Yes, thank you."

"Gosh, I hope my boobs get as big as yours when I'm pregnant," Jessica said as she eyed Julie's cleavage. "It's the one benefit of pregnancy, right?"

"Yes, it is! Julie used to be an A cup before she got pregnant!" I chimed in.

"Er, yes," Julie muttered under her breath.

"Well, I gotta run. It was great to see you, Clare! And congrats to you, too!" she said to Julie before swaying off toward the parking garage.

When she was out of eyesight and earshot, I turned to Julie. "Even?"

"Fucking even," she grumbled.

Tuesday, June 5
. . . .

Julie eventually forgave me yesterday but it took agreeing to step inside Abercrombie & Fitch so she could ogle the underage half-naked guys working. It helped that I told her to forgive me or I'd force her to be my date to Natalie's baby shower.

Julie may not want to attend, but Wifey1025 sure does. I thought about saying yes for a moment, just to enjoy introducing her to Marianne, but decided against it when visions of me hog-tied and gagged in her backseat flashed across my mind.

Friday, June 8
. . . .

Despite my bout of nausea during the meeting with Tony G., I really thought I was going to escape the Pregnant Plague. Due to my seemingly endless appetite, I figured I was one of those lucky people who don't experience morning sickness. But right after Jake and I watched a horrible movie, I started to feel horrible. I assumed that the rumbling, burning, twisting surge in my stomach was due to the craptastic acting in the movie, but this morning I woke up and felt like I'd drunk the better part of a bottle of tequila. Within seconds, my head was hanging over the toilet. I pray it was just a fluke because I can't spend the next thirty or so weeks with my head in the toilet. The second I start making frequent bathroom trips, Mule Face will make the assumption that I am (a) a drug user who uses the stalls to shoot up, (b) alcoholic, or (c) pregnant.

After I spewed every color of the rainbow this morning, I tried to get ready for work. Thirty minutes later, I gave up. It was no use— no matter how much concealer, blush, or mascara I shellacked on, the pasty white skin and purple bags under my eyes did not go away. Where the hell is the pregnancy glow? Or the shiny hair?

Despite the way the day started, I put it out of my mind because today was my first doctor's appointment. I made up a lame excuse about having a meeting with Jessica and Betsy and ducked out of the office. As I drove over, my heart raced from nerves because this would make it really, really real. Yeah, I've taken five thousand pregnancy tests, but once an actual medical professional is involved, oh so much more scary.

It didn't help my anxiety when a teenager in a Range Rover tailed me. She got really pissed off when I slowed down and stopped to let an ambulance pass. I stopped just for kicks and also because *it's the law*. At the next light, she pulled up next to me and gave me the finger. Normally, I would've laughed and blown it off, but a red, blinding, hormonal fury came over me and I rolled down the window and yelled, "Learn how to drive," followed by a word I have never, ever said. A word that I would never, ever let Jake use. A word all women hate. Which is exactly why I used it. Four letters, starts with a C and ends with a T. It's so horrible. I have no idea where it came from. It must be the hormones.

But, I've never felt like such a badass.

I can't believe it—being pregnant has turned me into a trash-talking hoodrat.

Feeling very feisty, I cranked up Dr. Dre and Snoop Dogg for the rest of the drive. I turned it down a little when I had the horrible thought of my unborn child hearing the lyrics and being born with a set of gold teeth and a clock around his/her neck à la Flavor Flav. I would have only myself to blame. I mean, the kid just heard his mother say the C word and crank up music about smoking pot.

I thought, *Hmmmm . . . must ask Dr. Clarke if it has ears yet.*

Regardless of my newly found badass status, the minute I walked into the office, the nerves returned. As I sat waiting for my name to be called, I discreetly glanced around the room. Immediately, I noticed the other pregnant women waiting. I also noticed almost all of them had their husbands/boyfriends/sperm donors with them, except for one girl who appeared to be a lesbian and had her female partner with her. Jake wanted to come, but I told him not to bother since I figured I'd just get the standard pamphlets and pap smear, so said the pregnancy books. But suddenly I felt like I did when I was in grade school and my mom forgot it was the one day we could wear our normal clothes instead of our uniforms and I was the only loser kid who showed up in a plaid skirt and kneesocks.

I'm already screwing up this mothering/pregnancy stuff.

"Clare Finnegan," the nurse called. She looked surprised as she said my name. She glanced at my chart again as I walked toward her, and she smiled. Once we were in the room, she said, "Congratulations! I didn't think we'd see you back so soon! You were just here a few months ago."

"Yeah, well, neither did I."

She took some blood and made me pee in a cup, which I screwed up like always and pissed on my new white cashmere pants. She asked me a million questions about my medical history and left. Dr. Clarke came in soon after.

"Well, Clare, welcome back!" She smiled at me.

"Yeah, well . . . thanks!"

"So, I hear you had a little scare a while back. How's everything been since?"

"Great. Well, except for the nausea. But good, otherwise."

"Good to hear. Sometimes those kinds of things just happen. But you were right to get it checked out. So, how did your dad react?" Dr. Clarke and my dad went to medical school together and occasionally run into each other at the hospital. The last thing I want is for her to tell my father.

"No one really knows yet." Isn't there some kind of oath that they take or something—she can't accidentally tell him or anything, right?

She saw my look and winked. "My lips are sealed."

"Thanks. The last thing my father needs is a heart attack. My sister already has that angle covered."

She handed me a packet with a bunch of leaflets and crap. I caught the word "incision" and quickly looked away.

"Here is a bunch of information on everything. Do you have any questions?"

"Um, yeah. A few."

"Shoot," she said, and sat down on one of those miniature stools.

"Well, I heard there's a bunch of stuff I'm not supposed to eat like cheese or something, lunch meat, caffeine . . ."

"Bullshit."

"Huh?"

"It's all bullshit. Unless you're eating a pound of bologna a day, you'll be fine. Everything in moderation."

"Really?" I love Dr. Clarke.

"Really. Our relatives in Ireland ate corned beef every day and drank stout and we all turned out OK. You'll be fine. Don't kill yourself trying to be perfect. Just limit the obvious ones, like alcohol." I seriously am in love with that woman.

"Do people ever give birth like on TV, with those blue sheets on and all covered up?" She just stared at me after this question and I wound up blurting out another, more ridiculous question: "Can you really get a brain aneurysm while giving birth, like I saw in a movie?"

Pregnancy has turned me into an idiot.

After more staring, some stifled laughter, and a bunch more leaflets, she gave me her estimate of the Scary Day, a.k.a. my due date: January 6.

Apparently, according to medical research, in January, an organism bigger than a cat will be forced out of me. It looks like my New Year's Eve is going to be a real hoot.

On my way out, I set up more appointments. I never knew pregnancy was so time-consuming. I was almost out the door when I saw Abby, my office's receptionist. She gave me a friendly wave and furrowed her brow in slight confusion. Probably because she knew I was just here a few months ago since Dr. Clarke's office called to confirm my appointment and she gave me the message. She's probably thinking I have some weird, untreatable STD requiring multiple visits, and will tell everyone about my mutated strain of venereal disease.

Sunday, June 10
· · · · · · · · · · · · · · · · · · · ·

The entire office gave me questioning looks all afternoon, no doubt due to Abby telling them about my contagious new disease. I'm going to let them think what they want for now, because I'm nowhere near ready to tell work since it would involve actually having a plan for maternity leave and such. Besides, I think my own parents should hear the news before Mule Face does. I'm planning on telling them tonight at dinner, although I have no clue how.

5:00 P.M.
Here we go again! Yes, my apartment has officially become Vomitville.

5:05 P.M.
Have. To. Pee. Again. Then. Puke. Again.

5:20 P.M.
It's time to peel myself off the bathroom floor and get dressed.

6:05 P.M.
Jake's hands are shaking on the steering wheel.

6:35 P.M.
"Great! You guys are here. The lasagna's just about ready." My mom looked busy as usual, tossing a salad with one hand and typing a PowerPoint presentation with the other.

"Do you need any help?" I asked as Jake immediately disappeared into the family room to commandeer the TV.

"Nope. I think I'm good."

"Where's Sam?"

"Oh, she's lying in bed. She was at a sleepover last night and is pretty tired so she's lying down." My mother lost about a thousand radar points and two thousand uptight points after I graduated from high school. If I came home from a sleepover totally hungover, the jig would've been up and grounding would've ensued. But Sam just gets a house full of whispered voices and a parental blind eye.

"How's everything with the in-laws? Natalie pulled anything lately?"

No, but I can't wait *to make that phone call,* I thought to myself.

"Not really." I tried to sound casual but my voice came out all squeaky.

"Everything OK?" She looked at me suspiciously.

"Yeah!" I said quickly. Goddamn it, I've never been good at lying to my mother, which is one reason why I spent most of my teenage years without phone privileges. I knew she wasn't going to let it go.

She just stared at me. "What's going on? Is everything OK?"

"Yes, Mom," I laughed.

"Did you get fired or something?"

"No. *Mom!*"

"OK. You don't have to tell me if you don't want to, but I know something is up." She shot me another wary look and clicked on her laptop a few more times.

"You'll know soon enough at dinner," I muttered under my breath. Then, a very, very bad thing happened: I let my guard down. I never should've done it—it's my mother's classic trick. She waits until I'm not paying attention and then socks me with some amazingly accurate question so I can't even attempt to cover up my reaction.

"Are you pregnant?" WHAM! My face turned pink and my stomach dropped. She didn't even look up from her laptop. "That's it, isn't it?"

"Uh, well . . ." I laughed again, feeling slightly hysterical. I would be so horrible in a military interrogation. All they'd have to do is bring my mother in and I'd spill the country's secrets.

She looked up from her laptop. "I knew it." She broke out into a huge smile and I got the pang in my stomach again. "I take it this wasn't planned?" I shook my head, unable to speak because I suddenly felt like crying. Maybe it was out of fear, maybe out of relief, or maybe because I knew this was something my mom couldn't make all better. I wanted my mom to fix it, but she couldn't. Because I was going to be a mom myself. Gah.

She put her arm around me. "Well, honey, it does change your life but don't be afraid of it. I know you didn't plan for it but the second you see that baby, you'll know everything will be OK. You weren't planned either but the first time we held you it was like . . . instant love." I silently nodded my head and the tears started to well up again. Before either of us could say anything else, the oven timer went off. My mom took the lasagna out of the oven and set it down. "I'm so proud of you," she said and kissed the top of my head.

Jake, my dad, and Sam all appeared, having heard the timer go off.

"Hi, hon," my dad said.

"Ew. Gross. You know I hate lasagna," Sam said, wrinkling her nose. She bent down and sniffed the dish and stuck her tongue out.

"I made it without meat," my mom said, wiping her hands on a dish towel as Jake and my dad discussed their early predictions for the World Series or something.

"MO-OM! I TOLD you I'm on an all-meat diet now. Like the one I showed you in last month's *InStyle*."

"All meat?" I asked her.

She turned to me, barely able to keep her eyeballs in her head. "DUH. It's only like the best diet ever." She examined her manicured fingernail. "I SO need an effing manicure," she muttered to herself.

"Let's eat, everybody," my mom said, giving my father and Jake a little tap.

Nobody even took their first bite before I cleared my throat and paused. Jake gave me a quick nervous glance.

"So, I have some news for everyone," I said, and smiled widely.

"You have spinach in your teeth," Sam said as she glanced up.

"What?"

"Spinach. In between your two front teeth. It's gross. Go look in the mirror."

Not wanting to get up and lose my chance to announce the news and not wanting to announce my pregnancy with spinach hanging from my teeth, I looked helplessly at Jake and raised my eyebrows. He shook his head and mouthed, "No."

"Yes," I hissed at him.

"No," he said, a little louder.

"What's going on?" my dad asked, his head ping-ponging between the two of us.

"Nothing, Dad." I smiled at him with my mouth closed. "Do it," I hissed at Jake.

Jake shook his head in silence.

"I'm pregnant." I tried to say it without moving my lips.

"What?" my dad said while my mom smiled and Sam examined her split ends.

I decided to screw the spinach and loudly said, "Jake and I are going to have a baby." Even as I said it, it didn't seem real. The second I got the words out, I started laughing hysterically.

My dad looked at my mom and she nodded. "Oh, well, um, yeah, um, congratulations!" he finally said.

Sam still didn't look up from her blond split ends.

"Sam?" my mom asked.

"What? Oh, sorry. I missed it. What did you say?"

"Your sister is pregnant," my mom said.

Her mouth dropped open. "You?"

"Yup."

"Well, are you going to have it?"

Jake and I looked at each other and rolled our eyes as my mom screeched, "Sam!"

"What? I was just wondering . . ." She trailed off and looked thoughtful for a moment. I thought she was going to say something nice or insightful.

"Can I have the new jeans you just bought? I mean, you'll have to wear high-waisted mom jeans now anyway. Oh, and your BCBG silver top?"

"Shut up, Sam. So, are you going back to work?" my mom asked.

"Yep. I'll take maternity leave, but I want to stay at my job and besides, having running water and paying our bills is important to us," I said as I fiddled with my earring.

"What are you going to do about child care?" my mom asked.

"Uh, we're still trying to get used to the idea that we're going to have a child. We don't know anything beyond," Jake said.

"How much is child care these days?" my dad asked.

"I don't know. Probably a lot. Let's not talk about that now, OK? We're not ready for that discussion quite yet," I said.

"Do nannies make a lot?" Sam interjected, looking thoughtful.

"I'm not sure. Probably." I shrugged.

"Like how much?"

"I have no idea. We probably won't be able to afford a nanny. But listen, like I said, we're not ready to have that particular discussion."

"I need, like, LOTS of money. I am effing broke," Sam said. "You can give me money to watch your kid."

"We will probably want someone who would actually WANT to take care of our baby. Would you?" I said to her.

"No. But I WANT money." She widened her eyes and pursed her lips.

After a million more questions that we couldn't answer, Jake and I drove home so we could continue sharing our news with other family members and continue to answer their questions in our half-assed manner.

10:30 P.M.

I just got off the phone with Mark. After I told him the news, he said, "Congratulations! Did Dad act weird?"

"Not really, why?"

"Because it's pretty much a confirmation you've had sex."

"I'm married, remember?"

"Yeah, but you've moved from 'don't ask, don't tell' to flamboyantly out of the closet now," he said.

"What are you talking about?"

"I don't know. I'm just teasing you. Listen, congrats. Tell Jake I'm proud of his swimmers."

10:45 P.M.

Reese is thrilled I'm joining the Motherhood Cult. She claimed she "knew" and her mother's intuition told her. I told her it wasn't her intuition but rather my quickly horizontally growing stomach. She laughed and said she's packing up all of her maternity clothes to give me. Score!

Now it's time to call the in-laws. . . .

11:00 P.M.

I wimped out and made Jake make the phone call to the Grandalskis.

"Well, dear! Congratulations. This is a surprise—what a surprise indeed! I can't imagine this was planned. Anyway, welcome to the mom club," Marianne said after Jake handed me the phone.

"Yeah, thanks."

"Have you thought about moving yet?"

"Huh?"

"Move, dear. You can't raise a baby in an apartment."

"We can't?"

"Oh, Clare," she laughed, "of course not. Babies need space and a lawn."

"I'll let you know." I'll let you know when I'm going to kick your ass, I should've said.

"When's your last day at work?"

"Well, my due date is in January, so sometime around then."

"I know being a career girl is important to you, but you'll see being a mom is the best, most rewarding job of all."

"I'm sure. I'm still going to be a career girl, though."

"You're still going to work? Really?"

"Yep."

"Oh, my. Well. How does Jake feel about having strangers raise his child?" I wanted to reach across the phone line and strangle her but I figured giving birth in prison would suck so I handed the phone back to Jake and let him deal with the psycho Donna Reed. I figure I have the rest of my life to hear about how selfish I am and how I'm permanently damaging my child by placing it in day care.

Besides, the lasagna was on its way back up.

1:00 A.M.

Despite not keeping an ounce of dinner in my stomach, tonight was pretty successful. I feel so much better now that my mom knows about the baby. Hearing her tell me it's OK, that I can do it, makes me feel like I can. Just like when she told me I could make the track team in eighth grade despite a bit of a weight problem. But she told me I could. And I did.

My mom's reaction was also a confirmation that despite not being planned, it is in fact supposed to be a happy time. I'm thinking I'll experience more of those "warm and fuzzy" feelings once I stop harfing up every shred of food I put into my body.

Monday, June 18
. . . .

I woke up this morning still feeling relieved that we told everyone the news last night. Although I make it a point to deal with Jake's parents as little as possible, I'm glad we told them and my parents. We're now finally out in the open. Out of the closet, to use Mark's words. It feels so much more real now that our families know, and especially now that my mom knows. At times, I'd felt like it wasn't really happening since she wasn't a part of it.

Despite the fact that our inner circle knows now, I'm not planning on telling anyone else for a while. Which has its negatives and positives. Positives being we can keep it our own special secret for a while, no hate e-mails from jen2485 and I don't have to deal with Mule Face checking my legs for spider veins just yet. Negatives being what happened today:

I dragged my sorry ass to the grocery store this afternoon in an effort to find something remotely appealing for dinner. I picked up a can of chicken noodle soup, debating whether or not my stomach and gestating embryo would allow me to keep it down. Just as my body reacted with a big fat "NO!" and my stomach heaved, a very nice woman dressed in a gorgeous cashmere shell approached me.

"Are you Clare? From the Internet?" she asked, smiling at me.

I froze, can of soup in hand, stomach in knots, cold sweat pouring down my face.

"Uh-huh." I nodded, afraid if I opened my mouth any further I'd decorate her lovely top with the contents of my lunch.

"My friends and I are big fans of your blog."

I nodded again, unable to meet her eyes.

"Where do you get all of your story ideas?"

I slowly raised my head and straightened my shoulders. Instantly, my stomach twisted again and I gagged, still holding the can of soup. Thankfully, nothing came out, but the nice woman hurried away pretty quickly.

So, in recap, a very well-dressed, professional-looking woman complimented my writing skills today and I responded by dry heaving while holding an aluminum can. Since the Internet doesn't know I'm pregnant, I'm sure she told all of her friends I'm some anorexic heroin addict.

Thursday, June 21
. . . .

The vomiting didn't stop last night until I fell asleep. I even woke up twice in the middle of the night to puke. I feel like I'm going to puke the baby right up.

I planned on keeping a low profile at work today: work on the last-minute details for the Gala this weekend and avoid Mule Face at all costs. However, as I walked to my office, Mule Face's head caught my eye. I looked and saw a beautiful sight: Mule Face now has a mullet. Seriously.

I think she asked for layers in the front and long in the back but it wound up looking all business in the front and party in the back. She said her hairstylist called it a "bi-level." The worst part is, she walked around the office all day and asked people if they liked her new look. Um, yeah, if she's planning on attending a monster truck rally/demolition derby this weekend, very appropriate. Every time I look at her, I picture her wearing acid-washed denim and standing next to a Camaro. Or vacationing with the Grandalskis at Lake Park Campgrounds.

I must take a picture of her hair and send it to Carrie. Maybe she can make an avant-garde mullet collage art project for the nursery.

Saturday, June 23
. . . .

It's here. Gala day.

I asked the baby if I could take a day off from puking, just one day, and it responded by making me heave up my breakfast.

Bad news: I won't be able to take the edge off with a few drinks.

Good news: After tonight, Carolyn Wittenberg, Jessica Greene, Betsy Fallon, and Tony G. of Tony G. Productions will all be in the past.

Bad news: My breakfast of corn flakes is all over the bathroom.

Good news: I wrote an awesome blog entry on corn flakes, thus again avoiding the whole "Hey World, I'm Pregnant" essay.

11:00 A.M.

I arrived at the hotel to begin setting up the silent auction and to crack the whip on the florist, linen rental company, and all the other vendors. Tony G. greeted me and looked me up and down and smirked while lifting an eyebrow. "Nice look," he said, and made a little *tiff* sound. What an asshole. I didn't need a reminder that no concealer will cover my dark circles, my hair was pissed off it rained so it decided to expand one thousand times the normal size, and the casual, yet professional outfit consisting of black capris and black flats I planned on wearing was crumpled up on my bathroom floor with bits of puked-up corn flakes all over it.

"Everything going OK?" I responded brightly, thinking of exactly which very sharp object I wanted to drill into his skull.

"We-ell, it's a good thing you're here. Things are already a blur. There's no room for my dancers to change, the dance floor isn't going to be big enough with those extra tables, and the acoustics are all wrong due to the ceiling draping," he said as we walked toward the ballroom.

I opened the doors to the ballroom and silently scanned the room, which looked amazing. The florists assembled Zen garden center-pieces with giant bamboo and palm leaves, surrounded by bonsai trees and red paper parasols hung from the ceiling. Custom lighting made each centerpiece look ablaze. Across the dance floor, a spotlight displayed the sponsor logos and Asian symbols. I stood back for a moment and enjoyed the sight of everything coming together. It was the moment when everything became sort of worth it.

It was more like half a moment, though, because Tony G. snapped his fingers. "Hello? Earth to the little lady. What are we going to do about my problems?"

"The dancers can change in the hospitality suite—room 1482. We can move the tables back a foot or two off of the dance floor. We can't do anything about the acoustics, but I'm sure you're such a phenomenal professional that you can work around it." He seemed pleased and left to go find someone else to harass.

I saw Jessica over by the silent auction display and walked over.

"Need any help?" I asked.

"Oh, God! Thank God you're here! We can't find the airline

package, the bid sheets are out of sequence, and none of the committee has shown up to help!" she said.

"Relax. I'll take care of everything. The airline package is in the accordion file and I'll reorder the bid sheets."

"You're a lifesaver. Listen, I have a hair appointment this afternoon, so . . ." She paused, waiting for me to jump in.

"Of course, of course. You go get beautiful and I'll take care of this."

"You're the best!" she called over her shoulder. Tony G. jumped out of the way as she rushed out.

3:00 P.M.

The auction display is up, the bid sheets successfully reordered, and Tony G. silent. Since I offered the hospitality suite to the dancers, I changed in the bathroom, which I found appropriate due to the amount of time I spend in the bathroom these days. I threw my hair into a clip and tried to apply some eye shadow but exhaustion began to creep in and the desire to look attractive quickly waned.

6:00 P.M.

Guests are beginning to arrive, because rich or not, these people always want to squeeze every dollar out of a five-hundred-dollar ticket. Jessica and her husband, Robert, were among the first here. She looks stunning in a silk Asian-inspired black dress with delicate embroidery and a plunging neckline framed by loosely waved hair. Betsy Fallon is wearing a bright red strapless dress that belies her personality, and Carolyn Wittenberg is sporting a blue taffeta-and-sequin dress accessorized with many, many carats of diamonds.

I'm sitting back and watching the rest of the crowd as the room fills. A woman with enormous breasts is wearing such a low-cut dress, I thought her nipple was going to pop out when she adjusted her earring. I've also seen some of the best face-lifts, brow-lifts, and second wives that money can buy.

A few minutes ago, I longingly stared at Carolyn Wittenberg's red wine, until she caught me staring and looked slightly alarmed, probably because it looked like I was staring at her cleavage.

6:30 P.M.

I'm so tired I don't care anymore. I already look like trash so I figure I might as well act like it and snooze in a stall in the bathroom. I can't imagine if someone walked in on me. They'd probably think I'm a crack whore who OD'd or something.

7:00 P.M.

My nap was wonderful. The silent auction table is running smoothly. The rest should be easy.

2:00 A.M.

Easy, my ass. Just after seven, the Junior Volunteers arrived and tried to appear eager for their assignments, although all they really wanted was a contraband drink from the bar.

"Hi, girls! Thanks so much for coming. I'm Clare, as some of you know, and if you need anything, I'm your gal."

The five teenagers flatly stared at me. Casey Nolan (daughter of William Nolan, net worth $200 million) flicked her hair back. "Um, just want to let you know, my dad wants to dance with me so I won't be able to help for very long."

"Sure, you can take a break, but it would be great if you could help out as much as possible."

"What*ever*," she whispered to Renee Kirkowski (daughter of Leslie and Rick, net worth $80 million).

"Casey and Renee, you get table one. Donna and Taylor, table two, and Paige . . ." I looked at Paige Bronstein (daughter of Steve and Laura, net worth $110 million). "You can float between the two." Poor Paige. She obviously wasn't in the inner circle.

"What school do you go to?" Paige asked me when the other girls left, gingerly touching her thick, coarse curly hair and adjusting her glasses.

"Well, I went to St. Mary's for high school but that was a good ten years ago."

"Ten years ago?" she asked, tugging at her dress.

"Why? How old do you think I am?"

"Like a senior, probably," she said.

Ha! It's probably good my stomach isn't showing yet. I wouldn't want to give the impression I'm some knocked-up teenager. It might slightly affect my credibility.

The cocktail hour ended at seven o'clock when waiters rang dinner bells and asked people to take their seats. I pushed past a throng of geisha girls holding silver trays of Singapore slings and mandarin martinis and mouthed, "Everything OK?"

"I'm sweating my balls off in this costume," one of them whispered back in a thick New York accent.

After the salmon salad with wasabi vinaigrette, Tony G.'s dancers came out and performed the dorky fan routine. It went smoothly until one of them tripped and almost ended up in Carolyn Wittenberg's lap.

The Chinese dragon and drums whipped through the room after the beef course. Everyone seemed to love it but that could be attributed to the approximately nine thousand drinks everyone had already consumed.

After dinner, Tony G.'s band started playing and I was able to slip my shoes off discreetly for a moment before I jumped up to close the silent auction. The Junior Volunteers were supposed to help close the auction and run the checkout process but I saw Casey Nolan and Renee Kirkowski downing cosmopolitans so I didn't think they'd be much help.

I looked around the dance floor and saw Betsy and Jessica dancing with their husbands to Tony G.'s rendition of Earth, Wind & Fire. Jessica had her hands in the air and was bopping around while Betsy kept her feet firmly planted to the ground and swayed from side to side. Carolyn Wittenberg and her husband were doing a routine that very closely resembled the Robot.

The pang of a full bladder hit me and I hightailed it to the bathroom and almost trucked over an old lady wearing close to a million dollars in diamonds. I waited for Casey Nolan to finish puking up cosmos before I could feel the sweet relief. I think I even let out an audible sigh, which probably caused Casey to think I was masturbating in the stall or something.

I picked my tired, nauseous, pregnant ass up and went over to the silent auction and sat down. People drifted out of the ballroom and began to check out and I started taking credit cards and giving out the prizes. Jessica and her husband appeared.

"This is her! This is Clare. Clare, meet my husband, Robert." Robert extended his hand and I warmly shook it as I noticed Jessica swaying.

"Nice to meet you. Great job tonight," he said, his bleached teeth glittering.

"Thanks."

"Oh! I almost forgot!" She turned to a beautiful couple in their twenties. "This is my sister Rachael Flynn and her fiancé, Ben Shepard. Isn't it great?"

"Yeah, sure!"

"I know! We'll have so much fun. It'll be like the Gala all over again. We can go to lunch and everything, right?"

"Right!" I had no clue what she was talking about.

"Gotta go! We'll talk Monday!" Jessica popped off, grabbing her husband's arm for balance.

Rachael leaned forward. "You did such a great job tonight. I know you'll make my wedding so special." I nodded and Rachael and Ben walked off, mouthing the words to Kool and the Gang's "Celebration."

My immediate reaction was: *Hi? Hello? Her wedding? Seriously. I'm sure to be nine months pregnant at this wedding. Because I am just THAT lucky.*

Carolyn Wittenberg was the last person to check out. "Hello, Clare," she said as she puffed on a cigarette and blew smoke in my face.

"You won number eight, right?"

"Correct."

"Well, we have your credit card on file, so just sign here." She scribbled on the paper, swiftly grabbed her prize envelope, and walked away, a blaze of navy blue taffeta and diamonds. I looked down at the bid sheet and started laughing. What a drunken idiot. She signed "Gala" instead of her name on the credit card receipt. That kind of made the whole night worth it.

After I arrived home, my feet resembled two wooden blocks, visibly throbbing. I poured myself a half glass of wine and lay down on the couch, happy Jake was out with his friend Bill-I-Still-Live-at-Home-with-My-Parents-and-Smoke-Pot-Every-Day-at-4:20.

The night was a success—I didn't slit Tony G.'s throat, Jessica and Betsy had a fabulously drunken time, I didn't pee or vomit on myself, and the event raised $650,000. I took a sip of the Merlot and closed my eyes. I thanked the dear Lord I was done with the Gala, with Carolyn Wittenberg, Jessica Greene, and Betsy Fallon.

Until . . . Oh, shit. I forgot.

Assuming Jessica and her sister weren't on drugs, they want me to plan her wedding. I so don't have the strength to do a wedding. Bride crying because the flowers are wrong, the mother screaming at the band, the drunk groomsmen, the wasted bridesmaids, the incompetent waiters, the sobbing father, and me in the middle, trying to keep the evening flowing. Oh, and add in a shitload of money, which means expectations. And one unborn fetus. New thought: What if it is after the baby's born? New set of fears: What if Christina makes me work the event while I'm on maternity leave? How will I manage that? What if I've just had the baby and my boobs are huge? What if I'm fat and don't have anything to wear? What if Jake burns down the apartment while watching the child?

Monday, June 25

• • • • • • • • • • • • • • • • • • • •

I'm still exhausted from the Gala and hoped today would be quiet. But no. So much for any downtime.

Today I suffered through what was officially the world's most pointless and boring staff meeting. By the end of it, I was flicking my Bic rollerball pen in between my fingers, thinking that spending an afternoon in the ER getting a writing utensil removed from my eye socket would be *much* more enjoyable.

I overslept and came into the meeting after it had already started. Christina gave me an evil look as I slid next to her. I mouthed an apology and sat down in my chair, which made a loud *crack* sound as I settled in. Jan, Christina's boss, stopped talking and looked directly at me before continuing to drone on about how we were already over on our printing budget.

Out of the corner of my eye I saw Mule Face hide a smile. She was wearing a purple polyester pantsuit that screamed Jaclyn Smith Plus Size Collection from Kmart. I glanced around the table at everyone, confirming by expressions they were all bored as hell already. I pulled out my budget and pretended to stare at it while playing a fun game of Check Out the Other Employees. Half of the staff works in another office across town, a fact for which I am eternally grateful since they are all kind of weird freaks.

I did a quick survey: Donna's tortoise-shell hair clip in the shape of a cat? Check.

Tracy's hot pink Lee Press-on Nails that look like Middle East torture devices used to scratch out POWs' corneas? Check.

Mary's open-toed orthopedic wedge pumps worn with reinforced-toe pantyhose? Check. (Why does she think it looks attractive? Does she think we can't tell she's wearing stockings? Maybe she wears them to make her legs look tan? These are mysteries of the universe that sadly, I am unable to answer.)

Jan finished her tirade about the budget by making us all promise to cut our expenses. I'm sure using fewer Post-its will get us back on track. She turned to Christina and asked her to begin her presentation. Christina got up and passed out a bunch of packets regarding clean-up work to be done by our IT guys—who exist solely to laugh at us and make us feel stupid when we can't access our e-mail.

Once Christina finished her presentation on our computer system, we all went around the table to report on our current projects like in kindergarten show-and-tell.

When it came to me, I reviewed how the Gala went and how I would be doing the Flynn-Shepard wedding. In a delusional moment, I briefly considered announcing my pregnancy, but chickened out. I finished my sentence and quickly looked to Mule Face to indicate that I was finished.

She smiled broadly and said, "Well, I do have something to tell everyone."

I thought she was going to resign.

No such luck.

She threw her left hand out into the center of the table with a dramatic slap.

"I'm engaged!" she screamed.

We all made fakey congratulatory noises.

"Big D proposed last night! I went to the grocery store and when I got home, he had set up candles and flowers and was down on one knee!"

I think that is officially the worst proposal story I've ever heard. The grocery store? How romantic. Not to mention he proposed on a Sunday night. I took a look at the engagement ring and almost puked. It's a heart-shaped diamond. It looks like it belongs to a three-year-old, along with her My Little Pony and Malibu Barbie collection.

I let the realization I'm going to spend the next several months of my life listening to Mule Face's wedding discussions sink in and suddenly I didn't feel so well, and this time it wasn't due to my unborn fetus.

When the meeting ended, I quickly walked back to my office, eager to get back to some quiet respite. Mule Face planted herself right in front of me, waving a *Bride* magazine.

"Look at this wedding gown. Wouldn't it look amazing on me?" She pointed to a model wearing a gorgeous silk form-fitting sheath that would show even the barest wisp of underwear, not to mention fat rolls.

"Yep!" I said brightly.

She beamed at me. "I knew you'd love it! You'll have to help me pick everything out. I want to learn from all the mistakes you made while planning yours." She waddled off, yanking her panties out of her crack as she walked away.

I wanted to chase her down and beat her over the head with her fifty-pound bridal magazine and tell her she was going to look like an overstuffed sausage casing if she wore that wedding gown.

Tuesday, June 26
. . . .

Mule Face hasn't shut up about her wedding for even a nanosecond. She's spent the morning being oh-so-productive by talking to her florist, bridesmaid, and Big D, saying things like, "Ooohhhh, I *love* it. *Oohhhhh* pink hydrangeas are *amazing*. Ooohhhh, yeah." She's even been making sexual grunts and rolling her eyes back in her head as she says "Mmmmm."

I swear, she could make a fortune as a phone sex operator.

When I walked past her desk, she looked weirdly at my midsection before getting up and waddling off to cram more Krispy Kremes into her pie hole. I know I can't wait much longer to tell anyone at work, but I still can't bear the thought of answering the asinine questions people will ask, like "Was it planned?" and "You're so young! Are you worried about losing your freedom?" or "You *do* know that you'll never sleep again, right?" and my personal favorite, "How bad do you want a glass of wine?" The answers: No, yes, in denial, and really freaking bad.

How do I bring it up? "Um, did you get that vendor contract yet? No? Hopefully it will come in soon. Why? Because I'm pregnant." I'd love to send out a mass e-mail but I'm pretty sure that falls in the "unprofessional" category. At least I have a little bit of time before they start gossiping about my stretch marks and baby names. Now they just think I've become a fat-ass and gossip about my love handles and double chin. (Which Reese and Jake swear aren't there but I think they're lying because they don't want me to cry like I did the other night when the Chinese takeout lady couldn't understand my order over the phone.)

Thursday, June 28
· · · · · · · · · · · · · · · · · · · ·

I called Reese today and waited through four rings until someone picked up the phone.

Silence.

Me: "Hello? Hello?"

Silence

Me: "Reese?"

Silence

Me: "Anyone there?"

A high-pitched voice: "TYLER!"

I had no idea who the hell Tyler was so I looked at my cell phone, but sure enough it said REESE HOME.

Me: "Tyler? What?"

Tyler: "I had some Oreos."

Me: "Um. Great. Do you know Reese?"

Tyler: "No."

Me: "You don't know who Reese is?"

Tyler: "My dog has a tail. Her name is Rudy."

Me: "Are there any grown-ups there?"

Tyler: "NO!"

Me: "If you find a grown-up for me, I'll buy you a pony."

Tyler: "A purple one?"

Me: "Yes! A purple one."

Tyler: "My mom—"

I heard muffled voices in the background and the sound of some-one wrestling the phone out of Tyler's vice grip.

Reese: "Hello?"

Me: "Reese—it's me. Who the hell was that kid?"

Reese: "Clare! I'm so sorry. I was in the bathroom. He's my friend Meredith's boy. I met her at a new Mommy and Me class Grace and I are taking. We babysit one day a week for each other now."

Me: "That kid is a brat."

Reese: "Clare! He's not a brat, he's four. He's perfectly sweet."

I heard Tyler in the background, yelling "WHO'S A BRAT? THAT'S A BAD WORD." I heard her yell, "Tyler! Don't throw that down the stairs!" followed by another crash.

Reese: "You're right. That kid's a brat. God, I can't wait until Meredith picks him up. So what's going on with you?"

Me: "Not much. Just wanted to make sure you were OK. I haven't heard from you that much lately."

Reese: "Everything's great!"

Me: "Are you sure, because . . ."

Reese: "Clare. I. Am. Fine."

Me: "OK, OK. Just wanted to be sure. So, are you doing anything fun this weekend? Any big plans?"

Reese: "Besides cleaning the house and doing laundry? No."

Me: "Well, Joel and Megan are having one of their famous parties on Saturday night and I was wondering if you and Matt want to come and be our dates."

Reese: "I'd love to. In that fabulous house they just bought?"

Me: "Yep. Five thousand square feet prime for partying. No kids

and every kind of booze you didn't know existed. Oh, and they're
getting a band this year. We'll probably just crash on the couch or
floor or wherever."

Reese: "Christ, I haven't been to one of those since—well, you
know. Before Grace. You'll know what I'm talking about soon."

Me: "Well, then we both need to get out. It's settled—we're all
going Saturday!"

Reese: "Who's going to be there?"

Me: "Julie can't go, if that's what you're asking."

Reese: "Oh, right. I don't care, I was just wondering. I don't
know if Matt will want to go. He doesn't like to go to parties anymore, but if we can find a babysitter we'll come. It's kind of short notice. I'll have to let you—"

Bang! The awful sound of glass shattering came from the other
end of the phone.

Reese: "OH MY GOD! THE CRYSTAL! I have to go."

After I hung up, I silently thanked Jake for talking me out of registering for Waterford crystal. The only things breakable in our place
are hideous gifts from Marianne.

I know Reese and Matt probably won't come on Saturday. I wonder if Reese will even tell him about the party. I doubt she has the
energy to keep up the act of perfect happily married couple with a
group of people who've known them since college.

Saturday, June 30
. . . .

Ugh. It's Fourth of July weekend. The fact I don't look pregnant but
merely fat and the temperature is ninety thousand degrees outside is
not making me excited at all for Joel and Megan's annual Fourth of
July party/barbecue. Normally, I'd be putting on some new cute tank
top or sundress and sandals, but now, in the alternate universe known
as pregnancy, I'm searching for something that covers my spare

tire/baby. Thankfully, I have many "tunic length" tanks from last season long enough to cover the blubber. The problem is the tanks are also "long and lean style" which makes me look "round and tubby," but I figure most of our friends know about everything so I don't have to worry about any misperceptions.

I really don't want to go, but Jake would die since Joel and Megan's Fourth of July parties are legendary. They usually last from around noon until dawn, when everyone passes out in various random positions. I'm pretty nervous about being one of the only sober people there. I'm slightly worried that the following will happen: (a) I will discover my husband is the most annoying drunk *ever*, (b) I will realize my friends are alcoholics and need to go to rehab, and (c) everyone will think, "Man, Clare really isn't any fun when she's sober."

2:00 P.M.
Percentage of drunk people at the party: 20.

OK, I'm doing well. Things have started out fine. Jake's "taking it slow" like he promised me by drinking only beer and refusing every Jell-O shot and mixed drink offered to him. Joel even tried to guilt him into taking a shot on account of the "former college roommate reunion," but he turned it down. For now.

I got a text message on my phone this afternoon from Reese: *Sorry. Can't make it. Sitter fell through. Have drinks for me!*

I'm so bummed. Even though I knew she probably wouldn't make it, I still held out hope she'd show up, sans Matt, and we could hang out.

I'm already getting tired of sipping on soft drinks and stuffing my face with Chex mix. I realized I'd never really eaten anything at this party before, minus the lone hot dog crammed down the throat to prevent gnawing hunger at four in the morning and dry heaves at nine in the morning. I've already eaten two hot dogs, some potato salad, and coleslaw. And I can pretty much guarantee this pattern will continue.

5:30 P.M.

Percentage of drunk people at the party: 40.

I've definitely swapped drinking and smoking for gorging on food, but otherwise everything is going well. Jake left to join a poker game and I've sprawled out on a lawn chair with Megan. After she stopped laughing when I told her about the In-Law Camping Trip, I figured it was time for another pop. And maybe another hot dog.

I wish I could update my blog. Wifey1025 would surely offer to come over and keep me company.

8:00 P.M.

Percentage of drunk people: 65.

People are starting to annoy me now. Megan accidentally spilled part of her cranberry vodka on me, so it looks like my boob is lactating. A wonderful sign of things to come. Megan's sister Jamie burped right in my face when she was telling me a story about how she never wants to have kids because she values her free time too much, and Jake keeps patting my blubber fat/baby in a weird drunken way. I think he's trying to be attentive but it looks more like groping. Oh, and my hands are shaking slightly from the eight gallons of caffeine.

12:00 A.M.

Percentage of drunk people: 99.9 minus one pregnant/fat girl.

Megan showed me her ass because she thought it would cheer me up. I spent a good twenty minutes recounting a good Mule Face story to Joel, about the time when she coughed and farted and tried to cover it up, and he laughed so hysterically, I thought, *Wow. I'm so funny. I'm a comedienne. People love my stories. I'm the funniest person here. I don't even need alcohol!* until I realized he was stoned and would've laughed at test patterns.

Joel and Jake have played "Bad, Bad Leroy Brown" approximately one thousand times, singing along while decked out in sunglasses and hats, using their beer bottles as microphones. A routine I've seen many, many times. Joel's sister Ava acted as their backup dancer, clapping her hands and twirling around unsteadily. If I hear everyone yell "Once more!" and "Fuck, yeah" and then "The south side of Chicago, is the baddest part of town . . ." one more time, I'm going to break a beer bottle and slit my wrist with the pieces.

"I'm having a baby! And I'm naming him Leroy!" Jake drunkenly yelled and everyone cheered, raising their drinks. "Isn't my wife beautiful? She's having a baby and it's sexy!" Jake shouted and everyone cheered again. I looked over my shoulder for someone, anyone, who thought this was just as weird/annoying/freaky as me.

2:00 A.M.

Percentage of people passed out: 32 and soon to include one tubby/pregnant girl.

Jake and Joel concluded their show by singing most of the Blues Brothers greatest hits. It's amazing how easily our friends are entertained. See, this is why I wanted to wait to have kids. I figured when we had kids, we'd spend our free time socializing with people who drink only a few cocktails and hold fancy dinner parties while debating politics and religion. A social life consisting of sophistication and intelligence. A social life with friends who drink only occasionally, so it wouldn't be such a big deal to be the sober one. Oh, and friends who also have kids. But instead, I'm at a party listening to Joel and Jake make plans to start a new business of selling house plants shaped like private parts they plan to market to college kids. And they kept asking for my help and opinions, so I nodded enthusiastically and smiled from time to time. I mean please, *someone* has to have a good time, but it would be nice to have at least one other person here who isn't drinking—like a parent, another pregnant lady, or a recovering alcoholic.

All in all, I'm pretty fucking proud of myself. I didn't kill Jake, although it became abundantly clear we would've never made it past the second date if I were a devout Baptist/teetotaler, and I didn't punch anyone in the face, even when begged to sing "Papa Don't Preach" around one in the morning. They wanted to hear me sing "But I'm keepin' my baby!" It was kind of frightening having a drunken mob of people try to persuade me to do something. I felt like the "good girl" being forced to play Seven Minutes in Heaven with the sketchy popular boy at a high school party in some crappy made-for-TV movie.

9:00 A.M.

Poke poke. Hmmm . . . I think he's dead. He looks dead. Poke poke. I must wake him up. I'm starving.

9:06 A.M.

I slowly pried Jake's left eyelid open and peered into his bloodshot eye. "Hlrjim" was all I got.

"I'm starving," I said. He didn't speak or even twitch. He looked dead.

"Jake?" I said, and he lifted his eyebrows up, eyes still closed. "Jake, wake up. I want to go home."

"Too early," he grumbled, then turned over and buried his face into the inflatable inner tube he was using as a pillow. I had no idea where the hell he got it until I remembered Joel and Megan's neighbor has a pool. My baby daddy is an alcoholic thief.

"GET YOUR ASS UP RIGHT NOW AND FEED ME, YOU DRUNK!"

That finally made him sit up. Well, that coupled with a ninjalike poke to his flank.

"Fine," he said. He got up and stumbled around while trying to put on his jeans. "Where the hell did this come from?" he asked, pointing to the inner tube.

"How the hell should I know? I went to bed when you and Joel were firing up the deep fryer to see if you could batter and fry Doritos."

"Oh, yeah," he said, and smiled to himself, fuzzily remembering his fry-cook creations. "I think we tried to fry up a pizza slice, too. It didn't work."

"DON'T CARE. NEED BACON."

"Fine. You might have to drive, though. I think I'm still a little drunk."

I've now become not only the sober driver, but morning-after designated driver.

Wednesday, July 4
. . . .

"Kill me. Please. Just kill me. Put me out of my misery," I moaned to Julie this morning. She came over to hang out with me since her apartment building is being fumigated for "water beetles," which is just a nice term for "cockroaches."

"Morning sickness still kicking your ass?" she asked from her bed on the floor, head covered in an ice pack.

"It's not just kicking my ass, it's freaking owning me. I thought pregnancy was a natural, organic bodily experience, not one my body seems to reject with every cell inside it," I said as I lay down on the couch and buried my face in a pillow. The cat hair on the pillow made my stomach turn and I tossed it across the room, narrowly missing Julie's head.

"Watch it! I feel like shit, too, remember?" She leaned over and glared at me.

"Yes, but you feel like shit because you were out until three o'clock last night, drinking and dancing your butt off. Wanna know what I did last night? Went to bed at ten P.M. Now I ask you, how is that grounds to feel like someone is sticking a knife in my head and punching me in the stomach?" I sat up and looked at Julie, awaiting her response.

She shrugged and moaned again. "I feel like I'm going to throw up."

"Well, you know where the bathroom is. Trust me, it's gotten plenty of action these days. I'm just thrilled I didn't puke at Joel and Megan's party. You should've come, it was a blast."

"Would've loved to. Had to work, remember?"

"Oh, right."

"So where's Jake?" Julie said as she adjusted the ice pack.

"Playing softball."

"In this heat?" Julie shrieked. "He'll die of heatstroke! Isn't he tired?"

"Julie, you need to remember not everyone on earth is hung-over. I know you're probably dying inside, but we got about ten hours of sleep last night, so I think he's up for a few hours of exercise."

"I got ten hours of sleep last night. Lot of good it did me," Julie muttered. She threw a blanket over her head. "You guys still doing it?" she asked casually.

"I wish," I sighed. "I feel guilty, but I'm way too exhausted and sick most of the time to muster up the energy to do anything remotely sexual."

"I simply cannot relate."

"I know. I tried to tell Jake to find a nice girl who'll have sex with him, but he turned it down. It's too bad, though. Since R—" I started to say Reese, but stopped myself. "—other women tell me men get a little freaked out by sex at the end. Hopefully I'll feel better so I can get some while the gettin' is good, so to speak."

"Rother women?" Julie eyed me suspiciously.

"Other. You know what I meant," I said quickly.

"Well, suck it up, sister. Remember what I said about increased blood flow."

"Please. Don't torture me."

"So, what's new with work? Have you told them yet?" Julie stretched her arms over her head like a cat.

"Not yet. I'm putting it off as long as possible. Although that might be a bit difficult if you don't keep your mouth shut in public."

"I apologized for that, OK? Besides, you should apologize to *me*. You told someone I'm pregnant. What if you cursed me and now I'm going to get knocked up, too?"

"It wouldn't be that bad. What did you say to me? Oh, yes, something about designer jeans and Reese Witherspoon. So, yeah! I hope you get pregnant, too!" I said, and smiled at her.

She pointed her finger at me and sat up. "You take it back."

"Really, why? I thought you said accidental pregnancies were very Hollywood." I looked innocently at her.

"Say another word and I'm leaving."

"Leaving? I don't think so. I'll blackmail you to hang out with me if necessary." I switched on the DVD player. "This should keep you here for a while."

The television screen flickered and George Clooney's gorgeous face filled the screen.

"You win." Julie sighed and snuggled down on the floor. "You have me for another three hours. Two for the movie and one to discuss his hotness."

"Deal," I said.

Friday, July 6
. . . .

Miraculously, I've felt better ever since Julie and I had the George Clooney movie marathon. I'm attributing it to his gorgeous eyelashes rather than the end of the first trimester. Although, according to every pregnancy book I've read, the second trimester is considered the honeymoon period. The first trimester is something like this:

Nature: "Hey, bitch—enjoy the upset stomach, cold sweats, and dry heaving."

Me: "But I didn't drink last night, Nature. Aren't you supposed to drink to get a hangover?"

Nature: "Ha, ha, ha! Don't you know that your body can't distinguish between three martinis or a tiny embryo? Enjoy the next nine months, *sucker*!"

And apparently the third trimester involves lots of waddling, water retention, and shooting hoo-ha pains. Can't wait!

To commemorate reaching the end of the first trimester, today is my second appointment with Dr. Clarke. According to the Internet, we will get to hear the heartbeat today. So naturally, I've spent all week worrying about everything from what if we can't hear the heartbeat because my stomach has gotten so fat the blubber muffles it to what if the baby's heart sounds weird and the doctor tells me it's because I've been eating goat cheese to what if there is no heartbeat, and in fact, despite already seeing the baby on the ultrasound in the ER, there is no baby and I've dreamt this whole thing and will need to be institutionalized due to early onset of dementia? (It actually happens. Some women have phantom pregnancies, a.k.a. pseudocyesis, according to Wikipedia. I also saw it on *CSI*.)

2:00 P.M.

OK, so there is a baby and it's not a phantom one, either. My theory of early onset of dementia is false.

Jake came to the appointment and became very shy around Dr. Clarke. I think he was just freaked out by the stirrups and diagrams of ovaries and uteruses (uteri?) everywhere.

She asked him if he would like to ask any questions and he said, "Um. Can it hear us?"

"Not yet. Hearing usually comes around eighteen weeks."

He looked relieved. He mentioned yesterday he was concerned about all of the rap music I'd been listening to and that the child's first word would be "crunk" or something.

After more peeing in a cup and blood testing, we finally got to hear the heartbeat. It really was amazing. First of all, because my stomach is not so chunky it obscures sound altogether and second because, a heart! My child has a heart! A real one! A teeny-tiny heart, but it works! And beats fast—like it had just run a marathon.

The room became very quiet and my skin became prickly when Dr. Clarke switched on the Doppler and turned up the sound for me and Jake to hear. I looked over at Jake and his mouth was open and I smiled at him, the same squishy and warm feelings we'd experienced in the ER washing over us.

I reached out my hand and he grabbed it and kissed it, still looking amazed. In spite of myself, my eyes filled with tears that I quickly wiped away, slightly embarrassed.

I'm pretty sure that Jake was emotional, too, based on the fact he bear-hugged Dr. Clarke on our way out.

As we left, we scheduled our ultrasound for August 13, which means in about T minus five weeks we'll know if we're having a boy or girl. It's so cool but a little freaky at the same time. Although we've pretty much accepted the pregnancy, knowing the baby's gender is just one step closer to having a real-life baby in our hands. And although pregnancy is OK in my book now, a wriggly infant is still not totally comprehendable.

I don't have much time to wonder over these miracles of my life. I need to focus on Natalie's Li'l Miracle since her baby shower is this weekend and I still need to assemble about fifty infant-shaped cupcake favors.

Saturday, July 7

Recipe for the Most Torturous Event Ever, also known as Natalie's baby shower:

- 70 bored women, assorted ages
- 5 old-as-hell women enjoying themselves

• 2 mothers to be, one nine months pregnant, weighing close to two hundred pounds, and the other four months pregnant, defiantly wearing four-inch stilettos and taking lots of pictures to post on her Web site
• 1 cake in the shape of a baby
• 250 pieces of confetti shaped like baby bottles
• 2 bottles of wine
• 3 lame shower games
• Assorted presents, all baby related

Separate the bored and old-as-hell women. Place bored women at random tables to discuss the weather, the cake, and when they can leave. Set old-as-hell women aside to discuss how late Clare's thank-you notes were and how she didn't change her name when she got married, but she'd better use that monogrammed kitchen utensil holder I bought her.

Place mother-to-be in the center of the room, loudly complaining that her feet hurt and her pelvic bone is throbbing while screaming, "Get me more cake!"

Mix in infant-shaped cake slightly resembling Rosemary's Baby. Take extreme satisfaction in cutting off baby's head when handing out the cake.

Sprinkle confetti around the tables so guests can find it in their purses, hair, and shoes when they get home.

Evenly distribute all of the lame gifts after they're opened. Force everyone to pass around gifts robotically and think of something original to say such as, "Wow! This breast pump rocks!"

Watch mother-to-be open your gift, which you spent an hour trying to buy on your lunch hour so you can see her smile real fakey and pass the godforsaken, heavy-as-hell motherfucking high chair to the next person.

Garnish with a generous helping of jealousy when mother-to-be receives Coach tote bag to be used as diaper bag. Smile too widely and resist the urge to grab the bag out of her fat fingers and run out the door.

Forcefully beat the guests with the lame baby shower games until they are so bored they start to offer you money in exchange for letting them leave.

Drizzle a large quantity of pop down Clare's mouth and voilà! You have Natalie's baby shower, known in some regions as the Most Torturous Event Ever.

Monday, July 9
· · · · · · · · · · · · · · · · · · · ·

9:30 A.M.
With Natalie's baby shower behind me, I called Julie to recap the torture this afternoon as I ate lunch at my desk. I barely said hello before she cut me off and went into a diatribe.

". . . came into the office on the first day wearing a sweater with Winnie the fucking Pooh fucking *crocheted* into it with the words 'Pooh Bear' written in cursive across the chest. The next day, she wore a sweater with a cat on it and hung a poster by her desk that has a kitten on it hanging from a tree branch that says, 'Hang in there.' Can you fucking believe it?" Julie said.

Apparently the "Metrotab" nurse got fired for distributing nude pictures of herself on the Internet during work hours and Julie had a new, even weirder nurse in her unit.

"What a freak," I said, twirling my salad around and examining a crouton. I thought: *Man, this crouton is huge. It must be like a couple inches wide. Hmmm . . . that's about the same size as the baby. Weird.* I popped it into my mouth. *Crouton. Crouton Finnegan-Grandalski. The baby doesn't have a tail anymore, so I should probably think of a nickname other than the Dragon.*

"I was really nice to her at first because I thought she was mentally challenged because when you talk to her, she just stares at you and smiles, looking back and forth a lot."

Wonder if Crouton will be a she or he. Would like a girl because cute! But a boy would be fun . . .

". . . knows quite a bit about the mating habits of dragonflies . . ."

Jake would love a boy to hang out with, although the thought of a teeny-tiny penis growing inside of me slightly repulses me.

". . . husband touches his crotch a lot while pretending to adjust his Mr. Rogers sweaters . . ."

Wish Crouton would stop messing with my bladder. Have to pee again.

". . . told work yet?"

"Huh?"

"Clare, are you even listening to me?"

"Uh. Yeah. Sorry, Christina just walked into my office," I lied. Crouton is already making me a bad friend.

"I said, have you told work yet?"

"No. I can't deal with Mule Face's pity and condescending looks yet."

"You'd better tell them soon so you can plan your maternity leave." I'd forgotten about that part. Despite the inevitable never sleeping again/diaper explosions/horrible labor pain/being alone all day with a human baby I'd have no idea how to care for and who would probably be smothered by my cat, three months off sounds pretty freaking good right now.

Friday, July 13
. . . .

Since indulging in the idea of maternity leave earlier this week, I've taken great pleasure in recounting everything I'm going to miss at work while I'm gone: the annual employee retreat, Mule Face's birthday lunch, taking on an administrator role while Christina goes on her annual two-week European vacation. Although I still have to coordinate the Flynn-Shepard wedding while practically in labor, I'm trying to focus on the positive.

As I happily penciled Xs in my calendar for my twelve-week maternity leave, I heard "Hey there, stranger!"

It was Reese. She stopped by my office to kidnap me on my lunch hour to get manicures and pedicures. Her mom watched Grace so we could spend some time alone together. She's such a great friend. She told me I'm pretty much the "cutest pregnant woman" she's ever seen and my hair looks very "shiny and pretty" and I'm going to be "all baby" and won't gain any extraneous fat.

She's totally full of crap, but I don't care. Hearing I look fabulous rules. Especially since all this bloating has turned my stomach, from boobs to hips, into one giant bloblike mass. As though all of the fat got together and colonized or joined forces in the name of love handles everywhere.

She also gave me a huge spa basket full of pretty lotions, soaps, and bath salts. She said I deserve it because she knows pregnancy is hard work and people who've never been pregnant sometimes don't understand. She's right. Jake bought tickets for next weekend to an improv show starting at eleven o'clock. Never mind my new bedtime is nine o'clock. He didn't say anything but I sensed his annoyance when I told him I would be happily dreaming of a world where men get pregnant, like seahorses, by the time the show starts.

Reese also mentioned she read my blow-by-blow of Joel and Megan's party on my blog. She looked really depressed when I reiterated how much fun it was, despite my sobriety. I tried to cheer her up by reminding her of how horrible her hangovers are, but she sadly said, "It would've been worth it," and gave me a small smile.

Saturday, July 14

. . . .

This afternoon, as I slathered on lotion from the basket Reese bought me, Jake appeared at my bathroom door with some news: Nine pounds, ten ounces.

That's how much Natalie and Doug's toddler-sized newborn girl weighs. Nine freaking pounds!

At first, Jake didn't have any reaction to the clearly ginormous size of this child, until I pointed out ten pounds is roughly the size of Butterscotch.

When we spoke to Natalie to congratulate her, she informed us her doctor told her it appeared to be the most painful labor she'd ever seen anybody go through and she deserves a medal for being such a champ. Never mind she took every kind of pain medicine legally available in the United States when she delivered.

She also said they've decided to name her Ash Leigh.

As in two words.

First word "Ash." Second word "Leigh." Middle name "Sierra."

The second I heard it, all I could picture was: "And now, appearing on Naughty Girls center stage, our featured performer: Ash Leigh Sierra!"

Poor girl. It's bad enough her parents are Natalie and Doug, now she has to live with an exotic-dancer name.

Doug got on the phone and described to us in exact detail all of the "gnarly stuff" that apparently came out of Natalie's crotch during birth, as if picturing her bottomless isn't frightening enough.

I'm so happy Natalie and Doug don't read my blog. The name Ash Leigh Sierra procured quite a few snarky comments.

After Jake hung up the phone with Doug, he looked at me, eyes wide. "Can you believe my brother had a kid? That he's a dad?"

"It's even weirder that Natalie is a mom." I shuddered.

"Whoa," he said, and slowly walked into the kitchen.

I followed him. "What?"

"It's just . . . weird." He shook his head as he opened the fridge. "They're going to have to pay for diapers and clothes and college."

I knew where this was going. I walked over to him and put my hand on my hips. "Don't. Just don't. We're going to be fine."

"Yeah, but—"

"No. Fine," I said, looking up at him.

"I know." He sighed and pulled me to him.

"Good," I said. I closed my eyes and leaned against his chest and silently wondered how the hell we were going to pay for diapers and clothes and college. I started to total it but gave up. I figured no need to add extra stress right now. Thinking about tomorrow is stressful enough since I'm going to tell my work about my bun-filled oven. So, I have enough to worry about, like Mule Face asking how much weight I've gained, without estimating college tuition circa 2028.

Monday, July 16

. . . .

Genitalia countdown: T minus four weeks.

Well, I did it. I'm a fearless career woman who deals with all matters, both personal and professional, in a mature, businesslike, polished manner. When I walk into a room, dressed in a crisp suit, hair neatly pulled back, people take notice and give me the utmost respect.

Well, at least in my dreams. It was more like my hair stuck up wildly due to hair-dryer/come-to-Jesus moment with styling crème coupled with extreme frizz. My pants not pressed neatly but wrinkled accordion-style around the crotch due to my expanding ass. And so, instead of my flawless and not-at-all uncomfortable pregnancy proclamation at work today, I stammered, red-faced and sweating, until I finally got it out. As expected, Mule Face overacted, giving me a huge hug and exclaiming loudly, "I *thought* you looked bigger! You seemed really worn out lately. I had no idea you were pregnant, though—I just thought you had a drug problem! Was it planned?" She even tried to pat my stomach while shoving a Chips Ahoy cookie into her mouth.

Christina said, "But you're so young! I thought you planned on waiting several years before you guys had kids."

"Yeah, well, best-laid plans, right?"

"Yeah, but when I think back to how immature I was in my late twenties . . . Whew! I can't imagine having a baby now, let alone back then. There are so many things I would've missed if I had a baby at your age. You poor thing." She sympathetically patted me on my shoulder.

"Er, uh, thanks."

As if that wasn't bad enough, Mule Face blurted out my news to George, our postman, as he came in this afternoon to drop off our mail. He looked at me and whistled. "Shit, girl! I read somewhere that babies cost forty thousand dollars the first year. You guys got that kind of money?"

I'm sure there'll be many more months of pitying looks and whispers behind my back about how fat I am, how I'll be a bad mother, how my child will probably be born headless with cloven hooves, but at least everyone knows now. Including the woman in the Wendy's bathroom who saw me hurling into the sink and said, "Oh, honey, are you pregnant?" To which I nodded and heaved again.

Most important, I can now announce my pregnancy to the Internet.

8:30 P.M.

Why the hell did I tell the Internet I'm pregnant? I've already gotten 150 comments and close to 200 e-mails. Most of which are of the congratulatory type, but a few are in the not-so-supportive category. Like this one from jen2485:

> Clare,
> I'm sure your hapy about the baby. While i'm hapy for u, what are you going to do for babysitting? U shouldn't go bac8k to work. but U will since u r the type to pick more designer purses over time with baby.
>
> jen2485

Tuesday, July 17
. . . .

I called in "pregnant" today. I figured I have a very small window of opportunity to slack off before the Flynn-Shepard wedding. I settled in this morning to watch some quality daytime television. After *The Price Is Right*, I figured I should get myself out of the house before *Montel Williams* started (topic: "Kids Who Have Rare Genetic Disorders." Not good for pregnant woman to watch.) so I called Reese to make a lunch date since Julie was at work. She sounded weird over the phone but invited me over anyway. When I got there, she answered the door all red-faced and puffy-eyed and I could hear Grace screaming in the background.

"Are you OK?" I said, closing the door behind me.

"Yep!" she said, but her voice cracked.

"Reese, you look awful. What's wrong?"

"Nothing."

Her face crumpled and I tried to put my arms around her to hug her but she backed away.

"Everything's fine. God! You look amazing," she said, and sniffled.

"Cut the shit. What's going on?"

"Not much. Except I think Matt might be having an affair."

"Huh?"

"Nothing. Just forget I said anything." She turned on her heel and walked toward the kitchen.

I followed her, not processing what she said.

"How do you know?"

"Oh, just something I found in his briefcase," she said. Grace continued to scream in her high chair.

"How do you know?" I repeated. She disappeared into the next room. I picked up Grace and tried to quiet her.

Reese appeared back in the kitchen, holding a piece of paper. She tossed it to me with a flick of her wrist and took Grace and rocked her.

It was an e-mail from someone named Leslie sent to Matt's work address.

> The Four Seasons is perfect for lunch and more. See
> you at 1.

"This could mean anything," I said too quickly. She grabbed the paper out of my hands, giving me five pretty serious paper cuts.

"Don't worry about it. I'm sure it's nothing. I was just surprised when I saw it. It's really no big deal."

"Reese, you have to ask him about it. It could be a misunderstanding; don't freak out until you know what's going on."

"I'm not freaking out. I was just acting silly for a moment. Must be the lack of sleep. Everything is fine."

"Reese, you have to talk to him." Grace finally stopped screaming.

"I don't think so. Oh, did I tell you the news?"

"What?"

"I'm pregnant again," she said.

"What?"

"I just found out last week. We wanted to wait a while before trying again, but last month we went out for margaritas and . . ." She trailed off. She shook her head. "Anyway! Isn't that incredible?"

"Congratulations! Oh my God! How exciting! How did Matt react?"

"I haven't told him yet."

"Are you kidding?"

She shook her head and grabbed my hand. "No. I'm just waiting for the right time to tell him. He's been so stressed-out lately and I don't want to worry him. I'm sure he'll be just thrilled when I tell him."

"Reese, what is going on? You're acting like a fucking Stepford wife or something."

Her eyes flashed with anger. "I said everything is fine. Now let's have lunch and you can tell me all about how you've been feeling. Oh, and don't worry, I'll still give you my maternity clothes."

"Reese . . ."

"Clare, I'm serious. Drop it. And don't you dare mention any of this on your blog."

"Of course not, Reese."

"Good."

"But I'm not taking your clothes. You'll need them."

"Fine."

She started to turn but I grabbed her hand tightly and pressed her bony shoulders to me before she could wiggle out of my grasp. "It's going to be OK," I whispered.

Wednesday, July 18
· ·

I didn't sleep much last night, as my conversation with Reese wafted through my head every time I started to drift off. After a few hours of tossing and turning, I snuggled up against Jake. Gratitude and calm washed over me and I finally passed out sometime after four.

I put my head down at my desk this morning, exhausted. Not only was I trying to survive on a few hours of sleep, but Mule Face hasn't shut her mouth about her wedding all morning. I'm going to throw myself out the window if she doesn't stop. I want to grab her by her pudgy muffin top and shake her and scream, "SHUT UP! I need peace and quiet to stress about being pregnant, worry about Reese's marriage, and freak out about my Visa bill and the cost of formula!"

She's gabbed on the phone all day about her bridesmaid dresses, loud enough for everyone to hear, since Christina called in sick today. Her dresses are a "beautiful bright purple, almost like a magenta."

She should just go all out and get matching hats if she really wants to humiliate them. I bet the guys will even have matching purple cummerbunds and bow ties to maintain consistency. I'm sure the bridal party is going to look attractive dressed as prom dates from 1987.

"It's OK. We're going to make it. I'm so sorry you have to hear this," I whispered to the baby after I heard Mule Face scream, "PARASOLS! THEY SHOULD HAVE PURPLE PARASOLS, TOO!"

Thursday, July 19
· · · · · · · · · · · · · · · · · · · ·

Dear Crouton,
First of all, I'm very sorry I ate that pizza thing with red peppers yesterday. I had no idea you don't like red peppers. I think you also owe me an apology because it was an honest mistake and I don't think hurling for four hours straight is an appropriate punishment.

OK, so now that we've cleared that up, um, like, so how are you doing? Is it comfy and all womblike in there?

Your dad and I are going to find out in a few weeks if you are a boy or girl. Your dad is betting girl and I am betting boy, and I should tell you right now I really hate losing so if there is any way you could really, really try to make a penis, that would be great. We haven't thought of names yet, but don't worry, we'll pick something good, something that won't get you made fun of on the playground.

Hmmm . . . what else? Oh, you should know I didn't mean it when I called your father that bad word the other day. He just ate all of the cookies from Wild Oats you and I like so much. Please don't ever use that bad word.

I know I'm probably not going to be the best mom in the world, but I'm sure as hell (don't use that word, either) going to do my best. We didn't expect to get you so soon, so I'm sorry if we mess up, but we're quick learners, I promise. Your dad and I love you very much and wish you would hurry up and grow so we can see your face. Speaking of which, the first time you see me I might not look very good, but don't be scared. I look great with a good makeup job and a blowout.

Well, anyway, I just wanted to say what's up and ask you what's the dealio. (Do you know what that word means? If you do, please stop listening to the music I play. Your father will have a heart attack.)

Love,
Your mom

P.S. I'm sorry I drank all those cranapple martinis before I found out I was pregnant with you. I hope you didn't get drunk.

Friday, July 20

· · · · · · · · · · · · · · · · · · · ·

Despite Mule Face's broadcast of her wedding plans, I managed to focus yesterday and pull together an event dossier for the Flynn-Shepard wedding, since today I met with Jessica Greene's sister, Rachael Flynn; their mother, Irene; and Rachael's fiancé, Ben Shepard. My face hurts from smiling so much. They want a typical black-tie blowout wedding in the city—reception at the Ritz, mile-high centerpieces with individual lighting design, custom-made chair covers, the works. Irene and Rachael did most of the talking while Ben stood outside the conference room on his cell phone with a business call. The meeting would've been very easy, but Irene Flynn has a penchant for long, inappropriate pauses during sentences; the kind lasting just a second too long, just long enough to make me hurriedly talk just to cut the silence.

Me: "Where is the location of the rehearsal dinner?"

Rachael: "We were thinking Morton's. Right, Mom?"

Irene: "Well, I . . ." (Long inappropriate pause as they both stare at me.)

Me: "So, Mortonswouldbereally—"

Irene (at the same time): "Yes, Morton's."

I felt like an idiot with zero communication skills.

The good news is they have a pretty clear idea of what they want and already picked their vendors so all I need to do is be the point person and tie up all the loose ends. Oh, and attend the wedding. One week before my due date. They made it very clear that they expect *me* to be the one to attend, no matter if nine months pregnant, baby hanging out of the birth canal, or wheeled in while still in a hospital bed. I'm expected to sport a walkie-talkie, gush over and provide encouraging words to the bride, keep the groomsmen away from the bar before the ceremony, bend over and take every insult slung at me from Mrs. Flynn and Mrs. Shepard, yell at the band if they play the wrong song, beg the florist to make last-minute changes, and possibly give birth quietly in the bathroom in between courses: "It's a girl! Oh, shit—the floral toss bouquet is the wrong color!"

When they informed me the wedding is on New Year's Eve, I calmly told them about my pregnancy and that my due date is the first week in January.

Irene looked suspiciously at me. "Oh, you're pregnant?"

"Yes."

"Oh, well are you . . ."

"Um, well, I—," I started to say.

"Even married?" she finished.

"Yes, I'm married."

"Well, at least you're married," she said.

She continued to stare at me and I suddenly realized she thought I was some knocked-up teenager who got married in a shotgun wedding.

"I'm twenty-seven," I finally said.

Irene and Rachael looked relieved. Irene said, "Well, then! I am so . . ." Long inappropriate pause. Happy? Nervous? Flatulent?

"Wellyeahitwillbeokand—," I started to say.

"Grateful you are due after the wedding and won't miss a thing," Irene said at the same time.

"Oh. Um. Yes. Although, sometimes babies come early, so we'll see," I choked out when I was pretty sure she was done and not just pausing.

Long stare from Irene.

"You will be the one present, won't you?" she finally said. "I can't imagine working with an event planner who won't be there the evening of the actual event."

I noticed Mule Face slowly inching toward the door, no doubt praying I'd give birth spontaneously at that moment so she could work on the account and get all the credit.

"Of course," I sighed, picturing Jake wheeling me into the Ritz-Carlton, still in my hospital bed and nursing baby attached to my boob.

Upon hearing I'd be coordinating the event, still-pregnant or not, Mule Face looked quite disappointed and went into the break room to heat up her lunch: a cheddar and onion bagel. Soon, the entire office became filled with the stench of cheesy BO. Believe me, Crouton and I were gagging, but the look of disgust on Irene's face made it all kind of worth it. Also knowing she'd walk around all day smelling like body odor and rotten cheese at the country club made me smile. Mule Face brought the bagel with her when she came in to introduce herself. Watching Irene and Rachael try to be civil while holding their breath almost made me love Mule Face. She certainly has impeccable timing.

Approximately ten minutes after Irene and Rachael left, Jessica called me to congratulate me on the news.

"How nice it is that you and your friend are pregnant at the same time!" she said.

I didn't have the heart, energy, or patience to correct her, so I simply said, "Yep! I hope my boobs get as big as hers!"

Saturday, July 21
. . . .

Today started out great. I sat on the couch for most of the morning, snuggled underneath my new cashmere throw, watching DVR'd episodes of *CSI*. After three straight hours, just as I determined "petechial hemorrhaging" is said in every episode and almost any crime can be solved with a black light and glow-in-the-dark spray, my cell phone rang.

It was Reese.

I contemplated not answering it, not wanting to disrupt honing my forensic skills, but I felt a pang of guilt and snapped my phone open.

"Hi, girlie," I said.

"Oh my God, Clare. You have to help me." Reese sounded frantic and I could hear kids screaming in the background.

"Tyler! Put that down. Your mommy would be very mad if I told her you broke the pretty vase."

"What's going on?" I asked.

"Matt just called and he got into a car accident. He's OK but the car is probably totaled."

"Oh my God—what can I do?"

"I have to go pick him up and I can take the baby but Meredith's supposed to come pick Tyler up in an hour. I can't leave him here by himself and I can't take him with me, so . . ." She trailed off, waiting for my response.

The last thing I wanted to do was babysit a toddler who needs to be on Ritalin, but I knew Reese needed me.

"Don't worry. Jake and I will come over and watch Tyler until his mom comes."

"Thank you! I owe you big time! Lunch on me!"

I basically threatened Jake's life (since the threat of divorce had little or no impact) to get him to agree to come with me. He was deeply engrossed in looking up videos on YouTube and not exactly thrilled to drop everything to go play Romper Room.

Reese threw about a million thank-yous over her shoulder when we got to her house. She grabbed Grace and pointed to a small boy and said, "That's Tyler."

I warily looked at him. His hair stuck straight up and he clutched a dripping Popsicle.

"Hey, Tyler! Why don't you let me clean that stuff off ya?" I said in a high-pitched, extremely unnatural-sounding voice.

He froze. He looked at me, then at Jake, and finally back at me. Figuring his silence meant acceptance, I took a step toward him. Big mistake.

"NO! NO! NO! NO! NO!" Mr. Hyde suddenly came out and he ran out of the kitchen.

Jake looked at me, his face clearly saying, *I gave up the Internet for this?*

I sighed and followed Tyler into the living room. He rolled around on the couch, the Popsicle placed on one of the pristine white cushions, melting icky red liquid into the material. "Hey, Tyler! Why don't we see if there are any cartoons on the TV?"

He gave me a blank look again. I racked my brain.

"Barney? Do you like Barney?" He looked at me with an open mouth and slowly nodded his head. The kid actually went for it. Now I needed to produce something.

I tore open Reese's media cabinet, desperately searching for anything I could pass off as Barney to the kid, while Jake worked on cleaning up the puddle on the couch.

Ten seconds later, Tyler started screaming.

"BARNEY! I want BARNEY!" He started howling and crying.

Jake gave me a look and tried to pick Tyler up to calm him down but he escaped and ran back into the kitchen.

"Whose kid is this again and why are we here?"

I gave up on finding Barney and turned to face him.

"Because Reese is my friend and I'm trying to—" I stopped. "What was that noise?"

"What noise?"

"It sounded like a toilet flushing."

We both ran into the bathroom and found Tyler, smiling and clapping, pointing to the toilet. *Oh, please, God, don't let it be anything important,* I prayed.

Jake peered into the toilet and started laughing.

"Hope you don't need to make any phone calls," he said.

"Wha?" I looked into the toilet and saw my new pink Razr swirling around in the bowl.

"TYLER! That's bad! That's not a toy!" I yelled, flustered, as I shamelessly stuck my hand in the toilet and pulled out my now worthless phone.

Tyler started crying again and began turning purple. Jake scooped him up and tried to calm him down.

"It's OK, buddy. Let's get away from the mean lady. She's mean, isn't she?" Still hysterical, Tyler nodded his head while Jake carried him away and left me with my dripping wet phone.

Half an hour later, the little monster fell asleep on the floor, surrounded by every toy we could find. After a major temper tantrum, four Popsicles, and eight million farmyard animal toys, he had officially passed out. Jake and I took the opportunity to tiptoe into the kitchen to raid the fridge for anything worthwhile.

Jake was halfway through an Amstel Light and I a bottle of Pellegrino when the lights dimmed.

"What the fuck?" Jake asked.

Then we heard a blood-freezing scream. We stared at each other for a split second before jumping up. We raced to the source of the shriek and found Tyler, awake, sitting on the floor next to a blackened electrical socket, looking stunned.

We stood there for a moment, everything frozen in slow motion.

I picked Tyler up and examined him. He seemed to have all of his fingers and toes and wasn't bleeding from any orifice. He immediately started giggling.

"Look!" Jake pointed to the floor, looking stunned, a plastic baby-proofing plug on the floor, next to a blackened penny. "I think he stuck it in the wall."

"OH MY GOD! He could've DIED. WE ALMOST KILLED HIM." I hugged Tyler to me, which only made him laugh even harder. I thought, *Oh, great, have given the kid brain damage.*

"He seems OK, I don't think he's hurt or anything."

"How can he not be hurt? WE ALMOST KILLED HIM!" Tyler stopped laughing and stared at me, transfixed, his mouth open.

"Did you stick the penny in the socket?" I asked him.

He stared at me blankly, probably thinking, *What the hell is a socket?* I grabbed his hand and examined it for any signs of damage.

"NO! NO! NO! NO! NO!" He leaped out of my arms and ran over to the eight million farm animals and started throwing them at the television.

"Tyler! Don't do—," Jake started to say.

"Jake, let him do whatever he wants. We almost *killed* him! I don't care if Reese's TV gets shattered."

Tyler's mother, Meredith, finally came to pick him up an hour later. We didn't tell her about the electrocution episode. I figure Reese can tell her. She did ask why Tyler was clutching my ruined pink phone. I explained what happened and the bitch didn't even offer to pay for it. She just said, "Well, that's what you get for leaving stuff within reach of a toddler!"

As he was leaving, Tyler gave me and Jake an angelic little smile and waved good-bye. I've never been so happy to see a kid leave before, other than my friend in second grade who came over and ate all of my Twinkies, but that's beside the point.

We left a note for Reese explaining why her couch is now tie-dyed red and one of her walls has singe marks coming from the socket. It read something like this:

> Reese,
> Hope Matt is OK. Tyler's mom picked him up at 4:30. He ate a red Popsicle on your couch and stuck a penny in the socket by the phone. He is fine, though.
>
> > Sorry,
> > Jake and Clare
>
> P.S. He threw my phone in your toilet.
> P.P.S. Do you know anyone who is looking to adopt a newborn in five months or so?

Monday, July 23

· · · · · · · · · · · · · · · · · · · ·

Genitalia countdown: T minus three weeks.

After our disastrous afternoon with Tyler, Jake and I slightly doubt our ability to be good parents. Granted, that kid is a toddler and somewhat of a brat, but the image of the blackened socket coupled with the real possibility he could've gotten seriously hurt is freaking me out.

I didn't have much time today to worry about all the horrible ways we could accidentally injure or kill our own child, because something very important is on my radar: I'm in maternity clothes now. Yes, scary stretchy-panel, tentlike maternity clothes. Up until now I've gotten away with wearing regular clothes in bigger sizes. I looked pretty good and even Julie told me two weeks ago I am still a fashionable knocked-up lady, which I took with the utmost pride. Now I've been banished from the land of cool clothes into Maternity Land, much the same way I was sent away from the cool kids' cafeteria table in seventh grade when I got the Bad Spiral Perm We Don't Speak Of. (I blame my mother—she should've known my naturally wavy hair + spiral perm = death to coolness. I mean, I was in seventh grade and didn't know any better. She was my mom and supposed to protect me from the boogeyman, pedophiles, and spiral perms. I swear, Crouton, I will never let you exercise poor hair judgment. I'm pretty sure when those spiral rods touched my hair, the gods ripped a black hole in the universe and destroyed part of the ozone layer as punishment.)

I now wear clothes that "show off the new cleavage" and "draw attention away from the stomach area with embellishment" like a huge-ass bow, or jackets that appear to have been molested by a Bedazzler, neither of which are appropriate for work.

Don't pregnant women work anymore? I have been completely unable to find a black suit that is (a) not polyester or made out of another highly flammable, nuclear-winter-survivable material, or (b) not ridiculously expensive for something I'll wear for five months. So, I have about four outfits as a result.

My dreams of being a stylish, well-dressed, classy pregnant lady have been flushed down the proverbial toilet. Along with my dignity, when I bought maternity underwear.

I complained to Jake we need more friends with kids and thus women willing to lend me maternity clothes and he reminded me Wifey1025 offered to send me all of her maternity clothes from when she was pregnant in 1995 if I would please, please just meet her in the parking lot of Bob Evans around midnight.

Tuesday, July 24

· · · · · · · · · · · · · · · · · ·

9:00 A.M.

It's a good thing I bought maternity clothes yesterday, since it's my birthday today and the only presents I've gotten so far are a stomach that, overnight, looks like I ate the Pillsbury Doughboy and an obnoxious call from Marianne.

My phone rang shrilly and I gave it a wary glance, debating whether or not I should pick it up. Usually, I let most calls go to voicemail this early but today is my birthday, so I answered it.

"Clare Finnegan."

"Hel-*lo*, darling. Happy birthday!"

Marianne.

"Oh, hi, Marianne. How are you?"

"It's *Mom*, honey! And I'm just fine. I wanted to wish you a happy birthday, dear."

"Oh, thanks, um, thanks!" Long pause. "Well, how's everything going?" I finally asked, desperate to end the silence.

"Oh, you know Dad and I, always so busy, busy, busy. We've been spending so much time with Ash Leigh and helping out Natalie. You know, grandparent stuff! Stuff we just can't wait to do with your little one. Speaking of which, are you taking birthing classes?"

"Birthing classes? I don't think so, why? I'm planning on having lots of drugs at the birth."

"You're not going to have a natural birth?"

"Well, any birth is kind of natural, isn't it? I just plan on having the assistance of all the drugs the good Lord gave us."

"You really should take a birthing class and reconsider. When I had Jake, Frank told me again and again how much he admired my strength. Wouldn't you rather Jake admired you instead of your epidural?"

I paused, not knowing how to answer. I simply said, "Not really," as I eyed a Snickers bar on my desk.

She clucked her tongue. "Well, consider it. Don't worry, should you choose to have a natural birth, I am planning on being there for you every step of the way. I will be your personal doula."

"Doula?"

"Yes, doula. A doula is a person the birthing mother hires to comfort and support her during delivery."

Screw. That.

"Um, I have to go." I started to unwrap the candy bar.

"You should get my birthday gift in the mail in the next couple of days. I can't wait for you to see it."

Every gift-giving occasion, Marianne gives us something for our apartment. The problem is she has quite possibly the worst taste in the entire world. This is a woman who decorated her living room in a jungle theme one year, complete with furry rug, zebra-print pillows, and weird palm plants her cats kept eating, which made them barf on said furry rug. Last year, she bought me a huge giant crucifix statue of Jesus, complete with blood dripping from the hands and feet. Since neither of us are particularly religious, it is buried in a drawer under the ugly plaid serving dish she gave us as a wedding gift. She also likes to give gifts she knows we already have, and then repeatedly ask why *her* throw pillows or knife block or shower curtain or whatever isn't out when she comes to visit.

Basically, I'm not too jazzed to see what she got me.

6:00 P.M.

Jake and I are on our way to dinner with my parents, Mark, and Sam. It's the only time during the year I can enjoy a fifty-dollar steak without having to fork over my own credit card and eat Hamburger Helper for two weeks just to pay for it.

Not surprisingly, Sam freaked when she heard I picked a steak place, because she's trying Madonna's macrobiotic diet she read about in *US Weekly*. And filet mignon is "so *not* in the diet" and she is "*never* going to lose two pounds" if we keep sabotaging her.

8:00 P.M.

"So how's work been going, Clare?" My mom looked at me, truly interested, but I knew my time was very, very short to answer, like on *Jeopardy*.

"Well, I'm working on a wedding right now and it's been going pretty well. I'm basically just the point person for everything and," I paused to take a breath, "the wedding is going to be held at—"

"Why do we always have to go to places *she* wants to go?" Yup, that was it. My five seconds were up.

"Because it's her birthday, Sam. You get to pick when it's your day." My father cut her off with a disapproving look. A lot of good it did.

"This place is gross. I mean, who wants to eat nasty cow meat practically bleeding on your plate? Ew. Make me puke. Why don't you just take me to a slaughterhouse?"

"Actually they didn't have any reservations. Sorry. Yum, I can't wait for my bleeding rare filet," Mark said.

"You guys are so retarded," she retorted.

"Sam," my mother warned.

"What? Oh, jeez, *sorry*. You guys are so stupid, is that better?"

"Yes, now shut up. I'm trying to talk to your sister." My mother still has hope we can go out to dinner together civilly even though I've tried to tell her Sam won't be normal until she has a lobotomy.

"Jake, how's your family doing?" My mom turned to my husband in an attempt to turn him into a performer rather than a spectator.

"Everybody's doing well. Parents are good, spending a lot of time with Ash Leigh."

"How's Natalie doing?" my mom asked, keeping one eye on Sam furiously texting on her phone.

"Great." She shot me a look and I met her eye, silently saying *she's as psycho as ever and I'll tell you later when he's not around and I can speak freely.* "Mmmmm," is all she said to Jake.

"Has Marianne read your blog yet?" Mark asked.

"What do you think?"

"Did you know ceramic ionic straighteners are, like, from heaven?" Sam asked.

We all looked at her silently for a moment, and thankfully the steaks came. Sam made a gagging noise as we all cut into our food, which prompted Mark to wave a piece of meat in her face until she created such a scene most of the restaurant wound up staring at us.

"Clare, Jake, we've been meaning to ask you guys, are you free the last week of August?"

I mentally paged through my calendar. "I think so, why?"

"Well, your father has a medical conference in Hawaii that week and we were hoping you two could housesit." What an incredibly loaded opportunity. Housesitting for my parents usually means one thing—supervising whatever party Sam decides to throw.

"Sure, we'd love to," Jake answered, grinning from ear to ear. He loves supervising high school parties since all of Sam's friends treat him like he's a god or something. All of the girls think he's "totally tight" and the guys think he's "the shit." Probably because he's socializing with them while I'm flipping out and running around picking up beer cans and kicking out people who are too wasted.

I noticed Sam's ears prick up like a dog's and she furiously began texting again, undoubtedly sending out hundreds of invitations as I cut into my strip steak.

"Great! We'll pay you guys as usual, since it's such a big favor." The money was really my only motivation for putting up with Sam for a week. There's a lot of things I'll do for five hundred dollars.

"How come you guys never ask me?" Mark said.

"Because I wouldn't dream of asking you to halt your postcollege party tour for a weekend," my mom said.

"Thanks, Mom. You rule."

"This is true," she said.

Now that Sam knew she had another party on the horizon, her mood perked up significantly for the rest of the meal. She still didn't really eat anything, but she managed to forcibly choke down some of her salad. She even managed to smile, which made me worry she's planning a true kegger.

1:00 A.M.
My phone beeped a few minutes ago. It was Julie wishing me a happy birthday. She was at Sauce's weekly half-off margarita party. She went on and on for fifteen minutes about how much she loves me and how much she loves Pedro, the bartender. Pedro even came on the phone to wish me a happy birthday, too. Except he kept calling me "Clear."

I missed the phone call because Jake and I were finally having sex. Finally. I was starting to worry my girl parts had vanished or atrophied and I'd become like a Barbie doll down there, which would make childbirth somewhat difficult.

Friday, July 27
· · · · · · · · · · · · · · · · · · · ·

"So, how was the birthday dinner?" Julie asked me today over the phone.

"Fine. Sam was her usual charming self. Jake and I had good birthday sex."

"Finally! Thank God. I was worried you'd become celibate."

"You're not kidding. So, what's going on?"

"Not much. Except I'm a drunken whore." She sniffed into the phone. "I made out with a married man last night."

"Julie, you didn't!" I said, and put my head in my hands.

"I did. I didn't mean to. I only meant to go out for a casual happy hour drink with my coworkers and then go dancing. Instead, I ended up doing tequila shots with Roger the Male Nurse/Married Man and tonguing him outside the women's restroom. I think everyone saw it so now they probably think I'm a giant dirty whore. I *am* a whore." She sniffled.

"No, you're not! Don't say that about yourself. It's not your fault at all—he's the one who's married. It's his responsibility to keep it in his pants," I whispered, fully aware of Mule Face loitering around outside my office, pretending to look for a floral order.

"Then, this morning when I came in, Roger gave me this creepy smile and asked when the next happy hour party is."

"Julie, listen. This guy's a slimeball. You shouldn't feel guilty at all. It's so *not* your fault. Don't let that prick make you feel uncomfortable. Just ask him how his wife is, that should shut him up. Oh! I know! If he doesn't lay off, tell him I'll do an entry on him, complete with pictures," I hissed into the phone.

Mule Face stopped pretending to look for files and leaned against the doorjamb of my office, shoveling microwave popcorn into her mouth. I gave her an evil look, which she misread as an invitation to sit down in my office.

"I feel like such a dumbass though. I mean, who does something like that? What kind of person makes out with a married guy?"

"I think the better question is what kind of guy cheats on his wife with a coworker during a happy hour party?"

I heard a lot of rustling and she said, "Clare, I have to go. I need to check on a patient. I'll call you later." I hung up the phone and Mule Face looked at me with an encouraging smile.

"So, what's going on? Who was that?"

"My friend." I started to straighten papers on my desk and hoped she would go away.

"Was that Julie? She's my favorite character on your blog."

I didn't have the strength to explain to her once again that the people I mention on my blog aren't "characters," but real people, so I just said, "Mmmmmm."

She didn't get the hint. She leaned forward conspiratorially and whispered, "Well, your friend isn't the only one to have had an affair with a married man. This one guy I dated a few years ago was married and used to offer to leave his wife for me but I didn't want to be tied down so I just told him to stay married. Just another episode in the life of a single gal!"

"Um, sure. It wasn't Julie though." Time to change the subject. "How's the Castle sweet sixteen party coming along?"

She licked butter off her chubby fingers. "Wonderful. Easy. Isn't it weird how my events are always so straightforward and yours always have so many problems?"

"Yeah. And isn't it weird how my events always get the best feedback from the clients?"

I desperately wanted her to react but she just smiled, popcorn stuck between her teeth, and shrugged. When she left my office, I saw a piece of toilet paper stuck to her shoe and I silently thanked Jesus for the small token.

Sunday, July 29
· · · · · · · · · · · · · · · · · · · ·

Julie's still depressed over making out with the disgusting married man. I've told her many times over that it's not her fault, but she's still upset. So, that makes two now. My two best friends are now officially depressed with their lives, for very different reasons.

Aren't I the one who's supposed to be emotional and depressed and hormonal? Instead, I'm trying to help them put fires out all over the place.

Since Reese and Julie have their own problems to worry about, I don't want to burden them with the latest "crisis" in my life: a complete inability to name my child.

After much introspection, I've discovered the reason for this: I watched an excessive amount of television as a child. And not the good, educational stuff like *Sesame Street* or *Reading Rainbow*, either. I'm talking every bad sitcom aired in the mideighties. I not only watched them, but absorbed and crammed into my brain every bit of information relayed to me. I mean, there are days when I can't remember my debit card PIN number, but I sure as hell can recite the theme songs from *Full House* and *Perfect Strangers*.

Besides taking up valuable space in my brain, these '80s television shows also crippled me in a much more serious fashion: they're the reason I can't find a suitable name for Crouton. Any name Jake or I think of evokes images of one of the characters from some horribly acted, laugh-track-filled sitcom aired between 1981 and 1990. An example: Jake came home last week and suggested the name Kevin. A perfectly benign, normal name, right? Negative. Kevin was the name of the tall, geeky son with the freakishly large Adam's apple on *Mr. Belvedere*, a show about a refined English male housekeeper and the wacky antics of the American family who employed him.

Next Jake suggested Nicole for a girl. Not bad, right? Wrong. I only think of the show *My Two Dads* when I hear the name Nicole. Nicole was the name of the main character, a teenage girl whose mom died before she found out if Joey, the wacky musician, or Michael, the straight-laced accountant, was her real dad. So, apparently they all decided to live together and both guys raised her. How's that for fucked up? I mean, her mom was a ho who didn't know who her baby daddy was and never bothered to go on *Maury Povich* for a DNA test?

Then I thought of the name Jamie. Another good one? Not exactly. Jamie was the name of the obnoxious brother on *Small Wonder*, quite possibly the worst show ever created (and thus also the greatest). If memory serves, *Small Wonder* was about a family who created a robot girl and raised her as their daughter. She was so lifelike, no one knew she was really a robot! Which would've been believable except for the tiny fact that she talked in a robotic voice: "HEL-LO. MY NAME IS VICKI. I LIVE IN A NUCLEAR HOUSEHOLD. I ENJOY DOING DOMESTIC CHORES AND HELPING MY PARENTAL UNITS MAXIMIZE THEIR LEISURE TIME." Amazing no one figured out the secret!

The irony is I was allowed to watch everything except for one show—*Three's Company.* My mother thought it was "sexist." I have no idea why. All I know is I wasn't allowed to watch it and so it became the only thing I wanted to watch. While other kids were trying to sneak to watch R-rated movies, I tried to sneak a peek at the antics of Jack Tripper.

So, when she thought another show I liked was sexist (*Just the Ten of Us*—apparently the daughters were "not good role models" and "objectified women as sex objects"), I went to my friend Adrianna's house. Her mother wasn't a feminist so we could watch whatever we wanted.

I asked my readers for some suggestions and jen2485 suggested we name him "Shithead" since his parents are clearly idiots and he will be, too. While I don't disagree Jake and I are idiots, I'm thinking of asking Wifey1025 to cut her up into little pieces first before trying to kill me.

Monday, July 30

Genitalia countdown: T minus two weeks. Still no name.

My birthday gift from Marianne came in the mail today. She bought me maternity lingerie and some stretch mark cream.

Her gift-giving streak continues.

Wednesday, August 1

Mule Face spent this morning picking out song selections for her reception. She pulled out a packet of paper five inches thick and asked us to pass it around and make notes next to the songs we would like to hear. The rest of the staff took it as an opportunity to reciprocate torture and requested songs like the "Chicken Dance" and "Macarena," but I just wasn't feeling it.

After the third e-mail asking for suggestions for her and D's first dance, I locked my computer, grabbed my purse, and walked outside. Thankfully, the blistering heat had broken for one day and it was actually tolerable outside. The sun was shining and a nice, cool breeze rustled through the trees. So, I decided to do something I'd always thought about doing, but never did. I grabbed a slice of pizza and a drink from the Italian restaurant on the corner, found a nice comfy patch of grass under an oak tree in the park across from my office, and had lunch.

Eating under a tree is so *not* me. With my obvious distaste for camping, picnicking under a tree always sounded nice, but visions of ants and mosquitoes and wildlife attacking me and stealing my lunch always deterred me.

It was actually quite nice. I leaned against the cool bark of the tree and closed my eyes.

"So, what's up? How's it going in there?" I said to my stomach. "I can't feel you yet, but I bet you're moving around in there, trying to send me a Morse code signal with your taps. We'll figure it out at some point. So, what's new?" I knew I looked completely ridiculous, shoveling pizza into my mouth and talking to myself, but no one was around. "Are you comfortable? I hope so. Because I'm sure as hell—I mean—heck—oh, whatever—I'm sure as hell not. Are you a boy or a girl?"

Nothing.

"I said, are you a boy or a girl? C'mon, you can tell me. I want to win the bet. I'd also like to narrow down the name choices, since, yeah, I think you've heard that conversation."

Still nothing.

"OK, fine. Be that way. You could at least give me some insider info, you know. I'm the one who's growing you, not your dad, so I'm the one who should be privy to these things first, don't you think?"

I think he fell asleep. I probably bored my own kid to death. I'm going to remember this trick when it's four in the morning and he wants to party all night long.

Saturday, August 4

Crouton's still not giving up the goods. I've tried to psychically receive messages about the gender from him/her, but nothing. I concentrated really hard tonight, but the only message I got was to go eat pizza. This kid is definitely coming out with pepperoni all over it.

After we had some pizza, Jake and I decided to treat ourselves and go out to see a movie tonight. Not just any movie, but a gory, disgusting horror movie. Jake first offered to go see the latest romantic comedy/chick flick starring an impossibly gorgeous and sweet leading man, but after weeks of being on the hormonal pregnancy crazy train, a romantic movie was out. I mean, I cried during *Never Been Kissed* last week, for chrissakes. (I couldn't believe Michael Vartan's character got stuck in traffic while on the way to meet Drew Barrymore's character in the end. I mean, what would've happened if there was an oil spill or something? He would've *never* gotten there in time and she would've walked away, rejected and depressed, and would've gotten drunk or high and slept with some random guy. I mean, *come on*.)

Anyway, I opted to see the most nightmare-inducing movie out right now. Plus, I figured there wouldn't be any obnoxious brats in a movie dubbed "the biggest scare you'll get all year." Man, was I fucking wrong. There were *three* kids in the theater, one of whom was under ten. All of these children were with their parents/guardians. I was shocked when I sat down and felt someone kick the back of my chair. I turned around, ready to let loose some expletives, and saw the sweet face of a little girl. In an R-rated gore fest at 9:30 P.M. on a Friday night. At one particularly bloody part involving a character getting his head ripped off with a chainsaw, the little girl screamed and her mother said, "Close your eyes, Charlene. Remember what I said—it ain't real." Not only were these kids probably traumatized for life, they spent the movie talking loudly, asking questions like "WHO IS THAT?" "CAN I HAVE MORE POPCORN?" "WHY IS THAT GUY CRYING?" "WHY ARE YOU SUCH HORRIBLE PARENTS YOU TOOK ME TO AN R-RATED HORROR MOVIE STARTING WAY AFTER MY AGE-APPROPRIATE BEDTIME?" (OK, the last one was mine.)

"But you brought your child," Julie pointed out later.

"Yes, but my child is the size of an onion and hasn't developed vocal cords yet, so it is too small and too mute to annoy anyone," I snapped back at her.

But seriously, these people thought this movie was appropriate for their kids? Those people must have "Parent Brain," a condition when someone has a child and loses all touch with reality. Parent Brain mainly shows up in places like shopping malls. Its symptoms include ramming one's stroller in a weaponlike fashion into innocent bystanders, strolling casually along with one's child while blocking everyone from passing, and ignoring one's child in public while talking to other adults, thus allowing said child to destroy everything within reach (sometimes followed by amused laughter rather than the appropriate horror/shock/embarrassment).

I must see if there is medication to prevent this.

Monday, August 6

. . . .

Genitalia countdown: T minus one week.

My mom agreed with my assessment of Parent Brain at the movies last night, and then surprised me by offering to take me shopping this afternoon for maternity clothes. I'd complained to her last week about my inability to find stylish maternity clothes that don't cost eight thousand dollars each and she offered to take me shopping and treat me to some clothes.

I met her at the mall around noon and found her talking on a business call in front of Expecting Style.

"That sounds good. Send over the proposal first thing." She looked at me and mouthed "Sorry." "Listen, John, I really have to go. I'm about to get on another call. I'll look for that e-mail." She snapped her phone shut and turned to me. "Ready?"

"Yep!"

We walked into the store and a pair of beautiful black wool pants immediately caught my eye.

"Aren't these gorgeous?" I said.

"They're beautiful. You'll need them for work," my mom said, as her phone rang again. She picked it up and checked the number. "Just let me take this for a minute."

I wandered over to the jean section and held up a pair of hip-huggers in a faded wash.

My mom reappeared. "Sorry about that. We have this huge presentation next week that everyone is freaking out about."

"No problem."

"How's everything been?" she asked as we walked over to a sweater display.

"Fine. Boring. Being pregnant is like watching paint dry."

"Be thankful for that. I was on bed rest for three months before I had you."

"Yeah, I know."

"How's Jake been handling all of this?"

"He's been great. He's pretty excited about everything. Well, everything except for the fact he changes the kitty litter himself now."

"Ah, yes. See? There are some pluses."

"Few and far between."

"Well, your father and I are just so excited for you guys."

"I know. It would be nice if Sam shared the sentiment."

"She does. She just doesn't know how to show it."

"Right."

"No, really. She is excited. She's just so focused on herself right now. It's the high school years. She'll grow out of it." She patted me on my back. "Just like you did."

"I was never as bratty as she is."

My mom silently looked at me.

"Please. I was never as obnoxious as her."

More staring.

"I think you're finally going senile, because she's so much worse."

"Honey, it's a miracle your father and I didn't sell you into white slavery when you were in high school."

"Watch it. I'm going to remember those comments when you're

old and decrepit and Jake and I have to choose between the state-run nursing home or the nice one without bars on the windows."

"Very funny. What do you think of this?" She held up a gorgeous pink cashmere cardigan.

"Gorgeous. But oh-so-expensive."

"Well, I'm treating."

"Mom, you don't have to—"

"Look, you should just say 'Thank you' and 'You're the greatest Mom ever' and accept the clothes."

"That's true. You might not have anything left after a few more years of supporting Sam. Thank you. You're the best mom ever."

Tuesday, August 7
· · · · · · · · · · · · · · · · · · · ·

As I twirled in front of the mirror this morning, admiring my new fabulous cream-colored maternity pants and blue seersucker top, I called to Jake, "Don't forget, we have dinner with Gwen and Alex tonight at eight."

He paused, razor held in midair, then sighed deeply and made fake sobbing sounds.

"I don't want to hear it. I sat through four hours of tailgating with Bill-I-Still-Live-at-Home-with-My-Parents-and-Smoke-Pot-Every-Day-at-4:20. You can deal with a few hours of dinner."

He rolled his head back and stared at the ceiling, as though he was a man on Death Row, left to contemplate his future during his last few hours.

Truth is, I'm not looking forward to dinner tonight, either. After graduation, Gwen and Alex suddenly aged approximately fifty-two years each, stopped drinking, and became way into book clubs, gardening, antiquing, and going to bed by ten o'clock. Which is completely strange, since they were two of the biggest drunks we knew in college. In fact, they met at a frat party and had bad drunken sex the same night. Slowly after college they started staying in more and more and going to bed earlier and earlier. Whenever we would all go out to a bar together, they would have approximately a quarter of their drinks, yawn, and leave. After a few frustrating experiences, we now just do things like dinner. I think they'll be the perfect dinner companions, seeing as how I'm not going to be dancing on tables anytime soon.

10:08 P.M.

Once again, I was very, very wrong in my assumption that dinner would be fun and relaxing. The words "horrific," "torturous," and "disaster of biblical proportions" are more accurate.

"Do we have to go? Seriously, can we just say we're sick or something? My grandmother's dead? We couldn't get a babysitter for Butterscotch? That it's my back-waxing night? That my balls are—," Jake whined as we drove to dinner.

"You're going," I cut him off. "Deal with it. These are our friends."

"They're not my friends! It's like having dinner with my parents— no, my *grand*parents, if they were a hundred and eighty-seven years old! Do you know that the last time we all got together, Alex told me he doesn't watch football anymore? Because he doesn't like to spend any time on Sundays lying around? What kind of a freak doesn't even watch football? And Gwen! She spent the last dinner we had with them talking about what flowers are in season in her garden and how to make marzipan cake decorations. Is any of this ringing a bell?"

"I put up with lots of crap from your friends. Like the time that you and Jonathan drank Jaegermeister and Red Bull all night and came home and puked up chicken wings all over the couch."

He remained silent.

I stared at him and he finally relented and grabbed my hand. "All right, fine. But La Dolce better have GALLONS of vodka ready."

"Don't be so dramatic. It's going to be fun," I said.

We were twenty minutes late due to an accident on the expressway and when we finally got to the restaurant, we were both humming with anger, shaking, and nearly drawing up divorce papers. Of course, Alex and Gwen were already there with half-finished glasses of wine in front of them. As we made our way over to the table, Gwen very pointedly looked at her watch and then smiled at me, shaking her head and waving her finger.

"Hey! Sorry we're late!" I said.

Gwen jumped up from her chair. "We were starting to get worried! We thought you might've gone into labor or something. Ha, ha!"

"Um, no," I stuttered out as she looked me up and down.

"How far along are you?" she asked.

I tried to answer but she cut me off. "Oh, no, wait, let me guess! Six months?"

"*Four* months."

She and Alex chuckled and he whispered a "Whoops" under his breath.

"Oh, well. You're either going to need a lot of stitches or a C-section because that kid is going to be *big*."

I signaled to the waiter and pointed to whatever wine was first on the list. I could feel everyone staring at me. I met their eyes and challenged them to say anything.

"Do you think you should?" Alex said.

"End up getting that car you were looking at a while back?" Jake asked, trying to change the subject.

The waiter brought over my wine and I took a big long sip. *Oh, how I've missed this*, I thought as the beautiful, smooth, velvety liquid went down my throat. *Love wine and Crouton does, too.*

"So, how's everything been?" Gwen asked.

"Great. Work is crazy but going well. We've been staying in more, relaxing."

"I noticed. You mentioned it on your Web site. So, do other people actually read it?"

"What do you mean?"

"Like people who aren't your friends?"

"They must. I don't have thousands of friends. It's kind of strange, actually."

"It's such an invasion of privacy, isn't it?"

"How?"

"Well, I can't imagine Jake wants his every move documented for the Internet. Nor your unborn child."

"I think Clare's a great writer and I'm happy to provide material," Jake said quickly.

"Well, OK. I guess some people choose to keep their marriage private," Gwen said with a small laugh.

After our food came, Gwen regaled all of us with her decorating stories.

". . . and then we picked up the most darling Waterford crystal bowl, which perfectly matches our wedding pattern, to go on the coffee table from Pottery Barn I told you about. It is just stunning in the sitting room next to that wine chest I e-mailed you a picture of. Remember?" Gwen looked at me and I nodded mutely for what felt like the frillionth time. My neck was already starting to cramp up.

"So how are you guys feeling about all of this?" Alex asked.

"What? The ravioli? It's great."

"Uh, no. You know, having a baby?" Gwen said.

"OK," I said, and prayed they'd shut up.

"Well, I mean, since it was a mistake." She and Alex exchanged looks as Jake checked the table to see if it was large enough for him to fit under.

"Excuse me?" I asked.

"We can't wait!" Jake threw out, hoping it would distract me long enough to drag me out the door without any carnal damage.

Gwen gave me one last prod and asked, "Aren't you freaked out at all?"

"Did you see the game last night?" Jake asked, in one last

desperate attempt to prevent the entire restaurant from being engulfed in hellfire and macabre suffering.

"Who the hell do you think you are? I'm sure you think all of this is super hilarious, but what would you know? You're both self-involved, condescending *losers*." I turned to Gwen. "And *you*. You *used* to be my friend. Now you're a stick-up-the-ass bitch no one can stand. You think we're pathetic and sad? Well, at least I didn't have butt sex with a townie while in college."

Gwen quickly looked at Alex, whose mouth hung open as he looked from me, the crazy pregnant lady on a tirade, to his Gwen, his girlfriend who did indeed have butt sex with a townie during school.

"You bitch. I told you that in confidence," Gwen said, her face turning purple.

"Oh, yeah? Well, don't worry. Everybody already knew. The townie told everybody. People used to call you Butt Sex Gwen behind your back."

Gwen looked at Jake, who nodded slightly. Ha-ha! I love Jake. He stood up and handed me my purse before dragging me out by my arm. Gwen didn't say anything, she just stared at me and wanted to rip my lungs out. I immediately burst into tears when I got outside. I sobbed, hiccupped, and snotted the whole way home until we stopped at McDonald's and got a McFlurry.

Of course, I'm devastated it happened. But I'm also relieved. Gwen was a good friend in college, but over the past few years she's made me feel like a loser every time we hung out. I don't want someone who will visit me in the hospital and tell me my child looks like Eddie Munster or something.

I read in one of those pregnancy books I might start to experience some rifts in friendships during my pregnancy. Apparently, it is true.

It is also true that McFlurrys make almost anything better.

Thursday, August 9
. . . .

I still feel like crap about dinner with Gwen and Alex. Jake said I should just let it go, that we've grown apart from them anyway, and they deserved everything I said. It's hard though; growing apart from any friend is difficult.

As much as I want to analyze the situation and replay it in my mind, I managed to focus on work today. I didn't really have a choice, since today was Rachael Flynn's wedding dress fitting at a snotty wedding dress boutique in the city where the dresses start in the ballpark of five grand.

I arrived right on time at two o'clock, despite having a serious incident involving my linen pants and Mule Face's cup of scalding hot coffee, to which she shrugged and smiled sweetly as she went back to boring everyone with her presentation of ring-bearer pillows. Anyway, I still arrived on time; burn-victim scar tissue, gestating alien child, and all. A lot of good it did me, as I waited for forty-five minutes before anyone showed up. Forty-five excruciating minutes while salesgirls pointedly stared at my still-warm coffee stain and snickered about the scuffs on my shoes. It didn't help I'd been fighting an escalating case of gas since I arrived. So, I sat and waited and texted Julie until Rachael and Irene flounced in, looking impeccable, well-rested, calm, and not coffee-stained.

"Hi! You're here!" I said brilliantly when I saw them.

Irene brushed back a lock of silvery-gray hair. "Oh, yes, dear." Long inappropriate pause. "We are."

One of the snotty salesgirls led Irene and Rachael into a room and soon Rachael emerged in a stunning strapless ivory ball gown, adorned with delicate gold beading on the bodice. She twirled, swishing the heavy fabric around like a peacock tail. She stepped up on the pedestal and admired herself while Irene furrowed her brow and tapped a perfectly manicured nail against her cheek.

Rachael looked stunning, but honestly, I was just trying to catch a glimpse of the price tag on the sample gown in the window. The ass-wad salesgirl ooohhhed and ahhhhed while kneeling down in front of Rachael and fluffing her skirt.

"Mother, what do you think?" Rachael asked.

"It's stunning, dear." Pause. "Quite lovely." Even longer pause. "It needs to be taken in here." She pinched at Rachael's waist.

"It fits perfectly," Rachael responded.

"I realize that, but the dress . . . and the waist . . . need to come in."

"That's why I have Paolo," Rachael said. I assumed Paolo was her trainer? Life coach? Plastic surgeon? Cocaine dealer?

"Remember . . . these pictures . . . are forever." Irene turned to me. "Clare, what . . ." Is your favorite sex position? Model is your dildo? Is the population of Rwanda? ". . . do you think?"

I remembered I was supposed to be bestowing the bride-to-be with compliments and not texting Julie about my strange gas pains.

"Gorgeous. Simply fabulous," I said, which seemed to be the only input required, as Irene went back to analyzing Rachael's body fat. I watched the salesgirl reapply her lip gloss and I felt the gas pain again. It was like my stomach was having a spasm or something. I rubbed my stomach again and shifted in my chair, hoping my stomach didn't make some weird loud embarrassing noise and cause Irene Flynn to pass out from shock.

It happened again. *Please, Crouton, could you talk to my stomach in there and ask it— Wait a fucking second.*

I grabbed my day planner and checked what week I am— eighteen weeks.

Between the eighteenth week and the twentieth week you should start to feel your baby move flashed into my brain from one of those pregnancy books.

Holy crap—Crouton? Not gas? Just then, Crouton kicked out an alien leg and I felt it again.

"Holy shit!" I muttered to myself. Yes, I actually said the S word in Bella Bridal.

The salesgirl jumped and Irene and Rachael stared at me. I think I mumbled something about Tourette's syndrome while turning beet red. I immediately went home and pulled out my pregnancy textbooks. After reading a few, it does seem what I thought was flatulence is actually Crouton moving around. Hooray! I don't have gas! Hooray! Crouton is athletic!

It's very strange to realize he/she has been moving around this whole time but was just too little for me to feel it. Which leads me to wonder what would happen if I were obese. Like five hundred pounds, can't get out of bed, have to be transported to a hospital in an ambulance after a crane rips out the side of my house and I have to be removed by a forklift? Would I never feel Crouton? Would I have felt Crouton sooner if I didn't have five thousand Nacho Bell Grandes this past year? Or did the Nacho Bell Grandes make Crouton big and fat enough for me to actually feel the kicks? These are the things I actually want to know, not how much the placenta weighs.

Saturday, August 11

Jake was so excited when I came home and told him I felt Crouton moving. He immediately placed his hand on my stomach to see if he could feel him, too. I tried to explain to him it would be a while before he could feel the baby, too, and he looked really depressed so I said a very, very stupid thing in an effort to cheer him up.

I said, "We can go to IKEA on Saturday."

I love IKEA just as much as the next person. In fact, I would totally have sex with the Swedish guy who invented it. Afterward, I would thank him profusely for inventing extremely affordable furniture made out of particleboard coated with plastic paint. Then I would ask him if it would be possible to construct it so it could withstand more than five pounds of weight. However, going to IKEA on a Saturday is dumber than a pregnant lady buying thong underwear.

We are foolish, stupid humans who deserved everything we got today.

Even though we knew it would be a mistake we rationalized it by saying we knew exactly what we wanted—an entertainment center for our bedroom—and could pop in and out while deftly weaving through the aisles o' crap. We even sat in the car for a few minutes after we found a parking spot approximately one state over, to meditate a little and chant: "Must not freak out in IKEA. Stay calm. We don't care how cheap the throw pillows are. We are only here for one thing. We will stay the course." We approached choosing an entertainment center in true commando fashion. We agreed we would not look at anything but entertainment centers, we would pick whatever one we liked, write it down, and for the love of everything holy, *get out*.

We leaped out of the car and joined the throng of people heading toward the enormous blue and yellow warehouse. (Aliens must think IKEA is a place where they give out free crack. Nope. Just furniture made out of tissue paper.) I noted looks of sheer defeat mixed with relief on the faces of people who were leaving; looks that said, *the IKEA god just kicked my ass. And I kinda liked it. Man I can't wait to put this end table together. Where is my car?* We went in and finally located the floor with entertainment centers via the aid of a giant map. I grabbed a piece of paper and one of those tiny pencils so I could write down FLOGERSHAM, or whatever the name of the model we chose.

Why can't it be called Black Entertainment Center? Too easy? Not fun for the employees because they don't get to watch customers try to pronounce Swedish words?

We raced over to the appropriate section, nearly knocking down a family of four speaking in a foreign language and examining bed frames. Jake got there first. He looked at me and said "DUNKER-FLO," while pointing to a unit.

I nodded my head and scribbled it down on my teeny-tiny paper. We almost made it back to the escalator when a stray bullet grazed my leg. *Oooohhhhh, picture frames for forty cents. Gee, maybe I do need fifty three-inch-by-three-inch picture frames, which are too small to hold a real picture without whittling it down to the size of a postage stamp.*

Jake looked over his shoulder and saw his comrade was hit. Like a brave soldier, he raced back to rescue me. He tossed the plastic-and-wood frame back into the bin and towed me to the escalator.

"But . . . I . . . we . . . might . . . need . . . someday . . . always . . . wanted . . . forty cents!"

My protests were ignored and we proceeded to the warehouse sector. This is when we got to helplessly wander the aisles, trying to locate DUNKERFLO in the color that we wanted. After thirty minutes, we finally found it and realized it came in three pieces. And box two of three was located in aisle four. So we went back to aisle four and wrestled the last box two of three from the hands of a weak college student. Ha-ha, screw you, blondie!

Back at home, two hours, eight hundred four-letter words, five holes not lining up, some tears, bruises, and some very creative usage of masking tape later, and it is assembled.

We had a panic attack as we realized the entire thing might crumble when we placed an actual television in it, so we decided to test it by placing books on it. It seemed to be holding up under the weight—unlike our dresser, whose drawer shelves buckle and bow when we put more than the equivalent of four T-shirts in them.

We then switched out the books with the television à la Indiana Jones in *Raiders of the Lost Ark*. It creaked and moaned a little and we thought the entire thing was going to explode, but it stabilized.

"Cool. So what do you want—," I started to ask.

"*Shhhhh!*" Jake hissed at me.

"What?"

"Clare, we don't know its limits yet. No sudden movements or noises or loud talking or too much disruption of the air around it until we know for sure how it will react."

Good point.

So, we stood there for another fifteen minutes, staring at our television, waiting for the unit to crumble like broken pie crust. Finally,

Jake allowed me to speak and turned on the television. What a coincidence, the Cubs game just started.

Regardless, we both breathed easier with the knowledge we have a new entertainment center for the next six to twelve months.

Or at least, we did until my parents stopped by a few hours later.

They came over to take us out to dinner and nearly made it out the front door without major incident. That is, until my dad walked into our bedroom and patted it. Hard.

"Looks pretty good!" he said, as he had heard all about the blood, sweat, and promising of Crouton to the devil it took to get it assembled.

He gave it another firm pat and Jake and I simultaneously winced right before one of the holder things on the shelf broke and the entire shelf came crashing down. Thankfully, it wasn't the piece holding the television up, but the whole thing swayed, as though warning us to NEVER TOUCH ME AGAIN, BITCHES!!!

Point made.

I blame my father's mistake (not only touching but firmly patting IKEA furniture) on the fact they are in their fifties and out of touch with the furniture trends of the poor.

The IKEA gods seem appeased now. Thank God, because I really do think I need some picture frames. For Crouton's supermodel-like baby shots, of course.

Monday, August 13
. . . .

I thought it would be one of *those* days. One of *those* days when I'd wake up and lie in bed, stare at the pillow next to my cheek, not wanting to twitch a muscle, not wanting to breathe because I knew once I moved, my day had begun. I thought I'd wake up slowly and allow my brain to wrap around the concept I was about to learn the baby's gender.

But no, I didn't wake up today with a sense of anticipation. My day began by being yanked out of a yacht in the Mediterranean where that cute guy on *The Office* was rubbing Hawaiian Tropic on my shoulders, by a deafening, panic-stricken sounding "Holy shit!" followed by a minor earthquake as Jake leaped out of bed.

I bolted straight in the air, cruelly ripped away from my European vacation.

I glanced at the clock. It was already 8:16 A.M. How the hell did we sleep so long this morning?

I had an 8:30 doctor's appointment before work. The *big* one. Or at least the biggest one so far. The Big One will probably be the one where a human comes out of my body. Apparently, Crouton's parts are formed enough for us to be able to see and photograph, which sounds gross and almost pedophiliac or something.

Jake kept insisting we keep it a surprise and find out at the birth, but seeing as how I'm the one who actually has to push this thing out, my vote counts as two. Overruled. I'd like to start calling the baby something other than Crouton. Like an actual name or something.

Of course, we haven't picked a name yet, but I wanted to narrow the field by 50 percent.

Instead of waking up, snuggling closer to Jake, and dreaming about buying teeny-tiny little baby socks, it was as if we were both shot out of a cannon and electrocuted at the same time. No time to shower. We ran around the bathroom, grabbing items out of the medicine cabinet as though we were escaping town before an impending alien invasion.

After seriously injuring a flock of geese and shaking our fists at a blind elderly woman driving a Cadillac, we made it to Dr. Clarke's office at 8:42 A.M. Not bad considering my meltdown over Butterscotch vomiting all over the carpet right before we left.

Ten minutes later, I was lubed up and we were staring at grainy pictures of Crouton. Jake commented how much it looked like a snuff film, which I agreed. I also concurred when he mentioned the extreme size of Crouton's head. Apparently this is normal, though. I was told all fetuses (feti?) resemble Skeletor from the *He-Man* cartoon on an ultrasound. I was very relieved to hear this, seeing as how I'm not sure how strangers would react to a baby closely resembling He-Man's nemesis. I mean, I'm sure it would be cute and all but a date for the prom would probably be out.

Yet the resemblance was so uncanny, I immediately changed the baby's name from Crouton to Skeletor.

The ultrasound technician, a lady named Catalina (like the island and the salad dressing) who was in desperate need of an upper-lip wax, smiled and looked at us. "Do you want to know the sex?"

I glanced at Jake, and silently asked him. He smiled and shook his head. I paused and looked at the screen, at Skeletor the Klingon Spawn. It felt like the moment before smoking the first cigarette after I "quit," the moment before doing the shot I knew would probably make me puke, the moment before handing over my credit card for the outfit costing more than my rent.

So I paused. But no way was I going to leave without finding out what kind of reproductive organs were forming inside of me.

"YES!" I shouted out. I looked at Jake and he just rolled his eyes and feigned surprise. I knew everything was cool.

"Well, see the legs there? I see three of them!" Catalina said.

We both just stared at her.

"Boy!" she said.

Nothing.

"B-O-Y," she said very slowly, her upper lip whiskers twitching. Our cue.

"Oh my God!" I screamed as Jake began immediately mapping out Skeletor's—I mean Mr. Skeletor's—future in the NFL. "I win!" I joyfully pumped my fist in the air. "Ha-ha! I knew it was a boy!" I pointed at Jake. "I rule!"

He laughed but couldn't take his eyes off the ultrasound monitor.

Yes, it's true. I have a very small penis growing inside of me. Which is sort of strange.

1:35 P.M.

I went back to the office for a few hours until I met Jake for lunch.

"So, a boy." I smiled at Jake as we settled into a booth at the tiny diner.

"No kidding." He folded his hands in front of him on the table.

"What do you think?" I studied his face for a reaction.

"I'd be happy either way. I'm just glad he's healthy and doing well."

"You don't have to be politically correct with me. It's OK to say you're excited he's a boy."

"I'm thrilled he's a boy, but honestly, I would've been thrilled if it were a girl, too."

"Oh, whatever. You're so diplomatic," I teased him, and rolled my eyes. "So, are you finally getting used to the idea that we're going to have a baby?"

"Well, that helps." He pointed to my stomach. "But, yeah. I think I am. I think I'm even excited. Screw that, I *am* excited. Some days, completely terrified, but mostly excited."

"Me too. Isn't it weird to think in a few months that will be us?" I gestured to a couple across the diner with a baby in a high chair.

"Yes. But it's also cool, you know what I mean?" He smiled at me earnestly.

"I think I do." I smiled back at him before I turned my attention to the menu, because *damn* did Mr. Skeletor want to eat.

10:00 P.M.

We never should've found out the sex. Our joy lasted a few hours, until we began to call people and tell them the news. Jake, of course, added, "He definitely was a boy, if you know what I mean," as if he could distinguish between Mr. Skeletor's arm, neck, or wiener.

Marianne immediately wanted to know if we were going to name the baby Phillip, after her father. Um, no.

My mom wanted to know if we'd "raise him right" and allow him to play with dolls if he wanted and dress him in pink. Yeah, good luck fighting with Jake.

Natalie wanted to know if I was aware boys have a statistically higher chance of birth defects and was I going to get any genetic tests done. Eat shit.

Sam asked if she could borrow my Jimmy Choo boots. No.

Mark said congrats and hung up to watch a recorded episode of *Lost*.

The IT guy asked if I was due next week. Fuck you very much, Joe, now please fix my Internet so I can buy more crap on eBay. And please don't tell anyone I found a way around the company's firewall.

Reese said she was running out to Tiffany to buy me something blue. I didn't protest.

And Julie said, "Just make sure that when he grows up he knows where the clitoris is. And that nothing under one carat is acceptable." Sure, right after potty training.

Tuesday, August 14

I've taken the newfound knowledge that I'm busy growing a boy and used it to justify the purchase of every single remotely useful baby item I find on the Internet. American Express *loves* me right now. They're all like beaming and shit and like, "Hey, Clare! Long time no see. We were getting nervous there for a while when you weren't using us. But now we understand it was a temporary lapse. We are so happy to have you back and please, keep up the good work."

I still have no idea what we're going to name said boy, but Jake's two suggestions—Richard and Peter—are not exactly winners. I'm perfectly happy calling him Mr. Skeletor for right now but everyone else in the world seems adamant that we pick a name and pick one RIGHT NOW GODDAMN IT.

What I say: "Back off, assholes, or else the kid will be named Skeletor, King of the Klingons. Why don't you all do something useful and turn up the air-conditioning?"

Wednesday, August 15

· · · · · · · · · · · · · · · · · · · ·

It's a good thing we're having a boy, because Jake will need another male to hang out with since Butterscotch is now officially a drag queen.

Seriously.

Whereas Jake and I were suspicious before, today his drag-queenness was actually confirmed.

It started a week ago, when we discovered Butterscotch no longer wanted to wear his very nice black collar. Jake or I would find it on the floor somewhere in the apartment and put it back on him, thinking it fell off. When we put it around his neck, he'd hiss and look pathetic for a few minutes. We figured he decided collars are out this season.

As a joke, Jake bought him a hot-pink collar decorated with beads spelling out "Princess." We laughed about it and threw it in a drawer. Then, this morning, before I left for work, I found his black collar right next to the front door. I picked it up and walked over to Butterscotch to put it back on. He looked really pissed as he saw me walking toward him with it. I stopped, remembered the pink collar, fished it out of the drawer, and walked toward him with it. The damn cat didn't even try to run away when I put it on. He squinted his eyes at me and purred loudly. He jumped off the couch and rubbed his face against my pants, thanking me for the beautiful present.

I shrugged and left for work, expecting to find it on the ground when I came home. But nope, he's still wearing his hot-pink "Princess" collar. He even jumped in Jake's lap and purred for a while this evening.

So, yes. The rumors are true. I'm thinking of buying him some fake eyelashes and falsies.

Friday, August 17

. . . .

The hilarity of Butterscotch the Gay Cat wore off quickly. Now? This is my predominant emotion: Hate.

All I feel is hate.

Why do I have to be knocked up in the middle of a record-breaking heat wave? I hate the sun, with its "I'm going to incinerate every last one of you." I hate the weathermen, with their "It's going to be a scorcher today, folks! Stay inside!" but then not telling us how to avoid going outside yet still go to our jobs. I hate my wireless connection, which has decided to punk out on me and stop working. I also hate jen2485, who told me she would pray for Skeletor since he obviously isn't going to have a strong male role model in his life.

I definitely hate my car's air conditioner, which decided to escape all of this heat and go on vacation, costing $750. Not to mention how awesome it was when it decided to crap out right in the middle of a traffic jam during rush hour. On a day dubbed "The hottest of the year so far!" I began to sweat profusely and pressed the automatic window button. I figured some circulation, even smog and exhaust filled, would help cool me down.

But . . . nothing.

I pressed it again.

Still nothing.

Beginning to panic, I tapped on the button repeatedly, with the same result. None of the windows would go down. I was trapped. In a car beginning to overheat. Desperate, I grabbed my cell phone and called Jake, who was already home, lying on the couch in front of the air conditioner while Butterscotch huddled for warmth in a corner.

"What am I going to do?" I screamed into the phone after I explained the situation.

"Shit, well, um . . ."

"Just tell me!" I could feel the sweat dripping down my back.

"You're going to have to turn on the heat, to relieve some of the temperature from the engine. Clare, I'm so sorry. Pull off at the next exit and I'll come and get you."

"You're kidding. I have to turn the heat on. Do you know it's *ninety thousand degrees* out?"

"Yeah, I'm so sorry. Just pull over, get out, and I'll come and get you."

I snapped my phone closed, said a quick prayer, and turned my heat on. I fearfully wondered if it was possible to roast the baby from the inside out. I had about twenty feet to go before I could pull off into a highway oasis, but those twenty feet were the longest of my life. Traffic came to a standstill after about eight feet and I could no longer bear the heat. I ripped off my work shirt, relishing in the air, albeit warm, hitting my back. At least I had a bra on.

I didn't care when other drivers began to stare at the nearly half-naked pregnant lady sweating profusely. I continued to stare straight ahead, focused on those twelve feet, until I heard honking next to me. I looked up and saw a man driving a Ford F-150, waving at me.

"Woo hoo! All right, darlin'!" he yelled out his window. As he opened his mouth, I could see he had nary a tooth.

Despite my situation, I smiled and waved at him. I figured, *Mr. Pickup Truck, even though you look like a child molester and probably have a severe case of genital warts, it's nice to be appreciated.*

Ten minutes later, I made the extra twelve feet and was able to pull off onto the oasis and get out of the car. Mr. Pickup Truck bid me adieu as I pulled off. What I mean is, he yelled something to the effect of he always wanted to "bang" a pregnant "broad." I'm not really sure. It was hard to tell with my windows up and the heat blasting.

Sunday, August 19

. . . .

The heat wave soldiers on. I think it's global warming. Damn it. I knew I should've recycled more, turned down my heat in the winter, and bought a hybrid car. When I met Julie for lunch today, even she was amazed at the sheer volume of sweat I'm able to produce these days. And she's seen me on spring break, in Cancun, in ninety-degree heat, pumped full of battery-acid margaritas.

"Are you OK? Jesus Christ, you're making *me* hot. Do you need a napkin or something?" Julie said as she surveyed my limp hair plastered against my forehead.

I sat down across from her at Emilio's, a tapas restaurant. "I'm fine. Just some water," I panted as my arms shot forward and I made contact with a glass of ice water. "Ah, so much better," I said after I gulped the glass down.

"You know, it's not even that hot out," Julie said disdainfully.

"Screw you. Yes it is. I'm dying. Skeletor is trying to roast me from the inside out."

"Are you having hot flashes? Like women in menopause?"

"Hot flashes, my ass. It's more like being punched in the face with a flame-thrower."

"So, what's good here? I've never been," Julie said as she opened her menu.

"Everything. It's tapas. You've done tapas before, right?"

"Nope." She shook her head. "To be honest, I thought you said 'topless' at first over the phone."

"It's like appetizer portions. You order a lot but it's all little plates."

"Groovy," she said, surveying the menu.

A waiter materialized and I silently pointed to my empty glass of water. Mercifully, a bus boy hustled over and filled my glass, which I chugged again.

"Order for me since you've been here," Julie announced.

I pointed to five dishes on the menu and when the waiter asked if there was anything else he could get us I said, "Water. And keep it coming."

As she watched me take down my fifth glass of water, Julie asked, "Do you think it's possible to sweat out your kid?"

I pushed my wet hair out of my eyes and glared at her.

"So, have you guys figured out a name yet?" she asked.

"Not yet."

"You should name him Ben," she said dreamily.

"As in Hot Dr. Ben?" I smiled at her.

"Hell yes."

Our food arrived and we passed the tapas plates around, sampling the delicious Spanish food.

"So how's Disgusting Married Man?" I asked Julie.

"Disgusting. Perverted. Still stalking me. Let's not talk about it, OK?" she said quickly.

"Oh, OK," I said. I searched my brain for something else to say. "Isn't it weird that Reese and I are pregnant at the same time?" I said before I could stop myself. "Uh . . . ," I stuttered.

"What?" Julie put her fork down and narrowed her eyes.

"Nothing. Reese is pregnant again," I said quickly.

"Is she really that fucking stupid?" Julie spat out.

"Uh . . ." I said. I lurched toward my water glass and chugged it again, trying to give myself a minute to regroup. "I don't know" was all I came up with.

"She'll be divorced with two kids before age thirty," Julie muttered. "She needs to get her head out of her ass."

"Well, she just . . ." I trailed off when I noticed a woman in her twenties, dressed in a gorgeous yellow sundress, walking toward our table.

"Sorry to interrupt, but I just wanted to come over and introduce myself. I'm Rian O'Toole and I read your blog every day. I love your writing," she said, and smiled at me.

"Thanks so much. Really, that means a lot. And thank you for introducing yourself. It's so great to meet you." I tried to flip my now crusty and wavy hair behind my shoulders.

"And you must be Julie! I recognize you, too!" Rian said.

"The one and only." Julie grinned at her.

"And congrats on the pregnancy! You look fabulous!"

I knew she was lying, but I accepted the compliment. Julie and I tried to continue our lunch after Rian the yellow sundress girl walked back to hers, but Rian's entire table stared at us the entire time. I guess they are readers, too. Never before have I felt so exposed, not only because I'm pregnant and I feel like the entire world knows, but because my pregnancy news is so intimate, not just the usual blog stuff about what bar I went to last Saturday and how hungover I am. It's becoming all very Internet-paparazzi-ish.

Monday, August 20
· ·

As I sweated this morning in my office, I decided to call Reese, since I knew she was one of the few people in my life who would truly understand just how on-fire my insides felt.

"Hello," she said, sounding breathless.

"Hey! Just calling to see how everything's going."

"Hey there yourself. Everything's going great. How are you feeling?"

"Melting in this heat wave, but other than that, pretty good."

"How's Jake?"

"Same old. How's everything with Matt?"

"Fine."

"Really?"

"Sure."

"You don't sound fine. What's going on?"

"Oh, it's no big deal. I was just cleaning yesterday and found another e-mail and it spooked me a little."

"You're kidding! From Leslie?" I asked.

"Yes, but I'm sure it's nothing."

"Read it to me."

"I threw it out."

"Well, what did it say?"

"Something about a great job on the Davis presentation and lunch and martinis on her today. Oh, and she liked his tie."

"What do you think it means?" I asked.

"I really don't know. It doesn't matter. I'm sure Matt wouldn't do anything to hurt our marriage." Right. And Matt didn't cheat on Reese five hundred times in college. I'm sure he outgrew cheating right after they took their vows.

"OK, well, you know best. I just don't want to see you get hurt."

"I'm not going to jump to any conclusions, Clare. It could be nothing."

"Are you going to ask him about it?"

"And say what? That I saw a couple of e-mails that may or may not be suspicious?"

"Yeah, that's exactly what you should say. That's what people do when they're married, talk to each other."

"I don't think so. I'm not going to turn this into a big deal. Because it's not."

"What was his reaction when you told him about the baby?"

"Nothing."

"Nothing?"

"Nothing, because I haven't told him yet."

"Well, um, when are you planning on doing that?"

"I don't know. When it's the right time."

"What is the right time?"

"I don't know. I'll figure it out. Listen, please don't tell Jake about any of this, OK? You haven't told him anything, right?"

"No," I lied.

"Good. The last thing I need is everyone gossiping behind my back about something ridiculous."

"Reese, we love you. No one is going to—," I started to say when she interrupted me.

"I have to go. I'll call you later."

I hung up the phone. I tried to tell myself it was nothing, it was all a misunderstanding, things were going to be fine, Reese was probably right, and I was overreacting. But I knew what Reese told me was probably just 10 percent of what was going on. A gnawing feeling reminded me how many times in college Reese suspected other women, how I'd always suspected but buried deep down into my psyche that Matt wants to have Reese as his trophy wife and still have something on the side.

I asked Jake what he thought earlier tonight. All he said was, "She should ask him about it," as he flipped back and forth between two baseball games.

"I know, but she won't. Tell me what you think."

"I just did."

"No, but tell me what you *think*." He flipped off the TV and looked me squarely in the eyes.

"Really? You really want to know what I think?"

"Yes," I said, suddenly cautious.

"And you won't get pissed at me when I say it?"

"Why? Are you going to say something bad?"

"You're not going to like it."

"Just say it. I want to know what you think." Although I was suddenly unsure if I wanted to hear his opinion.

"Fine. I think Matt is a complete fucking asshole." He stared at me, his eyebrows raised.

"You do?"

"He treats Reese like shit and he's the biggest egomaniac I've ever had the displeasure of coming into contact with." I sat back, stunned. I knew he and Matt weren't exactly close, but I didn't realize he hated him.

"What do you mean?"

"The guy's always talking about money, about how much his BMW cost or his house cost or what his Christmas bonus was."

"Yeah, I guess he does talk about money a lot. But I always think it's just because he has it."

"He's always 'on.' Whenever we get together, he asks me about how much is in my 401(k) and whether or not I took his advice to invest in a certain mutual fund or whatever."

"OK."

"He's constantly staring at other women when we're all together and says things like, 'That girl's tits make me wish I wasn't married. Are you with me?'" Jake imitated Matt's tone and threw his hands in the air. "Do you not see any of this?"

"I don't know."

"Wake up, Clare. This guy's a scumbag."

"You don't even know what—"

"Yes, I do. I can't stand the guy."

I folded my arms in front of my chest and glared at him. He shrugged. "I've never said anything because Reese is your friend. You asked for my opinion."

"I realize that. So what am I supposed to do?"

"Just be her friend. It's all you can do. And support her when she comes to her senses and divorces him."

I gave him a withering look. "Divorce? Doubtful."

"Oh, right."

"Yeah. Reese's dad had like fifty mistresses and her parents slept in separate bedrooms but they never divorced. Divorce just isn't done in Reese's family."

"Regardless, she better wise up."

I nodded and sighed heavily. I walked over to him and snuggled next to him on the couch. I buried my face in his shoulder, against his soft T-shirt that smelled like laundry detergent, and closed my eyes as he rubbed my back and twirled my ponytail.

I fell fast asleep.

Tuesday, August 21

. . . .

I woke up around midnight last night, thinking about Reese and Matt, worrying about the worst. Completely unmotivated to do work, I resumed my daily Internet surfing but started Googling things like "Signs your mate is cheating on you." I desperately wanted to ask the Internet for advice but I knew Reese would cut out my liver with a spatula if I so much as hinted at any problems.

During my hand-wringing, I remembered a Web site I used when planning my wedding: Bride Talk. There was a special message board for women having marital problems. Out of morbid curiosity, I read post after post about cheating spouses, abusive husbands, and overbearing mothers-in-law. (Man, was I tempted to post about that one.) After an hour, I became so depressed I stopped and almost clicked off, but the Baby Chat message board caught my eye. I clicked on it and saw posts titled "Lost my mucus plug! Yippee!" and "Just miscarried at sixteen weeks." I quickly closed the Web site.

Which lasted fifteen minutes before I went back on Baby Chat and furiously opened every post, soaking up information, fascinated and horrified at the same time. I was so transfixed I didn't see Mule Face come in.

"The florist from the Flynn wedding just called and their biggest grower is having problems securing enough cream flowers for the wedding. They want to know if they can use pale pink as a filler," she said.

I jumped and quickly closed my Internet browser, flustered as hell.

"Oh, um, yeah. I mean, no. That's not OK."

She stared at me and examined her nails. "I figured. Good luck with that one. God. My nails have gone to shit. I need a manicure." She looked up. "Oh, I almost forgot. Here." She thrust an envelope in my direction and clicked off, teetering in her inappropriate-for-work purple suede wedges.

I looked down. *Yes!* Mule Face's wedding invitation! I tore open the envelope and squealed with delight as I saw the iridescent gold lettering on red velvet backing and the enclosed card outlining where the couple is registered. Ahhhhh, the world might be going to shit and Reese's husband cheating on her, but at least I could still count on Mule Face to take tacky to a whole new level.

With a smile on my face, I cheerfully checked yes on the reply card and got back to reading stories about women who were permanently paralyzed from pain medication during labor.

Wednesday, August 22
. . . .

"When are we going on a babymoon?" I asked Jake as he was opening a carton of moo shoo pork.

He paused, holding the container in the air. "What?"

"A babymoon. When and where are we going?" I tapped my finger on the counter.

"I have no idea what you're talking about," he said as he spooned food onto his plate.

"You've never heard of it?"

He shook his head. Truth was, I hadn't heard of it either until yesterday, on Baby Chat.

"It's a trip we're supposed to take before the baby's born. You know, since we won't be able to leave the house ever again, let alone take a vacation."

"Babymoon? That doesn't even make sense," he said, handing me a plate of Chinese food.

"Why not?" I asked. I looked at the food and my stomach turned at the sight of wormlike lo mein noodles. I set the plate down on the counter.

"It's supposed to sound like 'honeymoon,' right?"

"I guess."

"A honeymoon is what you take after the wedding. So wouldn't a babymoon mean after the baby?" His mouth twitched as he looked at me.

"I don't know. I just know that we're supposed to."

"Supposed to?"

"It's not fair. Other people get to." Clearly, I am very mature and not at all like a whiny child.

"Fine. Let's see how much it would cost." He picked up his plate and walked into the living room and flipped on the television.

I followed him. "Oh. I don't really care if we go away. I just wanted to see what you thought."

"I know," he said, laughing, his eyes never leaving the TV.

Thursday, August 23
. . . .

With all this Reese drama, I completely forgot about this dinner tonight. Jake's old friend from high school, Grant, is in town with his girlfriend. I'm kinda tired and not really feeling well. I feel a little nauseous from eating a spicy taco for lunch. I was looking forward to watching television tonight. I don't know Grant well, but I think he's kind of boring.

What else?

Oh, his girlfriend is a disgusting ho.

No really, she is.

I met her a couple of years ago at a wedding. Jake introduced me and then was dragged away to do tequila shots so I was stuck talking to Grant for forty minutes. It wasn't so much us talking as me occasionally nodding while he droned on and on about his new kitchen remodel. *For forty minutes.* It was one of those conversations where I almost started to panic because I didn't know how I was going to get out of it alive and intact without having to do the verbal equivalent of chewing off my arm to escape captivity. I think I even blacked out for a while while he was describing his backsplash. I kept trying to desperately point to the bathroom and feign a full bladder but he ignored all of my cries. So, I was thankful when I saw a rather over-weight woman resembling Anna Nicole Smith wearing a teal se-quined dress approaching us. That is, until she walked over, licked Grant's face, and patted him on the crotch.

I swear, I almost puked up my five vodka tonics right there. (But I waited until later to do that.) I had to be polite and shake her hand when he introduced her as his new girlfriend. She shook my hand with the same one she used for grabbing Grant's package. Ew.

Later, we all enjoyed watching them bump crotches on the dance floor and I'm pretty sure I saw her stick her hand down his pants a few times.

Is that not the definition of a disgusting ho?

Since Jake possesses an inability to say no or blow anyone off, we are stuck breaking bread with these freaks tonight.

11:00 P.M.

I've taken five showers and I still don't feel like I'm clean enough. I wonder if overexposure to cK One causes permanent brain damage to an unborn child? If so, we are royally screwed. I think she wore enough perfume to kill every carbon-based life-form in a four-block radius. I got stuck sitting across from her so I watched the half-chewed food rolling around in her mouth as she told stories about her last boyfriend, "Tank." Grant entertained us all with an exhila-rating lecture on "The Time My Laptop Crashed and I Almost Lost a PowerPoint Presentation." I got through it by singing the lyrics to "We Didn't Start the Fire" in my head and texting Julie about Mule Face's honeymoon plans in Gatlinburg, Tennessee.

Julie sent me a text back that said, *You would die. Vince Vaughn is two feet away eating dinner. Call tomorrow for details.*

Julie was off having fabulous cocktails at a fabulous restaurant seeing fabulous movie stars and I was stuck listening to a story that involved the words "I mean, what was I supposed to do? So I told the guy, forget it, man, I'm going to Kinko's."

I also learned there is a kind of metallic paint magnets stick to. It makes me very curious—do other metal objects stick to the wall, like pots and pans? It could make for a very interesting art-deco theme.

I can't help but wonder if tonight was just a smaller microcosm of what's happening in our lives. Take the bore and the ho out of the equation and you have me and Jake at dinner, going home early, and Julie out at a hip restaurant, living a city-girl life that not too long ago, I lived, too.

When Jake and I got engaged and moved out of the city, we were ready to settle down a little, ready for a bigger place and an actual parking space. I knew I'd see Julie less and lose touch with the trendy clubs and restaurants but I didn't mind. But now, forget not only the hot new clubs and restaurants, forget any nightlife. At least for a while. I just don't want everything in my life to change. I know some things will and that's OK, but I still want to be *me* a year from now. And that "me" does not include the new back fat I've developed. The big, beautiful boobs can stay.

I don't know, maybe I'm just in a rotten mood because we have to babysit Sam this weekend. I can't mentally or physically deal with drunken teenagers right now. I have enough of that in my future when Mr. Skeletor is in high school and we have to start marking our liquor bottles.

Saturday, August 25
· · · · · · · · · · · · · · · · · ·

"Oh my God! You look just like Sam! Like, I could've sworn you guys were like *twin* sisters! Except that you're pregnant!" The sixteen-year-old girl looked at me with manic excitement, as though I just told her Sephora started offering free shopping sprees.

"Really? Because . . ." I tried to think of a way to respond since Sam and I look nothing alike.

"Oh my gawd! You guys even have the same effing voice! Kelly, come over here!" The girl waved over some other girl who was standing in the kitchen.

"*Wha*-at? What the hell do you want, Diane?"

"Totally listen to Clare speak!" They both stared at me, waiting for me to say something.

I stared back at them, amazed at how similar they looked. They were each dressed in long, tunic-style silky lingerie camisoles with lace trim and wide belts slung around their hips. Shimmery eye shadow, M.A.C. Lipglass, and hair flat-ironed so straight it swished when they walked.

"Um, I guess—," I began.

"OH MY GOD!" they screamed in unison.

It was all I could take.

"I have to find my husband," I said. I darted away before they could stop me.

I wandered around the house, past teenagers making out, looking for my departed husband. I finally located him in the basement, playing PS2 with three high school boys.

"Having fun?" I asked him sarcastically.

He didn't even look away from *Grand Theft Auto*. "Yep. Hey, can you get me another beer?"

I ignored his request and attempted to engage him in conversation, but it became pretty clear he was way more interested in socializing with his video game partners than me. The scary part is if I were a blind person, and if all of their voices were the same level and baritone, I would've put money on the fact they were all the same age.

Hmmm . . . will have to do Google research re: when the male brain stops developing.

I headed back upstairs to find Sam. I located her in the living room, whispering to her best friend Kristen.

"What are you guys doing?" I asked.

"Nothing. This guy we know totally has the clap, but whatever," Kristen answered.

I sank down into one of my parents' overstuffed armchairs.

"You're not expecting any more people, right?" I asked.

Sam and Kristen exchanged glances.

"Right?" I repeated.

"Totally. There may be like, one or two more guys coming but they're totally cool. You'll heart them," Sam said, avoiding my gaze.

"You know the rules, Sam. The second this gets out of hand or I get annoyed, I'm kicking everybody out. I'm pregnant, for chrissakes. This party is a gift," I said.

No sooner did the words leave my mouth than the doorbell rang and five more guys stood on the front step. Kristen jumped up and let them in as I turned to give Sam a Look, but she was already bounding across the room. She energetically hugged each of the guys.

Two hours later, three of Sam's friends cornered me again.

"OH MY GOD! WE'VE TOTALLY BEEN LOOKING FOR YOU! Diane, look at her ring. It is so beautiful!" The blond girl screamed—Diane, I assumed.

"Totally Tiffany, isn't it?" Diane asked and held up my left hand for the other two girls to see. They collectively sighed.

"Your husband is hot!" brunette number one said.

"Totally tight," brunette number two said.

I wasn't completely aware of the meaning of "tight" but I assumed it was good, so I said, "Thanks."

"Sam is so lucky to have you as a sister. My sister would never let me have a party," brunette number one said as she rolled her eyes and flicked her hair over her shoulder.

"Sam says you have a totally awesome apartment. Do you love it?" Diane asked.

I thought, *Sam? Sam who? She can't mean my sister Sam—the girl who'd rather show up for school without wearing any makeup than say anything nice to me.*

"Um, yeah. I *totally* love it. Sam said that?"

"Duh! She said you have like the coolest place ever and you guys are always going to parties and bars and stuff and you guys have a ton of friends and you're going to have the coolest baby," brunette number two said.

My sister? Said that? No, those girls must've inhaled too much nail polish remover and eyelash glue. There's no way Sam would admit to another human being there's something about me she actually admires.

"Sam told me that she hates my apartment. She thinks it's too small."

The girls looked stunned and then started giggling.

"What*ever*! You're so funny!" Diane said.

"Oh my God, she said your wedding was the funnest wedding she'd ever been to and that your dress was amazing!"

Sam's review of my wedding: "It was fine."

I never thought she told her friends something different.

And she thought my dress was amazing? The first time we went dress shopping, she talked on her cell phone the whole time. The second time she told me the dress I liked was hideous and the third time we left before trying on any dresses because she kept whining about her hunger pains and how much she wanted to go home.

I'm sure at seventeen I would've felt the same way, but it still made me feel like crap.

"So, what do you do?" Diane asked.

"I'm an event planner and I also have a Web site on the side," I said, suddenly uncomfortable.

"Event planning! How AMAZING! And a WEB SITE? That is so freaking cool! What's the address?"

"It's just clarefinnegan-dot-com."

"Is it popular?"

"Yep, it was featured in a story in *The Daily Tribune* a few months ago."

"OH MY GOD! So you're like, FAMOUS!"

Before I could respond, I heard the sound of someone throwing up. I pushed past a bunch of people and found Kristen getting sick in the kitchen sink. Sam was standing next to her, flirting with some guy.

I grabbed her arm. "Aren't you going to help her?"

She jerked her arm away. "NO! It's totally gross and she'll be fine."

"Nice friend. It's your responsibility to clean this up."

She rolled her eyes at me and turned back to the guy.

So much for any warm fuzzy sister-to-sister moments.

An hour later nearly everyone left except for the people spending the night. Sam helped Kristen to bed and cleaned out the sink and Jake was still playing video games in the basement. I'm still thinking about what Sam's friends told me. If she really thought those things about me, why wouldn't she just tell me? Why was it so hard for her to just say something nice to me? I figured these were questions I'd never fully figure out the answers to, like why men feel it's appropriate to adjust their balls in public. Or, I may get an answer, but it wouldn't be a good one. If nothing else, at least now I have a little hope my sister and I can have a normal relationship. Like when people say friends are "close enough to be sisters" or "she's like a sister to me." Because right now, the word "sister" in my family stands for "Person Who Annoys the Living Shit out of You."

Friday, August 31
. . . .

We survived. An entire week with Sam and no one murdered each other, nor did they kill themselves.

Yesterday, I casually said to Sam, "Your friends told me some nice things you said about me."

She shrugged her shoulders and opened the fridge without making eye contact. She grabbed a water bottle and took a big swig. Noticing me still watching her, she threw up her hands in exasperation as she slammed the water bottle down on the counter.

"*What?*"

"Nothing. It was just nice to hear you said those things."

"Whatever." She turned on her heel and walked out of the kitchen.

I almost followed her and pushed the issue, but her cell phone rang and she bounded upstairs, chattering in staccato about someone named Jane Jankowski and her bad highlights.

Score: Sam 1, sisterhood bonding 0.

Friday, September 7

. . . .

After our week spent as babysitters, Jake and I decided it was time to figure out arrangements for our own child. We got about two feet into the discussion before we realized we'd stepped into a minefield.

Day care. Nanny. Never once had I realized the intense debate/emotion/discomfort these words cause some people. Until this past week.

This week Jake and I began the dreaded search for acceptable child care for Mr. Skeletor. After I busted out the smelling salts and revived Jake from a dead faint when I told him the approximate cost, we began furiously researching options as to the best choice, a.k.a. the place least likely to kill our child.

We were able to quickly rule out one option: nanny. This would have been the most convenient option, but also the most expensive, like several hundred dollars a month more expensive. And while I don't mind giving up my *InStyle* magazine subscription for child care costs, I'm thinking having no heat, electricity, or running water would put a damper on our lifestyle. So, we moved on.

The next option: a yuppie day care center. I saw an article about this place in the newspaper and read about how they teach your kid a foreign language and how there's like a whole waterpark inside and everything. Of course, Mr. Skeletor won't be able to speak in English yet, let alone Latin, and he probably won't be going through a lazy river on an inner tube anytime soon, but I figure if they constructed stuff for older kids, they probably would be pretty good about changing the newborns' diapers and feeding them and shit, right?

We toured the center and liked what we saw. It was pretty cool—an outdoor play area with swing set, basketball court, volleyball net, and some pretty awesome toys I think Jake would've played with if the center's director wasn't with us. The infants have their own room full of cribs to nap in and a separate room where they could play or run around or stare at the walls or do complex geometric algorithms in their heads or whatever infants do when they're not sleeping.

All in all, we could actually see dropping Mr. Skeletor off there without a shred of guilt. Which means—how much and do you take American Express?

But alas, we wanted to check another place out: the home day care. We heard about this place from one of Jake's coworkers who brought her kid there. We wanted to look at it because it is much, much cheaper than the yuppie day care place. And, being that we are never ones to make a major decision without researching our options, we drove over to check it out.

As we pulled up, the wheels in my head started turning: *It's only five minutes from work, I could totally do this. And look at how cute this street is, it's like a little neighborhood. And how adorable are those neighbor kids next door? Mr. Skeletor would totally have like a million friends.* And then we committed our first error—we got out of the car. As we were walking up to the cute white house with pretty marigolds in the front, the mom/babysitter/whoever of the kids next door opened the front door, leaned out, and yelled, "KIDS! I told you it was time to come inside. Get the *fuck* back in the house!" Jake and I stopped dead in our tracks, whirled around so quickly we nearly got whiplash, and drove our car away from that horrible, horrible place where people use the F word. (I know. Am hypocrite.) I reasoned at the yuppie day care, at least they would be saying the curse words in Spanish. So, we're pretty sure Mr. Skeletor will be entering yuppie-ville in a few short months.

While the decision of where to send Mr. Skeletor was a pretty easy one, the fact that we're sending him anywhere at all has not been well received by Jake's family. Apparently, every time we mentioned the words "day care" or "maternity leave," they thought we really weren't serious and I'd stop being a crazy feminist and just make the decision to stay home already. Marianne reasoned, "Kids in day care are usually much less well behaved than ones whose mothers stay at home since they aren't disciplined well." That argument might've worked if I hadn't heard the story about Jake and Doug setting their neighbor's garage on fire when they were in grade school. Sorry, I don't buy that one.

I've also heard, "I think children should be raised by their parents and not a day care worker or nanny," from Natalie.

So I asked her, "OK, that's fine. Are you planning to homeschool your children, too?"

"No," she said tersely.

"No? Oh, well, I don't want my kids to be 'raised' by a school-teacher so I'm keeping them home all day, every day, only with me."

I don't think she understood the sarcasm.

Plus, let's get serious. When they all said they think one parent should stay home to take care of Skeletor, they weren't really talking about Jake, were they?

Seriously though—these people would rather me stay home and be a miserable, cooped-up woman addicted to *General Hospital* (which is exactly who I would become), than a happy, well-adjusted, although admittedly somewhat stressed working mother. I mean, I don't think I'm a bad person or I will be a bad mother because I will look forward to spending time with adults during the day rather than changing diapers. I also want to give my kid the best—vacations every year, a nice house, a paid college education. I don't want him to be a spoiled brat but I want to be able to give him the One Thing he wants for his birthday.

Maybe it's because I've been brainwashed because my mom worked. But God, I'll take that kind of brainwashing any day over the kind of brainwashing that means I'm responsible for laundering Jake's underwear. I want to be the best role model I can be for my son, and to me, that is being a working, professional woman. I hope I'll show him that while I love him and he is the absolute best thing in my life, the entire world doesn't revolve around him, and someday when he gets married, the housework and child-raising are shared responsibilities between husbands and wives.

And that is when his wife will send me a dozen roses every day.

Tuesday, September 11
. . . .

My oak tree beckoned to me again today. I had planned on grabbing a sandwich at the deli down the street, but I stopped as I saw the oak tree. Desperate to clear my head after all the day care drama, I bought a slice of pizza and plopped my huge self down on the ground. I figured winter is about to kick all of our asses, so I may as well enjoy the fall while it's still here for a brief period.

I rubbed my stomach as I watched a mom pushing a stroller across the park. I knew she was a stay-at-home mom. Her leisurely gait and her sweatpants gave it away. I decided to make sure Skeletor knows he's going to be well taken care of.

"Listen, Mr. Skeletor. I'm not going to be staying home with you after you're born. I know, it's kind of a bummer, because I'm sure you'll want to hang out with me and only me all the time." I laughed. He didn't respond. "But," I continued, "it's going to be OK. We found a wonderful day care for you that you'll love. The babysitters are so nice and they're going to love you. And when you get older, you can play with all the other kids and have best friends. Does that sound all right?" I waited until I got a kick. "Good. I just want you to know, though, that you're going to be the most important thing to me. Nothing, not work or money or friends or anything else, will come between us. Although I might work during the day, it doesn't mean I love you any less or that we won't be close. I will always make sure you have the best, even if it means your father and I don't. Sound good?" He kicked and I knew he understood.

Wednesday, September 12

. . . .

Jake didn't completely buy my story about having a conversation with Mr. Skeletor yesterday afternoon. He just doesn't get it. It's that women's intuition crap Reese is always preaching about. I *know* he heard me and I *know* he understood everything I said.

I couldn't debate my clairvoyant powers with Jake for any length of time after I got home from work last night because I had plans to meet Julie in the city for drinks.

"Thank God you're here! This jerk to my right kept trying to steal your seat," Julie said as she saw me walk into the restaurant. She jabbed her thumb toward a very fat and sweaty man glaring at her. "I almost put my new boots through his ass."

"Holy shit! I totally forgot; let me see!" I shoved the fat and sweaty man aside and sat down. Julie happily extended her leg and pointed her toe inside her brand-new buttery leather boots.

"Fab! I'm about to drool all over them!"

"Ugh. Please don't. They cost a fortune," she said.

"Lucky bitch. All of my shoe money will be going toward day care soon. What are you drinking?" I asked.

"Saketini. It's to die for and has enough alcohol to make me forget about Perverted Married Man."

"Ooohhh, do tell." I signaled to the bartender to bring me a glass of wine. He pointedly looked at my stomach and I just stared back at him.

"Well, he—"

"Wait!" I interrupted. "I need a drink first."

The bartender brought over my wine; I took a small sip and then looked at her. "OK, go!"

She took a long, deep breath in and exhaled while reapplying her lip gloss. She smacked her lips together.

"So! Disgusting Perverted Married Man finally stopped stalking me."

"What happened?" I asked.

"The freak gave me flowers last week that said, 'Hey, stud. Let's get together for another Happy Hour again.' What a loser." She wrinkled her nose.

"Not to mention the fact he has a wife who probably never gets flowers," I said.

"That, too. Anyway, that was the last move from the fuckwad. I took the flowers to his office, threw them at him, and told him I'd be happy to forward the card to his wife so she'd know what a pathetic shithead he is."

"So he left you alone after that?"

"No. He asked me to go on vacation with him. So I kneed him in the crotch. And then threatened to expose his cheating ass all over the Internet."

"That's my girl."

"So, what's new with you and Jake?"

"Besides my ass rapidly expanding? Nothing, except I have to deal not only with my own pregnancy but the excruciating torture of hearing about Ash Leigh's every diaper change from Marianne."

Julie gave me a sympathetic look. "That's why I'm never getting married. No in-laws to deal with, no wedding showers to attend. And I certainly don't have to worry about that stuff in my family— you know how they are."

Yes, I do. Julie's family parties usually consist of people drinking kegs of beer while watching NASCAR and listening to Toby Keith.

"Believe me, I would've married an orphan had I found one," I said.

"You guys see his parents so much. Doesn't it drive you absolutely insane?"

"Of course, but it means a lot to Jake so I try to do the best I can. But it's hard. Especially now that Natalie keeps sending me forwards at work with titles like 'Why Liberals Hate Christmas' and 'The Ten Commandments Belong in Public Schools.' "

"Natalie is a piece of work. Tell her to go fuck herself." She opened her bag and pulled out a compact and examined her dark eye shadow and adjusted her gigantic cleavage.

"At least she's still really big and fat and squashy from being pregnant."

"Well," Julie said, snapping her compact closed and throwing it back into her purse, "just remember she had to push a human being out of her cooter."

"Um, hi. I'm pregnant, remember?"

"Oh, yeah. Sorry. Oh my God! I almost forgot to tell you!" she suddenly shrieked, nearly snorting her drink out her nose. "I haven't told you about the new nurse who just started, have I?"

I gave her a blank look.

"Oh, Jesus. You're going to die. It's so disgusting. OK, so there's this new nurse who started last week and she's young, like early twenties, and mildly attractive though sometimes her eyebrows remind me of Russell Crowe's . . ." She trailed off, looking far away.

"Point?"

"Oh, yeah. Sorry. But her eyebrows *are* really weird. So, when she started working I noticed something really disgusting but I didn't know if anyone else noticed it so I didn't say anything. Clare, it's so bad."

"What?" I whispered, a look of horror on my face. I realized the bartender was washing glasses very slowly in front of us, hanging on Julie's every word.

"She has an, um, odor problem."

"Like BO?"

"Uh, an odor problem in a certain area."

"*No!*" I sat back in horror, noticing out of the corner of my eye the bartender still listening.

"Yes! Everyone else has noticed it, too. People have to hold their breath when she walks past." That did it. The bartender started gagging and walked away.

"Well, how do you think I feel?" she snapped at him.

"And the entire office talks about it?"

"Well, *yeah*! I mean, we can't even use the bathroom on our floor anymore because it smells so bad. I don't know what her problem is or if she doesn't shower or what. I feel bad for her but she's always talking about having one-night stands so you know there is something nasty growing down there. Oh! And get this—her name is Eve. Like Summer's Eve!"

"No!"

"Trust me, I couldn't make this shit up."

I always know whatever great story I come to dinner armed with, Julie will top it in about five seconds. I could come to dinner after winning *The Apprentice* and she'd tell me she gave Donald Trump a blowjob during her lunch hour.

My stories involve things like: I found a coupon for hamburger buns in Sunday's paper and *it was for forty-five cents. Can you believe it?*

"Man, that's nasty. I don't want to hear any more."

We realized that the bartender wasn't the only male listening to our conversation. A group of yuppie businessmen still dressed in their Brooks Brothers suits heard every word about poor Eve and her problem and were looking at us with complete disgust.

I whirled around on my stool. "Here's a solution: don't listen."

"Whoa, chill out, baby," one of the yuppie guys said.

"Assholes," I muttered.

"Hey, why don't you let us buy you a water and your friend a drink and we'll call it even, OK?" one of the other guys said.

"No, that's—," I started to say.

"Well, it's the least you could do!" Julie jumped in quickly, giving me a look that said *I will kill you if you ruin my chance for a free drink.*

"Thanks," I said tightly as one of the assholes handed me a glass of water.

"So, what are your names?" the asshole with the plastic hair and cosmically unnaturally white teeth asked.

"Linda," I said.

"Jane," Julie replied.

We turned to each other and started talking about a new BCBG dress I bought at an outlet last week for like fifty bucks.

"So, you're obviously taken," the asshole with the Cartier watch jabbed his finger at me, "but what about you? Do you have a boyfriend?"

"No, but I have a girlfriend," Julie replied and put her hand on my knee.

The assholes' faces lit up.

"Score! All right!" They high-fived each other. They bought Julie another drink and I gave her the Sign.

"I have to check my lipstick. Will you come with me?" I asked her. She looked at me sharply, seeing as how she was actually having fun flirting with these losers.

"Really?" she asked.

"Yes. Now." *I am too pregnant to pretend to be interested in what they are saying.*

We told the assholes we were going to the bathroom and promised on a stack of cocktail napkins we were not ditching them and then slipped out the back door of the restaurant.

As we walked out, my cell phone beeped.

"Mark wants us to meet him at Barleycorn's for a drink."

Julie raised her eyebrows.

"Forget it."

We arrived at Barleycorn's fifteen minutes later. As we pulled our IDs out of our purses to show to the bouncer at the door I heard a familiar voice yell from inside, "Don't let them in! They're underage!" The bouncer waved away my ID and stared at my stomach. The bright spot is apparently I don't look like a pregnant teenager.

I craned my neck to see Mark and spotted him at the bar, draft beer in hand, surrounded by guys in their early twenties. He waved me over.

"Hey, sis. Glad you guys showed." He put his arm around Julie. "And you brought my favorite girl."

"Too bad Clare will never let us consummate our relationship," Julie said, and rested her head against his broad chest.

"Don't even think about it. In fact, excuse me." I pushed them apart and walked in between. "Jules?"

"Apple martini."

"She's such a bitch," Mark said.

"An apple martini and a water," I yelled to the bartender, who completely ignored me to flirt with two girls with giant breast implants.

"I'm hitting the bathroom," Julie yelled to me.

"Yo, Steve—hook this girl up," one of Mark's roommates (Neil?) called to the bartender.

"An apple martini and a water," I said again.

"Steve! On my tab," Mark yelled.

"Thanks, bro. Web design lucrative these days?"

He smiled and sucked down half of his beer. "Not really. But remember—I live on ramen noodles."

"Unfortunately, so do I."

"Listen, I—"

"Lemon drop shots!" one of Mark's friends yelled. He thrust a tray containing what looked like five thousand shots in front of us. Mark picked up two.

"That for me?" Julie said from behind me.

"Yep. Here you go. Toast?"

"Sure. Here's to big tits," she said.

"Seriously, you have to marry me," Mark said.

"Marry? Dream on. Everything else is fair game."

"Fuck me," Mark said after he downed the shot.

"OK." Julie smiled at him.

"We have to go," I said, and grabbed Julie's arm.

"What? No way. I'm not ready to leave," she said, wiggling out of my grasp.

"C'mon, Clare, let her stay. I promise I'll be a perfect gentleman and get her home safe."

"I don't care about safe, I only care about *alone*."

"Sure," he said, and smiled sweetly at me.

"Not buying it. Let's go." I grabbed Julie's arm again and led her out the door.

"You really have to get over this overprotective older sister bullshit," she said once we were outside.

"Julie, I am too pregnant and too sober to deal with the consequences of you two hooking up."

"Fine. But after you're done being knocked up, game on."

"Don't hold your breath. I'm pretty sure I'm going to be 'knocked up' forever."

When I finally got home it was almost eleven. I collapsed into bed next to an already snoring Jake and promptly passed out.

Friday, September 14

. . . .

Seeing how supportive my in-laws were regarding the Great Day Care Debate, I really couldn't be happier they're staying with us this weekend during their kitchen remodel.

Jake and I spent the past two days cleaning, organizing, and straightening our place until it is overnight-guest ready. As if that wasn't bad enough, I realized sometime late last night I'm going to have to deal with my mother-in-law for an entire weekend without a drop of alcohol. I'm going to have to survive forty-eight hours without help from my friends Mr. Jack Daniels, Ms. Grey Goose, or Mrs. Heineken.

Monday, September 17
. . . .

So I present: *My Weekend*, a screenplay.

Friday, 5:38 P.M. Interior apartment.

Jake and I sit apprehensively, trying to watch the Weather Channel to distract ourselves from the incoming hurricane. I've already chewed off most of my nail polish and started on my cuticles. I start to regret the thirty-five bucks I just paid to get a manicure, seeing as how I've rendered it almost completely obsolete.

As if on cue, the doorbell rings and Jake and I look fearfully at each other, although not surprised since his parents know we get home from work around five thirty. We take a deep breath, look at each other, and open the door with huge smiles.

5:43 P.M.

Marianne (surveying the guest room we spent the better part of the week decorating and cleaning): "I see you took it to heart when I said you shouldn't go out of your way for us!"

6:07 P.M.

Jake: "So, we thought we'd take you guys out to dinner tonight."

Frank: "Sounds great. Where do you want to go?"

Marianne (turns to me): "You know, you're going to have to learn how to cook sooner or later [tinkling laugh]. You don't want to eat out every night when the baby comes, now do you?"

All three look at me. So, I look at Jake and say, "That's true. You should learn how to make dinner."

7:18 P.M. Interior restaurant.

I down another glass of lemonade, desperately hoping to catch a raging sugar buzz if nothing else. I look down at my shoes and a little sigh escapes from my mouth. Excellent planning to wear my new

Manolo Blahnik Mary Janes I bought off eBay because while sticks and stones and snide remarks may break my bones, no one can take my shoes from me. I'd fallen in love with them ever since the urban shoe myth episode of *Sex and the City* and stumbled across them on eBay for half price. It was truly a gift sent directly from the heavens above.

7:49 P.M.

Marianne: "Have you two looked at houses yet?"

Jake and I stare at her.

Marianne: "Houses?"

Again, she is met with *what the fuck* looks.

Frank: "Are you planning to move after the baby is born, Jake?"

Jake: "No."

Marianne: "You might want to consider it. You only have two bedrooms. You'll need one for the nursery and you'll need at least one more bedroom for your overnight guests."

Me: "We aren't planning on having any overnight guests right after the baby is born."

Problem solved.

Marianne: "Don't be silly. Of course, I will come and stay with you two for a few weeks after the baby is born to help you get adjusted to being new parents."

Simultaneous looks of fear and shock pass over our faces.

Me: "Thanks for the offer, but we'd like to keep it just us after he comes."

Marianne: "Well, OK. I just thought you might need some help."

Frank: "Where are you going to put the litterbox?"

Ah, yes. The litterbox. That is currently in the guest bedroom. The litterbox we temporarily moved to our bathroom while Frank and Marianne are staying with us, even though I was completely fine with telling them they had to leave the door open in case Butterscotch needed to come in and take a crap. The litterbox we will have to find a permanent place for after the baby comes. The litterbox

Butterscotch only occasionally uses, depending upon if he feels content with the attention he received that week.

Jake: "We'll figure it out."

Marianne: "I think children should be raised with a yard to play in, with—"

Jake: "Mom, we can't afford a house here. We don't have half a million dollars."

Marianne: "You could always move closer to—"

Me: "NO!"

All three turn to look at me.

Me: "Um, I mean, we like our neighborhood."

Marianne: "Well, Natalie and Doug's house is really coming along. She is such a great decorator and all of her furniture is restored antiques from the 1920s. She had all of her curtains custom-made and . . ."

Fade to black as Marianne drones on and on about Natalie and Doug's house and how "amazing" everything in it is. *Of course* it is amazing—you can practically build a house using expired Wal-Mart coupons out there.

Saturday, 1:28 P.M. Cubs game.

Jake: "Dad, want another beer?"

I give him a look of death, as I want more than anything an ice-cold beer to wash down my pride after hearing a lecture from Marianne on the importance of watching my weight during pregnancy. After she watched me scarf down a foot-long hot dog. Not to mention the fact that, seemingly overnight, my butt doubled in size.

Mark sends me a text message to look for him in the bleachers. I crane my neck to spot him but can't make out anyone specific among the mass of wasted people wearing Cubs shirts, so I call him.

Me: "Hey! Where are you? Wave."

Mark: "HEY, CLARE! HOW'S IT GOING?"

Me: "Fine. You sound like you're having a good time."

Mark: "WHAT? OH, YEAH! I'M HAMMERED."

Me: "Yep."

Mark: "WHERE'S HOTTIE JULIE?"

Me: "Not here. I'm here with Jake's parents."

Mark: "IS YOUR STICK-UP-THE-ASS MOTHER-IN-LAW WITH YOU? SHE'S A REAL BITCH."

Me: "Um, gotta go."

Marianne: "Who was that?"

Me: "My brother, Mark. Why?"

Marianne: "I heard the end of the conversation but I didn't catch who it was."

Me: "Oh. Um. Yeah. He's pretty drunk."

Marianne: "Does he have a drinking problem?"

Me: "No. He's twenty-two and at a Cubs game."

Marianne: "Binge drinking is a slippery slope, you know."

Me: "Thanks for the tip. So, Marianne, how are Carrie and Patrick's wedding plans coming along?"

Marianne: "Just fine, dear. I think it's going to be a beautiful wedding. Very large. They're planning on inviting all of the relatives, since they are so family-oriented and wouldn't want to leave anyone out."

Me: "We would've loved to invite everyone, too, but you know how expensive it would've been."

Marianne: "Yes, I know. You mentioned it. However, it was such a shame some family members were left out for the sake of money."

Me: "Yeah, a real shame."

Marianne: "What do you think you'll wear to the wedding?"

Me: "I'm not sure yet. I'll have to see what fits after he's here."

Marianne (after surveying my waist): "You'll probably have to buy something new."

10:02 P.M. Interior apartment.

The news comes on and Jake quickly reaches for the remote but it is too late. The lead story is about a roadside bomb exploding in Iraq.

Marianne: "I just don't know why it is only the negative circumstances constantly reported about Iraq. We have done so much good in that country with freeing the Iraqi people and removing Saddam from power but we never hear news stories praising those efforts. I am so sick of this media."

Jake: "Look! *The Three Stooges* is on."

Sunday, 11:31 A.M. Brunch.

Marianne: "Clare, I saw this book the other day at the bookstore and thought of you. Here it is: *You Can Do It! How to Be a Stay-At-Home-Mom on a Tight Budget.*"

Me: "Thanks, but I'm going back to work."

Marianne: "I just want you to make sure you're making an educated decision on all of this day care nonsense."

Jake: "Uh, Mom, we already figured all of that out."

Marianne: "I know, honey. I just feel very strongly that a child is best with his mother rather than at a day care center. A child is best raised by his parents."

Jake: "Mom, this isn't open for discussion."

Marianne: "Well, Natalie stays home with Ash Leigh every day and she is already so far ahead of other kids her age. I can't imagine leaving such a young child at a day care center with people you barely know. I can't imagine trusting—"

Frank: "Lay off, Marianne."

Random Woman with Horrible Timing But Very Good Taste: "Hey! Are you Clare Finnegan? Who has the blog?"

12:59 P.M. Exterior apartment.

Frank and Marianne's car is loaded and they are getting ready to get in the car and get the fuck out.

Me: "Thanks for coming."

Frank: "Thanks for having us."

Jake: "Anytime."

Marianne: "Now, remember, be sure to call us right when you go into labor so I can be there when he's born!"

Me: "Thanks, but like I said, it's just going to be Jake and me."

Marianne: "Oh. Is your mom going to be there?"

Me: "I'm not sure yet. Probably."

Looks of shock and dismay.

Jake: "Talk to you soon!"

We sighed as we waved good-bye to the Grandalskis. Once they were firmly out of sight, Jake turned to me and grabbed my hand. "I have a surprise for you," he said, then disappeared into the bedroom.

"What is it?" I called after him.

"Here," he said proudly as he held out a tiny package wrapped in tissue paper.

I took the three-inch-by-four-inch square from him and gingerly peeled back the paper.

"Perfect!" I exclaimed as I held up the miniature Cubs jersey. "When did you get this?" I asked him, incredulous.

"At the game. When you were in the bathroom. You made it easy since you went like twice each inning." He grinned down at me.

"This is great. Skeletor will be a Cubs fan from birth." I leaned forward and wrapped my arms around his waist.

"Well, then he'd better get used to lots of disappointment," Jake laughed as he patted my back.

"Oh, I'm sure he will be. I'm going to be his mom, remember? Disappointment all over the place."

"Don't say that. You're going to be a great mom. And if not, don't worry. I came out fine and my mother's pretty off her rocker," Jake said.

"That's true," I laughed into his shirt. I looked up at him. "You're probably going to win a Father of the Year award. You know that, right?"

He rolled his eyes. "I'll settle for not screwing up."

"We will. But we'll get each other's backs. We'll cover for each other." I released him and sat on the couch.

"Like in tag-team wrestling?" Jake said, and sat down next to me.

"Sure, if that analogy works for you."

"Great. I want to be Andre the Giant. Who do you want to be?"

"I don't know. That's not the point. I—"

"You have to pick."

"I don't even know any of their names, and frankly, I'm somewhat embarrassed that *you* do," I said.

"Fine. I'll pick for you. You have to be Hillbilly Jim."

"Why am I a hillbilly?"

"Because you had sex in the backseat of a used Ford Taurus."

"With *you*, remember?" I jumped up and put my hands out. "I don't want to be a hillbilly. I want to be someone else."

"No. It's decided. You're Hillbilly Jim and I'm Andre the Giant."

"Damn it. This sucks," I said as I sat back down on the couch and crossed my arms over my chest.

Tuesday, September 18
. . . .

Further building on the tag-team wrestling analogy, Jake and I banded together and started to tackle the task of clearing the crap out of the guest room/future nursery/Butterscotch's current litterbox.

We started by clearing out everything from the bottom of the closet, and came across a pile of what appeared to be very sparkly clothes covered in cat hair. It was several of my long-lost pieces of clothing. I immediately jumped up (which is getting more and more difficult to do these days seeing as how my ass is now growing a baby) and hugged all of my beautiful, formerly missing pieces.

Apparently, Butterscotch has been hoarding the clothes he finds particularly attractive and building a little nest. In college, I used to hide my favorite articles of clothing when I went to class since Julie was notorious for "borrowing" the skirt or shirt or whatever I was planning on wearing myself. Never once did I think I would have to hide my clothes from my cat. But at least he has good taste, especially in lingerie.

Thursday, September 20

. . . .

I gave most of the clothes Butterscotch stole to Sam. As I looked through them, I realized sequined tube tops, low-cut camisoles, and a velvet-and-leather bustier are probably not realistic fashion choices at this point since I don't see myself clubbing anytime soon.

So, Sam reaps the benefits of the life choices I've sown.

I'm embarrassed to say I'm a little depressed. It was like packing up my youth into a garbage bag and handing it over to my sister with all those good times still ahead of her. I mean, it's not like I actually want to go to a club or even bar-hopping, but it's still a little sad to have total confirmation those days are most likely squarely behind me.

As is the case these days, when my personal life takes a dip, my work life seems to dovetail. The invitations for the Flynn wedding arrived this morning and when I opened the box, I discovered "Flynn" was spelled "Flan," as in the Mexican custard dessert. Although flan is quite delicious and I found the misspelling slightly humorous, I sincerely doubted the WASPy Flynns would feel the same way. So, I called the stationer and screamed and ranted until they agreed to have them all reprinted and overnighted by next week.

Mule Face, of course, said, "Didn't you get a proof ahead of time? This kind of stuff always seems to happen to your events. It never happens to mine." Then, "Mmmm. Flan," in a Homer Simpson voice, and proceeded to buy four Snickers bars from the vending machine and wolf them down.

I found this deeply disturbing since there were none left for me.

Friday, September 21

· · · · · · · · · · · · · · · · · · · ·

With the wedding invitations in the process of being reprinted, I sat at my desk this morning and checked the news on my computer, when a window indicating a new e-mail popped up. I clicked away from the Web site and opened the e-mail. It was from Sam, one of those chain forwards with twenty questions you're supposed to answer about yourself and send back. I scrolled through the e-mail with no intention of filling it out, partly due to the fact forwards are Sam's primary method of communication with me. A few weeks ago, I'd e-mailed her to ask her what she was planning on getting our mom for her birthday and she replied with a chain letter forward I was supposed to pass on to ten people or suffer horrible luck for all of eternity. I didn't send it. Because I am a rebel.

I almost deleted the e-mail, but my name caught my eye. It was the answer to the question "What person do you most admire and why?" She answered, "My sister, Clare. She's a cool big sister and I def. want to be like her." A few tears actually pricked in my eyes as I read, "cool big sister" again. I thought, *She loves me. She looks up to me. She wants to hang out together and read magazines and get manicures.*

I immediately picked up the phone and dialed her cell phone since I knew she was off from school. She answered on the fourth ring, right before it went to voicemail.

"Hi, Clare," she said in a singsong voice.

"What's going on?" I said.

"No-thing." Singsong voice again.

"I just saw this forward you sent me."

"Oh," pause, "Leah just sent it to me." I could hear the trill of her instant messenger in the background.

"So, you admire me, huh?"

"What? Oh, yeah. Whatever. I mean, most everyone else put their sisters down, so I figured I'd just do whatever and just changed the name to yours."

"Oh. Well, it was really cool to read it."

"Yeah, I guess. Whatever, Clare. I have to go, I'm talking to my friend."

"OK, talk to you later."

"Yeah, whatever."

Tuesday, September 25
· · · · · · · · · · · · · · · · · · · ·

I spent the weekend moping around, complaining to Jake that Sam and I will never be close, we'll never have a good relationship, we'll never have a sisterly bond, and we'll never understand each other. I used this to justify a massive consumption of double-chocolate frosted brownies. Also, was for the *baby*.

As I shuffled home from work yesterday, down the hallway to our apartment, already dooming myself to another depressive evening, I stopped as I walked past our new neighbor's door. A giant banner plastered there proclaimed, CHAMPAGNE WAYNE IS BACK!

I relayed this to Jake. Immediately, we were curious. Who was Champagne Wayne? An alcoholic? Man just out of prison? Just another addition to our already freaky building?

Today, we actually met Champagne Wayne. Just how I pictured him: spiky hair coming dangerously close to an '80s mullet (excuse me, bi-level), leather pants, open purple silky shirt, and about forty pounds of gold chains. His eyes lit up when he saw us in the hallway.

"Hey there, neighbors!"

We were momentarily stunned, since none of our other neighbors have ever spoken to us.

"Hi," we replied in unison.

"I'm Champagne Wayne, your new neighbor," he said.

"We figured, from your sign," Jake said.

He ran his hands through his spiky almost-mullet and outstretched his arms, smiling. "I had to let everyone know I'm back!"

"Back from what?" I asked.

"From prison."

I looked at Jake with an *I told you so* look.

"The prison of being married to my bitch-ass ex-wife! Oh, sorry," he said, glancing at me. "I got myself a divorce and now Champagne Wayne is *back*! I'm having a party this weekend. You guys should come!"

We looked at him, trying to rein in our looks of *no fucking way*.

"We'll try," Jake said.

We made our escape into our apartment. We barely got the door closed before busting out in laughter.

"Can you believe that guy?" I asked, gasping for breath.

"Love the chains! And the chest hair!" Jake said, his face turning as purple as Champagne Wayne's shirt.

"Like we need another weirdo around here," I said.

"Oh, honey, pot meet kettle," he said, and kissed me.

Wednesday, September 26
· · · · · · · · · · · · · · · · · · · ·

I think I've discovered why Champagne Wayne's bitch-ass ex-wife left him: because he never sleeps!

The man has been throwing parties nonstop since he moved in. At all hours of the night and into dawn we hear the thumping of old-school early '90s rap music, people cheering during drinking games, and women shrieking. I don't mind a neighbor who likes to throw a party every now and then, but I do mind when the party lasts for four straight days. And when I can't attend because I'm pregnant.

Neither he nor any of his attendees presumably have jobs, because the fun doesn't usually end until around four thirty in the morning, or at least that's when they usually pass out or lose the ability to speak.

As I was leaving for work today, I saw a trio of scantily clad women with hair matted to their faces and mascara running down their cheeks trying to sneak out of the building so they wouldn't have to do the

Walk of Shame past people who actually work for a living. (Edited to add: Maybe they do work for a living. As hookers.)

Tomorrow, I have a 7:30 A.M. breakfast meeting with Irene and Rachael. Sorry, Champagne Wayne, the party's over.

12:30 A.M.

OH. MY. GOD. How many times do they need to hear "Baby Got Back"? Jesus, people, it's a fun song but this is the seventh time you've played it in the last two hours.

That's it. I've finally had enough. I have a meeting in seven fucking hours and I haven't slept at all.

12:35 A.M.

I made Jake go over to kick some ass.

I didn't hear him knock, but I did hear the music turn down a few notches and some muffled voices through the wall. Within a few moments, there was a loud cheer and the music came back on full force.

". . . you can do side bends or sit-ups, but please don't lose that butt . . ."

12:45 A.M.

Jake still isn't back.

1:15 A.M.

Oh my God, they've killed him. They've knocked him unconscious, he's lying on the floor and bleeding and they're just stepping over him as they do Jell-O shots. Or maybe they kidnapped him and are using him as bait so I'll come over and they'll have us both. Then they can perform weird religious rituals on us.

Champagne Wayne doesn't seem like the violent/religious freak type, but one never knows.

1:35 A.M.

He. Is. So. Dead.

I lay in bed for a few more minutes before finally deciding to rescue my husband. I made sure I had my cell phone in my hand and pounded on Champagne Wayne's door, which was covered in glitter and streamers. A Very Drunk Man answered the door, swaying a bit. He squinted at me and attempted to focus on my face.

"Es?" he asked, slobbering on my arm.

Before I could even open my mouth, I saw Jake on Champagne Wayne's couch, smoking a cigarette, sporting a cowboy hat, and drinking what appeared to be a Tom Collins. I shoved the Very Drunk Man aside and he stumbled backward, crashed into an end table, and slumped onto the floor. I stomped over to Jake and stood in front of him, arms crossed tightly against my chest. He looked up guiltily.

"Sorry," he said.

I continued to stare at him. By then we'd attracted the attention of the entire party, who were crowded around us, praying something exciting would happen.

"Let's go" is all I said to him.

He sheepishly removed the cowboy hat and tried to hand it to a drunk guy wearing an ABBA T-shirt and black jeans whom I recognized as Champagne Wayne.

"Oh, no, buddy! That is yours! Cowboy Jake! You've got one helluva husband, Mrs. Jake." He put his arm around Jake, who looked nervous.

"Um, that's OK. We really need to go to bed. Would you guys try and keep it down? My wife has an early meeting."

"Sure thing, partner!" He made a gun sign with his thumb and forefinger.

We wordlessly walked out of the apartment, stepping over the Very Drunk Man who was not able to get up and passed out on the floor.

"Clare, I'm sor—," Jake began as soon as the door was closed.

"Don't!" I held up my hand to stop him. "I just want to sleep. We can talk tomorrow."

"No problem, partner," he said.

Thursday, September 27

. . . .

Jake called me at work today to apologize profusely again for being such a dumbass last night and promised to make it up to me by cooking me a special dinner tonight. Since I'm unaware of any dish he is able to make besides scrambled eggs, spaghetti, or hot dogs, it should be an interesting meal. With possibly all three things combined.

His explanation of what happened last night was he didn't want to be rude. Apparently, we don't want to offend our neighbor who throws wild parties until the crack of dawn and has guests throw up in our hallway. I walked into my meeting with black circles under my eyes and puke on my kitten heels but at least Champagne Wayne wasn't offended.

To be honest, though, if I didn't have an early meeting this morning or a baby gestating, I probably would've stayed and had a drink, too, so I can't be too pissed off.

6:00 P.M.

I got home from work and the entire apartment smelled like bacon and sausage. I breathed in deeply and recognized the aroma of a "Jake's special," which is basically scrambled eggs with bacon and tomato and a side of sausage.

"Hey!" Jake said, coming out of the kitchen carrying a glass of wine. "I figured you'd need this. Or you could just throw it at me." He handed me the wine.

"Like I'd waste good wine." I took a sip of it as I followed him back into the kitchen. "Wifey1025 offered to 'take care of the problem' with Champagne Wayne. I told her my husband is the bigger problem. I'd start looking over your shoulder."

"Thanks."

"Did you get that stuff on the list on the fridge while you were at the store?"

"Yup. Look—I even got the paper towels on sale!" He proudly

thrust a roll of paper towels in my face, pointing at the "buy four rolls, get 50¢ off" sticker.

"Great, you got to use the coupon, right?"

He looked at me, confused.

"You took one of those coupons off and used it at the register, right?"

He stared back at me.

"Um, yeah," he said. "That's what I did."

I opened the freezer and four packages of frozen mixed vegetables whacked me on the head, one after another.

Apparently, those were on sale as well.

Friday, September 28

· · · · · · · · · · · · · · · · · · · ·

As I got into the office this morning, late due to a serious crisis involving my hair, a round hair brush, a hair dryer, and permlike waving, my phone was already ringing. I silently prayed it wasn't Christina calling from her conference and picked it up, trying to sound like I'd been there for an hour already.

"This is Clare."

"Hi, Clare."

"Hey, Reese! What's going on?"

"Well, um, I . . ." Her voice cracked.

"Are you OK?"

"Yes, I'm fine," she said, and cleared her throat.

"Did something happen with Matt?"

"Sort of. I told him."

"Told him what?"

"About the baby. I told him that I'm pregnant."

"What happened?"

"Well, he didn't say anything. He just stared at me and left. I told him and he left. Like I told him it was supposed to rain today. He just left."

"Did he say anything?"

"No."

"Reese, tell me exactly what happened."

"I just did."

"Be specific."

"I'll try. I wasn't planning on telling him this morning but I was just sitting there feeding Grace as he was packing up his laptop and I looked at him and he looked so cute and sweet and then I looked at Grace and she looked so happy in her high chair and it just came out. I just said, 'I'm pregnant,' and he stopped and stared at me. So I said it again but he still didn't say anything. He just kept staring at me and he kind of dropped some stuff out of his hand and he said, 'What?' and just looked at me and picked up his stuff. Then he gave me this really weird smile and said, 'Oh. Great' and patted me on my head and left. That was it. He just walked out the door and went to work. And that was it."

"Oh, honey. I'm so sorry, but maybe he was just surprised, you know? Maybe he didn't know what to say. Maybe you should just give him some time and see what he says tonight when he comes home."

"That's exactly what I was thinking. I'm sure he was just surprised."

"Of course he was. Just give him some time. It took you weeks to even tell him about the baby. You've had some time to process all of this, he's had five minutes. Just give him some time, OK?"

"Of course."

"Good. Now calm down and try not to worry. Don't freak out until you know what exactly to freak out about."

"OK."

"Reese? Did you ever ask him about Leslie?"

"No."

"Are you going to?"

"No."

"Are you sure that's the right decision?"

"Yes. Please don't ask me about it again."

"It's going to be OK, I promise. I love you," I said.

"I know. Love you, too."

I hung up the phone, knowing I had no clue if it was going to be all right or not, but I didn't know what else to say. I wanted to grab her bony arms and shake them and bring her out of the fog of denial.

She called me later and told me Matt came home from work early, with a bouquet of lilies, and apologized for his reaction. I could still hear a catch in her voice but at least she sounded happier. Once again, I was at a loss for what to tell her, so I just told her again everything would be OK and I loved her.

She said, "I love you, too. Everything's going to be fine. Let's talk about something else. Like the fabulous shower I'm going to throw you."

"What? Hell no. I don't want a shower."

"Bullshit. You need one."

"No, I really don't want one. Natalie's baby shower was enough for at least ten years."

"I don't want to hear it. It's done."

"But—"

"No. Don't. You guys need stuff for the baby, don't you?"

Fuck. She had me there.

Silence.

"That's what I thought."

Crap.

Tuesday, October 2

. . . .

Dear Mr. Skeletor:

For the love of God, please let me sleep for longer than forty-five minutes at a time. The sooner you learn your mother needs sleep, the better off we'll both be. This would also be a good time to train yourself to sleep until at least ten on the weekends. This whole dragging my sorry butt into work each day on only a few hours of sleep just ain't working. So please, stop karate chopping my bladder all night long.

I'm sorry we haven't decided on a name for you and we're still calling you Mr. Skeletor. But it's much better than some of those names your father suggested. Trust me on this one. I promise we'll think of one soon.

Oh, and I'm sorry I ate at Chipotle the other day. Although, I think you owe me an apology, too. I'm not sure I can look some of my coworkers in the eye ever again. So, let's just call it a truce, OK?

I'd also like to remind you I'm cooking dinner for my parents this Friday night, so please, please, please, don't make me puke or fart or make any other embarrassing bodily function while I'm cooking or while everyone is eating.

Oh, and one last thing—I hear it's pretty cozy in there and I hope you have a nice stay during the next thirteen weeks. However, I'd like to remind you that your lease expires at forty weeks, so keep that in mind when January rolls around, m'kay?

Love,
Mom

Friday, October 5

How is it Friday already? What was I thinking when, in the midst of a manic hormonal episode, I invited my parents over for dinner tonight? Friday seemed so far away when I told my mom to "Be there at seven" in the midst of surfing Rachael Ray recipes online. I found a great recipe for steak with goat cheese crumbles and balsamic vinaigrette, mashed potatoes, and steamed asparagus.

My mom called yesterday to say they were coming at six thirty now since my dad had to see patients at the hospital later that night. Seeing as how I usually don't get home until five thirty, it is going to be a challenge. But I am using a Rachael Ray thirty-minute-meals recipe so I should have everything ready. Maybe I'll even have time left over to do some laundry before they arrive.

5:45 P.M.
Don't panic. Don't flip out. I'm sure the person whose car is totaled is very sorry they smashed into the other car and ruined everybody's lives by turning Ogden Avenue into a parking lot.

6:07 P.M.
I'm finally home. I'll be fine, right? I mean, I'm doing a thirty-minute meal, right? Time to get started.

6:17 P.M.
Why did we have to leave the potato peeler at the Grandalskis last Christmas when we made the sweet potato pie? It's really hard to peel potatoes with a tiny paring knife. It's also really hard to peel potatoes using a tiny paring knife when my finger is sliced open.

6:28 P.M.
Potatoes peeled and boiling on the stove. Asparagus steaming in steamer pot thingy we got as a wedding present. Steaks pan-seared and put in the oven. Pregnant lady sobbing hysterically.

6:35 P.M.
My parents are here. Jake pours glasses of wine as I longingly stare at a beer in the fridge.

6:45 P.M.
The oven is smoking. Holy shit!

6:47 P.M.
A pan was on fire. Parents and Jake came running to the kitchen as I threw the pan, steak and all, into the sink and turned on the faucet. My mom looked at me and said, "You put a nonstick pan under the broiler?" Oops. I'm sorry I almost incinerated everyone with my stupidity. Oh, well, we can still have the potatoes and asparagus.

6:56 P.M.
Fark. Asparagus stalks steamed for too long and are now stuck to each other to form one giant globular green mushy mess.

7:15 P.M.
Why aren't the potatoes done yet? They're still rock-hard and resemble Styrofoam.

7:17 P.M.
Maybe it would've been helpful if I had turned the stove on. That might've helped them cook faster.

7:45 P.M.
Potatoes are done. Seeing as how I set the steaks on fire and steamed the asparagus until it became oatmeal, looks like I'll be serving the potatoes with some oriental-flavored ramen noodles, the only edible thing in our cabinets.

7:54 P.M.
Ramen noodles and mashed potatoes are on the table. Just as we all sat down to eat, my dad's pager went off and he and my mom left so he could admit one of his patients into the hospital. They didn't look too disappointed about missing my gourmet meal. I'm *so* not Rachael Ray.

I was cheered, however, when several readers assured me they, too, had once put a nonstick pan in the oven, causing life-threatening emergency situations.

Wednesday, October 10

· · · · · · · · · · · · · · · · · ·

As if dragging Jake out of Champagne Wayne's Party O' Losers wasn't the horrifying highlight of the month, I just read something that totally tops it.

I read on Baby Chat about something called a Lotus Birth. Apparently it is when a baby's umbilical cord isn't cut at birth, but instead left intact and attached to the placenta until it detaches on its own several days or weeks later. These parents believe it is more natural and comforting to the baby. They carry the placenta around in a shoebox until it detaches.

How freaky is *that*?

What do these parents do when a visitor holds the baby? "Be careful not to touch the soft spot on his head; support his neck and . . . the placenta so it doesn't fall on the floor"?

To all pregnant women: I know pregnancy is emotional and difficult, but let's try to keep it together, OK? Keep those thinking caps firmly in place, ladies.

Friday, October 12

· · · · · · · · · · · · · · · · · ·

After my venting about a Lotus Birth, I felt very high and mighty about being a calm, prepared, normal, and all-knowing pregnant woman who totally has her shit together. Yet today, I was knocked down off my proverbial high horse by that bitch Karma.

As evidence, this is the e-mail I sent Julie tonight:

> I was wondering if you know where I left my dignity?
> Oh, really? You mean it just flew right out of my office when I wasn't looking? Did it say where it was going? Because I'd really like to have it back. No? You're sure?

I thought today would be pretty easy. A Friday—not too much work to do coupled with looking forward to hanging out with Julie all weekend since Jake is in Vegas for some nerdy technology conference.

I was so, so wrong.

One of the first things I did this morning was e-mail Jake to see how his flight went. It went something like this:

> Hey! Just wanted to see how everything is going. Work's boring as usual. I miss you already and can't wait to see you! Call me as soon as you get a chance.
>
> Love you,
>
> Clare.

Then I e-mailed Josh, this dude who's selling us our new, pimped-out yet child-friendly SUV (Sadly not the convertible I wanted. I acquiesced when Jake pointed out the ass-freezing Chicago winter and the possibility of Mr. Skeletor getting launched, car seat and all, from the vehicle if God forbid there should ever be an accident.) to see when we could pick up our new car.

Ten minutes later, Josh called.

Josh: "So, Clare . . . I just got your e-mail."

Me: "Great. What do you think?"

Josh: "Well, it's certainly flattering."

WTF?

Josh: "Clare?"

Me: "I'm here. Josh, I really—"

I stopped suddenly as I caught sight of my e-mail outbox, displaying the subject of the e-mail to Josh as "miss you!" Crap. I sent Jake's e-mail to Josh instead. Outlook must've automatically filled out Josh's e-mail address instead of Jake's when I typed "J" in. I had just told our car salesman I miss him and can't wait to see him.

I awkwardly tried to explain what happened, but I'm pretty sure he still thinks I have the hots for him. What is also completely disgusting is he sounded somewhat into a fling with a pregnant lady. It's too gross to even contemplate. So, I'm just going to forget about it and work on fine-tuning my list of baby items to include in my registry. I asked Julie to go with me since Jake's out of town. I thought about asking Reese, but I didn't want to bother her with my own, very insignificant issues considering her personal crises.

Jake was pretty disappointed I picked this weekend to register. He claimed he wanted to help pick out everything for Skeletor, until I whipped out my PowerPoint presentation about *why* we should register for the expensive stroller (biggest reason: it's awesome) versus a much more economical version, and his eyes started to glaze over. After ten minutes, he said, "OK, go ahead and register this weekend. I trust you. Pick whichever one of those go-kart things you want."

"Go-kart things?"

"Strollers. You know what I mean."

10:00 P.M.

Julie was supposed to come over after work. She was supposed to call me when her train got in so I could pick her up at the station. We were supposed to hang out and order a pizza.

She called me at six and I grabbed my keys.

"You here?" I answered.

"Well, um, no." She sounded a little drunk.

"What?"

"I went out for a few drinks after work, just for *one* drink, ya know. And my coworker insisted on buying everyone a shot of tequila. And then beautiful Hot Dr. Ben showed up—" I heard rustling in the background. "Here, I have one."

"Julie?"

"What? Oh, Clare, sorry, I'm in the bathroom." Calling me from the bathroom definitely meant she was drunk. "Anyway, he keeps buying me drinks. But I swear I'm leaving after the next round. Just one more drink and I'll be on the next train so we can hang out."

Yeah right. I knew even if she did make it to the train station after another drink the odds of her getting on the right train were pretty slim and she could end up in Milwaukee.

"Don't worry about it. It's Hot Dr. Ben, I understand. Just stay in the city tonight and come out tomorrow morning."

"No. I'll be on the next train."

"Seriously, no. Stay tonight and get fabulously drunk and get some ass."

"Really?"

"Hell yes! One of us should be doing something worthwhile."

"OK, I love you and I'll see you tomorrow."

"Use a condom!" I shouted into the phone before hanging up.

It is probably best this way. In the old days, Julie would come out and we'd hang out all night, drinking wine and apple martinis and watching snippets of movies in between pouring more drinks and smoking cigarettes outside. Now, even though we've been friends for years, who wants to hang out with a sober pregnant lady or a mom, even a cool one? I know we'll always be friends, but the thought of us no longer being as close breaks my heart. I'm going to banish those thoughts out of my head and be grateful Julie is giving up her weekend, most of it anyway, to hang out with me in the suburbs and help me register for baby stuff. If that doesn't equate to friendship, I don't know what does.

I'm going to go flip on a movie and settle in with a pint of Ben & Jerry's.

Sunday, October 14

. . . .

Julie finally called from the train station around noon yesterday, dying from a hangover. Seeing as how I'd been up since seven due to the world's fullest bladder, I was ready when she called. When I arrived five minutes later, I spotted her. She had her sunglasses on, Starbucks in hand, and was wearing a maroon sweat suit and gray T-shirt. Her hair was thrown carelessly into a loose knot on top of her head. She still had on shoulder-dusting sparkly earrings from last night. She opened the car door and sat down.

"Hey." She grimaced as she closed the door.

"Wow. Good night?"

"Oh my God. You don't even understand. I am so motherfucking hungover right now but I don't even care because last night I had the Best. Sex. Ever. Seriously." She flipped off her sunglasses and stared at me with her bloodshot eyes. "Seriously," she repeated. "I think I'm still a little drunk. And somewhat chafed. But I don't care. It was so worth it."

"At least someone had a good night last night. I spent my evening sitting on my fat ass, eating gummi bears."

"God, I'm so sorry I bailed on you last night." She leaned back and closed her eyes and slowly opened them. "I really wo— PULL OVER!" She sat straight up.

"What?" I asked, nearly driving off the road.

"Dunkin' Donuts! Can we stop there? I'd sell my soul for a breakfast croissant right now."

After we stopped at Dunkin' Donuts, I finally got Julie up the stairs to my place, her wincing all the way. She flopped down at the kitchen island and practically inhaled her sandwich, peppering the air with details about last night's sexual escapade.

"God, I can't wait to see him again. He's so perfect—totally hot, great body, athletic but not one of those meathead guys who works out all the time, white teeth but not plastic soap-opera-star white, amazing skills but not porn star–ish. I swear, he's . . ." She trailed off.

"He's what?" I asked. I followed her gaze to the refrigerator, where last week I'd hung up a picture of Grace. I stayed quiet and waited for her response. I saw a look of sadness cross her face as her eyes softened but it passed quickly and she rolled her eyes and shook her head.

"Anyway, it was amazing."

I wanted to bring up the Reese subject, but I knew better and just smiled.

"So, are you ready to pick out some baby shit?" I asked her.

She crumpled up her sandwich wrapper, jumped off the kitchen stool, and clapped her hands together. "Hell yeah, I am. Bring it on!"

We arrived at the mouth of hell, a.k.a. Baby World, an hour later since we mutually deemed it necessary to arm ourselves with Icees. Julie and I paused and glanced at each other before we walked in. Immediately, we were assaulted in each of our sensory organs with all things baby—a vomitous mass of pink and blue clothing, sounds of screaming children, and the smells of overripe diapers.

"Fuck this," Julie said, and tried to turn around and bolt but I grabbed her jean jacket collar and hissed into her ear.

"Leave me here alone and I'll slit your throat."

Before she could respond, a perky salesgirl appeared.

"Hi! I'm Kayla! Can I help you two with anything today?"

We pasted smiles on our faces. "Sure, Kayla. I'm here to register today."

Kayla clapped her hands together. "CONGRATULATIONS! Oh my goodness! What a *miracle*! How overjoyed you must be!"

Julie shot me a look that clearly said, *this bitch is crazy.*

"Yeah, um, thanks. So, can I have one of those gun zapper things?"

"Well, dear, we just need to get you all started. Follow me." We walked past a somewhat frightening display of what were called Exersaucers but looked like spaceships for children. "OK. So. Will the father be joining you today?" She smiled at me and I wondered how many uppers she took before her shift.

"No."

"No?" She frowned.

"No." I realized she thought I was some unwed crack whore. Judgmental bitch. "No, there is no father. Good thing the baby will have two mommies!" I elbowed Julie hard and she woke up and jerked.

"What?"

"Honey, I was just saying how lucky our boy is to have two mommies."

Julie didn't miss a beat. "Yep, honey!" She grabbed my hand while Kayla tried to cover her disgust.

"OK, well, who should we put as the coregistrant?"

Julie smiled and stuck out her hand. "Hi, I'm Jake."

After a few more comments from Julie about frozen sperm and turkey basters, Kayla released us on our own recognizance to go forth and register. Julie immediately ran over to the aisle containing breast pumps. She grabbed one off the shelf and put one of the cups on her boob. "Oh, baby, yeah. Right there, harder!" she yelled as though in the throes of an orgasm while a woman next to her gave her a dirty look. "Oh my God—look at this! Nipple cream! Is that for sex or something?" she shrieked in the loudest possible voice. She noticed the woman giving her looks of death. "What? Relax."

Not wanting to have to break up a fistfight in Baby World, I grabbed Julie's sleeve and dragged her over to the high chairs.

"OK. This is the one that is supposed to be good according to the Internet. What do you think?" I said, and pointed to one of the high chairs.

"Looks good to me," Julie said.

We turned the corner and walked down the bouncy seat aisle.

"What the hell are these?" she asked.

"Um, they're seats that bounce. They're supposed to keep the baby quiet."

"Look, it vibrates!" Julie said, as she switched the display model on. "It's like a massage chair for babies!"

"That's a must-have," I said, zapping the bar code with my registry scanner gun. "Skeletor will need a good, relaxing massage after he realizes he has idiots for parents."

So we moved around, zapping things that looked good and rolling our eyes at things we deemed psychotically unnecessary. Like baby wipe warmers.

"Who would buy this crap? Some people will buy anything," I said.

"Twenty-five-piece knife set."

"What?"

"You heard me. Ron Popeil. Last year. Twenty-five-piece knife set," Julie said.

I thought she forgot about that. I have a soft spot for (read: uncontrollable need to buy) anything Ron Popeil is hawking on an infomercial. The rotisserie oven, the food dehydrator, name it and I'll not only buy it but obsessively watch the infomercial every time it's on. I ordered the Ron Popeil Automatic Pasta Maker five years ago, used it once, and quickly realized I had no desire to make my own pasta and shoved it in a drawer. But by God, every time that infomercial comes on, I say, "Jake, look at how cool it is!" Then he says, "We have the fucking thing, remember?"

Last year I came home drunk and ordered the Ron Popeil twenty-five-piece knife set at three in the morning. I didn't even remember doing it until the box showed up and I pretended it was a surprise gift for Jake.

So, I guess I have no right to question why people buy useless crap, because if there was an infomercial hawking the wipes warmer, holy hot damn, I'd order four of 'em.

We finally finished registering two hours later after taking the strategy to register for everything and I could tweak it later online. I think Julie registered for some gum at the checkout counter.

We went back to my place and collapsed on the couch.

"God, I can't believe all of the crap you need for a small baby," I said.

"Well, hopefully you'll get most of it at your shower."

"Uh-huh," I murmured, suddenly uncomfortable.

"Don't worry, I'm going to throw you the best fucking shower ever. And I'll kick the ass of anyone who doesn't give you an expensive gift."

I thought, *Oh, man. How am I going to tell her Reese is throwing me one, too?* I was too drained to mention it.

"Great. Sounds like a plan. What do you want for dinner?" I asked, changing the subject.

"Sushi."

"Sounds good to me. It's a date."

We spent the rest of the night munching on goma ae, shrimp tempura rolls, and spring rolls while watching *Wedding Crashers*. At one point, I started to doze off but was jolted awake as Julie rehashed her sexual experiences from last night in graphic detail. There's nothing like the words "rock-hard cock" to bring me back to earth. After the movie, we turned out the lights and talked more in the dark before we fell asleep, like we used to in college.

All in all, it was a pretty great night, one of the best we've spent together. And not even a drop of vodka was involved.

Monday, October 15

. . . .

Although my weekend with Julie was something I sorely needed, I woke up this morning with a spiny ball of dread I couldn't wash away, no matter how many Diet Cokes I chugged. Ever since Saturday night, when Julie mentioned throwing me a shower, the level of my stomach acid increased tri-fold. The thing is, there's no way they can each throw me a shower. For starters, I don't have enough people to invite to split the guest list in half. I thought about it all weekend, which basically meant I shrieked, "WHAT AM I GOING TO DO?" the second Jake walked in the door from his trip. He's the one that came up with the Final Solution: they have to do the shower together.

Just the thought makes me want to crawl into the closet, give birth in there, and emerge six months later. I'm envisioning bloody chunks of hair flying everywhere, biting, chairs being used as weapons à la *Jerry Springer*, the works. With me in the middle throwing holy water on everyone. Pretty much my worst nightmare. But I've thought about it and they're just going to have to deal because I love them both and they're my two best friends and we're all adults and their feud is childish and they should both just shut the fuck up and do it, OK?

Yeah, something like that.

I figured Reese would be the easier one to crack, seeing as how

she's all distracted with her own personal tragedies, so I started with
her. After stalling at my desk and checking my messages for the
thousandth time, I picked up the phone.

"Hello?" she answered.

"Hey! It's me. How's it going?"

"Clare. Hi. Good."

"Really?"

"Well, no, not really, but aren't you supposed to answer that question with a positive?"

"I guess. Have you asked Matt about the e-mails yet?"

Silence.

"Why not?" I asked, exasperated.

"Because I'm scared of what he'll say," she finally said in a wavering voice.

"I know, hon. But you have to ask him," I said gently.

"I know. I'll figure it out. Anyway, what's going on with you?"
she asked, her voice perking up.

"Well! I went and registered this weekend."

"Ooohhh! That's great. I'll have to look it up online later. I'm
sure you picked out some wonderful things. Speaking of which, you
need to pick a date for your shower."

"Yeah, well, that's what I wanted to talk to you about." I could
feel my face start to get hot and a bead of sweat dripped down my
cleavage just as Skeletor gave me a swift kick. "Just hear me out and
don't say anything until I'm done, OK?"

"What's wrong?"

"I know you and Julie don't exactly care for each other these days
but I've stayed out of it, even though it's been really hard on me." I
stopped and gulped some water down, camel-style. "But I love both of
you. And you both want to throw me a shower, which I am so, so
grateful for. But I can't have two separate ones, it's not fair to my other
friends or family. So, I'd like you guys to work together on this."

Silence.

"I'm done now," I said.

"You know I love you," she started out slowly, "but Clare, she's such a bitch to me. She thinks I'm some 1950s housewife because I stay home with my child."

She was right; I couldn't refute it.

"I know. I'm sorry that you guys have your problems, but you do have something in common—*me*! We all used to be friends until you two declared war on each other for some reason and it has sucked for me ever since. Please do this for me, Reese. It would mean so much." There was another long pause and I threw in another "please" for good measure. I heard a huge sigh of exasperation.

"Do you know what she said to me at your bachelorette party? She told me to go home and masturbate to *Desperate Housewives* since my husband clearly wasn't fucking me."

"I'm so sorry she said that. You know how she is. She's always been a little jealous of everything you had. I really do think she misses you."

"Right."

"Please, Reese. For me?"

"*Fine*. I'll do it."

"Oh, God, thank you so much!"

"But this doesn't mean I'm going to keep my mouth shut if she says anything to me. I just hope she can refrain from saying the F word at your shower."

"Fine. Just please don't kill each other. I don't have time to visit you both in jail on a regular basis."

"Funny. Hey, what are you guys doing on Saturday night?"

"Blockbuster and takeout, why?"

"Let's get together, the four of us. We haven't been out in ages."

"Sure. Um, oh, wait. I forgot. I think Jake has some work thing we need to go to," I lied.

"Oh, really? That's too bad. I wanted all of us to meet up. Maybe another time."

"Yeah, definitely."

I hung up with Reese and immediately began fanning myself

with one of the Flynn-Shepard wedding invitations. I felt horrible I
lied to her but I don't want to fake my way through a dinner with
Matt when I really want to cut his balls off and feed them to Butterscotch.

I put my guilt aside and concentrated on my next task: calling
Julie, who I knew would be less easily convinced.

"Hey!" she answered.

"Hey," I said.

"Oh my God, Clare, I was just going to call you. Hot Dr. Ben just
e-mailed me."

"You're kidding!"

"No. I'll read it to you: 'Julie, I had a great time on Friday night.
Let's get together again soon. Are you off on Saturday? If so—dinner
and drinks? Ben.' What do you think it means?"

"Probably that he wants to have dinner and drinks on Saturday."

"You know what I mean! Do you think it means he just thinks
I'm easy so he wants to hook up again, or something more?"

"Well," I said thoughtfully while I chewed on my pen, "I think it
means something more because he asked you out for dinner and drinks,
not just drinks. Plus, he didn't say anything like, 'Let's do it again soon,'
you know?"

"Yeah. That's what I think, too. What am I going to wear? I need
to cut out early and go shopping. I need an outfit that says classy but
not stuffy. And I definitely shouldn't dress sexy, well, since I already
gave away the farm on that one."

"Yep. Hey, I wanted to ask you something."

"Yes?"

"Well, it's more like I wanted to tell you something." And . . .
cue the sweating. "Reese mentioned she'd like to throw me a shower,
too, so—"

"That bitch! I knew she would—," Julie exploded.

"Shut up a minute. Listen to me. I'm sick of this shit between you
two. I've put up with it for years now and I've had it. I love you both
but this ends now. You both want to throw me a shower and that

can't happen for a number of reasons. So, I'm asking if you'll do one together."

"Are you kidding?" Her voice was black and flat.

"No. I'm not."

"So, you want me to call up Mrs. June Fucking Cleaver and pretend to be all nicey-nice and ask her about, oh, I don't know, what it feels like to have accomplished ironing your husband's pants that day? You can't be serious. You're insane."

"Julie, cut the shit. We all used to be friends. You two used to be friends. I am *still* her friend. Do this for me."

"Should I call her up and tell her about how Matt tried to kiss me?"

"What?"

"Oh, yeah? I didn't tell you that? He tried to make out with me when he was wasted."

"No. You didn't tell me. When was this?"

"About three weeks ago. I saw him at Le Passage. He was tanked with some work buddies. I went up and said hello and he told me about how fucking boring his life is and how he just wants to party. And then he leaned in and tried to kiss me."

"You're joking. What did you do?"

"Nothing. I told him to go fuck himself and to go home to his wife and kid."

"You did?"

"Yeah. Then I poured my drink over the crotch of his pants and left."

"Oh my God, I can't believe this."

"Are you serious? Matt's always been a slimeball. I don't know why you keep giving him the benefit of the doubt. Or why Reese married him."

"You know how Reese is. She was looking for some stability. She thought Matt could give that to her."

"A lot of good it did her. I'm not going to feel sorry for her, though, that bitch is sitting up there in her million-dollar mansion and passing judgment on the rest of us fuckers."

"No, she's not. She's just—"

"Don't even start. Another word and there is no way in hell I'm doing this baby shower."

"So you'll do it?"

"God, I hate you."

"I know."

"Fine, I'll do it. But you so owe me."

"Anything you want."

"Yeah, well," her voice changed, "then you can lend me your black pearl necklace for Saturday."

"As long as you don't use it as some kind of sex toy."

"Forget it then," she said, and laughed.

"Whatever, so you'll do it?"

"Yeah, I'll do it. Only because I love you. Not because I hate her any less."

"Fair enough."

I hung up the phone and collapsed back in my chair. I debated calling Reese and telling her what Julie said about Matt, but I knew the message would get lost in translation. Reese is never going to face reality until she really wants to. That was a lesson I learned years ago. Regardless, this is going to be one interesting baby shower.

Friday, October 19
. . . .

Shower dread aside, I had to go over to the hospital today for the infamous one-hour glucose test. Apparently it tests for diabetes during pregnancy. When I got to the hospital lab, a nurse handed me a cup filled with orange liquid tasting like Orange Crush. I actually enjoyed it until the nurse checked her watch and instructed me to "Chug it!" since I was supposed to drink it all within five minutes or something. Being the former flip cup champion, I chugged that baby down in record time.

While waiting out the hour, I sat in a very uncomfortable chair until they could draw my blood and release me into the general population. I had prepared by bringing several *People* magazines, but read very little since I was totally distracted listening to another pregnant woman describe in detail how her diarrhea was so bad she was afraid of pooping her baby out and could the nurses please check to make sure the baby is OK? Then, her husband and three-year-old came to wait with her. The three-year-old threw herself down on the ground and screamed while the parents ignored her and read *Parenting* magazine. I found it very ironic since the cover story detailed how to discipline toddlers.

Finally, an hour was up and the nurse drew my blood. I winced a little when the needle went in, as I always do. I would much rather they take blood from any other body part, eyeballs included, than my inner arm. It always skeeves me out for some reason. But, being the compassionate caregiver, the nurse chastised me and said, "Honey, you think this is bad, just wait until your epidural wears off while they're stitching up your episiotomy cut. Now quit moving around."

We, as a human race, need to invent a better way for babies to be born. Like a way not involving vaginas or stitches or needles. I must ask Dr. Clarke about this at my appointment on Tuesday.

Tuesday, October 23

. . . .

Dr. Clarke said two very scary words at my appointment today: "third" and "trimester."

It's true, I'm really in it. Which means Mr. Skeletor is just about two-thirds of the way done, and I have close to zero things done for his arrival. Like, oh, small things—pick out a name, get the nursery ready, cover up sharp pointy things in my apartment, move the cases of wine currently occupying where his crib will go, actually buy a crib, etc. Like I said, small things.

So yeah, I know I said he needs to pack his shit up and move out at forty weeks, but I'm willing to extend the lease for a while. We can try it on a month-to-month basis, as long as he respects the management and doesn't throw wild parties or anything.

One of my readers did put it into perspective, though. She said, "Think of it this way—two-thirds of the way done means only one-third longer until you can drink again." That does help because while I'm terrified of actually having a baby who I'll have to protect from choking hazards and poisonous materials, I'd sell my kidneys—*both* of them and probably Jake's, too—to drink a pitcher of margaritas.

Wednesday, October 24
. . . .

To celebrate my third trimester, Mule Face brought in cupcakes for everyone today. (How did she even know? It wasn't like I told her. She must be tracking my pregnancy on her own. Scary.)

Well, she said it was to celebrate the third trimester, but the cupcakes were decorated with little "Here Comes the Bride" designs on them, as if anyone could forget she's getting married next weekend. She has stopped doing any form of work since last week and started cornering innocent coworkers in their offices, the conference room, even the bathroom to blabber on about last-minute details. She talks for so long I start praying my phone will ring so I can get rid of her. Or, at least wonder if I can discreetly grab my cell phone and dial my own office number.

The greatest part about her bringing in the cupcakes today was she sent out a blast e-mail to everyone saying, "Cupcakes in the conference room. First come, first severed." To which Tom, one of the interns, hit Reply All and said: "Severed? I don't think so. I'd like to have a cupcake but I don't feel like getting anything cut off so no thanks."

Mule Face just laughed and thought Tom was flirting with her, but the rest of us all know she makes him want to cut out his eyes with a spoon so he won't have to watch her eating strawberry frosted Pop-Tarts every morning. That's a direct quote.

Friday, October 26
. . . .

I think I have a hangover from all the sugar on Mule Face's cupcakes. In spite of myself, I ate close to five yesterday. I didn't want to eat so many, but the *baby* did. Being a good and indulgent mother, I went ahead and allowed him the treat.

He's been flipping around like crazy today and tapping my cervix periodically. I'll be sitting at my desk and suddenly an electric jolt will run through my body. It's like having a portable internal lightning rod.

I asked him to please chill out so I could make sure the Flynn wedding invitations went out today but he ignored my request and gave me a swift kick to the ribs for good measure.

Disobeying me already? Not a good sign.

After the invitations went out this morning, Irene called and said she and Rachael would be in this afternoon to discuss favor details. I walked to the bathroom to check my appearance before they arrived. I looked awful so I went down to my car and grabbed my makeup case for a few touch-ups.

Christina was in the bathroom. "Hi, Clare. I hear the Flynns are on their way over."

"Yep. They should be here shortly." I placed my makeup bag on the vanity with some hesitation. I pretended to adjust my contact lens for a few moments until Christina snapped her purse closed and raised her eyebrows at me.

"Good luck," she said, then patted me on the shoulder and walked out.

Immediately after she left, I opened my makeup case and reapplied my eye shadow. I hate pulling out my makeup in front of other people. I wish I could be one of those women whose makeup is all one brand, like Laura Mercier or M.A.C., and it's all shiny and new-looking and kept in a pristine case so when someone asks to borrow something, I could say "Sure" with ease and hand them a gorgeous shade of blush. Instead, my bag is filled with a mish-mosh of drugstore brands mixed in with a few expensive brands. I also have eye shadows with the plastic covering popped off, so every now and then I reach into my case and come out with a nail bed full of plum eye shadow.

So it is understandable why I wouldn't feel my most professional if I were standing next to my boss, applying Wet 'n' Wild eye shadow with one of those plastic applicators that comes in the compact.

Someday, maybe someday, I'll be one of Those Women, a woman who only has beautiful silk underwear and thongs in her underwear drawer, instead of half nice and half junky stuff. A woman with no skeletons in her beauty closet. But for now, I'll just have to look like one, since I doubt Rachael Flynn buys any of her makeup at Walgreens.

Monday, October 29

. . . .

Julie texted me this message this morning:

> Black pearl necklace worked. Ben was a dream and even better the second time around. So hot. So good. Just wanted to give you an update.
>
> J.
>
> P.S. Talked to Reese. Do you know if she has scheduled her sorely needed stick-removal-from-ass surgery yet? Let me know. I'd like to send flowers.

Well, at least they spoke.

Wednesday, October 31

Along with the lightning rod cervix kicks, Mr. Skeletor has also blessed me with an overwhelming waterfall of emotion.

Suddenly and out of the blue.

On today of all days. On Halloween. The holiday for strange happenings, hauntings, and ghoulish occurrences. In the true spirit of Halloween, I thought of something truly bizarre today: Jake and I will have a child to take trick-or-treating next year. Of course, he'll still be a wee one and we'll probably have to carry him from house to house and then we'll steal his candy, but still. A kid. To dress into a costume and take out into the world.

I saw all the little trick-or-treaters as I drove home from work today. Dusk was just beginning to settle and as I saw the groups of pumpkins, witches, and zombies trekking up and down the block, I felt a pang. A pang because someday, Skeletor is going to be one of those little kids. I got a little teary-eyed and switched on the radio, hoping I'd hear some Eminem or something so I could focus on the profanity-filled lyrics rather than my overflowing emotions.

Eminem was not on the radio.

The Beatles were, however. "In My Life," to be exact.

Well, that did it. The lyrics about loving someone more than everything that had come before just about killed me. The tears overflowed and rained on my steering wheel. I tried to brush them away quickly, lest they impair my vision and I run down some kid dressed as Harry Potter.

I was still crying as I walked into our apartment. Jake was already home.

"What's wrong?" He jumped up and bounded over to me as soon as he saw my tear-streaked face.

"Song . . . Beatles . . . Halloween . . . witches . . . Eminem . . . love you more . . . things that went before . . . . *so moving*!" I blubbered.

"Er, yes." He patted me on the shoulder.

"You don't understand! I'm talking about our child here! Don't you care?" I shouted at him, hands on my hips.

He stared at me, not sure how to proceed. "Of course I care. I love the baby," he finally said.

"Good. Me too," I hiccupped out. "I love the Beatles, too."

"Er, yes," he said again, totally bewildered.

Saturday, November 3
· · · · · · · · · · · · · · · · · · · ·

I woke up this morning feeling awful. At first I thought it was still the lingering effects of a Halloween candy hangover, but I quickly realized my discomfort had more to do with my sudden enormity than too many mini Three Musketeers. After the requisite bathroom trip this morning, I lay back down in bed and wondered if I'd be allowed to join *Celebrity Fat Camp* after I had the baby.

It appears as though, literally overnight, I've become huge. Even Jake muttered an exclamation under his breath when he saw me this morning.

The worst part about turning into a tank overnight is I can no longer squeeze myself into a good portion of my clothes, including the cocktail dress I planned on wearing to Mule Face's wedding tonight. It literally came down to a choice between buying a new dress this afternoon or throwing a bed sheet over myself in a nouveau toga-style dress. Since there was no way I wanted to spend money on a dress for Mule Face's wedding, option A was out. Since we didn't have any clean sheets, option B was out. So, in conclusion, as much as it seriously disappoints me, we aren't going to the wedding.

I am so depressed. I was so looking forward to laughing at the iPod hooked up to speakers operating as the DJ, the hideous bridesmaid dresses, and the fried chicken buffet. Everyone at work on Monday is going to be recapping the wedding and I'm going to be clueless. Maybe it's just as well. Watching Mule Face and Big D do their choreographed dance to Aladdin's "A Whole New World" might drive me to drink.

So, Jake and I are going to have dinner and get some Cold Stone Creamery, Skeletor's favorite treat now. He'd better knock it off soon though, I don't want to have to work off three gallons of cake batter ice cream after he's born. I've already gained thirty pounds, and twenty-nine of that had better be baby.

Oh, and speaking of Skeletor, Jake suggested another name last night: Corbin. I asked him if he was on drugs, which he took as a no.

Monday, November 5
. . . .

I bounded out of bed this morning, eager to arrive at work and hear the reviews of Mule Face's wedding from my coworkers. As I left my apartment, I saw Champagne Wayne in the hallway. It was about eight thirty and he looked like he was just getting home, dressed in a purple suit reeking of cigarettes and carrying a glass with brown liquid in it.

"Heya!" he slurred.

"Hi, Wayne," I said, and tried to walk past him.

"Hey! Wait! You looksh good!" He patted my stomach.

It's nice to know I've still got it.

I was only at my desk for ten minutes before my phone rang. I let it go to voice mail and listened to the message. Just as I thought, it was Reese.

"Clare, sorry to bother you with this, but I have to get your opinion about something for the shower. Julie wants it in a bar, which I think is totally inappropriate for a baby shower. I was thinking we could have it at the Four Seasons and do an afternoon tea. Well, call me and let me know what you think."

Just another daily phone call asking me to take a side. I ignored all of the phone calls, e-mails, and text messages and just told them to work it out; I didn't care. Because I don't. I truly don't care where it is, who is invited, or what color the tablecloths are. All I care about is that we all get through it so I can have this baby already.

Wednesday, November 7

. . . .

With a few short weeks until the deadline, not even half of the Flynn-Shepard RSVPs are in yet. Irene assured me their guests are always very prompt in responding to invitations but I'm thinking she's never the one managing the process. It's probably her assistant or some poor event planner. I'm praying a crapload more come in before next week because I do not want to call all of the Flynns' equally rich and snotty friends.

I was just about to pick up the phone and make my daily phone call to Irene when Julie called.

"So, aren't you going to ask me how my date with Ben was?"

"Oh, God, I totally forgot. Sorry, it's been crazy. How was it?"

"Fabulous. Amazing. We went to Tavern on Rush for dinner and then met his friends out at a bar."

"That's great. How were his friends?"

"Most of them were OK, but the girls were bitches and looked me up and down and then ignored me like I was trailer trash."

"Did Ben notice?"

"Of course not. Typical guy."

"So, what exactly is going on between you two?"

"Oh, who knows. We're just having fun. Nothing serious."

"Well, I'd love to meet—"

"Oh! I forgot to tell you!" She cut me off. "Reese wants to give out favors of little engraved—"

"Julie, cut it. You remember the rule."

"Fine. But you're going to laugh so hard when this is all over and I can tell you what's really been going on."

"Sounds good."

"I gotta go. Amanda, our new nurse manager, has taken it upon herself to send out an e-mail chastising everyone on their excessive use of computer paper. I need to go kick some ass."

Thursday, November 8
. . . .

When I got home tonight from work, Jake was sleeping on the couch, face covered by a throw pillow. He claims he's still exhausted from me keeping him awake with my shower worries the other night, but I swear, he's the most well-rested person on the planet.

"Message hsmmmmm," he said.

"What?"

"Message on machine for you," he managed to roll out of his mouth before turning over.

I walked over to the blinking answering machine and pressed Play.

"Hi, Clare, this is Kyle Tiesdale, reporter for *The Daily Tribune*. If you recall, I interviewed you a while back for the piece we did about your blog. We got a great response from the article so we'd like you to give us a call back to discuss a few things. Thanks."

"JAKE!" I screamed across the room.

"WHAT?" He bolted straight up on the couch.

"Did you listen to this message?"

"No, I heard it was for you and stopped it. Who was it?"

"*The Daily Tribune*. They want to talk to me about something."

"About what?"

"I have no idea. They want me to call them."

"So, call them back."

"What do you think it's about?"

"Has to be something good, right?"

"I guess."

"So pick up the phone."

I grabbed the cordless phone and walked into the bedroom and closed the door behind me.

"Kyle Tiesdale," she answered on the first ring.

"Kyle, hi. It's Clare Finnegan."

"Hi, Clare! Good to hear from you so soon."

"Thanks."

"Listen, we're still receiving feedback from the piece we did several months ago about your blog. You have quite a loyal fan base."

"I do. They're great." My heart started to quicken.

"We're interested in having you do some occasional pieces for our Life & Style section. Would that be something you're interested in?"

Um, are you fucking kidding me?

"Wow, yes. Of course I would."

"Great. Why don't you pull together some writing samples and e-mail them over to me so I can show my editor and we'll go from there."

"Sounds great. Thanks so much, Kyle."

I hung up the phone and started screaming. Jake ran into the bedroom, looking more than slightly alarmed. I barely squeaked out the news before he hugged me. I picked up Butterscotch and twirled him around. He responded by growling at me and biting my hand. I didn't mind, though, because I'm going to be a world-famous newspaper columnist!

Only problem is, I have to pull some writing samples out of my ass. But I'll worry about that later. It's much more fun to plot my future as an award-winning columnist.

Friday, November 9

My celebration was short-lived when I realized my baby shower is to-morrow and I'm about to be forced to open gifts in front of everyone and discuss why we haven't picked a name yet.

Hmmm . . . maybe I can write a sample article on the perils of baby showers?

Saturday, November 10

My alarm went off at 9:30 this morning but I was already awake. I went to bed at midnight but visions of pink and blue confetti and old women demanding more cake kept me awake. I spent most of the night throwing myself around the bed and sighing loudly, hoping Jake would wake up and notice. He just snored away, oblivious to my impending doom and mattress gymnastics. So, I spun like a chicken on a rotisserie for hours while he dreamed about the Bears winning the Super Bowl (and probably a world where his very cranky wife is twenty-five pounds lighter).

I elbowed him when the alarm went off and he jerked suddenly out of his deep sleep and mumbled "Mhhrrhrr" and put his pillow over his head.

"Not today, buddy," I said as I grabbed his pillow off his head.

"Five more minutes," he said sleepily, and threw the cover over his head.

"Dream on. This shower is for both of us, so get up."

Still covered by the duvet, he stuck one hand out and grabbed my thigh. "Shower. Both of us. Yes. Good idea," he said.

Our sex drives are still going strong during the pregnancy, so no way I passed that up.

Jake and I arrived at Reese's right at noon for the party. I smoothed my print jersey wrap dress and adjusted my four-inch heels before ringing the doorbell. I had fidgeted the whole way over and still couldn't relax.

Reese appeared at the door, dressed in fitted tweed pants covering a tiny bump and a perfectly pressed silk blouse.

"Hey there!" she said brightly, showing a bit too much of her gums. She hugged both of us and led us inside, her baby blond hair swishing with every step.

Julie was inside, standing in front of the George Bush photo, wearing a suede skirt, knee-high boots, and a very low-cut cashmere wrap top, laughing hysterically.

"Hey, gorgeous," Julie said, wiping her eyes and giving each of us a kiss on the cheek. "Have you seen this shit?" She pointed in the direction of the photo.

We both shrugged, smiled, and rolled our eyes.

She shook her head and handed Jake a baby blue drink. "Have a babytini."

"A what?" Jake said, holding the drink up and examining it.

"A babytini—Hypnotiq, watermelon schnapps, and pineapple juice. You'll either die from the alcohol content or the sugar content," she paused and took a swig, "or both."

Jake took a sip. "Whoa. You might be driving home," he said, and handed me the keys.

I looked at Reese, who shrugged and mouthed "Sorry." I smiled and shrugged. I knew the cocktails were Julie's idea. I'm sure it was one battle Reese chose to give up, considering the shower was at her house and not a sports bar, like Julie had wanted.

"Congratulations to the both of you!" said a male voice behind us. We turned and saw Matt standing there, holding Grace.

My heart skipped a beat and we both awkwardly said, "Thanks," not really meeting his eyes. I wanted to reach across the room and choke Matt with my bra for being a lying, cheating bastard.

"Hi, Matt," Julie said.

Matt looked nervously at her and gave a small wave. We all stood around silently for a minute.

Julie drained her glass and said, "Jake, another one?" He looked relieved and nodded and followed her into the sunroom. I saw Matt blatantly stare at Julie's ass as she walked away. Grace began to fuss and Matt patted her diaper. "Oh. I think she needs to be changed." He gave Reese an expectant look and she stared back at him. "Can you help me?" he sputtered out, waiting for Reese to jump and rescue him.

"You can do it. It's your day today. I have to get ready for the shower," Reese said. They continued to stare at each other and I became acutely aware I was witnessing some kind of weird marital standoff.

The doorbell rang and I practically tripped over myself, running toward it and yelling, "I'll get it!"

It was my mom and Sam.

"Hey, honey," my mom said, and stepped forward and hugged me. I closed my eyes and breathed in the scent of Marilyn Miglin perfume and for a second, the world stopped. There is something about my mother's perfume that makes me feel like I'm five years old again, watching her put on her makeup before going out to dinner.

Then she let go and I was brought back to reality.

"Hey, Sam," I finally said to my sister, as she had yet to acknowledge my presence.

"Oh, hey. What's up," she said flatly. Turning back to her phone, she walked into the kitchen. "Oh, I *know*. She is such a bitch and—"

Julie walked into the foyer and saw my face. She stepped in front of Sam and grabbed the phone. "This is mine until the party ends."

Sam put her hands on her hips but Julie extended a babytini toward her. "Trade?"

Needless to say, she shut up.

Within a half hour, all of the guests had arrived, including evil Gwen, who I acted all fake happy to see while silently praying she'd tuck her skirt into her underwear or something while in the bathroom.

Matt finally left with Grace, making Jake the only male at the party, not that he noticed since he'd already had four babytinis by then.

We did all of the standard baby shower things: ate crustless sandwiches, scarfed cake, and made pointless small talk. Everyone wanted
to know what we are going to name Mr. Skeletor and when I would say
we haven't decided yet, they seemed to think it was an invitation for
suggestions. Sorry, I'm not going to name my kid Billy because Jake's
weird aunt has "always loved the name."

Unfortunately, I was forced to open gifts in front of everyone and
this time it was Julie's turn to give me a sympathetic look, as it was
clearly not her choice. It was fine, though, and we actually got a lot of
good shit. Reese got me a day of pampering at a salon, Julie got me a
bottle of Belvedere vodka (for after the baby's born, she explained)
and gold leaf earrings, and my mom and Sam bought us the Bugaboo
stroller. So our dear child can rest his head in a stroller more expensive
than the combined total of everything I'm wearing. Carrie gave us
adorable clothes; well, mostly adorable except for the I LOVE CAMPING
T-shirt. Marianne and Natalie bought us our high chair and car seat,
having sent their regrets since Ash Leigh was sick and apparently it
takes both of them to care for one small kid. I'm pretty sure Marianne
is just pissed I refused to let them throw their own shower. Sorry,
thanks but no thanks. I get enough torture being kicked in the ribs
all day long without adding Jake's family to the mix.

The gift opening went pretty quickly and painlessly and pretty
soon everyone was gone and it was just Jake and me, Reese, Julie,
and my mom and Sam.

And 50 percent of us were drunk.

My mom left soon after, carting Sam out to go home and sleep it
off. I knew this was my shot.

"Reese. Julie. Come into the kitchen with me." I grabbed Reese's
arm and shook it until she let go of the garbage bag she was using to
clean up and grabbed Julie's babytini with my other.

"Oh, God. Come to Jesus meeting. Come to Clare meeting. Whatever," Julie said as she waved her arms.

"Come into the kitchen," I ordered, and they followed me, rolling
their eyes. "Listen. Guys. I don't expect you two to be best friends

again. But I love you both and it means so much to me that you did this together. And it was a beautiful shower, even more so because you guys both did it. I just wanted to tell you."

Julie rolled her eyes and Reese took a deep breath and stepped forward.

"I love you, too. I'm so glad you liked the shower. You've been such a great friend and it was a little bumpy, but I think we pulled it off."

"You guys did more than pull it off, it was the best shower ever."

I looked at Julie and she suddenly became very interested in Reese's countertop.

"Julie?"

"What?" she said innocently.

"I'm trying to say thank-you to you guys."

"What?"

"I'm trying to thank you guys for the shower."

"You're welcome."

"It wasn't too terrible to work together, was it?"

"Piece of cake," Reese said.

Julie took a long swig of her drink and set it down.

"Julie?"

"Like she said, piece of cake."

Knowing this was as close as they would get to a truce, I didn't push any further. I was in such a good mood I didn't even mind when I found Jake passed out on Matt and Reese's bed, empty martini glass in hand.

Sunday, November 11

. . . .

We lugged everything back from the baby shower and stacked it into the spare bedroom. I poked Jake awake this morning and forced him out of bed. I appointed today The Day We Shall Set Up the Nursery or, more appropriately, The Day When Jake Gets Mad and Says Fuck a Lot While Clare Eats Ice Cream and Cries.

We rented our apartment almost two years ago after moving out of the city. At the time, we were so accustomed to city prices we were shocked, *shocked*, at how much more space we could afford by moving to the 'burbs. We were all, "Oh my God—there are *two* bedrooms! And *two* bathrooms! And closets! There are closets! For clothes! And a kitchen! Yippee!"

We thought we would never fill 1,200 square feet of space with just little old us and our little old belongings, plus one obese cat. We were thrilled we didn't have to sleep next to the cat's litterbox and both of us could be in the kitchen at the same time instead of cooking dinner relay-race style.

So, we moved in.

Our amazement lasted approximately six weeks.

All those closets we thought we'd never fill? Done.

Our joy at having a place for the litterbox? Short-lived. We realized we needed the second bedroom to operate as just that occasionally, as opposed to our cat's twenty-four-hour toilet.

The kitchen we vowed to use daily to make gourmet meals because *dude*, we have a garbage disposal? Yeah, pizza is still easier.

After a short while, the walls of our new spacious place began to close in on us. But we put off moving because it was something we could do after the wedding. And then we figured we'd live here just a bit longer and then buy a place. Besides, moving meant Scary Mortgage.

So now, since we are very, very organized, we have one extra bedroom housing our junk mail, the cat's shitbox, Jake's clothes, and old power strips, cords, and extension cords knotted together in ropelike fashion. Plus a bunch of old boxes containing things like fifty empty CD cases, receipts from 1999, and beer bottle caps.

I started the process by grabbing a big trash bag and throwing out every piece of paper I saw. This worked fine until Jake came in and started going through the bags and taking out stuff he "needs."

I have discovered my husband is secretly the male equivalent of the crazy cat lady who hoards her money under her mattress because she doesn't trust the government. We threw out bags upon bags of old credit card receipts, years-old bank statements, every single credit card offer Jake ever got in the mail, and I'm pretty sure every piece of paper he's come into contact with since birth. Apparently, every time he got a piece of mail he didn't want to throw out, he shoved it into the spare dresser in the guest room. He claims he didn't want to throw any of it out due to the possibility of identity theft, to which I quickly pointed out no one is desperate enough to want to steal either of our identities. He acquiesced and agreed to pitch everything but every time I tried to throw something out he would grab it and say, "Wait! I think I need this!" Again, my comparison to the crazy cat lady: "But he's my favorite cat! You can't give Fluffy to the pound, Mr. Officer. He's all I've got left!"

Then began the always fun-filled task of putting together furniture. Well, Jake put it together while I hovered over his shoulder, asking him each time if he could tighten the screws one more time. I'm pretty sure he wanted to stick the screwdriver in my eye, but I had visions of our crib collapsing on top of Skeletor and trapping him. Which immediately evoked visions of the scene in *Happy Gilmore* when the window air conditioner falls out of the window onto the elderly woman, so I started laughing hysterically.

I'm going to hell for comparing a life-threatening baby situation to an Adam Sandler movie.

Jake finally got all of the furniture assembled and in place while sweating profusely. It looks amazing, like a room a real-life baby would sleep in. Except for on top of the dresser, within reach of Skeletor's little hands, is a varied assortment of what I would classify as Not Child Appropriate due to the fact each can be at least one of the following: (a) swallowed, thereby killing child; (b) used as a weapon, thereby killing parents; or (c) porn. Such as: Jake's golf clubs, speaker wires knotted together, an old cable box, a screwdriver, and a fiftieth-anniversary issue of *Playboy*. I'm thinking all that's missing is a makeshift meth lab and a loaded handgun.

1:00 A.M.

We can also add cat urine to the list since Butterscotch is upset we moved his litterbox and continues to piss in the spot where it used to be: right under the crib. I think the cat urine smell will be perfect to mask the smell of cooking methamphetamine.

Monday, November 12

. . . .

Mule Face got back from her honeymoon today. She strolled in pretending to be exhausted and spent most of the day making exasperated noises and claiming, "I'm *so* tired." She passed around this big packet of souvenirs she got from Gatlinburg, including pictures of Big D sitting in a hot tub shaped like a champagne glass. Plus he has abnormally large nipples.

She even e-mailed everyone the link to a Web site with her wedding pictures. It amazes me she believes anyone cares that much. When I got married, I never assumed people wanted to see my pictures because hello? Boring. It's like the baby picture thing. Seeing fifty pictures of little Joey on your front lawn is so not interesting. I must remember this over the next few years.

Wednesday, November 14

. . . .

Who cares I've spent the last two days listening to Mule Face's honeymoon stories? Or Skeletor loves to perform a rendition of Michael Flatley's *Lord of the Dance* on my cervix all day long. It doesn't matter because the world is a beautiful, amazing place filled with good-hearted and loving people.

Several of my readers chipped in and bought me a bunch of items off my registry, including our oh-so-expensive but oh-so-beautiful bedding set and a cashmere blanket. They called it my "virtual shower." I immediately posted a slightly blubbery entry thanking everyone, complete with pictures of Butterscotch looking disgusted when I wouldn't allow him to lounge on Skeletor's new blanket.

Friday, November 16

. . . .

Jake remarked today that I'm in the "home stretch." I rolled my eyes at him and declared him to be crazy. Because, obviously, I have tons more time left, right?

Uh, no.

He pulled out the calendar and counted down the number of weeks for me until I started to have a mild panic attack. I pulled out my pregnancy books, hoping to find a chapter on "Third Trimester Psychosis," but all I read was a bunch of congratulations on the baby being viable outside the womb were it to be born now. And while that's great news, I guess, it made things worse.

Most people say they're terrified during the first trimester something will go wrong; they'll miscarry and lose the baby. Of course, we had our moment in the ER when we thought we lost the baby, but the first trimester was mostly about trying to come to terms with having a child. While we were scared, the fear was nowhere near as crippling as it is now.

The real fears have started for me now that I'm in the last leg. I know if he was born now, he'd have to stay in the neonatal intensive care unit for weeks and probably would have serious disabilities to overcome. For some reason, that thought is a jillion times more frightening to me than miscarrying when I was six or eight weeks. Because he's a real person now.

I don't even know what I'm talking about. But I know I can't talk to Jake about it and I certainly can't blog about it; jen2485 would just twist my words and imply I'd rather have no baby than one with disabilities. There's just no good way to explain to anyone what I feel right now. But don't worry, Mr. Skeletor, I'll do everything, including sew my knees together, to keep you cooking in there as long as possible. I want nothing more for you than to be a big, strong boy who can run, play, and romp around with all the other kids.

Monday, November 19
. . . .

We're still nowhere near agreeing on a name. I'm still offering suggestions but Jake's shooting every name down. Like today, when I watched *Legends of the Fall* and drooled over Brad Pitt's gorgeous long hair and Aidan Quinn's eyes.

I started thinking *hmmm . . . Aidan.*

As Jake left to run an errand, I said, "What about Aidan?"

He stopped and looked at me. "Were you watching *Legends of the Fall* again?"

"Um, yes. Why?"

"Because every time you watch that movie you come up with a freaky new name like Tristan."

"You don't like Tristan?" I called after him.

Tuesday, November 20
. . . .

Today was a horrible day. Awful. I want to crawl under my covers. Or travel to a secret fantasy land with rivers flowing with mint chocolate-chip ice cream and the only men are the nice ones. Not the ones that ruin your best friend's life and cause you to get into a giant fight.

The day started off fine until Reese called to thank me for sending her flowers after the shower. (Only Reese calls people to thank them for a thank-you gift. It's like a never-ending circle of gratitude.)

"They're just beautiful. I can't believe you remembered peonies are my favorite."

"Of course I remembered. They were in your wedding bouquet."

"Good memory," she said.

"Reese, was everything OK after the shower?"

"What do you mean?"

"I mean between you and Matt. Things seemed kinda tense before he left with Grace."

"I have no idea what you're talking about."

"It just seemed like you guys were fighting about something."

"Clare, everything is fine."

"Are you sure?"

"Yes. You're imagining things."

"Well, not really. I know things have been strained for you guys."

"Clare. Everything was fine. Let's drop it."

I took a deep breath. I could drop it for the frillionth time or I could keep pushing her and hope she would come out of the fog.

"I don't want to drop it, Reese. You're obviously hurting. You need to talk about this."

"No, really, I don't."

"Please don't shut down again. I'm here for you. Talk to me."

"Clare. Stop. My marriage isn't your concern."

"Like hell it isn't. *You* are my concern. That includes your marriage. I'm worried about you."

"Don't be. Worry about Julie. She's the one who needs help. I'm perfectly fine." Her voice began to rise, something I've rarely heard. I knew I should stop. But I didn't.

"No, you're not. I've never seen you this miserable." There was silence on the other end.

"I'll help you through this, if you let me. Please, think of Grace."

After a long pause, she said, "Clare, I have to go. I can't discuss this anymore," and hung up the phone.

Monday, November 26

I submitted my articles to *The Daily Tribune* today. I'm pretty sure they blow. Kyle told me to write them in the same style as my blog, but without the excessive use of the F word. Which was much, much harder than anticipated.

Fuck.

Wednesday, December 5

Poor Jake. He's been a surrogate therapist, butler, maid, cheerleader, and emotional rock for me since I turned in my articles. This entire situation is very, very Clare. Not only do I have the stress of being almost ready to give birth to my very first, unexpected child, but I'm stressed about two additional things: finishing the details on the Flynn-Shepard wedding and securing an awesome column in the *Tribune*.

What, worrying about feeding, clothing, birthing, naming, and caring for a newborn baby wasn't enough?

Jake, of course, isn't worried about anything. He spent the evening dozing, watching sports on the couch while I made a list of possible names. "What do you think of George?" I asked him.

He didn't even open his eyes. "George who? Costanza?"

"George Finnegan-Grandalski."

"Oh," he said, "funny."

"What?"

"Oh. You weren't kidding?"

I guess George is out.

Tuesday, December 11

. . . .

What with being convinced our child is going to enter first grade as Mr. Skeletor, my mood did not improve when Dr. Clarke told me today that by the end of the week I'll be considered full term. Full term means the baby can come out if it feels like it and be healthy, but it probably won't. So, full term does not mean I get to be done with this pregnancy stuff anytime soon. Which is good and bad. Bad because if I gain any more weight, I think my body will be able to be used as a flotation device in case of an emergency airplane water landing but good because I'm nowhere near ready to care for a newborn.

Holding a helpless little baby in my arms without an instruction manual scares the shit out of me.

Things I'm also afraid of: giving birth, forgetting I have a child and leaving it somewhere inappropriate like a Victoria's Secret dressing room, forgetting to feed it and letting it starve to death, having an ugly child, having a child who thinks I'm ugly, being an uncool parent, being a parent who won't let her kid watch an R-rated movie, being a cool parent who buys her kid beer, and accidentally killing or maiming it.

The last one is a horrible, although valid fear. I killed my turtle when I was seven because I noticed when I put it in hot water it would move around a lot, which I thought was "dancing." My friend came over and I wanted to show her my pet's trick, so I put it in the hot water and boy, did it dance. And then it stopped. *Forever.* It wasn't dancing. Boiling alive does not equal dancing.

My panic was not assuaged when I turned on the news tonight and the first story was about a newborn baby that had been kidnapped while the mom was shopping in the mall. Immediately, I began worrying about Skeletor being snatched away by some mentally ill person. By the time Jake got home from dinner with a client, I was lying on the couch, my face buried in a tissue while sobs wracked my body.

"What's wrong? Are you in labor?" Jake said. He threw down his laptop case on the hardwood floor and a loud *crack* echoed throughout the room as he rushed to my side.

"What was that?" I said, and sat up halfway.

"Forget it. What's the matter? Is something wrong with the baby?" He grabbed my hand and I could feel his palm beginning to sweat.

"Seriously. I think you just broke your computer," I said as I struggled to pull myself up into an upright position.

"Fuck it, Clare. What's going on?"

"Oh, uh . . ." Suddenly, I felt very silly. "It's just . . . this story . . . um . . . kidnapped baby . . . so sad." I stared at the crumpled tissue in my hand.

Silence.

"There's nothing wrong with the baby?"

I shook my head.

"And you're OK?"

I nodded, still looking down.

"Well, that's good." He sat down next to me on the couch. "But my laptop's pretty much screwed."

"Sorry. But who cares about a laptop when your child is kidnapped?"

"He isn't kidnapped, remember?" Jake pointed to my beach-ball-sized stomach.

"You're missing the point. He could be. There are lots of sick, demented people in this world. People who we can't protect him from. I mean, I couldn't even protect my turtle. From *myself*." I threw my hands up in the air as though I'd lost all hope. I stared at Jake and waited for him to throw himself against the couch in distress and agony, but he simply stared at me. So, I pulled out the most clichéd pregnancy line I could think of: "YOU DON'T EVEN CARE, DO YOU?"

He tried to explain that yes, he would care if Skeletor got kidnapped, but that he isn't going to worry about it because it isn't likely, and we are going to be great parents blah, blah, blah. I gave up and waddled to the kitchen to eat a Popsicle. Jake was almost to the bedroom when I let out the Fat Pregnancy Scream Heard 'Round the World.

He'd eaten all the Popsicles.

He doesn't care if I kill the baby or if the baby gets kidnapped, and he certainly doesn't care about his chubby pregnant wife.

Wednesday, December 12
. . . .

Thankfully, the pregnancy psychosis ended when I woke up this morning and I apologized to Jake and took back everything I said last night. Well, at least this one: "You ate those Popsicles on purpose because you hate me. You think I'm fat and ugly. You know what? I hope someone kidnaps you."

Although I don't want Jake to get kidnapped, I do worry if Jake thinks I'm fat and ugly right now. Every time I look in the mirror, once I get past the World's Largest Belly, my eyes migrate to the lovely dimpled cellulite now colonizing on my thighs and butt. He can't think it's attractive. But having a big stomach is kind of like having giant boobs, I'd imagine, in the sense that there's something else to distract him from any other flaws.

It doesn't help that he's become too freaked out to have sex anymore. He claimed it would be too weird. Actually what he said was: "I'd feel like the baby could stick his hand out and grab me or something." That statement alone pretty much killed my sex drive along with his.

At least I can always count on Wifey1025 to boost my self-esteem when I'm feeling like Aaron Spelling's house in human form. She e-mailed me today and asked what plan I've followed for pregnancy fitness since I'm, in her words, "So small and petite and in shape."

I couldn't bring myself to admit my fitness routine is clocking how many doughnuts I can fit into my mouth at once, so I was vague and said "cardio."

Thursday, December 13

. . . .

Reese met Matt our freshman year of college at one of those gigantic fraternity parties where I ran into everyone I knew and proceeded to say really stupid things to classmates and pray they were just as wasted as I was and wouldn't remember a thing I said.

I don't remember how they started talking, but Julie and I found them sucking face on the dance floor. We congratulated her and snapped a few requisite photos before leaving to go back to the dorm and pass out.

Reese came home around nine the next morning, still a little drunk and smiling widely. They dated for the next six years, and two years after graduation, Matt proposed. We all cried and bought cheap champagne and watched *Father of the Bride.*

They got married exactly one year later in a huge beautiful wedding ceremony with four hundred guests. It was Reese's fairy-tale wedding and she was the princess.

Reese quit teaching when she became pregnant with Grace. She loved her job, she loved her students, but happily walked away to raise her daughter. She thought getting married and having a family was enough. The marriage, kids, big house, expensive car, and housekeeper would be enough. Matt cheating on her didn't fit into the equation, so it was ignored.

The only thing scarier than the rumors being true is her world becoming gray.

But she's going to do it.

She's confronting him tonight.

She called an hour ago and asked if I could watch Grace tonight.

12:00 A.M.

I'm exhausted. I feel like crying and vomiting at the same time.

Reese brought Grace over after I got home from work.

"Is there anything I can do? Are you OK?" I asked her after she handed Grace to me and showed me eight million times how to make a bottle.

"No. I think I'm good." She gave me a wavery half smile and I was struck at how young she looked.

"What are you going to say?" I asked, shifting Grace to my hip.

"I don't even know. I think I'm just going to ask him about the e-mails and see what he says. Like I said, I'm sure it's nothing but I have to ask." She shrugged.

"What made you change your mind? I mean, last time we talked, you were so angry and then I got your message today . . ."

She studied the scuff marks on the ceramic tile in our kitchen and slowly raised her eyes to meet mine. "I thought about what you said."

"What did I say?"

"What you said about Grace. About thinking of her."

"Oh. Reese, I'm sorry if I upset—"

She held up her hand and shook her head. "No, it was good. It made me think of my mother. She's been miserable her whole life. She thought she stayed with my father for us, but really, she stayed for her. Because she was too afraid to change her life." She gave me a rueful smile and smoothed her hair back. "I don't want to be like her. I can't be like her. I won't let myself turn into her."

My eyes filled with tears. "I love you," I said.

"I love you, too. Are you sure you're going to be OK with Grace?"

"Piece of cake."

"Even without Jake?"

"Oh, please. He'd just sit on the couch and watch TV anyways. We'll be fine," I said, and gave Grace a little pat on the butt.

"Well, OK. I'll be back soon," she said.

I hugged her tightly, as tightly as I could with my beach-ball stomach and Grace.

The second the door closed, Grace screamed. I tried to feed her, burp her, sing to her, change her, offer her a drink, but nothing worked.

Her face contorted and turned purple. I barely heard the doorbell ring over her screams of fury.

"Hi!" I said brightly as I let Julie in.

She looked confused. "What is all that noise?"

"Oh. That's Grace. I'm watching her for Reese."

"Oh, God. Why? Oh, wait, is she asking Matt if he's doing other women?" she asked as she walked straight into the bedroom. "So, where's the shirt?"

"In the second drawer."

"Great," she said, and started for the dresser.

"But I'm holding it for ransom."

"What?"

I raised my eyebrows and gestured toward the still screaming Grace.

"Fuck no. I don't need to borrow the shirt. Forget it." She tried to walk out the door but I grabbed her arm.

"Please, Julie. I need some help. Jake isn't here and it's impossible for me to take care of her with this giant stomach. Please," I pleaded, "I will so owe you."

She folded her arms.

"I have vodka!"

She softened a little.

"I'll consider letting you make out with Mark." I'm a horrible person for pimping out my brother but I was desperate.

"Deal."

I poured Julie a hefty vodka tonic and we finally got Grace to shut up so we flipped on the television to watch *Grey's Anatomy*. After it was over, I put Grace to bed (it was so weird to see an actual baby in Skeletor's room) and came back to the living room and collapsed on the couch.

"You're huge, you know," Julie finally said.

"Thanks. I know."

Julie flipped to MTV. A rerun of the Video Music Awards was on and Jared Leto's band was playing.

"Gawd. Remember when he used to be hot?" Julie said.

"Oh! I know! He made me want to kill myself, he was so hot. Remember him as Jordan Catalano on *My So-Called Life*?"

"Yes!" she shrieked. "So hot. Now he's all gothic and wears eye makeup." She flung herself back on the couch and sighed. "Ben looks a little like the old, hot Jared Leto."

"Really? Damn, if that's even somewhat true, I'll sleep with him."

"Yep. I'll get a picture tomorrow night. Your pink boob shirt should be a winner."

"Your boobs aren't even going to fit into that shirt."

"That's the point, my dear."

"So what's going on with you two?"

"Nothing serious. Other than we have seriously good sex. And he's seriously hot. But just having fun. The other day, he did this thing . . ."

Before she could finish, I saw Reese's car pull into our apartment complex. Shit. I didn't think she'd be back so early. I planned on kicking Julie out before she got here. Immediately, my stomach began to cramp up and my heart to pound.

"How did it go?" I asked her as I flung the door open before she had a chance to buzz in.

She looked terrible. Her mascara ran down her cheeks and pooled around her chin and her nose was bright red.

"Not so good," she said quietly.

"What happened?" I asked, closing the door behind her.

"I showed him the e-mails and he denied everything. He said nothing was going on between him and Leslie and I was overreacting."

"Isn't that kind of what you expected?"

She dried her eyes on a wadded-up Kleenex as I glanced nervously toward the living room, where Julie was undoubtedly listening.

"He denied it but started saying all of these other things. Stuff about how he didn't do anything with her but that he thought about it. About how getting married so young and having Grace makes him feel like he's middle-aged. How he blames me for pressuring him into being a husband and father before he was ready. He said he feels like he's trapped and I need to lay off and give him space." Her face crumpled.

"Oh, honey. I'm sorry. You know that's not true, don't you?" I asked.

"What's not true?"

"You didn't pressure him into anything. He's lucky to have you as his beautiful wife and father to his kids."

"I don't know. I don't know what to—" Her head snapped up and I followed her gaze.

Julie appeared around the corner. She held a glass of wine in her hand.

"Fuck him," she said, and extended the drink to Reese. Reese looked surprised but took the drink and wordlessly gulped it down in one long pour. She met Julie's eyes and started to tear up again. Julie stepped forward and hugged her tightly.

They both stayed for another hour, until Jake got home from work. That whole time we both just sat silently and listened to Reese talk. Talk about how much she loves Grace, about how she has everything she thought she wanted, about how she doesn't really have anything she wanted. Talk about how she doesn't know what she's going to do now.

I felt like I'd been treading water for hours by the time they both left. I felt like crying for Reese, because even if Matt didn't cheat this time, I doubt their marriage will last. I don't want it to last, but I wish I could make it all better for her. Even just for a moment. She deserves it. She deserves to be happy. Not just regular happy, but pure bliss, floating on a puffy cloud happy.

I emptied the dishwasher and went into the bedroom. Jake was lying on his stomach in bed, checking his e-mail on his laptop. I walked in and placed my cheek against his bare back and listened to the whoosh of his breathing.

Monday, December 17

I've been so distracted with helping Reese emotionally that Christmas is quickly sneaking up on me. I announced to Jake this afternoon that I would be going out Christmas shopping alone, since I wanted some peace and quiet, not to mention exercise. He didn't argue.

Wanna know how it went? Here's the entry I just typed for my blog:

> You know those dumbasses who wait until the week before Christmas to do all of their shopping? You know, those idiots who end up standing in line, cursing under their breath, noses red from the extreme cold outside and hair plastered to their face due to the extreme warmth inside? The people who go to Sharper Image asking about some stupid car gadget thing and get laughed at by the sales clerk because the car thing is like, the most popular gift this year and they sold out weeks ago. The schmucks who, in an oblivious haze, actually set foot inside Toys 'R Us and then quickly leave, running back to the child-free safety of their motor vehicle, throwing holy water on themselves and praying in tongues God will let them forget a place like that exists on this good earth.
>
> Yeah.

Wednesday, December 19

Seriously. How long does it take to read a few articles and then send off an e-mail saying, "We hate your writing. We think it sucks. Actually, we think you as a person suck and should be banned from ever picking up a pencil or composing so much as an e-mail ever again.

We do not like you and we think you are ugly. P.S. We most definitely do not want to offer you a column."

I am *dying* here. They need to just give me the answer, good or bad, so I can have a reason to eat the entire quart of cookie dough ice cream in the freezer.

Thursday, December 20
. . . .

Dear Dr. Clarke:

Re: My Birth Plan

If you are wondering what to give me for Christmas, please read the following suggestions:

I have no wishes of greatness. I do not buy organic shampoo, I don't wear hemp clothing, and my favorite food is Taco Bell; I am not an advocate for anything "natural." Thus, please be aware I have absolutely no qualms about using every legally available drug to numb the pain of childbirth. I am also open to illegal drugs, should the need arise. I also realize this child is supposed to come out of my vagina and would like to discuss some other options, such as: if there is any way you could wave a wand and make the baby magically appear without any of that gross hospital stuff, I would like to sign up. Please let me know what my options are re: magical birth on pink puffy clouds.

Clare Finnegan

P.S. If there is any way you could wave your wand again and make me bikini ready immediately after the birth, that would be awesome. I'd also like a pony.

Saturday, December 22

The Christmas joy continues. I went to Target this morning to pick up a few last-minute gifts and nearly got knocked over by a lady who threw her body in front of me to get the last set of Christmas lights and then said, "Sorry! For my kids. You understand, don't you?" I looked at her, wishing that I could strangle her with aforementioned Christmas lights and poke ornament hooks in her eyes, but then the headline "Crazed Pregnant Woman (Who *Is* Horrible Writer) Kills Shopper in Target and Then Eats Hot Dog" might not portray me in the best light so I just ate the hot dog instead.

I stomped into our apartment after the whole debacle, ready to spew hate and fire during my recollection of my morning, but Jake was sitting on the couch, head in hands. The reason being one of the greatest stories I've ever heard:

Jake and a few of his friends chipped in and bought an old busted van to use for tailgating at Bears games. They all got the bright idea to take it in and have it painted orange and blue with the Bears logo on the side. Jake went this afternoon to go pick the van up from the detailer. When I got home, I looked out the window.

"Why is the van still white?"

"They hmmmmhmsh," he said.

"What?"

"They. Painted. The. Wrong. Van."

Apparently they got his van mixed up with another one belonging to a nice family about to go on a road-trip vacation and just in for an oil change, and Jake got the oil change and some poor family has to drive down to South Carolina in an orange and blue van with a bear head painted on the hood.

It's so awesome.

Sunday, December 23

· · · · · · · · · · · · · · · · · · · ·

In light of my rapidly approaching due date, my mom insisted on having a holiday tea with her "girls" to do some female bonding while I still have time and am not covered in head-to-toe baby vomit. Sam initially balked at the idea, but I think my mom threatened to return a few of her Christmas presents if she didn't come.

I met my mom and Sam at the Peninsula Hotel at noon. I tried to look as put together as possible, which wasn't easy since most of my maternity clothes are now too small. It unfortunately leaves me with the option to either buy new ones or parade around in the same two outfits. I've chosen the second option so this morning I squeezed my huge butt into a pair of black pants and a boxy sweater.

Sam surveyed me up and down when I met them in the lobby and said, "God, I hope maternity clothes get better when I'm pregnant."

I smiled at my mom and then looked at Sam. "They are better. I'm just nine months pregnant so I can't fit into most of them."

"Oh," she said as she narrowed her eyes. "Do you think the baby's really big or something?"

"I hope not, but we'll see," I said as we walked toward the tea room. "But at this point, I don't really care. I just want to be done."

"Ah, a sign of a woman nine months pregnant," my mom said to me.

We approached the hostess stand and were led to our table.

"So, what do they have here?" Sam said as she suspiciously eyed the tea menu.

"Uh, tea," I said to her.

"That's it? But I don't like—*ew*!" She pointed to my stomach, which was visibly moving in waves.

"Oh, yeah. He doesn't like these pants. Whenever I wear them, he gets really pissed and pushes back and rolls around a lot." I shrugged my shoulders and tried to ignore the throngs of well-dressed women now staring at our table.

"That is so effing weird," she muttered.

"That's just what happens when the baby's big and just about ready to be born," my mom said to her. "What kind of tea are you guys getting?"

"The lemon," I said, and closed my menu.

"Can I get champagne instead?" Sam asked.

"Nice try. No," my mom said.

We ordered our tea and immediately a waiter placed a tiered tray of goodies on our table. "This is a pregnant woman's dream," I said as my swollen fingers gained artificial intelligence and jerked out and grabbed a fistful of scones before I even knew what happened.

"So, are you getting excited?" my mom asked. She spread cream on a scone.

"Yes and no. I'm excited to be not pregnant anymore but I'm a little nervous about caring for a baby. But I'm excited to see the baby and finally meet him. But I'm nervous to see what my body's going to look like after he vacates the premises. I could go on and on. So, how's that for an answer?"

Our waiter reappeared and set steaming cups of herbal tea before us. I took a moment to breathe in the scented steam, hoping it would revive my pasty complexion, before sipping delicately.

"Yum," I said as I set my teacup back into its porcelain saucer.

"It is. So, Sam, aren't you excited about the baby?" my mom said.

"What?" Sam was still eyeing her cup of tea with skepticism.

"About the baby? Aren't you excited?"

"Oh." She paused for about ten seconds before she nodded her head. "Yeah. Yeah. I am. It'll probably be kind of cool."

My mom smiled triumphantly at me.

"Really?" I said carefully.

"Yeah, yeah. Why wouldn't I be?" She rolled her eyes and leaned forward to grab a cookie.

"I don't know, you just haven't seemed that into it," I said, and sipped my tea.

"Whatev. I am. You don't know how I feel. I think it'll be good," she said.

"Well . . . thanks. That means a lot." I awkwardly patted her hand.

She smiled at me and we locked eyes. I was certain she was going to launch into a diatribe about how much she loves the baby and wants to be the baby's godmother and be best sister friends. I smiled back at her, waiting.

"You know what?" she said.

"What?" I responded, my hopes soaring.

"These cookies are, like, amazing."

"Yes. Yes, they are." I laughed.

Tuesday, December 25
· · · · · · · · · · · · · · · · · · · ·

Merry effen Christmas.

I'm sorry, but I'm dying.

Skeletor has decided Christmas is truly the season of giving and his gift to me is making me feel like I've been kicked in the crotch. Repeatedly.

Nothing fits me anymore except for some gross black stretchy pants and a few short-sleeve tops, which has made for some interesting wardrobe choices at work. I haven't slept more than two hours straight in a week despite feeling ready to fall asleep all of the time. My eating choices have been limited to Popsicles, the only thing that I can keep down since my stomach is compressed to the size of a pea.

I also found my first stretch marks this morning. I made the huge mistake of turning around and looking at my butt after I got out of the shower. I have four or five purple lines on my right ass cheek. Why only on the right one? I'm so glad I spent one hundred dollars on stretch mark cream last week. It seems to be working so well. Although, it's really not as big a deal since my sex life decided to take an extended vacation.

Both Julie and Reese called to see if I wanted to exchange gifts but I told them unless they were planning on bringing over a scalpel to cut this child out of me to stay away. Not surprisingly, they did.

I can't even get excited about any of my gifts, even though I did get some great stuff. My parents bought me a beautiful armchair and ottoman from Pottery Barn for the nursery and Jake got me a gorgeous necklace. Sam didn't even tell me I look fat. But I just want to sit here and feel sorry for myself.

I started crying last night to Jake how I couldn't believe it was Christmas already and how I didn't even get to make Christmas cookies or watch *How the Grinch Stole Christmas* or drink cider. He wisely put me to bed. This morning when I woke up, I found a plateful of Christmas cookies in the kitchen. Jake stayed up all night baking them. They were a delicious breakfast, even though most of them were burned since Jake fell asleep while they were in the oven.

I am also getting worried because I've heard having a newborn is much harder than being pregnant. I pretty much hate being pregnant right now. Does this mean I'm going to hate being a mom? That I'm going to hate having a newborn even more than I hate being pregnant? Oh, God.

I haven't heard anything from *The Daily Tribune*, despite sending several e-mails in which I tried to sound both professional and witty at the same time. I'm giving up. I'm going to eat that quart of cookie dough ice cream. Because that is something I don't hate.

Thursday, December 27
. . . .

Walking has now officially become waddling. No thanks to the massive quantities of ice cream I consumed last week.

Rock on.

Something else I'm thrilled about? The stranger in Starbucks this morning who gave me a fearful look and asked me if I was due yesterday. It took all of my strength not to squirt gingerbread latte into her eye sockets and scream "TWO MORE WEEKS!"

Then the UPS guy who delivers our mail at work said, "Dayum. You gonna have that baby any day now."

Later, Mule Face was in the middle of a story about how her sister nearly died from pain during labor when I got another Braxton Hicks contraction and grimaced. She flipped out and screamed, "OH MY GOD. YOU'RE IN LABOR!" before I could shut her up.

I'm also getting at least fifty e-mails every day, asking if I've had the baby yet and offering tips to start labor.

At my appointment with Dr. Clarke this afternoon, she told me everything's fine but there is no progress so far, which means jack is happening down there. She asked me if I was working from home yet and I told her I had to pull off a huge black-tie wedding first. She said not to worry, since I'll most likely still be pregnant for a while. Then she told me she'll wait until I'm two weeks overdue to induce me. I swear, if my reflexes weren't a little slow these days due to massive water retention, I would've wrapped my fat fingers around her neck.

I think the ninth month of pregnancy is designed to make women so miserable, they stop worrying about (a) the pain of labor, (b) caring for a newborn, or (c) never sleeping again. I'm convinced it's like a divine boot camp for new moms. The constant peeing means about two hours of sleep a night, I'm weepy and emotionally fragile about 99 percent of the day, and my lady parts are taking quite the beating due to Skeletor's gymnastics. I can't imagine childbirth and being a first-time parent being much worse. So, I asked Reese for her opinion.

"Trust me, it is" was all she said.

I'm not buying it.

Tuesday, January 1

Well, it happened. Just like Ryan Seacrest said. A new year is here. Which means one very important thing: the Flynn-Shepard wedding is over; Ms. Rachael Flynn is now Mrs. Rachael Shepard.

The wedding went fine, which I can say since it is *over*. I spent a good majority of the reception policing a very intoxicated bridesmaid who drank too many vodka tonics before the ceremony even began. As a result, I was on my feet for close to twelve hours straight. By the end of the night, I resembled Miss Piggy with my engorged foot fat nearly busting the seams of my poor shoes.

It was also my first sober New Year's Eve in about ten years, although Jake did not join me in my sobriety, and he's been on the couch napping for most of the day.

The wedding is over so I will be working from home, which is a very good thing since I no longer fit behind my desk.

Another implication of this year rolling around is this is the year when we meet our human child. I've moved beyond the whole freaking out, oh my God we're going to have a kid soon stage to THIS KID BETTER COME SOON BECAUSE I'VE BEEN PREGNANT FOR ONE HUNDRED YEARS.

Improvement? Jury's still out.

Thursday, January 3

I'm working from home today and besides fielding a few follow-up calls from the Flynn-Shepard wedding, I've spent the majority of the morning with Bob Barker, in awe over the actual retail price of Ricola cough drops. Jake offered to stay home with me today, but I practically shoved him out the door because Please. It only takes one of us to sit around, feet tapping, staring impatiently at my stomach.

In preparation for Never Leaving the House Again, I've ordered groceries online and done every shred of laundry in sight, both of which took me an hour. So, in search of other ways to pass the time, I came up with a to-do list.

1. Watch *Flip That House.*
2. Read new *US Weekly.*
3. Blog about suggestions for items to include while packing hospital bag.
4. Check e-mail.
5. Name child.
6. Nap (although I've done this so often, Jake's referred to the ninth month as the "dormant period").
7. Call Jake and whine how I'm still pregnant.
8. Screen Marianne's and Natalie's calls.
9. Pack hospital bag.
10. Hysterically cry when Jake questions items included in hospital bag.
11. Try to forget article I read about woman who had a fourteen-pound baby.
12. Stop reading news stories about widows. I had a soul-crushing panic attack last night about what I'd do if Jake died and I became a single mother. Again, I thought back to the turtle story and realized I'd have to get remarried immediately, to provide the child with a parent who probably won't accidentally kill it. I also forbade Jake from driving after dark or when there's rain, snow, or fog.
13. Go into labor.

Friday, January 4

No baby yet. I think Jake is starting to give up hope that he's ever coming out.

I woke up late last night to pee again, and saw the light on in the nursery as I walked to the bathroom. My bladder forced me to go to the bathroom first before I went inside. Then I pushed open the door to the nursery and found Jake, standing next to the crib, staring at it.

"What are you doing in here?" I said, and shielded my eyes from the light.

"Just picturing him in here," he said softly, putting an arm around my shoulders. "When's he going to come? I'm sick of waiting."

"I know. Me too. Believe me. Soon, hopefully." I leaned against his chest. "Let's go to bed."

"In a minute," he said. He released me and sat down in the fluffy chenille armchair we put in the corner of the room. He held out his hand for me. I reached over and snuggled beside him in the armchair, wedging my belly between us. Skeletor immediately woke up and started pushing against Jake.

"You're smashing him," I said.

"That's OK. Just for a minute," he said.

I closed my eyes and Skeletor settled down.

The three of us fell asleep until morning.

Saturday, January 5

I've had my share of embarrassing public moments. When I was waiting in line in high school to get my senior portrait taken, I suddenly and unexpectedly got my period, ruining my favorite pair of pants. In college, when I wore a new dress just a wee bit too small to Jake's fraternity formal, my boob popped out like Punxsutawney Phil on Groundhog Day in the middle of a story. When I went on my very first post-college interview, I got out of my car and slipped on some podlike leaf creation and slid halfway underneath my car, exposing my white granny panties and ruining my brand-new suit. Oh, and the president of the company witnessed it since his office faced the parking lot.

Shit, I'm even good at inadvertently embarrassing other people in public, starting with when I was five and my mom took me to Neiman Marcus and I knocked over a mannequin. Smashed body parts littered the shoe section and we were asked to leave. Reese will never forget when we were college freshmen and went to Kappa, the hot guy fraternity. She whispered to me to act like we belonged right before I tripped and tumbled down an enormous staircase while wearing a black skirt and knee-high boots. Apparently at one point during the fall, my feet were behind me and I was surfing headfirst down the stairs. We didn't get invited back. Reese was not happy.

I thought all these years of public humiliation would be just a precursor to a great climax involving my water breaking all over the five-thousand-dollar couches at Pottery Barn and giving birth on the Amherst dining table surrounded by Voluminous Vases.

But no.

I gleefully and expectantly dragged my ass from place to place today, positive I was going to feel a pop and a burst and look down and see fluid pouring from my nether regions. And I would've welcomed the humiliation, thank you very much. I traipsed through the grocery store, Target, Nordstrom, and Bed Bath & Beyond.

Nothing.

Finally, in a last-ditch effort, I went to Taco Bell and loitered around like a drug-dealing teenager. Still nothing.

All I managed to accomplish today was seeing the doctor. I tried to limit my food intake before the appointment, to avoid the scale getting pushed farther and farther to the right, into the "Fat Ass" numbers, but it didn't work. I gained three pounds this week for a grand total of forty-five pounds. To add insult to injury, Dr. Clarke told me I haven't progressed at all so she fully expects to see me next week.

I am now drowning my sorrows in a Burrito Supreme.

Oh, and to everyone at *The Daily Tribune*: I hate you.

That is all.

Sunday, January 6
· · · · · · · · · · · · · · · · · · ·

My due date.

Well.

Huh.

Excerpts of some e-mails I've gotten:

> If you haven't had that baby yet, you should really try
> drinking castor oil.   —MCK89

> Are you scared about labor? Like, the pain and
> stuff?   —Emily4.0

> Please, please can I be in the delivery room when
> you give birth?   —Wifey1025

> How much wait u gained? 50 pounds?   —jen2485

> I had my son at forty-two weeks.   —CincyJane

What's the point of even having a due date if it's not right? Why don't they just call it: "I have no idea so I'm going to close my eyes and whatever date my finger lands on is when your child may or may not vacate your body."

Am I bitter about this whole no-progress shit? Fuck no. I hope I'm pregnant another month. Scratch that, another *nine* months.

It didn't help that this morning I woke up, looked down, and saw my stomach had exploded with stretch marks. Deep, angry red lines now radiate from my belly button. Those, coupled with the fabulous new spider veins on my legs, are making me feel just great about myself. This kid better come soon, or else my body is going to look like I survived a knife fight. Forget wearing a bikini ever again, I'll be lucky if I can wear shorts. I'll be like my grandmother, who wears double-knit pants to the beach.

My phone's also been ringing nonstop. Julie rambled on and on about how she thinks it's over with Hot Dr. Ben since she found out last night he thinks Tara Reid is hot and ew. I'm suspicious if it also has anything to do with the fact one of his friends asked her what her parents do for a living and looked disgusted when she told him her dad's a truck driver. Reese told me Matt bought her a two-carat anniversary ring but she's not sure if he did it just out of guilt. Marianne called to again ask me when she can stay with us after the baby's born. (How about never? Are you free then?) My mom called to "reassure" me since Sam was ten days overdue and then Sam got on the phone and asked me if I was freaked out about labor because "You know, it's supposed to be the worst pain you will ever feel." Thanks, very helpful.

I think I'm going to give birth by myself in a field to escape all of these freaks.

Never one to wait patiently, I've started Googling ways to make labor start, none of which are possible because (a) spicy food will make me hurl and unless this baby's coming out of my mouth, no thanks; (b) there's no way I want to have sex right now. I don't know what whale sex looks like, but I'm sure it would be pretty close; and (c) walking around is painful and makes me gasp for breath. Besides, a *Judge Judy* marathon is on.

But if smelling excessive amounts of cat urine is a catalyst for labor, it should be any day now since Butterscotch is all, "I love peeing in that other room. Thanks for always forgetting to close the door."

Monday, January 7

. . . .

While lying around, feeling very sorry for myself today, I got the phone call I'd been waiting for. Kyle Tiesdale called to let me know the status of my *Daily Tribune* submissions.

"Sorry it's taken me so long to get back to you, but I was in Mexico over the holidays."

"Oh, no big deal. So what's the situation?"

"Well, I talked to my editor."

"OK . . ." I was dying, dying.

"She loved your pieces."

"She did?" I jumped up and started pacing around the room. Well, I moved as quickly as my fat pregnant self would allow.

"Yes, she did. We'd like to bring you on as a guest columnist."

"Shut up!" Not my most professional moment, but true to character.

"Now, it would just be an occasional piece, not a full-time job or anything. The pieces would be centered around the challenges of being a new mom."

"New mom?" I stopped.

"Yes, the fears, worries, anxieties, joy, etc."

"I don't know anything about being a mom."

Kyle started laughing. "That's the point. We all feel that way."

"Really? Are you sure?"

"Positive. We love your voice."

"OK, when would my first article appear?"

"We'll figure all of that out after you finally have that baby. Are you taking three months' maternity leave?"

"Yes, but I can work on the articles before I go back to work."

"We can figure all of that out soon. Let's talk in another two weeks or so, OK?"

"OK, Kyle. Thanks so much for this opportunity."

"Absolutely."

I hung up the phone and sank down on the couch. I enjoyed the quiet moment and rested my hand on Butterscotch. I listened to him purring and the crackle of excitement in the air before I picked up the phone again and started dialing everyone I'd ever met.

OK. So I'm going to be a journalist, with a real-live newspaper column. A journalist who talks about mom and baby things. I'm going to be just like Carrie Bradshaw on *Sex and the City*, except my writing will be a lot less about sex and more about diapers and crap.

Tuesday, January 8

. . . .

I felt horrible today. I lay around all day like a big fat sloth, periodically getting up to pee or shove another cookie into my mouth. As an added bonus, I had painful false labor contractions, a fun precursor. In my opinion, false labor contractions are completely unnecessary. I already know labor is going to be a bitch, okay? I don't need a reminder.

I finally whined to Jake enough on the phone and he came home after lunch.

All day long, the contractions continued sporadically. Every time I'd have one, Jake would sit straight up and stare at me, to which I would wave my hand dismissively because *please.* I so will know when I'm in labor.

It wasn't until we started watching old episodes of *Real World* that I realized the contractions were twenty minutes apart. I kept my mouth shut because I was positive they would stop and I could watch *Access Hollywood* uninterrupted. But no, right as a juicy segment on Brangelina came on, another one of those fuckers came. I looked at Jake and said, "Maybe. But don't get your hopes up. They'll probably stop now that I've said it."

He nodded and casually got up, carefully placing his *Sports Illustrated* on the coffee table, and slowly walked toward the bedroom. As soon as he was out of sight, I heard him rushing around and banging his drawers open and shut. I rolled my eyes, still positive I was going to be right there on the couch in two hours, watching *Law & Order: SVU*.

Once they hit ten minutes apart, I wordlessly began walking around the apartment, cleaning up the never-ending puddles of cat pee, vacuuming, and painting my nails.

Then, they were seven minutes apart.

I took a shower, blow-dried and flat-ironed my hair. Then I trimmed my cuticles.

"This can't be it. We don't even have a name yet," I said to Jake.

"I don't think the baby cares," he said as he grabbed my hand while I winced in pain.

"No. He does. I know it," I said as I exhaled. "How the hell am I supposed to breathe? You know, like that Lamaze crap? What am I supposed to do? Why didn't we take birthing classes like your mom said?"

Labor officially made me a madwoman. One who agreed with my mother-in-law.

"I asked but you said you didn't think you needed—" He stopped when he saw a look of fiery anger flash across my eyes. "Never mind. Um, um . . . just breathe slowly."

We sat on the floor in front of the television, silent. I intermittently scrunched my face and tried to breathe as Jake clutched my hand.

"OW!" I yelled.

"What? Is the baby coming? Oh, shit! Is it coming out right now?" Jake jumped up and eyed my pants.

"Yes, it's coming out right now. Catch it. No, you dork. You were squeezing my hand so hard my engagement ring dug into my knuckle."

"Oh, sorry," he said, and sat back down.

Five minutes apart.

Jake and I looked at each other and shrugged, smiling goofy, crooked smiles. We called Dr. Clarke, who gave us the go-ahead to go to the hospital, which immediately caused me to go into raving freak-out mode.

"Where's my hospital bag? Where's my purse? Where's the checkbook? Where are my shoes? Where's my makeup? I need to update the Internet! They'll be worried!"

It was like one of those dreams where my house is burning down and I only have a few minutes to save a few things.

When Jake finally wrestled a six-pack of bottled water out of my hands, promising the hospital had modern amenities such as running water, and swore he would update the Internet from his laptop at the hospital, I gave up and got into the car.

We called my parents and arrived at the hospital, where we were given a room. One of the nurses, whom I dubbed Nurse Shithead because her bedside manner consisted of berating me for not taking birthing classes, came in and asked me to fill out an admitting form. I paused when I got to "weight."

"What's wrong?" Jake asked, sweating profusely.

"Is it OK to lie?" I wondered out loud.

"About what?" Jake said, and tried to turn the form toward himself.

"My weight."

"No, you should tell the truth," he said emphatically.

"Crap," I said. I wrote the number down in very tiny, dotlike script, shielding the paper with my hand.

"Lemme see." Jake grabbed for the paper again.

"No way." I jerked my hand away.

"C'mon, it can't be that bad."

"Oh, yes, it is," I said, and held the paper over my head.

"What is this horseplay?" Nurse Shithead appeared at the door, sternly glaring at us.

"Uh, nothing. Just filling out the form," I mumbled like a scolded child, and pretended to study the form some more.

"Done?" She held out her hand.

"Yep," I said. I offered the form while glaring at Jake.

"I'm going to check you," Nurse Shithead said, and motioned with her hand. I wasn't sure what that meant until she sat down on the side of the bed. Jake looked away and pretended to check his e-mail on his BlackBerry.

I was four centimeters.

Another nurse walked in and started hooking me up to a bunch of beeping machines. At this point, I became terrified and just wanted to go home. I started wondering why I thought home births were for hippies and freaks when Nurse Shithead told me, "Sit up and stop screwing around."

And then a contraction came and I felt like the wind got knocked out of me and I thought, *Oh, yes, this is why I'm in a hospital—drugs.*

"When can I get the epidural?" I asked miserably, hoping if I sounded pathetic enough she'd feel sorry for me.

"Not yet," she said, and snapped off her gloves and walked out.

I looked at Jake and my eyes started to water. He kissed my hand and rubbed my shoulder. I reminded him of his promise to update the Internet and he pulled out his computer. He posted an entry about being at the hospital and he would update as soon as Skeletor was born. Immediately, new e-mails began pinging into my inbox, but Jake shut the laptop before I could wrestle it out of his hands.

He turned on the television and flipped on *Monday Night Football.* Just as I was about to yell at him this was one time when watching sports was NOT OK, my mom walked in. Seeing her instantly saturated me with relief. She hugged me and promised to get me a cup of water, no matter what Nurse Shithead said with her "No Fluids Ever" policy.

I could hear her out in the hallway talking to the nurses. They weren't relenting.

"I'm sure it will be OK, I used to be a nurse. I know how this works," she said in a condescending voice. They relented but said they wouldn't be responsible for whatever happened. (Like what? If I spilled it everywhere and ruined my fashionable hospital gown decorated with honeybees? If I used the water as a weapon and threw it at Nurse Shithead?)

The anesthesiologist came in shortly after and gave me the epidural. Originally, I was somewhat freaked out at the idea of a needle going into my spine, but at that point I was all, "Put it wherever you want it. In my eye? OK, sounds reasonable. Just make this pain *stop!*"

After the epidural, Jake and I fell asleep for a while and my mom went down to the cafeteria to get some coffee. Well, at least I slept. I think Jake stayed awake and watched football for a while.

The second shift of nurses started and we traded Nurse Shithead for Ms. No Habla Inglés, who spoke zero English and just nodded her head to everything.

"How many centimeters am I now?"

Nod.

"Is it time to push?"

Nod.

"Is global warming truly going to be our generation's biggest legacy?"

Nod.

My mom handed me a magazine and they checked me again. Before I could even read an article, I was told it was time to push and before I knew it, Jake had one leg and my mom had the other and I was being told to push.

Not just "push" but, "PUSH, BITCH! DON'T YOU WANT TO HAVE THE BABY? PUSH!"

I wanted to tell them to go screw themselves.

I had no idea if I was pushing or not; I couldn't feel a thing. Everybody kept saying what a good pusher I was, so I guess something was happening.

So I pushed. And then I pushed some more.

Everyone was right in my face and this time, I did tell them to go screw themselves.

Dr. Clarke came in and scrubbed up and smiled and said, "Few more and we'll have a baby."

Jake and I looked at each other and he pushed back my hair and kissed me on the forehead. My mom squeezed my hand and told me how proud she is of me. We saw them wheel in the infant warmer and I realized it was for *our* baby and what felt like a tennis ball formed in my throat. I also had a flash of fear sweep through my brain, like *I'm not really sure I really want to do this, um, can we just come back like next week or maybe like next year?*

"Do you have any more ideas?" Jake asked me.

"What?" I said as I grabbed some ice chips.

"Ideas? About what to name the baby."

"Seriously? You're seriously asking me this now?" I stared at him.

"Do you like Daniel?" he said thoughtfully.

"NO!" I said.

"Why not?"

"Because Daniel is a stupid name and reminds me of my first-grade boyfriend and—SHUT UP! Let me have the kid first and then we can argue, OK?"

"OK, sorry," he said sullenly. My mom shook her head at him. "What? I think Daniel's a good name," he whispered to her.

Before I could yell at both of them, another contraction came. Dr. Clarke and Jake and my mom were all yelling at me to push, but I just went quiet. I went quiet and pushed, thinking about seeing Mr. Skeletor.

The next thing I heard was everyone scream and Dr. Clarke said, "Happy birthday . . . little GIRL!"

The screaming stopped and the room buzzed.

What?

"Girl!" she repeated, and held up this pink, wiggly, squirming baby who was most definitely a girl.

Jake and I looked at each other, eyes wide open and mouths slack-jawed.

Girl?

Miss Skeletor?

What?

Then we both welled up and I think he kissed me before I sent him over to see her and my mom hugged me and grabbed my hand. Both of us craned our necks to try to see her, and sputtered a little when we heard her cry.

I knew right then she would be OK.

A nurse brought her over and handed her to me. "Seven pounds, ten ounces. Congratulations, Mom!" she said.

I reached my arms out but stopped for a moment. I thought, *Mom? Who's she calling Mom? I'm too young to be a mom.* I immediately felt panic bubble up through my body. *What am I supposed to do with her? Am I holding her right? What if I drop her or something?* Then these people would all know what an imposter I am and not the best mother ever but rather an irresponsible clueless idiot.

I looked down at my daughter. She felt so tiny, but just too big to have been inside of me minutes ago. I looked up at Jake and I saw him gazing down at his daughter, a pure, true, unconditional, instant, no-questions-asked love.

I still wasn't sure what to do, so I just kissed her head and let her curl her tiny fingers around mine. She opened her eyes and locked her gaze on me. It felt like I'd been stabbed in the heart.

"Hi, I'm your mom," I said to her. The words sounded strange even as my mouth formed them. She yawned and stretched out her tiny, birdlike legs. I peeked into her swaddle and caught of glimpse of her feet, toes spread out. "There's no way." I looked up to Jake and smiled.

He lightly stroked the blond wisps atop her head as he asked, "No way what?"

"No way those tiny feet could've caused all that kicking," I said as I kissed her again.

Jake smiled down at me and covered my hand with his. I put my daughter's cheek up to mine and closed my eyes.

I knew life would never be the same.

It would be better.

Wednesday, January 9

· ·

The last twenty-four hours have been the strangest, world-spinning, "I feel like I'm in the outer limits and wouldn't be surprised to see Rod Sterling walk into my room and say, 'Having a baby is an everyday occurrence in . . . *The Twilight Zone*'" experience.

My dad and Sam were the first to arrive this morning. My dad gave me a hug and kiss and did the whole "We're so proud of you" speech I've heard from my mom eighty-seven times already. It will never get old.

Sam repeatedly asked me, "Aren't you *so* glad you had a girl instead of a boy?" in between texting her friends that she is free tonight. When she held Unnamed Baby Girl Finnegan-Grandalski, she said, "Do you ever notice how all newborns look like frogs?" Seeing my face, she quickly added, "At least she's not ugly. Some babies are soooo fugly.

"Your life is like, decided now," she said.

"What do you mean?"

"Like, I could still go and be anything I want. I could marry a royal prince or have a five-carat engagement ring. You're married and have a baby. You already know what your life is."

"It's great," I said.

She looked at me and rolled her eyes. "Whatever. I have my whole life ahead of me."

"I wouldn't be too sure, Sam. Your life could end right here if you don't shut up," I seethed.

My dad quickly jumped in. "Sam, be nice. Apologize to your sister."

"Jeez, sorry. You guys take everything I say the wrong way."

"She's beautiful," my dad said as he held the baby.

"I know. Isn't she so calm? She's so peaceful," I said proudly.

"She is. Just a word of warning though. Babies tend to wake up a little a few days after they're born. They're still kind of dazed at this point."

"Maybe. But I have a feeling she's going to be a laid-back kid," I said firmly.

"OK," my dad laughed.

Sam held the baby for a minute until she started to squirm, then quickly handed her back to me. "She's fussy," Sam declared.

"No she's not, she's just changing positions and yawning," I said. "Do you want to hold her again?"

"Not really. Everyone always makes you hold a baby and then stares at you."

I couldn't disagree with her, so I let it slide.

My dad and Sam left a few minutes later, just as Mark called Jake to tell him he's planning on coming to the hospital tonight after a work happy hour party. I'm thinking it might be best if he doesn't hold Baby Girl lest a drunken-uncle/dented-newborn-head incident occurs.

I managed to sneak in a quick nap while Jake talked to Mark until Marianne and my mom arrived at exactly the same time. Marianne said she could only stay for a minute because Natalie and Ash Leigh were waiting in the car. Of course, we wouldn't want to inconvenience Natalie. The best part was when my mom said to her, "We missed you at the shower and now you can only stay for a few moments. Such a shame your other grandchild takes up so much of your time that you have so little left to spend with this one."

Marianne looked at her, red-faced, and stammered out, "Oh . . . well . . . Natalie . . . Ash . . . Leigh . . ."

My mom put her hand on Marianne's shoulder and said, her voice oozing with sarcasm, "Of course. We understand."

I love my mom.

Reese stopped by with a big, almost embarrassing bouquet of flowers. She looked fabulously put together in a gabardine maternity pantsuit but I noticed dark circles under her eyes.

"Hello, gorgeous," she said breathily, leaning forward and giving me a kiss on the cheek.

"Hello yourself," I said back to her, adjusting my tentlike hospital gown.

She spotted Baby Girl and practically knocked Jake over as she ran to the bassinet. She picked her up. "Ooohh, God. I forgot how little they are. I can't wait." She closed her eyes and breathed in deeply. "The newborn smell."

"Yup. Even better with a clean diaper," I said. "Jake was just about to go out and get some contraband McDonald's. Do you want anything?"

"Nope, I'm good. My mom's watching Grace so I can't stay too long."

"Remember, I want one of everything!" I yelled to Jake as he left.

Reese held my hand and looked down at me and smiled.

"What?" I asked.

"It's just, I'm so . . ."

"Proud of me?" I finished.

"Yes," she nodded.

"Why does everyone keep saying that? What are you proud of me for? I got knocked up and had a baby. Just another day," I said, smiling.

She shook her head and laughed.

"Pretty soon it will be your turn," I said.

She smiled a little smaller, a little sadder, a little more hesitantly. "Yep," she said.

"Anything new with . . ." I didn't have to finish the sentence.

She shook her head slowly and shrugged. Her face brightened a little.

"I do have some great news, though."

"Do tell!"

"I got accepted into DePaul University's master's program. I'm thinking about going back and getting my master's in teaching."

"You're kidding! That's amazing! You never told me you applied! When did you do this?"

"Recently. I applied on a whim, just to see if I could get in. I never planned on actually going, but I think I might."

"Oh, Reese, that's so great. You should do it. You deserve it."

"I know. It's such a huge change. I mean, I never thought I'd go back to work but I never thought Matt . . ." She trailed off.

"Honey, this is the best decision you ever made. I can feel it."

"Thanks, it feels good to hear you say that. Listen, I'll fill you in later. I have to run and pick up Grace."

I hugged her tightly and kissed her on the cheek. I tried to say everything, to let her know that I'd always be there, how proud I was of her, in the hug.

"I love you," I said, and she nodded.

Reese left and Jake came back with the illegal McDonald's and I about fainted from the smell.

"Fries." He handed me a large red sleeve of beautiful salty, crunchy treasures.

"Coke." I grabbed the sucker and took a long slurp, enjoying the way the carbonation burned my throat.

"McNuggets." I practically pulled his shoulder out of its socket.

"Tiffany," he said evenly, and handed me a blue box.

"What?" I said, staring at the beautiful blue color.

"Open it." His eyes twinkled.

I grabbed the box and gingerly opened the top and peeled back the tissue paper. Inside lay a sterling silver baby rattle. I lifted it up and immediately the floodgates opened and tears began streaming down my still-puffy face.

Jake welled up, too. "See here," he said, and pointed to the rattle, "here is where we can engrave her initials," he paused, "whenever we figure them out."

"It's so amazing. Thank you, I—"

"Oh my God! Is that Tiffany?" came a voice shouting from the doorway, startling Baby Girl.

Julie rushed over in her scrubs. "Oooohhh, it's so beautiful!" she shrieked as Jake got up and picked up the baby and tried to soothe her. My heart flopped a little as I saw him pick her up so carefully, kiss her head, and whisper "Shhhhh" into her ear.

"So. Mom," Julie said.

"Yep. Isn't it totally weird?"

"Um, yeah. Freaks me the fuck out so bad I can't even discuss it."

"How long can you stay?"

"Not long. My shift starts in a few minutes, but I'll come up and say hey when I can."

"So, how do I look?" I asked.

Julie narrowed her eyes. "Please, bitch. Two of your thighs still don't equal one of mine and your hair looks fabulous."

"Really?" I asked, grabbing for my compact.

"Yeah. You're lucky tousled waves are in right now."

She's right, I thought as I admired my Kate Hudson hairdo in the mirror. *I'm a total MILF.*

"So, a girl, huh?" she said, and grabbed the mirror out of my hand to apply her lip gloss.

"Yeah, who would've thought?"

"Is Jake disappointed at all?" she asked.

It was a fair question, but one only Julie has enough balls to ask.

"Oh, please. He's over the moon. She's so never going to be allowed to date."

"Or wear high heels or makeup or anything other than Disney character sweaters," Jake jumped in.

"Well, just don't let him get like Jessica Simpson's dad and all virginity promise ring and stuff," Julie said to me, and jabbed her finger in Jake's direction.

"I'll see what I can do," I said.

"How are the nurses treating you here?"

"OK, I guess. Better than Nurse Shithead."

"Yeah, she's a real bitch. Let me know if they aren't treating you right and I'll kick some ass."

"I'll consider you my personal bodyguard."

"You should. So, let's see the little thing," she said, and surprised both of us by walking over to Jake, her blue scrubs swishing.

"Hand her over, Dad," she said.

Jake paused for a moment, his eyes flashed to me, and he handed Julie the baby.

"Hi there. I'm Julie. I'm the cool one. I'll buy you beer and take you to get a tattoo and give you condoms," she whispered into the baby's ear, "and I say the F word a lot. But so does your mom."

"Shhhhh!" I said. Truth be told, I didn't care what Julie said; I was thrilled she even held her.

"Swaddled babies always remind me of Glow Worms. Remember those toys?" Julie said.

"Oh, yeah! You're right. I remember the commercial—the little girl holding the softly glowing cute stuffed green worm. They were supposed to light up after the faintest touch but my friend's only lit up after you sat on it or pressed your fists into its stomach."

"I'll tell you right now, Julie—babies don't glow," Jake said.

"Thanks, smartass."

"So, how's Hot Dr. Ben?" I asked.

She snorted and rolled her eyes. "Please. Tara Reid."

"Yeah, that's bad," Jake said while stuffing a handful of fries into his mouth.

"So over," she said without a hint of regret. "So, now that Hot Dr. Ben is officially Ex-Hot Dr. Ben, what about that promise to let me go out with Mark?"

"Julie, my foolish friend, don't you know I'll lie through my teeth when under duress?"

"Is that a no?"

"That's a no-fucking-way no."

"So, no word on the name yet?" Julie asked.

"Nope. We couldn't figure out a boy's name, let alone a girl's. She's going to be called Baby Girl for the rest of her life."

"You could call her B.G. for short."

"Like a rapper?" Jake said.

"I don't think so," I said.

"Just don't name her one of those weird yuppie, made-up names.

One time, I had a woman in the ER and she named her baby Meconium Sunrise. You know what meconium is, right? It's essentially baby shit. So, this idiot named her child Shit Sunrise."

Jake and I stared at her.

"What?" she said.

"Thanks for the tip," I said, and shook my head.

Once Julie left, I sent Jake home to pick up a few things I'd forgotten, and a nurse who resembled Star Jones pre–gastric bypass came in to bring Baby Girl to the nursery so I could get some rest. As I watched Star Jones wheel the bassinet out of the room, I felt an all-encompassing, visceral longing to have my baby back next to me, where she belongs. I cheered myself though by watching Star Jones's large ass leave the room. Because I would die if I had to look at a cute perky nurse's ass when my own is the size of South Carolina.

I opened up the laptop and composed a long tearful entry about my new daughter and how amazing and beautiful she is. I couldn't stop the tears as I read congratulatory e-mail after e-mail. I was happy not to have any e-mails from jen2485 and didn't even get creeped out when Wifey1025 offered to be my night nurse.

After I closed my computer, I sat there, restless, waiting for Jake to come back. I flipped on the television but wasn't in the mood to watch either the Weather Channel or the channel continuously fixed on the hospital's chapel. I'd already read all of the magazines I'd brought and wanted to see Baby Girl again. *Screw it*, I thought. I swung my legs over the side of my bed and put on my robe.

I thought to myself, *I'm fine. I can totally walk around and do whatever.*

Oh, by the way? I'm an idiot.

I made it as far as the nurses' station before my legs buckled and I was all, "Heeeeelp meeeeee!" and a nurse had to help me back to my room, scolding me the whole way. Then she saw my smuggled McDonald's and man, was she pissed.

Good thing Jake walked in right then because she pretty much blamed him for everything. Before she left, I asked her to bring Baby Girl back, seeing as how I was practically on lockdown now. I looked at Jake, shaking snow out of his hair and dusting off his shoulders. I felt like there were so many things that I wanted to say to him—how I love him, how he's the best husband ever, how lucky I feel to have him, etc., but Star Jones appeared with Baby Girl. Jake lifted her out of the bassinet and walked over to me and placed her in my arms. She was asleep, sighing occasionally, dreaming about Lord knows what, probably giant bottles or boobs or something.

"Isn't she beautiful?" I asked Jake smugly.

"Absolutely. The best-lookin' kid around," he said proudly, touching her teeny-tiny fingernails.

We're pretty sure she's going to be a supermodel.

"Come here," I said, and tugged on his shirt and scooted over in bed.

"In bed?" He looked at me quizzically.

"Yes. Right here." I patted the bed next to me.

He hoisted himself into bed and laid his head down on the pillow. Our faces were inches apart. We gazed down at our daughter.

"Hey, I thought of a name," Jake said.

Oh, man, here it comes, I thought.

"What about Sara?"

Sara. No '80s movies or television shows flashed in my head. It was a miracle.

Baby Sara.

I knew.

"Baby Sara," I whispered. I looked down at our baby and she gave another little half sigh and I knew she approved. "Baby Sara," I said firmly, and nodded.

We lay there for a while, silently admiring Sara, occasionally looking at each other with grins that couldn't possibly convey our emotions.

I closed my eyes and lay back. I thought back to when I found out I was pregnant, back to the moment when everything changed. I was so scared. Scared of what my body would become, of what I would be like, of how Jake would cope, of how we were going to figure all of it out.

I looked at Jake, now soundly asleep, and Baby Sara, who was just beginning to stir.

I would do it all over again.

"I love you both," I whispered to my husband and daughter.

I feel like this is when my life really begins. Everything else has just been preamble, albeit a long, drunken, very fun preamble.

Sam was right. My life is sort of decided now.

But in a really great way.